Flight

Flight

Fran Dorf

A DUTTON BOOK

DUTTON
Published by the Penguin Group
Penguin Books USA Inc., 375 Hudson Street, New York, New York 10014, U.S.A.
Penguin Books Ltd, 27 Wrights Lane, London W8 5TZ, England
Penguin Books Australia Ltd, Ringwood, Victoria, Australia
Penguin Books Canada Ltd, 10 Alcorn Avenue, Toronto, Ontario, Canada M4V 3B2
Penguin Books (N.Z.) Ltd, 182–190 Wairau Road, Auckland 10, New Zealand

Penguin Books Ltd, Registered Offices: Harmondsworth, Middlesex, England

First published by Dutton, an imprint of New American Library,
a division of Penguin Books USA Inc.
Distributed in Canada by McClelland & Stewart Inc.

First Printing, August, 1992
10 9 8 7 6 5 4 3 2 1

"The Sound of Silence" Copyright © 1964 by Paul Simon. Used by permission
of the Publisher.

"The Weight" Copyright © 1968, 1974 by Dwarf Music. All rights reserved.
International copyright secured. Reprinted by permission.

 REGISTERED TRADEMARK—MARCA REGISTRADA

LIBRARY OF CONGRESS CATALOGING-IN-PUBLICATION DATA:
Dorf, Fran.
  Flight : a novel / by Fran Dorf.
    p.   cm.
  ISBN 0-525-93482-0
  I. Title.
PS3554.06715F55 1992
813'.54—dc20   91-48237
                                                               CIP

Printed in the United States of America
Set in Aster
Designed by Julian Hamer

For my family;
And for S. P., wherever you are.

ACKNOWLEDGMENTS

Many people offered support and encouragement in many different ways during the writing of this novel. First, I want to thank my husband, Bob Dorf, for everything. I want to express my appreciation to Renni Browne and Dave King for their enduring patience and valuable insights. I couldn't have finished this book without them. Many thanks to Peggy Dorf and John Hawkins, for their careful suggestions. Also, thanks to Jaime Redniss, for the gift of sharing. And thanks to my dear and trusted friend, Nancy Sinacori.

Despite its format, *Flight* is a work of fiction. The people and events depicted herein exist only in my imagination. Certain places in the book, most particularly the Shawangunk Mountains in upstate New York, do exist but are used here fictitiously. The town of Comity and the Drummond Rehabilitation Center are my inventions, and I offer my apologies for plunking them down in the middle of New York State.

Part One

Lana

LSD is Western yoga. The aim of all Eastern religion,
like the aim of LSD, is basically to get high; that is,
to expand your consciousness and find ecstasy
and revelation within.

—Dr. Timothy Leary

1

The rap went something like this: "What if we could, like, stop time? Imagine it, Lana. Everyone would freeze and you could walk around and look at everything. You know what I'd look at? Bodies. All kinds of bodies. I'd go up real close and look, so I could see the little—what do you call them?—pores in people's faces. Close up, they'd look like giant black holes. Weeeeeeohh, I'm about to fall into a big black crater. Or, like, people's noses?

"And nipples. The way girls' nipples get all wrinkled up when they're cold. And the colors? Some are pink, and some are brown, and some are that real light cocoa color, like yours, Lana. If you look at them up close they're mountains and valleys. Grand Tetons. (LAUGHTER)

"Or, like, what if we could get into the reality of flying? We could be birds. We could do some real good in the world if we could fly. We could, like, grab all the bourgeois pigs out of their beds at night and transplant them, like to Biafra or someplace like that. That would teach 'em a thing or two. Flying would be cool.

"Hey, Lana, like, all we need is to understand what's wrong with this society. If we'd all just come out of our own little boxes, we'd be able to share and love each other. You know what they say, make love, not war. Wow! Like, can you imagine telling like your mother how we're all going to love each other? She'd just call you all those names, like *slut*, like *whore*. Which is pretty fuckin' funny, your mother calling you all those names. But those names will have no meaning in the new reality we're gonna create. Like, drop acid in all your mother's vodka bottles, then she'd

3

understand. Then we could watch her get crazy. Middle-aged crazy. Far fucking out! Then you could go up and look at her nipples. (LAUGHTER) Old-people nipples.

"It's like our friend here, Lana, he needs some of that love we're all gonna have too. Share the love, that's what I always say. Share it all, then we'll be, like, one big happy loving spiritual family, all over the world. Like we were at Woodstock. Wasn't that something?

"What about it, Lana?"

(SUSTAINED LAUGHTER)

She leapt over the scum-coated rocks at the edge of the sand, a lone bird, extending her arm-wings to their full twenty-foot length, flapping in a steady beating motion of the humerus. She could feel the wing membrane fill with the updraft; hollow-boned, she achieved lift. She rode the current, gliding in spirals high above the surface of the water, crossing her legs at the ankles for a rudder, for balance. Soaring, she became nearly motionless, every muscle taut, every tendon and ligament gathered to the flight. She could feel the contraction of her powerful breastbone, her heart pumping, lungs filling with air, and she gained height like a high flier, like a condor. Practicing technique, she banked left, she cambered, she soared, hovered, glided, swooped. And like a condor she searched the water as it swept beneath her; then, trimmed her wings, nosed down, and dived. At last she skimmed along the surface of the water, braked, and alit for a moment before catching the updraft again. Whoosh, like the wind, she would be gone, high above her enemies, into the breathless clouds.

"Lana?"

A voice. And a sound, the sloshing of water, a natural waterfall over the barnacled rocks.

"Lana?"

Who was Lana?

She had to rise again, gain altitude, or she would be lost, smashed into the rocks. Or worse: become prey to the enemy. But she was blind. How could she catch the updraft blind? Why couldn't she see?

"Lana?"

A name. Someone was calling a name. A human name. But she wasn't human.

Yet she felt suddenly so heavy. Why couldn't she catch the updraft again?

There was something cool and damp on her head. A wet cloth.

And five fingers pressing in. Someone was breathing, just above her, breathing hard.

"I tell you, she's coming out of it."

Whose voice was that? Not the enemy. It was a man's voice, sounding clear and deep against the call of flight. Tonight she would soar. Tonight, when sleep came again.

She turned toward the sound of the voice, struggled to focus. She could feel his hands on her, strong hands. Slowly, very slowly, she focused. A man.

She folded her arm-wings in.

There was that sloshing sound again. The water. It was a human sound. She remembered it. A bath? Or was it the faucet? The flight was calling her back—to soar. She had to practice, perfect her technique, escape, survive.

She struggled to see, to turn darkness into light. But there were footsteps now, moving away. And then a door swinging shut; she could hear the squeal of the hinges.

She remembered a door that had sounded exactly that way, when she was eight and fell down the stairs and broke her leg. Was that before they moved to Comity, or after? The squeal of the hospital door was just like that. Was she eight now?

"Lana, move your leg."

She wiggled her leg, as he said.

"Look, doctor, she's moving her leg." Another voice. A female voice.

"Lana, are you there? Lana?"

Lana was there, and not there. She was soaring over barnacled rocks.

"Can you move your hand for me, Lana?"

She looked. It was a hand, a human hand coming into focus. She moved the muscle that moved the fingers. That was easy.

The female voice said, "Look, doctor, she's moving it."

Slowly Lana turned and focused on a woman.

Yes. She remembered now. It had taken them only two rides to hitchhike to Woodstock. She and Ethan got a lift off of Route 6A out of Comity with a couple named Dave and Sweet, in a van filled with incense and sitar music. Sweet didn't say how she got her name, but she was short and stocky and rolled monster joints that Ethan kept calling mad reefer logs. Sweet and Dave weren't going to Woodstock. Bourgeois, they called it. Three days of peace and love and they were charging admission, making money off the people's music, when it should have been free.

Lana and Ethan left Dave and Sweet somewhere north of Kingston, then picked up another ride all the way to Bethel in a schoolbus with some people who'd come from Maryland. There were sixteen of them in a bus painted green with white polka-dots. They'd ended up in a line of cars and vans and buses that stretched out from Yasgur's farm way out of Bethel nearly eight miles. Half a million people, they said, from all over the country.

Dave and Sweet should have come. Woodstock turned out to be free after all.

And that was long after she broke her leg, wasn't it?

"All right, take it easy now, Lana. Prepare the shot, nurse— goddammit, she _is_ coming out of this. Lana! Look at me!"

The light was blinding. He was sticking her skin with something, a needle. She felt it go in, but it didn't hurt.

"There now," the man, the doctor, said. "That didn't hurt, did it?"

She looked at him. A nice-looking man in a white coat. Deep green eyes, bushy brown hair trimmed very short, the sideburns, especially. He might have been called handsome, but he was middle-aged. At least forty.

She opened her mouth to respond, but what came out sounded more like a grunt than speech. If only she could speak. No. She had to make sure she had a way to escape.

A cool delicate breeze blew in from the open window, white curtains billowing out around it. She could escape through there.

The thought was comforting. If she could, she would speak. She tested the muscles of her mouth.

"Where am I?" The words formed easily, though her jaw hurt for some reason. But she _was_ human, after all.

The doctor broke into a huge smile. He looked at the nurse, who was about Lana's own age, eighteen, maybe a few years older. Her tag said her name was Betty. Betty put her hands together and clapped.

"You're in a hospital," the doctor said.

Was that something to clap about?

"What kind of hospital?"

"The Drummond Chronic Care Rehabilitation Center."

"I . . . was a bird."

The nurse looked at the doctor. "It explains that posture."

The doctor nodded.

"Was I in an accident?" she said.

"Yes."

"What kind of accident?"

"Why don't we leave that for later?" the doctor said. "Okay? Betty, go and call her parents."

"Not later. I want to know now."

"Well, we know you took some LSD."

LSD? She'd never taken LSD. Sure, she and Ethan had smoked plenty of grass, but *acid?*

Suddenly she remembered the very tall man with dark long hair, down past his shoulders. Dungarees with an American flag patch at the knee, no shirt, a beaded headband he wore Indian style. He had set up a tray table: grass, downers, uppers, acid. Purple Haze. Best there was.

"Yes, I remember. Acid. I got it from a guy at Woodstock."

"Who?"

"He . . . he had a far-out name. I'm trying to—"

"That's all right, Lana. It doesn't matter."

But it seemed like it did matter. "It was an unusual name," she said. "Like a nickname. Like . . ."

"Don't strain yourself, Lana. It's not important."

The doctor was touching her shoulder. He looked concerned— she had started to get out of bed. Gently, he helped her to lie back.

"I'd like to examine you now. Okay?"

"All right." Her mouth tasted funny, she was thirsty. "Could I have something to drink first?"

The doctor went into the bathroom and turned on the faucet. That was the water sound she'd heard before. He brought it back to her, helped her to sit up, though she didn't need help, held it for her while she drank it down; then he set the glass on the table by the bed.

"Now, look straight ahead."

She did as she was told, aware of his face very close to hers as he prodded her, shined a tiny sharp light in her eyes. She reached out and touched the skin on his cheek, withdrew her hand quickly. She closed her eyes, squeezed them shut against the memory. All boys, all men, even doctors, had that dirty, unwashed smell, the smell of sweat and swagger. She could hear those boys' voices even now, she would never forget them: Greg Horan, Denny Hartigan, Randy Slessenger, Jack Wells, Alan Wells. Especially Alan.

No. She wouldn't think of that. She had told herself she wouldn't, although sometimes she would lie in bed and concoct elaborate revenge fantasies. She particularly liked the one in which she invited Alan into her bedroom and tied him up to the bed, then made him hard with her hand, then left him there with his penis erect and watched while all of Comity filed in and pointed at him. Thinking of that helped sometimes. But she'd never even told anyone what had happened that day—except Ethan, of course, but he had been there. He saw it.

She'd never wanted to keep anything from Ethan. He had a different smell, anyway.

The doctor turned off his light, backed away.

"Jonathan Baldwin, M.D.," she said.

"How do you know?"

"I read your tag."

"That's good, Lana. Really good."

Why was he surprised that she could read? She had always been a good student. She could have gone to college if she'd had the money. If Ethan had had the money.

"What happened?" she asked.

"You don't remember anything?"

"Little bits. Pieces. I was still tripping when we got back to Comity, I think."

The doctor was flexing and unflexing her arm, which felt stiff.

"Who do you mean, 'we'?"

"Ethan and me."

"Your boyfriend?"

"Yes. Do you know where he is?"

"No, Lana, I'm afraid I don't. Do you remember anything else?"

"Not really. It's all kind of a blank."

"Can you lift your arm up for me, Lana?"

She lifted it. Her arm felt very heavy.

"It's amazing her muscles didn't atrophy."

He was talking to the nurse, who had come back.

"I couldn't reach her parents," the nurse said. "I told Ann Mahoney to keep trying, and to have them come right away when she gets them."

Lana looked at the nurse. "My parents? That's a joke." She turned to the doctor. "What happened after Woodstock?"

"You don't remember anything?"

"We hitched a ride back from Bethel. I wanted to go to High Exposure. I was into this thing about, you know, flying. We came back and we . . ." All she could remember was standing in Devil's Meadow. She and Ethan had been arguing about something. But she couldn't remember what.

"Tell me what happened, doctor."

The doctor glanced down at the clipboard he was holding.

"It might be better if we wait to tell you the details."

"Wait for what?"

"There was an accident, Lana."

She strained to understand what the doctor was saying to her.

"Do you remember falling?"

"I remember flying."

"Then you don't remember falling from High Exposure?"

Lana started to laugh. Baldwin and the nurse just looked at each other.

"It must have been an acid rap," she said. "You know."

The doctor obviously didn't know. He was looking at her the way her mother looked at her, usually just before she got the back side of Ellie's hand across her cheekbone.

"Oh, wow, that must have been some rap," Lana said. "You know, like one time, a guy I knew took some acid and threw his television set out the window because he decided it was on a different plane of reality than he was."

"In medical school," the doctor said, "I read about a man who put an electric drill through his head because he wanted to 'continue' time."

"Wow, man," she said, "I knew there was a reason I never took that shit. I—wait a minute. Are you saying I *jumped* from High Exposure?"

"No."

"But I fell?"

He hesitated, then said, "You were pushed."

"*Pushed? By who?*"

"Ethan Skitt. He tried to kill you, Lana."

"That's impossible."

The doctor put his hand on her arm in a gesture of sympathy. "I'm afraid it's true, honey."

"But Ethan loves me," she said. "We had a ceremony, he would never have done that." If only she could remember what they had been arguing about.

"I only know what it says here on your chart," the doctor said. "I'm pretty new in this place."

"New?"

"A year."

"I've been here a year?"

"No, Lana, longer than that."

"How long?"

"Why don't we wait until your parents get here? As soon as we thought you were coming out of it—"

"Out of what?"

"Wherever you've been."

"I was flying." Lana could feel the beating of her heart, the flapping of wings. No. That was only a dream. "But what have I been *doing* here?"

"You've been in a state we call a catatonic stupor."

"Yes, I remember I had to fly, to save myself. But I also remember being here. There was a nurse, Nurse Mahoney, who was always very gentle with me . . . It's all so confusing."

"No need to think about it now, Lana."

There was a long silence. Maybe she should try to go back to the rocks. The call of flight was strong.

She leaned back against the cool sheets and closed her eyes. She would try to sleep now.

No. It was too late. She opened her eyes. The doctor was still standing there.

"How long?" she said softly.

He stared at her for a moment; then, without ceremony or preface, he said, "Twenty years, Lana. In fact, it's twenty years ago today."

2

Twenty years ago, the graduating class of my high school, Comity High, class of 1969, put on *West Side Story* as its spring play. It was as amateurish as such productions usually are, but it was relentlessly energetic, and my brother, Alan, with his authoritative manner and open good looks, made a convincing Tony. Lana Paluka and Ethan Skitt, easily the most notorious couple in our school, and a pair whose ignominy would expand well beyond the boundaries of our town a scant few months later, came into the school auditorium late, just as my brother began singing "Something's Coming," in his fine, strong tenor.

For some reason, this was the memory that flashed through my mind the day I got the call about Lana. Even though it was a twenty-year-old memory—a fleeting one, since I had immediately shifted my attention back to my brother's performance—I could picture the scene in detail: the lights from the hallway behind Lana and Ethan illuminating their faces as they entered the darkened auditorium; Lana's wild mass of frizzy blond curls and the white embroidered peasant dress she wore; the braided rawhide band around Ethan's forehead and the dark hair that reached his shoulders; the scowls on the faces of the parents caught in the wedge of light, annoyance bordering on anger. Although this was the sixties, when a certain rebelliousness was prevalent among young people in general, Ethan Skitt's reputation as a troublemaker was already well established in town. He made no secret of the fact that he was heavily into drugs, and he was sullen, aloof, unswervingly arrogant in the face of authority. He'd been suspended from high school three times that I knew of, once for an altercation with my brother in the parking lot, another time for painting the words STOP THE WAR in huge red letters on the sidewalk in front of the main entrance to school, a third for an outburst of profanity during a discussion in a history class, one at which I wasn't present, but I heard that it ended with Ethan saying "Fuck you" to Mr. Fetterman, the history teacher. In short, Ethan Skitt was bad news, already a juvenile delinquent. A criminal in the making.

The couple came into the auditorium noisily, making no effort to diminish the impact of the doors as they closed behind them. They were giggling and obviously stoned, covering their mouths with their hands, as if no one else could possibly intrude in their world of two. Someone in the audience hissed, loudly, "Shhhh." Ethan gave him the finger and a wild glare, which brought a renewed burst of giggles from Lana before they finally sat down at the back.

This was an odd memory, really. There were other more salient, more sensational, certainly more lurid images of Lana my mind might have conjured up. Apart from Ethan, Lana Paluka had her own reputation. She was the girl everyone whispered and snickered about, the one everybody said would spread her legs for anyone. Several years earlier, I had personally participated in the event that established Lana's reputation as the school slut, a reputation she never lived down despite the fact that she apparently never went near another boy afterward except Ethan Skitt. And although I wasn't present the afternoon of the summer we all graduated, when Ethan tried to kill her, I might well have first remembered something about that.

And yet, given everything that's happened since the day I got the call, it seems somehow fitting that I would first think of them together that way.

I was in my office at the Westchester *Herald*, struggling with a feature on Elmond Dixon, the recently murdered financier and alleged pedophile. The piece just wouldn't come together. My lead was weak, my sentence construction choppy—the whole damned thing read like a recent journalism graduate's attempt to write a controversial story without taking any risks. Deadline for the Saturday edition was less than an hour away, and I simply couldn't organize my thoughts, translate my notes, overcome my guilt over what I'd had to do to get the story.

It had taken me all of Tuesday and Wednesday of that week to get the background I needed for the series I was doing on the case. I kept looking for a new angle I could break myself. Unfortunately, except for the uncorroborated account from the defendant herself, the Dixon children weren't talking about their father to the press. Nor were Dixon's wife, his friends, or his business associates, all of whom essentially called twenty-four-year-old Alissia Dixon a lying murderer. It was on Thursday that the detective I'd hired succeeded in tracking down a one-time Dixon maid named Georgina White.

I showed up that evening at the door of her third-floor walk-up in the seediest part of Mount Vernon. She answered the door on the third knock, but opened it only about six inches.

"Who're you?"

I pulled out my press card, held it up to the small crack in the doorway. "Ms. White? My name's Jack Wells. I'm with the Westchester *Herald*. I understand you used to work for Elmond Dixon."

She opened the door a few inches wider—a black woman in her fifties. "Yeah, I worked for 'em, for two years. Until 'bout eleven years ago."

"Why'd you leave, Georgina?" I asked.

"Got a better job. At a restaurant."

A good answer. Better than being fired, which might mean she had an ax to grind.

"You didn't like working for the Dixons?"

"Oh, I liked it fine. All of 'em were pretty nice to me. 'Cept him, of course."

"Why's that?"

"That Dixon guy was a son of a bitch. Treated me lower than a piece of dirt on the floor. An' that poor Alissia. Always did feel sorry for that poor kid, with an old man like that. Even if they was rich."

"Why'd you feel sorry for Alissia?" I asked. "Did her father treat her badly?"

"I told you, he was a son of a bitch. Just 'cause he was rich don't mean nothin'."

"Did you ever see him touch her, Georgina?"

"Once. I seen it once." She opened the door wide enough for me to go in, then took a seat on a couch that was so old and ratty it would have been rejected by the Salvation Army.

"What I seen was twelve years ago." She was looking not at me but out a filthy window. "Always felt sorry for that kid, like I say. Any daddy who'd do that . . . Course, Alissia ain't a child no more, and even if she was, nothin' don't excuse murder."

"How come you never told anyone?"

"Shit. It was only once, and I needed that job. I'm gonna go report the troubles of some rich white folks? Got my own troubles."

"Is this the truth, Georgina?"

"All you white folks think 'cause we're black that automatic means we liars. I ain't got no reason to lie. I'll testify to what I seen in court, if anybody ask. You can use my name if you want."

I would. And I would let both the county D.A. and Dixon's defense attorney in on it the next morning.

"What'd you see, exactly?" I asked.

For a moment she just stared at me.

"How bad do you want to know?" she said finally.

"It's important, Georgina."

"I need some money. I'm kind of strung out right now."

"How much?"

"A hundred."

I happened to have a hundred and twenty-odd dollars in my pocket. I handed her all of it except a twenty. She crumpled the money up in a ball, closed her fingers around it.

"It was in Dixon's kitchen," she said. "Dixon thought I wasn't there but I was in the little room they had right off the kitchen, Miz Dixon used to call it the sewing room, but mostly she kept canned stuff in there. It was only that once, but I seen him hug her—like real close, you know—and rub his hand up and down her back."

"And that's it?"

She glared at me. "It wasn't like no daddy would. Lissa was real upset by it, I could tell, and she was trying to get away from him, like wiggle away, but he kept on holding her that way, like he owned her. Then he leaned over and kissed her, right on the lips." She shook her head sadly. "It wasn't like no daddy would kiss his child. Gave me the creeps."

Fucker.

When I left, Georgina White was still holding my money in a little ball in the palm of her hand.

Let me digress for a moment. A hundred-dollar payoff is the least of what we reporters do, all the time. Far worse, I think, is camping out in front of some poor woman's house in order to be there for a comment on what it feels like to have your son murdered. Or printing something about a basically good person that we know will destroy his or her political career. Reporting the news. Finding the truth, regardless of the method or consequences.

Consider the reporter who befriends an accused murderer in order to write a book, a state of affairs about which there has been some discussion in recent years. The objection has been raised to the morality of keeping the fish on the line—claiming to believe the accused's account of his own innocence, until the story is finished and its subject "betrayed" in print. My situation with the Lana Paluka case might easily have offered certain parallels, had my "fish" been a stranger to me, had I even known there was a fish. But none of these people were strangers and, as things were, betrayal wasn't an issue, because I had no idea at the outset what I was getting into. It was a "story." That's all. And, although I had known Lana almost all my life—as indeed I had known all the players involved—it was not my intention to become embroiled in these events. When I first got the call about Lana and, later, when the publisher called to explore the possibility of my writing a book about the Lana Paluka case, it never occurred to me that I would suddenly find myself a prime player in this thirty-year drama. I considered my mission the reporters' mission: I would be objective, detached, interested only in uncovering the truth, then re-creating it dramatically, in the way true crime stories are being done these days. I admit at the outset, not without a certain shame, that when I sat down with Lana that first afternoon out by the lake—she with her Bible on her lap, I with my tape recorder—I made very little distinction between her and all of the others I had interviewed or planned to interview for the project: the police detectives, the lawyers, the nurses, the doctors. I assumed Lana had agreed to tell me her story for the money, and even as the interview hours with her piled up, I never looked for a reason why she would so readily tell me the most intimate and painful details of her life. I am a reporter. People tell me intimate details all the time.

But I'm getting ahead of myself.

The day after I bribed Georgina White, I was sitting in front of my computer screen staring at the headline I'd just written: "WITNESS TO DIXON SEX ABUSE TO TESTIFY." Even the district attorney, Dan Randall, hadn't managed to dig up Georgina White. How the hell had I gotten so lucky? What if Georgina asked Randall for money too? On the other hand, my instincts had served me well in the past, and they told me Georgina was telling the truth.

The Dixon trial was the kind of case that could make a reporter's career. It had all the elements—a prominent Westchester family, money, sex, murder, even child abuse. This one could do it for me. I had paid enough dues. I was a good reporter, goddammit, and I was thirty-eight years old. Too old to be working for peanuts for a second-string newspaper, even if it was the largest circulation daily in the state outside of New York City. I wanted to work for the *Times*, had wanted to ever since leaving Comity almost twenty years ago.

Comity, New York. Only claim to fame is its proximity to the

Shawangunk Mountains, whose cliffs attract hundreds of climbers every summer. The Gunks, and the Lana Paluka affair.

"Hey, Jack, you have space-out cookies for lunch?"

The high-pitched voice belonged to Joette Larson, who'd recently come to the *Herald* from a large midwestern daily and for some reason appointed me her personal rival. I looked up from behind my computer and saw Joette's mop of red hair.

"Just thinking, Joette," I said, smiling. "Try it sometime."

She laughed and went back to her work.

Joette was going up to Comity that weekend to cover the opening of my twin brother's latest real estate venture, the West Farm Mall.

"There's a *mall* in Comity?" I said when Alan first told me about it. I had been only dimly aware that he was spending less time on medicine and more on real estate development over the last few years.

"Well, sure, Jack. The town's got to move into the twenty-first century sometime. And I'm going to be the one to take it there. We open next month. We've got the lieutenant governor coming to cut the ribbon. Angela Allwin, too. Ever hear of her?"

"Afraid not."

"Neither had I," Alan said, laughing. "She's some actress nobody every heard of, supposedly had a small part in—what was that movie last year about the singer?—well, whatever. She's a knockout, though. And we've got a Ferris wheel, for the kids. And a Dixieland band, for the gomers—"

"What?"

"Gomers?" He laughed. "Stands for 'Get out of my emergency room.' It's sort of medical slang. You know, old people who whine about their aches and pains a lot and drive six miles an hour in a no-passing zone . . . And a rock band, for the teenagers. Hey, maybe you could talk to some people over at the paper, get them to cover the story. We could run some ads, they could give us some play. Of course, we've hired a dynamo PR lady to work with the press. But it can't hurt to have an in—right, kiddo?"

"I'm sure we could plug your mall without the quid pro quo, Alan."

Actually, I was far from sure that a mall two counties north of Westchester would be of any interest to Jim Harling, my editor. As it turned out, Harling was interested enough to assign Joette to the story when I said I didn't want it.

I looked back at the computer screen. If I hadn't gotten the Georgina story, there were hordes of hungry reporters who would have, including a few at my own paper—Joette Larson for one. And if I wasn't above the occasional payoff, at least I hadn't sold my soul to promote toothpaste or dog food the way some of my college buddies had.

Journalism was an honorable profession. It was for the good of the public. And the public needed to be informed about the epidemic of child abuse in America. What was a hundred dollars slipped to some woman who really needed it in exchange for something the public needed to know? And if Georgina ever mentioned a payoff, which she wouldn't, it would be my word against hers.

I glanced at the clock on the wall of the newsroom. Enough. A little cut-and-paste and it would be fine, better than fine. I punched the keys to transfer my copy to Harling so he could read the piece before it went to copy edit, then flipped off my computer. One-thirty. Half an hour before deadline.

The phone was ringing.

I picked up the receiver on my console. "Newsroom. Jack Wells."

"Jack?"

I recognized the voice—Ann Mahoney, a nurse I'd dated when I first got back from Akron. Nice lady. Great body.

"Good to hear your voice, Ann," I said. "What's it been, a year?"

"Almost."

"How are you?"

"Fine, Jack. I'm getting married in a month."

Surely she hadn't called to tell me that.

"I'm happy for you, Ann. You still on staff at Bellevue?"

"No . . . I changed jobs a few months ago. Now I'm upstate. I'm working with chronic care psychiatric patients, at the Drummond Rehabilitation Center. Maybe you've heard of it?"

I could see Jim Harling motioning to me through the glass walls of his office. He wanted to know where the Dixon feature was.

"Drummond's up near Ossining, isn't it?"

I held up my index finger and pointed to the computer; Harling nodded and sat down at his own terminal, from which he could call up my copy.

"Well, actually," Ann said, "Drummond Rehab is more north, in Dutchess County."

Was this a geography lesson? "Ann, we're coming up on deadline right—"

"I called because I wanted to tell you about something, Jack. I don't know why I'm being so nice, except you're the only reporter I know."

Ah. "I appreciate it, Ann. No hard feelings—"

"Actually, you did me a favor, Jack. Really. Thanks."

Thanks?

"So what's the story you've got for me?"

"Okay, here goes. Do you remember about twenty years ago, in a little town upstate, there was a girl who was pushed off a really high—"

"You mean *Lana Paluka?*"

"How did you know?"

"She was from my hometown, Ann. I . . . knew her since she was nine years old. We grew up together."

"That's right, you told me you were from Comity, and I knew she was. But I never made the connection. Well, then, you must know all about the case. And you remember her?"

"I remember her, Ann." It wasn't likely a guy would forget the first girl he had sex with, even if everything else hadn't happened.

"Did her boyfriend really push her off that cliff?"

"My brother and another friend of ours were witnesses."

"Really?" Ann said. "Yes, that's right, there *were* a couple of witnesses. But the boyfriend said he was innocent, didn't he?"

"He was lying. Didn't even care that two people saw him do it. The guy was a criminal from the word go. And a lunatic, too. He made up some story that Lana was tripped out on acid and jumped off that cliff."

"Remember all the stories back then about kids tripping out on acid?" Ann said. "What LSD is doing to our young. Parents get tough on drugs. Timothy Leary."

"Tune in, turn on, drop out. Look what we started—but what we did then seems pretty benign now, doesn't it?"

"I don't know about that," she said. "Kids tripping out and jumping off cliffs doesn't seem all that benign . . . Her boyfriend had that odd name—Sitt? Or was it Skatt?"

"His name was Ethan Skitt."

"That's it," Ann said. "Ethan Skitt. I remember they held up his trial for a long time, hoping she'd come out of it and testify against him. He was convicted, wasn't he?"

"Attempted murder," I said. "They let the fucker out after only thirteen years."

"You sound bitter about that, Jack."

"I am bitter. When he got out, he murdered one of the witnesses who'd testified against him. Just for revenge. My friend Randy Slessenger. Should I love him?"

"I suppose not. I didn't know about that part. But I remembered the rest of it when I saw her."

"What do you mean you saw her?"

"She's here, Jack! At Drummond. She was in some sort of catatonic state for years."

"All this time? Wow! I thought it was a coma, though. What's the difference?"

"A catatonic state is a psychiatric condition; a coma is a physical one."

"What does that mean?"

"It means that for all those years she was technically conscious but didn't acknowledge anyone's presence, look at anyone directly, or speak a word. It means that for twenty years she never went to the bathroom herself, fed herself, dressed herself, did anything for herself, even after her legs healed. If you took Lana Paluka's arm and raised it over her head it would stay there until you took it and moved it down again—for days, even weeks."

Christ Almighty! I'd had no idea.

Harling was motioning me again. Damn. The conversation seemed to be going nowhere—Lana Paluka was my *private* nightmare.

"Ann, thanks for the tip, but twenty-year-old stories aren't exactly hard news."

"Twenty years has to be one of the longest catatonic states on record, Jack. But she's not in it anymore."

"What did she finally die of?" I asked.

"She didn't die, Jack," Ann said. "Last Saturday Lana Paluka woke up."

*The point was to open up a new space, an inner space,
so that we could space out, live for the sheer exultant
point of living. Go to class stoned, shop for food
stoned; go to the movies stoned—see, all is
transformed, the world just started again. On these
luminous occasions, the tension of a political life
dissolved; you could take refuge from the Vietnam
war, from your own hope, terror, anguish. Even if you
weren't political you had something in common
with those who were. Drugs planted utopia
in your own mind.*

—*Todd Gitlin*, The Sixties

3

AUGUST 1989
DRUMMOND REHABILITATION CENTER
DUTCHESS COUNTY, NEW YORK

Dr. Jonathan Baldwin stood in the doorway of Lana's room, watching his patient study her reflection in the bathroom mirror. He was thinking of his brother. It had been twenty-four years since he'd arrived home from school one day to find Eddie sprawled on the bathroom floor in a pool of his own blood—two slashed wrists, the result of a mescaline-induced psychosis. The note beside the body read, "The buttons made me realize how utterly hopeless life really is." Baldwin couldn't help wondering what his brother might have done with his life, if he'd been given a second chance, the way Lana had.

Baldwin glanced down at the stack of paper he was holding in his hand: Lana's medical records, entered into the master files in the Drummond computer when they switched over a few years ago. Baldwin had gone through it yesterday and printed out a copy. The thing was a book. Twenty years of notations by at least eight different doctors in four different facilities. She'd been brought into Comity Hospital on the afternoon of August 18, 1969, in a catatonic stupor. Dr. Edmond Reinman admitted and examined her, found a fracture of the right tibia and fractures of the left fibula, patella and tarsal bones—her only physical injuries. Blood tests revealed that the patient had ingested lysergic acid diethylamide within the previous twenty-four hours. There was also a note by a Dr. Donald Clayfield to the effect that the patient upon being brought to the hospital had experienced a period of agitated excitement in which she stood and threatened attendants in the emergency room with a scalpel before returning to her stupor. *She stood on two broken legs?*

The legs had healed within the year. For the next twenty years, Lana remained more or less in a near total catatonic stupor, broken only by occasional periods of extreme psychomotor agitation: fits of screaming, foot-stamping, tongue-clicking. Except for the occasional fits, during which she screamed over and over, "Save me, save me, help me," words that no doubt had some symbolic significance within her inner belief system, she'd remained totally mute, often striking odd postures but allowing herself to be fed and led about. Eventually she'd been transferred to a state-operated psychiatric facility in Ulster County, New York, then to one in Green County when the first institution was shut down. She had just been transferred to the Brody Institute in Massachusetts when the chief of staff at Drummond received a letter from a blind trust out of New York City called the Miracle Foundation. The letter, signed by a Douglas Enworth, stated that the foundation wished to pay for Lana Paluka's care. The only stipulations given for this largesse were that she be transferred to Drummond, one of the best chronic care psychiatric hospitals in the country, and that no attempt be made to determine her benefactor's identity. On January 2 of every year since, a check for $250,000 had arrived, drawn on a New York City bank and signed by Enworth. The Miracle Foundation.

Baldwin flipped through the sheaf of papers to the more recent notations. Over the years she'd had surprisingly few medical problems. She'd responded to none of the standard courses of treatment, including shock therapy, insulin therapy, and barbiturate therapy. Even a course of the L-dopa drug that Dr. Oliver Sacks down at Beth Abraham Hospital in the Bronx had been so successful with had proved ineffective. She did often exhibit the waxy flex common to catatonics—in which a limb placed in an unnatural position will retain that position for a short while until, like melting wax, it gradually returns to a natural position. Early last year she'd developed a stasis edema of the legs after she stood in a corner for a month, posturing and grimacing.

Baldwin looked back at Lana, who had not taken her eyes from her reflection. She was running her fingertips over the contours of her face, over her mouth, nose, eyelids, cheeks. It was the first time in the year since Baldwin had been head of psychiatric services at Drummond that he'd seen her features relaxed, without that fixed stony expression she always wore, or the blank stare. It was hard to believe this was the same patient Baldwin so often saw being led through the halls with that shuffling, ambling gait.

He realized now that she was quite attractive. Strong, even features and a full well-shaped mouth. Her eyes were blue, her hair a striking pale blond. She was a pretty girl.

Girl? This "girl" was almost forty years old.

The damned thing was positively weird. Catatonics didn't just wake up like this. Not after so long.

Jonathan Baldwin had been a psychiatrist long enough to know that occasionally even the most incoherent schizophrenic, the most regressed hebephrenic, the most chronic depressive simply recovered, sometimes even without medication. But this was more than simple recovery.

By all rights her muscles should have completely atrophied, even with the continuous physical therapy the staff provided. And it wasn't just that her body showed little sign of deterioration due to her illness, it also showed no signs of aging. The girl didn't look a day over eighteen. Of course, Baldwin hadn't seen Lana when they first brought her in—he was barely out of college himself then—but it looked to him as if she hadn't aged a day. The staff had made every effort to provide enough nourishment, supplementing what food she would take by mouth with intravenous feeding, but she should still have looked emaciated. Lana looked more . . . lean and lanky, like a newborn colt.

"Could I see a newspaper, please, doctor?"

Baldwin hung the chart back in its place.

"Of course, Lana. I'll get one from one of the nurses for you."

He appropriated Ann Mahoney's *New York Times* from her desk at the third-floor nurse's station. Lana was still examining her reflection when he came back in, tendrils of matted hair drifting across her forehead. Her hair, in fact, was the only physical reminder of what she'd been like before. In March the nurses had trimmed it very short, a haphazard cut for ease of maintenance that left her looking rather like a porcupine. But it had grown in some and was wild now, a mass of frizzy blond curls.

He handed her the newspaper, wondered if she was thinking what he was thinking: that it had been twenty years since she'd looked in a mirror, twenty years since she'd looked at a paper, twenty years since she'd really looked at anything.

She skimmed the front page of the paper, then handed it back to him, turned again to the mirror.

"I'm thirty-eight years old." She crossed to the window, looked out for a moment. "It's summer. I remember it was summer before. Before my accident."

"Yes, that's right." After Saturday's reaction, Baldwin had decided not to push her to acknowledge the truth, that it had been anything but an accident. The mere fact of her recovery after so long had to be difficult enough to handle, for now. She would accept the rest of it in time. Of course, who knew what would happen when her parents finally showed up?

Damn! They were paging him.

Baldwin excused himself and picked up the phone at the nurse's station.

"John?" It was the hospital administrator, Marcus Gilbert. "Douglas Enworth is here."

"Who?"

"Lana's benefactor."

The Miracle Foundation had been paying for Lana's care for a very long time, since long before Baldwin got to Drummond, yet he knew that never once had a representative shown up in person. Why now? Had someone called them, let them know she'd made a miraculous recovery?

Baldwin hurried over to the administrator's office, where Gilbert introduced him to a smiling middle-aged man so flawlessly groomed that he fairly sparkled. His nails were immaculately manicured, the dome on top of his bald head was so shiny it looked polished, his smile was almost blinding. He was wearing a beautifully cut dark gray suit with a white shirt, and a green silk tie in an elegant peacock feather print.

"Very nice to meet you, doctor." Enworth had a vigorous handshake and a voice that suggested breeding built in rather than studied.

The three men sat down, Enworth and Baldwin in the chairs facing Marcus Gilbert's desk, Gilbert behind it.

"I understand there's been a profound change in Miss Paluka's condition," Enworth said.

"On Saturday she came out of the stupor," Baldwin said simply. "She's now completely responsive."

"Is that usual in this type of case?"

"I know of no other case like this one."

"How so?"

Baldwin gave him a lengthy description of Lana's current condition, explained that she now—suddenly—seemed to have a rational grasp of events and of her situation.

"I'd have to say, based on fifteen years of experience in the practice of psychiatric medicine, that this patient appears to be free of major mental illness, catatonic or otherwise. Her memory of the past twenty years is almost nonexistent, though. And she also has almost no memory of the events that took place around the time of the fall."

"The party I represent will want a complete report, doctor. I'd like to know what, exactly, she *has* remembered."

"Lana says she remembers a green bus," Baldwin said. "She says she hitched a ride to Woodstock, and after that she remembers a man who gave her some LSD. And that's about it."

"A man?"

"A hippie. You remember them, Mr. Enworth. They wore long hair—"

"I remember the hippies, doctor. I want to know about this one."

"He had dark hair and wore an Indian headband and jeans with a patch of the American flag on one knee. That's what Lana remembers."

Enworth laughed. After a moment, he said, "How does she account for her surviving that fall?"

"She says she flew to the bottom."

"Flew?"

"Yes, she's mentioned it a few times but this morning told me that she had confused a dream she'd had—"

"A dream about flying?"

"A very common dream, Mr. Enworth. Having to do with power and control."

"Yes, I suppose it is rather common," Enworth said. "I myself have dreams of flying. Would you like to analyze them sometime?" He laughed again.

"You have to understand that this girl—woman—has lost half of her life to date," Baldwin said. "She was in a state of consciousness that neither you nor I can ever fully understand. Some degree of confusion is to be expected, Mr. Enworth."

Enworth got up and walked over to the bookcase, looked over the titles for a moment, then turned back.

"Yes, of course, I understand. The party I represent only wishes to make sure that she is getting the best care. Do you have any idea why she has suddenly recovered? Why now?"

"None whatsoever." It was easy enough to describe the absence of clinical symptoms, to chart the results of the few neuropsychiatric tests he'd had time to give her, to chronicle the patient's apparently normal brain function including an ability to concentrate he himself envied. Easy enough to describe, not so easy to explain.

"And do you expect to release her from the hospital soon?"

"Well, it's not a simple decision. On the one hand, extended periods of time in institutions are considered something of a last resort nowadays. Drummond is considered a last resort. I don't want her to become 'institutionalized,' as they say, so that she'll never be able to adjust to life on the outside. On the other hand, I want to make sure she can handle—"

"But she's been in institutions for twenty years. Isn't she already institutionalized?"

"Perhaps. But she seems almost like a different person from the one who's been here all these years."

Enworth smiled his blinding smile. "Is that a professional opinion?"

"No, a personal one . . . I was wondering, Mr. Enworth, what sparked your interest in Lana?" Baldwin asked.

Enworth seemed genuinely surprised by the question.

"The party I represent became interested in the case after reading about it in the newspapers."

"Who *is* the party you represent?"

"The Miracle Foundation."

"We know the name of the foundation, Mr. Enworth. But what does it mean?"

There was a silence.

"Miracle as in God's miracle?" Baldwin said.

"Do you believe in miracles, doctor?"

"I don't know. Do you?"

"The Miracle Foundation is dedicated to helping deserving people regain their lives," Enworth said.

"But where does the help come from? When did it begin? What other work does the foundation do?"

Enworth smiled and held up his hand, glanced over at Marcus Gilbert.

"The foundation still retains its wish to remain anonymous, doctors. I trust you will continue to respect that wish."

"Absolutely," Marcus Gilbert said. "And we are most grateful."

"I'd like to see her now."

"Yes, of course," Jonathan Baldwin said. "If you'd just wait outside for a moment, I'll take you right down to her room."

After Baldwin showed him to the reception area, he stepped back inside Gilbert's office and closed the door, keeping his hand on the knob.

"Did you call him, Marcus?"

"Not I. Someone else must have let him know."

"But who knows about the Miracle Foundation?"

Marcus Gilbert shrugged. "It's not something we talk about, Jonathan, but everyone in this hospital knows."

"Well, if we don't find out who has the loose lips, we're going to have the press breathing down our necks in very short order." He opened the door. "I'll take you down there now, Mr. Enworth."

Baldwin led him to Lana's room, where they found her standing by the window, staring out.

"I've brought someone to see you, Lana."

She turned around, looked at Enworth. Baldwin introduced them.

"Would you excuse us for a few moments, doctor?" Enworth said. "I'd like to talk to Lana alone."

"Is that all right with you, Lana?"

"Sure."

Baldwin left the room but stopped short just outside the door. What if this Douglas Enworth was an imposter? What if he was the guy who'd tried to kill her so long ago, come to finish the job?

"You all right, doctor?" Nurse Chemona, passing by in the hall, gave him a strange look.

"Yes, yes, I'm fine," Baldwin said. He decided he was being ridiculous. If Enworth was the boyfriend who'd tried to kill her she'd have recognized him, even after twenty years.

Jonathan Baldwin went on about his business, but not before asking Nurse Mahoney to go in and check on Lana in a few minutes.

4

Lana's hair was the color of a yellow pearl, but it was of a certain coarse texture, full and thick and curly, even frizzy. At around the age of twelve, she cut it very short for a brief fling as a tomboy. She tried to ease her way into our gang, which consisted primarily of my brother and myself, our cousin Denny Hartigan, Randy Slessenger, and Greg Horan, but her effort to join us on an equal footing failed miserably despite her excellent batting arm. As she developed physically, she tried to hold on to her shaky place in our group with a new tack, cultivating a gutter mouth that outdid us all and using makeup heavily, white lipstick, eyes rimmed with heavy mascara and black liner. When we all started smoking pot up on Devil's Meadow at the top of High Exposure, Lana always inhaled the deepest, talked the dirtiest, made the raunchiest suggestions. The effects of marijuana exaggerated that low throaty laugh of hers.

She started having sex with my brother at fourteen, by which time she had already begun to grow out her hair. At the in-between stage it seemed more frizzy than anything else, but by the time she was with Ethan several years later, it reached the middle of her back. She tried to tame the thick unruly mass with a ribbon tied low, the hair hanging out below it like a tail. With wisps of pearl-yellow hair escaping from the ribbon, more wisps drifting across her forehead, and those floor-length peasant dresses she wore, she always reminded me of a heroine in an eighteenth-century novel.

Through the glass walls I could see my editor reading the Dixon copy on his computer screen, munching away at potato chips, wiping his hands with a napkin he kept on his desk. Jim Harling always had a big bowl of chips on his desk, which was always filled and from which he helped himself freely all day. He wasn't exactly fat, but he had a large paunch and more than one chin. I liked him, thoroughly enjoyed his almost childlike enthusiasm for the movies, his children, and, especially, the newspaper business.

Possible story angles on Lana raced through my mind as I headed into Harling's office. I hadn't even thought to ask Ann Mahoney if Lana had said anything about what had happened on High Exposure. And Harling might not be interested in Lana Paluka, whether she was catatonic or chattering like a magpie.

I stood there watching him read the Dixon piece on the screen, scrolling down as he went.

"Great stuff," he said a couple of times, without looking up.

But I wasn't thinking about Elmond Dixon. I was thinking about the day, not long after I began my freshman year in college, when I got the call about Lana and Ethan.

It was very late in the summer of 1969. I had already left for college; my twin brother, Alan, and I were going our separate ways for the first time in our lives, Alan to Harvard, I to Boston University. When the call came, I was already moved into a room in one of the huge dormitories on Commonwealth Avenue.

"Jack, something's happened." It was my mother on the phone.

"What is it? Is Alan all right?"

"He's fine." A pause. "You remember Lana Paluka?"

"Of course, Mom."

"Well, yesterday Ethan Skitt tried to kill her."

"What?"

"He pushed her off the cliff at High Exposure."

"You're kidding."

"No, Jack, I'm not."

I hesitated a moment, trying to adjust to this news, then suddenly realized what my mother had said.

"What do you mean, *tried* to kill her?"

She sighed. "I don't know how, dear, but she survived."

"That's crazy, Mom. Nobody would survive a fall from up there."

"Well, that's why I'm calling you, really. I know it seems impossible. But your brother and Randy were there. The two of them saw the whole thing. Alan's going to have to testify."

So there I was, separated from my twin brother for the first time in my life, scared, excited, happy to finally be able to shine on my own. And within the next year or so I would have to go home and watch Alan testify in a murder trial.

* * *

"So how'd you find Georgina, anyway?" Jim Harling finally looked up from the computer.

"Just a lucky break, I guess." No point in mentioning the private detective I'd hired.

"Did you call Dixon's defense attorney after Dan Randall said he'd subpoena her?"

I nodded. For some reason, I suddenly wanted to confess giving Georgina the bribe. I didn't.

Harling grabbed a chip and popped it in his mouth.

"Well, this is great stuff, Jack. You outdid yourself on this one."

He punched up the keys to save and transfer the story, turned off the computer, and waved me into a chair. I filled him in on Lana Paluka.

"I covered that story," he said. "Back when I was starting out in this business, my first job as a reporter on a paper in Albany. I was in that courtroom every day. Fascinating case . . . You knew the Paluka girl personally? How?"

I wasn't about to say "in the biblical sense," though I thought of it.

"My twin brother was one of the witnesses."

"Really? Which one?"

"The tall, good-looking one," I said. All my life, people had been telling me how tall and good-looking my twin brother was. One girl in high school told me she'd do anything—anything at all—just to get Alan to smile, just so she could get a look at those dimples. Not that I'm so bad-looking myself, but I'm a redhead, and shorter, stockier, taking after my mother's side of the family, all redheads except her. Alas, I got freckles instead of dimples.

Harling laughed. "Ah, identical twins."

"Very funny," I said. "Anyway, the other witness was our best friend, Randy Slessenger."

"Well, how about that," Harling said. "Were you in the courtroom?"

"Only when Alan and Randy testified. I went back to college right afterward. Both of us did."

"We must have been there at the same time," Harling said. "Small world, huh? And she's alive. What was it, 'sixty-eight? No. It was right after Woodstock. 'Sixty-nine. I can't believe she survived this long. She should have been dead—falling from that height."

"She should have been scrambled eggs, Jim. High Exposure is almost two hundred feet high. Nothing but jagged rocks at the bottom."

"So you knew the place?"

"Yeah, you could say I knew the place."

"And now you're saying she's come out of the coma?"

I explained the psychiatric distinction between a coma and a catatonia.

"Sounds like a coma to me," Harling said.

"I thought I might go on up to that hospital and check it out. Might make a good feature."

"You could do a followup on the key players, too. 'Where are they now?' sort of thing. That Skitt kid served time in the state penitentiary, didn't he? You know what happened to him after he got out of prison?"

"Yeah, I know exactly. When he got out, he went after Randy. Shot him in the head."

"For revenge?"

"Who the hell knows why? I suppose for revenge. And he probably would have gone after my brother, and Lana, too, if they hadn't caught him and thrown him back in prison, where he belongs."

Harling nodded. "I've always been fascinated by that kind of killer. Even as long as I've been in this business, I still wonder what goes on in a mind like that. The serial killer. The hitman. The cold-blooded monster. I mean, to really get inside that mind . . ." He laughed. "You know, Jack, I've already got Joette going up there to cover your brother's mall opening."

I smiled. "That's all right, she can still do that."

He laughed again. I really liked Jim Harling.

"Call me when you see the Paluka woman," he said. "Then head over to Comity. Drummond Rehab is fairly close to Comity, isn't it?"

"Fifty miles or so."

"Right. Get some additional background there, get some good quotes from the people who knew her well, who remember her. Fax it in for the Sunday edition if you want to stay up there for the weekend and visit your family. Story ought to be a snap, since you probably know exactly who to see, plus they'll all be willing to talk to you. Easiest assignment you ever had. Right?"

Wrong.

When I got home, the first thing I saw was half a squirrel—just the head and midsection—lying in the hallway. Reggie had obviously been out hunting that morning and left me a present. No sign of the rest of the squirrel. Or the cat.

I came in, tossed my keys and briefcase on the wicker chair in the hall, then went into the living room to get the fireplace shovel. Trying not to think about where the rest of the squirrel might be, I scooped the remains up and threw them into a pile of leaves in the woods behind the house. I could see Gerta Pearce watching me from her usual kneeling position in her garden, all three yippy Yorkies at her side.

"Reggie's at it again, I see," she yelled across the yards.

"I think he just likes killing." Last week it had been a field mouse and a chipmunk.

I was still carrying the shovel when I walked over to Gerta's yard. She was wearing a polkadot gardening hat and bermuda shorts.

"How's the garden coming?" I asked.

"Okay, except my gladiolas are sulking."

"I wanted to ask you a favor, Gerta."

"Feed Reggie?"

"I guess you know me pretty well by now." I gave her a fairly sincere sheepish look. Since my divorce, I'd always kenneled Reggie when I traveled, until one weekend when I had to leave in a hurry and asked Gerta. She said she didn't mind—her children were all gone now, she had only the dogs to take care of. And her husband, of course.

"Really, Jack, it's fine." She picked up one of the Yorkies and stroked it. "Reggie is such a sweet kitty."

I stifled a laugh. "You sure?"

"Positive."

"I'll only be gone a couple of days. I should be back by Monday."

"No problem at all. Be glad to. I just hope he doesn't bring me a squirrel, too. Or something worse . . ."

I decided not to mention the time Reggie brought me the skunk.

"Where are you going? Out on a story?"

"Just home to see my folks," I said as I headed toward my yard. "You're a terrific neighbor, Gerta. Thanks."

I leaned the shovel against the back porch, where I hoped it would miraculously clean itself of dead squirrel cooties without my having to wash it, then went back inside.

Reggie was asleep on my bed. The white Angora fur on the purple satin quilt, a reckless purchase inspired by my divorce three years ago, made quite a picture. All it needed was squirrel blood dripping from Reggie's claws.

I stroked the cat's fur. "Reg, you're a cold-blooded killer."

Cold-blooded killer.

It was what the district attorney, Dave Bonsall, had called Ethan Skitt during his opening statement. *This young man, ladies and gentlemen, who sits now before you, is a cold-blooded killer. Heartless, remorseless, brutal. It does not matter that his victim—*

*an innocent young girl—somehow miraculously survived and at
this moment lies in her hospital bed. It is the intent that matters.
And of that there can be no doubt . . .*

Innocent young girl? Lana?

The State of New York vs. Ethan Skitt lasted nearly a month.
The trial was held in the old stone courthouse building in Kingston, in a courtroom crammed every day with reporters, with people from Comity, with parents, friends, supporters, detractors,
and the merely curious. The crowds got bigger every day, as did
the headlines.

During the long wait for the trial, Alan and I completed our
freshman years. I was studying in the communications school at
Boston, having wanted to be a reporter for as long as I could
remember, even though Dad had always expected both of us to
follow in his footsteps. "The practice is already *there*," Dad
had said. But I had never liked the sound of it—Doctor Wells
and Sons—nor the prospect of returning to the town where I
grew up, only to spend my days touching the flabby bodies of
Comity matrons. Alan was smarter, more personable, more motivated, and a lot more popular. He would make a good doctor, I
wanted to be a reporter. I should say, though, that it did surprise
me to see Alan actually return to Comity and take over our father's practice. I had always assumed he'd prefer a bigger stage.
Park Avenue, perhaps.

Dad drove to Boston to get both of us when it was time for
Alan to testify. We could have gone on our own, but Dad welcomed the opportunity, as he saw it, to recapture that sense of
closeness we'd always had as a family.

So Kevin Wells and his boys drove down from Boston as if on
a family outing, though Alan was uncharacteristically quiet during the long ride. I asked him if he was scared, he said he wasn't.
To which Dad boomed, "Nothing to be scared about. It's your
civic duty to tell what you saw."

Which, of course, it was. Still, I knew my brother really *was*
scared, though he wasn't one to admit that kind of thing. Certainly no one in the courtroom would have guessed it from the
relaxed, composed way he answered the prosecutor's questions.
But I knew.

Reggie opened one eye and looked at me, stretched, curled up
again, and went back to sleep.

I threw a few things into an overnight case and went downstairs to make a call to the Drummond Rehabilitation Center for
directions. Then I called my parents.

Dad answered the phone. When I heard his voice, I realized I'd moved back to this part of the country over a year ago but some-how managed to visit my parents and brother only twice, not a much better record than my yearly visits when I'd lived in Akron.

"This weekend?" Dad said. "Really?"

"Guess I'll be coming to Alan's mall opening after all."

"You going to cover it for the paper?"

"No, Dad. I'm a little past mall-opening stories."

"Well, this is great news, Jack. Your mother and I were just saying how much we miss you."

After I hung up the phone, I considered calling my own twin boys back in Akron, Craig and Chris. The last time I talked to Craig, he wanted to know if it was all right to have his ear pierced. My ex, Donna, said that if I gave the go-ahead she would too. The whole idea depressed me, not only because I couldn't believe my sensible sixteen-year-old wanted to do it but also be-cause the lecture that came to mind sounded so much like the lecture Dad gave me the time I walked in from college with my hair down to my shoulders. I told Craig I'd think about it. That was nearly a week ago. I decided another few days wouldn't hurt.

I locked up, got the Saab out of the garage, and headed out into the warm afternoon.

Once one has experienced LSD, existential revolution,
fought the intellectual game-playing of the individual
in society, of one's identity, one realizes that action is
the only reality; not only reality but morality as well.
One learns reality is a subjective experience.

—*Free*, Revolution for the Hell of It

5

It was already dusk by the time Douglas Enworth left Lana's room. He'd been very nice to her, offering her congratulations and good wishes, but she still couldn't understand why a man like that, or anyone for that matter, would want to take care of her all these years. No one had ever taken care of her, except Ethan.

She stood at the open window looking out over the parking lot, at the sweep of lawns beyond it. Enworth was down in the lot now, getting into a small silver sports car. She listened to the dull thud of the car door closing, the muffled hum of the engine, the gritty crunch of the gravel as the car backed out from between the painted white lines. The car stopped for a moment, then started back up again, moving forward now, easing first into a dip in the blacktop, then coasting onto the road leading away from the parking lot and finally disappearing from view. She wondered where he was going, where he lived.

What was out there for her?

Slowly, Lana raised her right arm in front of her, brought it down, then up again in a graceful arc. First one arm, then the other. She imagined a membrane filling with air, expanding, contracting. She imagined the wingbeats.

She could divide her life into three distinct parts now. There was the "before time." She could remember it exactly.

She is ten. She comes home from school on a winter afternoon and hears strange noises from the apartment—banging, thumping, cursing, the sound of heavy footsteps. Standing at the bottom of the stairs, she looks up. Her mother is in the apartment, crashing about in a drunken fury. Suddenly, Ellie appears at the top of the stairs, holding onto the branches of the small Christmas tree that has been in the corner of the living room. Only two nights ago she and Ellie and John had all decorated the tree with strings of popcorn and shiny golden balls.

Ellie doesn't seem to notice Lana standing there as she hauls the tree down the steps. Her eyes are moist and half-closed, and she is holding one arm out in front of her like a blind woman, as if guiding the way, steering clear of collisions. The tree bumps down each step, rustling the branches, breaking ornaments. Popcorn is flying everywhere.

Lana steps out to block Ellie's way.

"Mom! What are you *doing?*"

Ellie glances at Lana for a moment, then pushes past her, opens the back door, and drags the tree into the small yard in back of the bar. She is wearing a thin white blouse with short puffed sleeves. It is freezing outside. She sets the tree on its side in the dirt, turns, and runs back into the house. Lana knows what is happening; she knows it from the look in her mother's eyes.

Lana runs into the bar screaming for her father to come and help her. No one is there. The bar is closed, locked up tight. Why is the bar closed in the middle of the afternoon?

She will have to be the witness. She runs up to the apartment. A table is overturned in front of the sofa. A small porcelain statue of a dog has been smashed on the floor. Lana pleads with her mother to stop. She begs and cries but her mother only laughs at her and shoves her out of the way. Now, Ellie grabs the Christmas stockings, and the presents, too, scooping it all up in an armload. She keeps dropping things on the stairs on her way down, then stooping down to pick them up and dropping others, cursing the whole time at Lana, at John, at her own mother, at life.

"Mom, stop it! What are you doing?" Lana keeps screaming.

Ellie ignores her and sets about her task, tossing each present on top of the tree in the backyard, one by one, a red and green and gold heap on the grass. Then she throws open the shed under the stairs where the lawn mower is and pulls out the gas can.

"Why?" Lana gasps, at ten still thinking there a reason for these things.

Finally her mother stops, whirls around, gazes at Lana, her eyes diminishing in her face, narrowing to slits.

"If you don't know I'm not going to tell you. You miserable little shit. You disrespectful, ungrateful—"

With one sweeping motion Ellie pulls a pack of matches from

her pocket and lights one, tosses it onto the heap. With a muted "whoof" the entire mound erupts in flames that swallow Christmas in a roaring bonfire. Ellie's face seems to glow in the light of the flames. She stands watching for a moment; then, when Lana begins to sob, she turns and glares at her.

"That's what disrespectful little girls get."

Then she turns and stumbles back into the bar, leaving Lana to stand and watch the orange flames leap up into the freezing air.

Later, sober, maybe the next day, Ellie comes into Lana's room and puts her arms around Lana and cries. She always cries afterward and begs Lana's forgiveness in a litany of moist sorrows. And Lana forgives her. Of course, at ten she forgives her.

Yes. Lana could remember that time perfectly, chronologically, accurately: the Christmas-present burning, the drunken tirades, the men in the bar, the brawls between Ellie and John.

She never had figured out what it was that she had done wrong that time. It took her many years to realize that what she had done could have been anything, anything at all. Something big or small, real or imagined.

With Ethan's help, fear and embarrassment had given way to rage; rage had given way to loathing. And at the end, Ellie had had no power to produce sympathy in Lana but for her tears, and even the power of Ellie's tears had long ago dimmed.

She remembered the last few days, too: waking up, as if from a night's dream, Dr. Baldwin, the nurses, the visit from Enworth.

But she could remember almost nothing about the void, the big dark space of time from when she and Ethan got to Woodstock to waking up here. The void everyone said lasted twenty years.

She listened. Other cars were pulling out of the parking lot now; she could hear the heels of shoes (high heels, flat women's pumps, men's shoes) clicking on the asphalt, the sound of muffled voices. Her senses were very sharp; she could recognize individual voices from very far away, even hear what people were saying. There, out in the corridor, Nurse Mahoney was telling someone that Mrs. Erickson needed her bedpan changed. It was somehow a familiar sensation, this intensity of perceptions, as if she had experienced it before. If she could only remember when, and how.

Later, Lana would find out who Mrs. Erickson was, maybe go and see her.

She turned and went to the bathroom, emptied her bladder,

washed her face in very cold water. Staring at herself in the mirror, she filled the glass from the tap. As she drank it down, she remembered the way her father would stand at the bottom of the back stairs and yell: "We got customers, Ellie. You think you could get off your ass and come down and help?" And Ellie, sitting at the kitchen table, her bottle of vodka beside her, would giggle in her pathetic little defiance, and take a last swig before slamming the glass down on the table and weaving her way downstairs.

Lana studied herself in the mirror. Her whole being had changed. It was subtle, at least no one else seemed to notice it. But it was real. Her eyes were no longer blue. They were azure. She now had a narrow, gaunt-cheeked look. She had the same features she always had, yet they didn't add up the same. The color of her eyes. The way her forehead protruded. Her profile. Her nose, which had always been prominent, now looked slightly hooked, like a beak. She wet the brush, slicked her hair back so that the shape of her head showed. She was slim, toned, primed, fit . . . She could soar, she could fly high over this place without fear, up into the sky, out over the landscape to search for Ethan. She could see him from the sky.

She remembered a story from school, a myth: the goddess Minerva had intervened for Perdix when his uncle Daedalus tried to kill him by pushing him off a tower. Minerva saw Perdix fall, and saved him by changing him into a bird. Of course, Minerva changed Perdix into a partridge—a shy, retiring bird, afraid of high places. She, Lana, would be a condor, an eagle, a killer. With her prey already spotted.

If only Ethan were here, he could explain it all to her.

She turned away from her reflection in the mirror. The doctor said she was free to go anywhere in the hospital. Time to go explore.

The hospital library was a small windowless room lined with books on all four walls. She had found it easily, merely by asking. There were so many people to ask, everyone was very nice to her. Everyone shook her hand, congratulated her. They all seemed to know her. And she, locked away somewhere in her mind, knew them.

A large woman with thick ankles and a moonish face was sitting behind a desk.

"May I help you?"

"What's that?" Lana pointed to the square box on top of the woman's desk that looked like a television.

"It's a computer."

"And that?" She pointed to the strange flat typewriter next to it.

"That's the keyboard. Watch."

The woman pushed a few keys on the typewriter, and the letters she punched appeared on the screen.

Nice trick. "What's it for?"

The woman laughed. "Well, it has a lot of uses. We type on it. Or we can use it like a giant file cabinet, it has all sorts of information inside—"

"What's your name?"

"Elizabeth Norton. I'm a volunteer here."

"Do I know you?"

"Sometimes I go into your room and talk to you."

"Do you? What do you say?"

"Oh, anything. Anything that comes into my mind." She smiled. "Sometimes I tell you things about myself, if I've had an argument with my husband, or if I'm having a bad day. I think I told you things I've never told anyone."

"Because I didn't hear?"

"I suppose so."

"Will you tell me something now?"

Elizabeth's face became flushed and she was silent.

"That's all right," Lana said. "You don't have to."

"It's so much nicer this way, Lana. You can talk back."

"But I don't have a fucking thing to say."

Elizabeth hesitated a moment, then said, "I'd like to help you, Lana. If you want anything, you just ask. All right?"

"I want to see a book," Lana said. "About birds."

Elizabeth got up and walked over to the far wall, scanned the titles for a moment, then pulled down a large blue volume, held it out. "This is a book about birds. It has some beautiful color plates. Is this what you want?"

Lana nodded, took the book, and sat down on one of the chairs in the room. It was called *Basic Ornithology*. The letters on the cover were gold. She opened it, thumbed through the pages. Vibrant colors flashed by her eyes, reds and greens and blues and browns, all on a white background. So many different kinds of birds were pictured here, all of them beautiful. And they had lovely names, too. She whispered them: kingbird, lark, wren, thrasher, gull, sparrow, owl, tern.

She turned to the table of contents, found a chapter heading called "The Aerodynamics of Flight." The chapter was all about things like "lift" and "drag" and "thermals" and "gravity." It said birds had hollow bones.

She closed the book. It was ridiculous, her being a bird. *Basic Ornithology* said human bodies weren't suited for flying. The bone structure was wrong; there were no wings, the chest cavity wasn't right. Humans didn't have feathers like the birds, or even membranes, like the bats. Aerodynamically speaking, the human body was pathetic.

But Lana couldn't think of any other way she could have survived. Maybe they were all lying. Maybe she had never fallen from High Exposure in the first place. Maybe the whole thing never even happened.

Maybe this was a dream—a nightmare—and she and Ethan had been together all these years.

"I heard you had a visitor this afternoon, Lana," Elizabeth said.

How did everyone know so much about her, when she didn't know anything about them?

"Why do you think a man like that would be interested in me, Elizabeth?"

"He's the head of a big charity, from Manhattan. At least that's what everyone says. They help people who need help."

"That's what he told me," she said. No use wondering about it. It was just one more thing Lana didn't understand.

Lana handed the book to Elizabeth, and turned to go.

"Nice to see you, Lana," Elizabeth called after her. "You seem so much better today."

Better than what? A silent catatonic hulk? Certainly better than that.

"Lana," Elizabeth said, "I'll tell you something that I told you once, when you didn't hear."

Lana turned around and looked at the woman, a stranger.

"I had a very unhappy childhood," Elizabeth Norton said. "I felt ugly and unloved. I never had a date until I was nearly twenty, and my husband was the first and only man I ever went out with. Sometimes I'm sorry for having married him out of desperation. I was afraid no one else would want me."

It was Ethan's idea to perform the ceremony up at Devil's Meadow. He said it would be a closure for them.

It took them about half an hour to walk there. When they got to the meadow, Ethan sat down crosslegged in the grass, brushed the hair away from his face. His hair had grown long now and he usually tied it back with a rawhide band, but he wasn't wearing the band today. His black hair shone in the sunlight like polished ebony.

"Are you ready?" He pulled a razor blade from the pocket of his jeans, took it out of the cardboard.

Lana was startled for a moment, but she sat down across from him. He smiled. It wasn't a winning smile, like Alan's, not a flashy smile. There was something somber around the edges of Ethan's smile.

They needed each other, she and Ethan. Lana knew that.

"I'll make a cut on your fingertip," he said, "then you'll make a cut on mine. Not a big cut. Then we'll touch fingers. We'll mix our blood. They did it like this in a book I read a long time ago. Soulmates."

It was a powerful sensation, the quick raw slash with the blade, the pain gone in a moment. The blood oozed out, twin globules, deep and thick and red; then they touched.

He said, "Always I will love you, Lana. Forever. Forever. Forever beyond the stars." He looked at her. "Now you say it."

"Always I will love you, Ethan . . ."

When she finished saying the words he kissed her gently on the lips. "And I'll protect you," he said . . .

"Lana?"

She opened her eyes. She had been half-dreaming, thinking of another life, in the time before all this happened. In this life, Dr. Baldwin was standing in the doorway of her room, and she was lying on her bed. It was Wednesday morning.

"Fine. I was just thinking, doctor, dreaming. About Ethan."

"What were you dreaming?"

"We got married. We made up a ceremony, cut our fingers. Mingled blood."

"You were young, Lana."

"Do you know where Ethan is?"

"No, I'm afraid not, Lana. He might be still in prison. Maybe he's married by now. Maybe has children."

"No. He wouldn't have done that. He wouldn't have left me."

"He tried to kill you, Lana. Can you face that?"

"But you don't hurt a person you love."

"You don't remember it?"

She strained to remember but all she could get were flashes. Rain. A hot breeze. A lake. Sky. They were arguing. "How could you do that, Lana?" Ethan had said. If only she could remember what she had done. Her brain still worked. It was a matter of starting with the outcome, then figuring out why the outcome didn't fit with the facts, couldn't possibly fit. What *was* the outcome? Ethan had been convicted of trying to kill her—

"Lana?"

"No. I don't remember. But I know it isn't true."

"Sometimes the things we believe when we're eighteen don't have much to do with what we know when we're almost forty."

"When can I leave?"

He smiled. "Give it time, Lana. Give yourself a chance to get adjusted."

The doctor was keeping her here, insisting she become a part of the hospital rhythm. It only *seemed* as if she could go anywhere.

"Are you angry, Lana?" he said.

"Why would I be angry?" she said. *Don't tell him anything. Outsmart him.*

"I don't know. You just seem angry to me. It's perfectly understandable. Been having any more of those dreams?"

Why in the world had she ever told him about flying?

"Oh, no, doctor. I'm settling in."

She would say no more about flying, surviving. If she did he would never let her out of here. And she had to get out. She had to find Ethan.

"How do you feel about your parents coming, Lana?"

Her parents?

"They won't come."

"Nurse Mahoney got in touch with them last night. They said they'd be here in the morning. This morning."

"I'll believe it when I see it."

"Why do you think they wouldn't come?"

"Have they ever come to see me?"

"They've been here a few times. You have to remember, Lana, that it must have been very painful to see you that way."

Sure.

"The last time I saw Ellie she was screaming at me."

"About what?"

She shrugged. "Oh, the usual."

"What was the usual?"

"Oh, that I was too fat. And that I was to be home early. And where was I going. I didn't even tell them I was never coming back. See, we had some money saved, and after Woodstock, we were gone."

"Where were you going to go?"

She shrugged. "Oh, just anywhere. Away from Comity, from everything."

"Was it so bad there?"

"Not when I was with Ethan."

"Well, you never *did* go back."

She looked at him, laughed. "Yeah, that's right. I never did."

"What happened at Woodstock?"

She closed her eyes, tried to remember. Sarah told them not to go to Woodstock with all that money. Ethan agreed, took their money out of the pocket of his backpack, and handed it to Sarah. His mother was still holding the bills when they walked away.

The rest was mostly blank.

She opened her eyes again. There were two old people, an old man and an old woman, standing in the doorway of her room now. They were peering in at her.

"Look at this, John," the old woman said. "She really is back."

The voice sounded familiar—

"It's a miracle, Ellie."

Her mother? This puffy old woman?

She squinted. But they couldn't be her mother and father. They looked more like a grandmother and a grandfather. The woman came toward her. She was all dressed up in a pink suit that looked like something out of the thirties, from one of the movies Ellie used to watch all the time. Something Carole Lombard would have worn.

The old woman came toward her. Soft flabby arms encircled her, a smell of perfume and hairspray. No liquor on her breath. It couldn't be Ellie.

"It's a miracle, Ellie," the old man said again.

Ellie Paluka. Her mother. She'd gained some weight and her jowls were soft. And she was gray. Well, wasn't that the ultimate irony—Miss Radio City Music Hall goes gray.

Ellie must have told her three hundred times how, once, Cecil B. deMille came backstage after the show, and how she wasn't dancing the night deMille came looking for girls to be in the movies, and if she had been dancing, it would have changed everything. "Imagine, Lana! Cecil B. deMille! If he'd have seen me that night, my whole life would have been completely different," Ellie used to say, as if Lana cared *what* Miss Radio City had to say. Would she say it now, in front of this doctor?

"We're glad to have you back, Lana." The old man hugged her.

Why did everyone keep talking in riddles?

"From where?"

"Well, the doctors could never really give us a good answer, Lana," he said. "Mostly you just sat. Sometimes you thrashed around, but mostly you sat. And a lot of the time you had your arms out." He raised his arms outward from his body, imitating a bird.

She started to laugh.

"You don't remember any of it?" he said.

She remembered the times he made Ellie beg, like a dog.

No. She didn't want to remember that. She wanted to fly through that window and be gone from these people.

"Go away!" Lana said.

"Now, just a minute—"

"You must give her some time, Mrs. Paluka," Dr. Baldwin said.

"Lana, please," Ellie said, now pleading, pale eyes in a paler face. "Please talk to us."

"I never wanted to see you again. And now here you are."

"But you don't have anyone else but us," Ellie said. Her voice sounded wheezy.

"What's the matter with your voice, Ellie?"

"Your mother has a lung disease," John said.

Was that supposed to make her sorry?

Suddenly Ellie reached into her purse and held out a small box wrapped in silver paper with a red ribbon.

"I brought this for you, honey."

Lana glanced down at the present, then looked into her mother's eyes, which were resplendent with hurt. Her hair had receded back from her forehead; it looked thin and brittle. She was an old woman, maybe even dying. Did that mean Lana had to forgive her, love her?

"Take it, Lana," Ellie said, tears streaming down her face. "It's for you."

Lana looked down again at the offering. It was that time with the presents that had started everything.

Lana shook her head, drew her knees up to her chest. She would hold onto loathing Ellie, and her father too, even if she didn't have anyone else.

"Lana, give your mother a chance," John said.

Lana laughed, looked over at the doctor, then at Ellie and John.

"Anybody got a match?"

She searched her mother's eyes for some sign of recognition of her joke and found none. Ellie probably *didn't* remember. It was thirty years ago to her. Lana had to get that concept into her brain.

"Your mother's changed, Lana," John said, pretending he didn't remember either. "She's been in AA for years. Alcoholics Anonymous. She hasn't had a drink for a very long time."

Lana stared at her mother. The idea of Ellie without her bottle of vodka—

"I'm completely clean," Ellie said. "And it was all because of what happened to you, Lana."

Did she think that would make up for everything? It didn't matter one way or the other to Lana. There was some satisfaction, though, in hearing the sound of Ellie's wheezy voice.

There was a long silence. What did these two strangers want from her? Instant love?

"Where's Ethan?" Lana said.

Ellie and John looked at each other; then John said, "You weren't here all the time. First your legs had to heal, you were in another place, but then the insurance ran out . . ."

"I asked a question," said Lana.

Another exchange of looks between the two of them. Finally, John said, "The bastard is in prison, Lana."

"And he'll rot there forever, if I have anything to say about it," Ellie added putting the present down on the table by the bed.

"But I thought the doctor said I was here twenty years. Ethan's been in prison that long?"

Ellie crossed her arms over her chest. "As far as I'm concerned he shouldn't have spent one minute in prison. He *should* have fried."

"You always hated Ethan, Ellie. You hated him because I loved him."

Ellie clicked her tongue on the roof of her mouth, sighed. "No, Lana, that isn't true. I hated him because he wasn't good for you. He was no good, Lana, I always told you that."

Why was she lying? She had *always* hated Ethan.

"You're acting like a child, Lana."

"I am a child."

"Tell her, John."

John Paluka sat down on the bed next to her and said, "Lana, you must listen to me. Ethan Skitt is a bad man. He tried to kill you."

"No," she said, tears coming swiftly. "I won't listen. And I won't believe it. I don't care what you say."

"Oh, for God's sake, John," Ellie said. "You've got to tell her what happened in '82. Then she'll know what kind of a boy she thought she loved."

Part Two

Priestman
Winter 1982

*From that hour, Siddhartha ceased to fight against his
destiny. There shone in his face the serenity of
knowledge of one who is no longer confronted with
conflict of desires, who has found salvation, who is in
harmony with the stream of events, full of sympathy
and compassion, surrendering himself to the stream,
belonging to the unity of all things.*

—*Hermann Hesse,* Siddhartha

6

The man they called the Priest had done his time. It was the
highest achievement available in a world where time wasn't
counted by a clock, or by days and nights, but by years. Time
didn't just pass; you had to do something to it—kill time, defeat
time, conquer time, triumph over time. Time was the enemy, even
more the enemy than the guards and the cages. Also, there were
no women, no mirrors, and you couldn't wear blue.

Only the guards wore blue.

The superintendent had taken away mirrors last year when he
discovered that a broken bit of a mirror could be used as a
weapon. A man died for the superintendent to discover that.

There was no natural light in the place, so you could never be
sure what hour it was. The blare of the bells and the clanking
groans of a hundred cages opening and shutting in unison were
the only reliable indication that time was passing. You counted
your life by years. Scoggins was doing nine to twelve, McGregor
one to three. If you asked any man how much time he had left,
he always had it figured, to the day. Three years, two months, six
days.

Except the man they called the Priest, who told anyone who
asked, "It doesn't matter when the Priestman gets out. Priestman
is already dead."

Priestman always talked about himself in the third person. It
was one of the things that contributed to his crazyman rep.

* * *

"Priestman wants bellbottoms."

The Priest stood in the doorway of the parole-clothing department. He had come to turn in his state-issued clothes and prison radio headphones and to pick up the civilian clothing provided to each departing prisoner. He was going home today. Not that he would have a home to go to anymore; few would after thirteen years in the joint. But he'd maxed out his time, and the superintendent had no choice but to release him. Even if he *was* fuckin' nuts.

Two guards were on hand: Oscar Lafitt, the rotund C.O. who was going to drive Priestman to the bus depot, and Bernard Reichevic, the C.O. in charge of parole clothing, who was working on a crossword puzzle at his desk near the row of high shelves along the back wall. Both wore blue.

Priestman wore the inmate's green. The clothes hung on him; the pants were held up with a rope belt. He had a rawhide band wrapped around his forehead, like always, and he was unshaven.

Standing next to Oscar Lafitt, Priestman looked like he'd just gotten out of a Nazi concentration camp. Mostly, this was his own doing; other men inside managed to eat well enough, but Priestman was skin and bones. His head was nearly bald, his skull littered with sparse patches of dark brown hair and raw-looking scabs, the result of the "haircut" a couple of screws had given him a few months ago. One of the gashes was oozing something yellow-greenish. Until the screw haircut, the Priest's hair had reached halfway down his back.

Arnold "Reds" Scoggins, a huge man with a mass of kinky orange hair, glanced up from the December *Hustler* he was reading.

"Bellbottoms?"

The Priest's intense dark eyes were focused right on him, which pissed Scoggins off. Everyone knew you didn't look a man in the eye in here unless you were his buddy, or unless you were conning him or fucking him. Of course, everybody also knew that the Priest was a goddamned lunatic and had been for years. Given seven to ten for attempted murder, he should have been out in four, five years max, but he'd knifed a guy who was trying to rape him less than a month into his term. You had to respect a man for protecting himself, especially since he was only nineteen at the time. Still, the Priest was the strangest cat who ever walked in any joint Scoggins had ever been in, and he'd been in a few.

The other inmate in parole-clothing was called H.Q., for Harry Quinton DeWitt. DeWitt, who'd been eating a doughnut and peeking over Scoggins's shoulder at the *Hustler* centerfold, was looking at the Priest now.

"We ain't got no bellbottoms," DeWitt said. H. Q. Dewitt had no respect for a man who couldn't hack it. You can't pay the time, don't do the crime, was what he always said. And that included the ones who cracked up, too.

"Why not?" Priestman said.

"Because bellbottoms went out with flower children, man. Don't you know that?"

"Priestman doesn't care," Priestman said.

"Look," DeWitt said, "you get your gate money and whatever's in your account. You get a pair of pants and a shirt and a belt, and a pair of socks and shoes. And if it's winter, like now, you get a coat. You don't get to choose the style. This ain't fuckin' Macy's."

"DeWitt's got a point." This from the back of the room, where Reichevic had stopped doing his puzzle and was walking over to the Priest.

"Bellbottoms? Fuckin' guy's gone," Lafitt said to Reichevic, who nodded.

H. Q. DeWitt and Arnold Scoggins concurred with this assessment, possibly the only thing they would have agreed with their guards about. The Priest was a total gonzo. There was the way he looked, for one thing. Not that everyone in the joint didn't have a similar kind of look, a kind of emptiness about the eyes that came from the sameness of life, from boredom. But in the Priest, you could see a certain ghoulishness, too, maybe because in him boredom mixed with derangement. Or maybe it was because of his misaligned nose, broken a number of times and set badly. Or because he was always making religious-type comments that no one understood. Or, possibly, because he was so thin, like a man in the last stages of cancer.

You could tell from the contours of his face—the cut of the jaw and cheeks, the strong profile, the hardness of the brow—that it had once been a handsome face. But now, Priestman's face was all angles and planes; it made you think of the bones underneath rather than of flesh and skin.

If the Priest *could* have had a mirror, he would have seen why people reacted the way they did to him.

Of course he didn't talk to himself like some of the lunatics did; still, you could tell there was nothing sane left in the brain by the way he looked at you. Through you. And then there were the noises that sometimes came from his cell at night: clicking noises, beating noises, fluttering noises. And also, sometimes, a low chanting, the sound of "Ommmmmmmmmm." No one knew why the Priest made these noises or why he thought he made them, but his penchant for making them had gotten him into trouble more than once in his thirteen years. He'd been beaten up more times than even *he* could count. The fact was that Priestman had spent over half of his time in solitary confinement, mostly for his own protection from the three hundred or so men in his cellblock who were the captive audience to his strange nightly noises. In the hole for all those years: the three at Attica after the knifing incident, four years at Great Meadow, the last six here at Green Haven. And much of the time the Priest wasn't in the hole he'd spent in prison hospitals on psychiatric observation or recovering from a beating he got when he was finally put back on the cellblock.

"Priestman wants what he wants," Priestman said.

"This is 1982," Scoggins said. "No one wears bellbottoms anymore.

"It's 1982 for you, man. Priestman died back in '69 with Lana."

Scoggins looked at him.

"So," the Priest said evenly, "you got bellbottoms or not?"

"You'd stand out in bellbottoms," Scoggins said. "Like a pig out of shit."

Which struck the Priestman as funny; it struck all of them as funny.

"It's Priestman's karma to stand out like a pig out of shit," Priestman said as soon as the laughter died down.

"Karma? What's karma?"

"It's what a man *is*," Priestman said. "It's like whether you do good, or do bad. Like you, Scoggins. Say you go out with a cart to pick up some boxes in the storeroom, if you're carrying good karma that day the screws might let you go at the checkpoint without looking at what's inside your cart. And if your karma's bad that day, they're gonna get you for swagging."

Scoggins looked over at Reichevic, then laughed.

"You ain't gonna get me for swagging, are you, Reichevic?"

Reichevic snorted. "Depends on your karma."

"So, what about you, Priestman?" Lafitt smiled. "How's *your* karma?"

"Priestman's got some real bad karma. Priestman's karma was what put him in here."

"What karma?" Reichevic looked over at Lafitt. "Shit. Fuckin' guy threw his woman off a cliff."

"Yeah, that's why Priestman's here, all right," Priestman said.

Lafitt laughed. "But Priestman never done it. He was unjustly accused, ain't that right, Priestman?"

Priestman said nothing, only stared.

"Where'd I hear that innocent rap before?" Reichevic said.

"Yeah, how come we got no one guilty in this institution?" Lafitt said.

The Priest was looking around the room, eyes darting along the shelves.

Scoggins was ready to explode. The fuckin' screws. Everyone knew it was a man's prerogative to talk about why he was in the joint, or not. Maybe his woman was two-timing him and that's why he killed her. It was one thing to jab at him while he was inside, but a man deserved some respect as he walked out the damned door.

"Sheeee-it," Scoggins said finally, "what about those boxes we got in yesterday? Maybe there's some bellbottoms in there."

The two guards and DeWitt stared at him. DeWitt shrugged, then went back to eating his doughnut and checking out *Hustler*. Scoggins began rummaging through the boxes.

"You ought to get that head looked at, Priestman," Reichevic said.

The Priestman smiled. "Priestman did, yesterday. They gave him some goop to put on it."

Scoggins had opened a third box. Where the hell did they get this stuff? A whole box of chartreuse pants. And in the next box, a load of shirts. Purple, red, orange, white. Never blue. You'd think that when you were getting out they'd give you something blue just because you hadn't had it for so long.

Finally, Scoggins turned around.

"Sorry, no bellbottoms. Guess you'll just have to take what we got."

He walked over to the shelves and began collecting the things the Priestman would need. Usually he asked a man what size he needed, tried to fix him up with the best he could, which wasn't much given what he had to pick from. But at least a man deserved something that fit when he went out on the street. In this case, it didn't matter. The Priest would be back very soon, or else he'd end up in mental. Or dead.

Scoggins put the pile of clothing he'd collected on one of the benches, then went to get the bag with Priestman's personal effects. After thirteen years, most guys had a shitload of stuff. Priestman's bag had only a few toilet items, a worn suede hat with a large floppy brim, and a framed picture of himself and a blond-haired girl. Babyfaces, the both of them, wearing bellbottom jeans and T-shirts. They had their arms around each other. They were smiling. Priestman's hair reached his shoulders in the picture. He was wearing the rawhide band.

The Priest took the bag from Scoggins, opened it and lifted out the picture. He ran his fingertip along the glass atop the image of the girl, touching her for a moment.

"That your woman?" Scoggins asked.

Priestman nodded, put the frame back in the box and set it down on the bench.

"Was."

"Looks like a girl to me."

"Eighteen."

"She ain't eighteen now."

"Yes, she is."

The four men looked at one another and grinned. The Priest always talked in riddles.

"So, Priestman, what you gonna do when you get out?" Scoggins asked.

Priestman took off his shirt, laid it down carefully. His chest seemed almost concave.

"Find her," he said, sitting on the bench to take off his pants.

"Who? The girl in the picture?"

Priestman stood up, now completely naked. He reached for his shirt, then pointed to the box and nodded.

"Lana."

Scoggins suddenly felt sorry for the man. No girl would wait that long. Especially since the man who was coming out didn't even vaguely resemble the kid in the picture. And anyway, the Priest never had any visitors.

"And what you gonna do after you find Lana, Priestman?" DeWitt said. "Fuck her brains?"

Priestman stopped buttoning up his shirt.

"Lana's dead."

There was a silence as they all realized that the woman he'd killed and the woman named Lana were one and the same. The guy was carrying around a picture of a dead woman.

DeWitt started to laugh. "I thought you said you were going to find—"

"Hey, give him a break, H. Q.," Scoggins said.

DeWitt backed away. "Sorry, man."

The Priestman buttoned up his pants, which hung miserably on him.

"Don't be sorry, DeWitt," he said, smiling. "It's your karma to be a pig—"

"You fuckin' goon—" Harry Quinton DeWitt made a move toward the Priest. The screws reached for their sticks, but Scoggins grabbed hold of DeWitt's shoulders, held him back.

"The man is gone, H. Q.," Scoggins said. "Don't start something."

"Fuckin' guy called me a pig," H. Q. said, his voice several octaves higher than usual.

"But you *are* a pig, DeWitt," Priestman said. "See, truth is part of karma, too. Might as well accept it. Fighting against karma is just fighting."

DeWitt struggled against Scoggins's restraint. "Shut your fuckin' face."

"Hey, man, cool out," Scoggins said. "Get the fuck outta here, Priestman."

Priestman shrugged. "I'm going. I'm just trying to tell you something—"

"We had enough of your preachin' bullshit," DeWitt said. The veins were standing out on his neck; the two guards were alert, poised.

"You ain't never gonna have to listen to it again, H. Q.," Scoggins said. " 'Cause you ain't never gonna see the Priest again. Ain't that so, Priestman?"

Priestman shrugged, tucked his shirt into his pants and started for the door, hugging his bag to his chest. Lafitt turned to go with him.

DeWitt harumphed, pulled away from Scoggins, and went back to his chair at the desk.

"Wait a minute," Reichevic said, "you still didn't tell us what you're gonna do out on the street."

Priestman turned and looked at his guard, focusing on him in a way none of them had ever seen the Priest look at anyone before.

"You really want to know?" he said.

"Wouldn't have asked if I didn't."

"I've got a score to settle."

There was a moment's silence; then Scoggins laughed. "Don't we all," he said. "Don't we all."

They all laughed again; they laughed until tears streamed out of their eyes. But it wasn't lost on any of the four men in the room that the man they called the Priest had suddenly stopped referring to himself in the third person.

"Don't be thinking about revenge, Priestman," Lafitt said. "All that gets you is the quickest way back in."

"I'm going to find Lana."

"Fuckin' guy's lost," DeWitt mumbled. He stood up. "Where you gonna look, Priestman? The cemetery?"

"Yeah," Scoggins said. "You said she was dead."

"Not dead. Only half-dead. See, man, Lana lived."

Lafitt said, "Well, don't be thinking about finishing the job, Priestman. That'll get you back here even sooner."

The Priest stared him down and smiled. "All I'm gonna do is make the karma right," he said. "It's been dead wrong for a very long time."

7

The man they called the Priest had a single thought repeating in his head from the moment the big iron gate of the prison opened to let him pass through. Thirteen years. The two words seemed to drown out all other thoughts, a triple-tone pulse in his brain, a terror-sound he was powerless to stop, like a scream on one of the tiers in the night. Thirteen years.

It was a cold December morning, the kind of morning where merely breathing produces cloudy white puffs in front of the face. It had snowed all last night, until a warm front moved in from the north and changed the snow to freezing rain before quickly moving on, leaving the sky cloudless and blue by the time day broke. The thin crust of ice atop the snow blazed in the morning sun.

Now and then, as the Oldsmobile sped along the highway, the Priest looked out the side window, at the flash of whiteness rushing by, but mostly he just sat, staring ahead at the open road.

Oscar Lafitt, his massive bulk taking up more than his share of the front seat, occasionally glanced over at him.

They passed a small lake about half a mile from the bus depot. It was completely frozen, very still. Evergreen trees laden with snow bent inward toward the sheer white surface of the lake.

"So, Priestman, where you gonna go?" Lafitt said.

The Priest didn't respond. He touched the brim of the suede hat he was wearing.

"Hey, you deaf or something?"

"New York City," Priestman said just as the car pulled up in front of the bus depot.

Oscar Lafitt turned off the ignition and opened the door. "New York City it is."

The bus depot, built at the same time as the state correctional facility—back in the forties—had never been updated or changed. It was a squat cement building right next to the highway, with rectangular windows set high off the ground and a worn mud-colored awning out front above the cement platform. If the outside of the building was unremarkable, the inside was even more so. Bare gray walls, a ragged American flag in one corner, a ticket counter, a few plastic benches, some vending machines, most of them broken, some magazine racks. It was just as cold inside the building as outside, maybe colder. A woman in a bright purple coat sat on one of the benches with a little girl. She was reading a copy of *Good Housekeeping* magazine. At the sound of the door opening, they both looked up. The woman turned away when she saw the two men who entered, but the little girl stared. Everybody knew the prison was nearby. A man on his way out was a regular sight at the bus depot. This one was something else again.

"Mommy," the little girl said, "look at that funny man."

The Priest glanced over at the child as he came in. His eyes lingered for just a moment too long. Or so the mother thought.

"Want some candy, honey?" She pulled a chocolate bar from her bag and handed it to the little girl.

"Cold enough for you today, Sam?" Oscar Lafitt asked the man behind the ticket counter, who was all bundled up in a coat and a hat. The two men were friends, played poker together on Friday nights, occasionally took their wives bowling.

"Goddamned heat isn't working right in here," Sam said. "They oughta pay me double in this."

"Yeah, well don't hold your breath." Oscar Lafitt laughed. "Got another one heading for the Big Apple today."

The ticket seller looked at the Priest, then back at Lafitt.

"Yeah? Where'd he get that hat?"

"It's Lana's," Priestman said.

"Who the hell's Lana?"

"His woman."

Lafitt made a circular motion by his ear with his finger. The ticket seller smirked. He and Lafitt often took bets on the departing prisoners, on which ones would be back again. Lafitt would never bet on the crazies. It was too sure a thing.

"How's your wife, Sam?" Lafitt asked. "She didn't look too good last Friday."

"Ah, she's all right. Just got a cold is all."

Oscar Lafitt nodded, then turned to the Priest.

"So, what're you waiting for, Priestman? You got money. Give the man your money."

"That'll be thirty-six dollars one way," the ticket seller said.

Priestman pulled the seventy-six dollars he'd gotten from the superintendent out of the pocket of his pants. He fumbled with the stack of bills for a moment, then counted out thirty-six dollars.

The ticket seller punched out a ticket.

"Bus'll be here in fifteen minutes."

The Priest started walking toward the door.

"Well, take care of yourself, Priestman," Lafitt said.

Priestman smiled. "Remember, Lafitt, fighting against karma is just fighting. If you surrender to the karma, miracles happen."

"Yeah, Priestman," Oscar Lafitt said with a frown. "I'll remember."

The Priest stood under the awning in front of the bus depot and looked around. The little girl and her mother were sitting on the bench near him. The girl, about ten, was humming to herself. Rose used to sit on the front steps of the pink house and hum to herself.

Priestman looked down at the child on the bench. Such beautiful skin. So clear, so smooth. When was the last time he'd been close to a child?

There it was again. He was thinking of time. He had to stop thinking of time.

"Mister, where'd you get that funny hat?"

"A friend of mine gave it to me," he said. "What's your name?"

"Cindy! Get away from that man." The mother grabbed the girl and yanked her back over to the bench.

The Priest looked away. What was most amazing was the colors. The world had been reduced to two colors for so long: green, the color of the walls, the color of the pants; and gray, the color of everything else, even the sky you could see from the yard. And here, less than five miles away, the world was brilliant-hued. He'd forgotten how many colors there were. There was the white paint on the trim of the building at the depot. And the white of the snow. The little girl's pants were yellow. Bright yellow, like a canary. And the color of the coat the child's mother was wearing was called lilac. Li-lac. It reminded him of the color of the oil Sarah used on her skin. He whispered the word. It felt good rolling off his tongue.

He'd forgotten.

There seemed to be a fine golden layer of dust coating everything, too. Gold was another color he'd forgotten.

Standing there, he realized for the first time that he was alone. Being in the hole wasn't being alone. You were still surrounded by men and by walls and by guards.

It felt good.

No. It couldn't feel good. He had work to do before anything could feel good.

Suddenly he whirled around and went back into the building. He walked up to the window again, handed the man his ticket.

"Changed my mind," he said. "I'd like to go to Comity."

The man took the ticket back, counted out change from the cash register and held it out.

"That'll be eleven dollars, one way. The bus to Comity is coming in now."

Less than fifty miles away, in the town of Comity, New York, at just about the same moment as the Priest was getting onto his bus, a woman was leaving her house for a pilgrimage she had made every day for the past thirteen years. The woman was the Priestman's mother, Sarah Alexandra Newcastle Skitt, and she was a familiar figure in Comity, in her shawl and her long dress and heavy man's boots, walking along the highway that bisects the town, heading east, up into the mountains.

The town of Comity, New York, lies in the shadow of the Shawangunk Mountains, a smaller range of mountains than the more northerly and more famous Catskills, but steeper, more concentrated. The town is known primarily for the series of spectacular cliffs that lie just to the east, and provide a mecca for daredevils and true mountain climbers.

The mountains are visible from everywhere in town, stretching out across the horizon like the bony armor across the back of a stegosaur. The whole area is naturally wooded, laced with streams and creeks, all tributaries of Mohonk Lake. Very little of the woodlands were left in the town itself, most of the land having been cleared for development, but surrounding areas remained untouched, the pristine woods just as they were when the Indians hunted and fished here. The place to which Sarah headed each day was called Devil's Meadow. It was a name coined back in the fifties by the mountain climbers, and neither the townspeople who used the name now, nor the climbers who coined it, were aware of its particular irony. Centuries ago the Indians who lived in this part of the country believed a guardian spirit lived in this meadow and performed certain of their sacred ceremonies and rituals there, particularly coming-of-age ceremonies for young boys of the tribe. They called it the Place of the Spirit. Sarah, also unaware of this bit of history, nonetheless believed that Devil's Meadow was a holy place. Each morning she went there, making a treacherous hike over difficult terrain that only a woman of great heartiness and forbearance would attempt, a walk that took her several hours and made up the major part of her day.

Sarah usually left her house just after breakfast, wrapping her fringed shawl tightly over her head and shoulders like a woman grieving, taking long, purposeful strides. On this particular morning, her stride was slower than usual; her sorrows weighed more heavily on her, though she would only later find out why. She had already begun calling herself "Woman of Many Sorrows," testimony both to her own sad history and to her Indian heritage, or what she believed to be her Indian heritage. All Sarah had of that heritage was the tale she used to tell to her children of a particular ancestor, an Iroquois shaman named True Face whose great wisdom and healing magic were said to have aided the great prophet Handsome Lake. That, and a very old beaded moccasin in the Iroquois style.

Her children were all gone now, and whether her tale of her ancestor was true and the moccasin authentic would never be known. Yet Sarah's Indian heritage was surely where she had gotten her looks, her tall sinewy body, her black, black eyes that seemed to reflect no light, her dark coppery skin. Her black hair, although flecked generously with gray, was thick and coarse and full, and she still wore it long, almost to her waist, though it was hidden beneath her shawl.

At the rusty tin mailbox next to the highway, she turned right and walked up the interstate for about two miles until she came to the intersection of Canyon Flats Road, where she turned right again, following in the direction of the SCENIC OVERLOOK sign. She headed upward for about a mile until she came to another turnoff, then turned there and made her way up more sharply now along a narrow winding mountain road called Canyon Lane. Eventually she reached Lookout Point.

There, Sarah stood for a moment in the crisp air. Then, silent as a snowfall, stealthy as an Indian scout, she turned and disappeared into the woods. The only sound she made was the crunch of her boots on the forest floor.

It took her about ten minutes to reach the meadow, a vast expanse of space covered in snow, so high up it seemed to meet the sky, which was clear that morning and very blue. Though the snow was deep, it was frozen and crusted over and her feet sank in only inches as she made her way across the meadow. She walked right up to the edge and stood there on the precipice, peering out over the ledge, as if expecting to find something in the sky. Then she looked down over the sheer rock wall that jutted inward from the edge at an angle of about fifteen degrees, ending over two hundred feet below in a jagged rocky ledge.

After a moment, Sarah stepped back and sank down to her knees in the snow, raised her face to the sun, closed her eyes, and prayed. She stayed that way for a very long time.

Had anyone seen her they wouldn't have been surprised. In Comity, New York, Sarah Alexandra Skitt had always been known for her exotic beauty, her proclivity for having babies without benefit of marriage, and her general eccentricity. She moved into her aunt Ethel Mason's house back in '55, and it was only a few years later that it became known just what a loon she was. In 1960, she appeared at the mayor's office and made a scene that had become a local legend, demanding that the town fathers build a church on the very spot at which she now prayed. Then there was the time she barricaded herself inside her house for nearly seven months eating only macrobiotic foods, and serving only them to her children, until the school intervened and provided hot lunches of a suitable and nourishing nature: frankfurters, shepherd's pie, bologna sandwiches, and soup, real lunches like the rest of the children in Comity ate.

Sarah had had six children, and had only been married for the birth of two of them, and even the names she gave them were odd, or so the people of Comity thought: Laban, Ethan, Nathan, Adam, Joshua, and Rose Petal.

All of Sarah's children had left her now, as mother's children do, but it was not of the two who had simply moved away that she thought when she went to Devil's Meadow each morning. Nor was it of the two who were dead and buried, nor even of the one who had been at a state mental hospital for twenty years now. It was for her second son that Sarah prayed, for her son Ethan, a son she had loved and hadn't seen in thirteen years. Her other children were in a state of grace. Ethan was the one who needed her prayers, for he had committed the gravest of sins. The jury convicted him of attempted murder, but it was the same as murder to Sarah, for it was only through God's divine intervention, through His blessed miracle, for His own unknown reasons, that the girl Ethan had pushed from this place had been spared. And it was here on this very spot, on the spot that Sarah believed was holy, that it had happened. Every day of her life she reminded herself that she had raised a bad man, a man who would commit such a sin and then lie under God's oath, in a court of law, despite evidence against him that was solid, irrefutable. Sarah had tried to teach her children goodness, but Ethan hadn't learned.

And it was because of this, because of her own failings, that

Sarah Skitt made her pilgrimage each morning, even in winter, placing her shawl over her head and walking nearly five miles over rugged terrain to a place called Devil's Meadow, a place that in spring fairly burst with tall grasses and wildflowers but which now was frozen and still. And there, alone, she prayed for her son's immortal soul.

8

The Priest stretched out in the seat as the bus bounced along the open road, passing farms, meadows, fields, the endless space of the open country.

Sitting across the aisle were the woman in the lilac coat and her daughter. The woman was sleeping, the coat folded neatly and stowed in the overhead rack, her head resting on the window, her mouth open. The Priest watched her for a moment, the rhythmic breathing, the rise and fall of her chest, her breasts. He hadn't been with a girl—a woman—in thirteen years. He wondered if he could.

The child was holding a small black box with a hinged lid, rummaging through it, taking objects out of it one at a time. A bracelet, small human figures, a plastic bird. She examined each object closely, held it up to the window—now a tiny plastic cow, now a plastic figure of Pinocchio, now a pair of earrings. She put the earrings up to her ears, her hand grazing the skin on her neck. The earrings, tiny purple glass prisms, glittered on the little girl's cheek.

It had been a very long time since the Priest had seen junk. There'd been no place for junk earrings and little objects in prison.

"Mommy, that man with the hat is watching me."

The woman woke up, took her daughter by the hand, and led her down the aisle to a seat many rows back.

The Priest looked out the window for a few moments, then lay back and slept more soundly than he had in years, awakening only when the driver brought the bus to a halt and yelled, "Hey, mister, we're in Comity. You gettin' off?"

* * *

The Priest got off the bus at the western edge of town and walked east along the interstate highway. The town seemed very different than he remembered, for the land, originally cleared for farms, was flavored with signs of development: new subdivisions, fast-food restaurants, convenience stores.

Some of the landmarks seemed more familiar as he came into the center of town; there was the string of shops along Copson Way—Pringle's Flower Shop, Annette's Lingerie, a few others he recognized—the post office, the old movie theatre, but now it was something called a triplex. What did that mean?

He whispered the word, but he said it wrong, giving the "i" the long vowel sound so that it came out "Trigh-plex."

He crossed over to Main Street, which was now an open air market with a cobblestone street lined with little shops, then headed toward Bromfield Square. As he passed in front of the State Street Bank, a woman pushing a baby carriage turned to stare at him. He recognized her too; they had been classmates at Comity High, class of '69. Averting his eyes, the Priest walked on, crossed through the park inside the square. A flock of ducks in the small lake were honking and making a huge commotion. He walked briskly now, as if he knew exactly where he was going, and emerged from the park on the southwest corner, just next to a place called Woody's. There was a pink-and-white-striped awning over the door. There were a lot of pink-and-white awnings, in fact. All over the square. It was late afternoon now, and the sun was sinking slowly behind the mountains. Priestman remembered that, the cool orange tinge of the landscape, the mountains and the sky.

He stood watching the door for a few moments. Several times the door opened and someone went in or came out. It looked crowded—no one would notice him in the dimly lit bar. He decided to take a chance and go inside.

It was almost exactly the same. The mahogany bar had a few more nicks and scratches, and the glass beads that had always hung between the bar and the back room had been replaced by a curtain. The other change was that John Paluka was no longer standing behind the bar. In his place was a fat, balding man with a tattoo on his right forearm and a round, pleasant face. He was talking to a bespectacled man who had a briefcase leaning against the barstool under his foot. Someone was playing a jukebox in the back, and he could hear sounds from back there, talking, laughing. There were two men sitting at one of the tables.

"Help you?"

Keeping his head down, the Priest sat on the far stool.

"Beer." He began to get out his roll of money.

"What kind?"

Priestman tried to think what kind he wanted but for some reason couldn't remember any names except Budweiser.

"Budweiser."

"Draft?"

He nodded.

The bartender filled a tall mug, set it down in front of the Priest, and went back to his conversation with the traveling salesman. Priestman took the first frothy sip, letting it fill his mouth with the bitter taste, remembering how many Sunday nights he had spent in the apartment over this place. Lana's mother always had the television on, like a background beat to living, and he would sit in front of it for hours. Lana said she didn't understand his fascination with television, and he didn't really understand it either, except that Sarah had never had television in their house. He even put up with Ellie's obvious disdain for him. Lana would say her mother didn't want her to be with him because his people were crazy. He hadn't wanted Lana to know that about him, and yet it was why they were together. Didn't she know that? How could she have betrayed that?

He took another sip of beer, suddenly remembering how spectacularly drunk he and Lana had gotten the night they announced there would be a lottery for the draft in the fall. Lana had always said she would never touch alcohol because of what it had done to her mother, but that time she had made an exception.

It was early in the summer when John Paluka invited them into the bar. John kept handing around drinks. "Have another for a little luck." Ellie was there too, prancing around that night, enjoying the way all the men looked at her.

"Hey, Ethan baby." Ellie sidled up to him. "Lana tells me you and she got something special. That right?"

He nodded.

"Well, us Paluka women don't know from special, do we, Lana?" She glanced over at John, who was mixing a drink behind the counter.

"Stop it, Ellie," John Paluka said. "If the kid gets a low number they could ship him off to Vietnam the very next day."

"It's all in the numbers," a man sitting at the bar said.

Ellie shrugged.

"Why do you hate me, Ellie?" Ethan had been very drunk or he wouldn't have said it.

"I don't hate you. I don't have feelings for you one way or the other."

But he knew how to tell what people thought. It was in their eyes. He knew that what she really wanted was for him to get shipped off to Vietnam and come back in a wooden box so her daughter would be free to marry someone else. Lana had told him as much. But, drunk as he was, he'd decided to drop it.

"You want another one?"

Priestman realized that he'd been thinking about something that had happened so long ago it was beyond mattering. Right now what mattered was the small compartment under the sink behind the bar. It was hidden from view, accessible only by pressing the button on the floor next to the sink with your foot. The Priest wouldn't have known about it except one time John Paluka showed it to him. "See, kid, look at this." It was so very long ago. But he remembered. He remembered the way John Paluka had touched the object inside, tenderly, running his stubby fingers over it as if he were touching a woman he loved.

"What're you lookin' at?" the man behind the bar said.

The Priest averted his eyes, then got off the stool.

"Nothing," he said. "Nothing at all."

The Priest walked on, heading east along the interstate highway. About a mile from the edge of town, on what used to be the Opatcho farm, a huge subdivision was under construction—West Farm Acres, street after street of colonial splits, those closest to the road very nearly finished, those farther back less so. There was a guardhouse out front, and an enormous sign featuring barn-red letters, a farmer, and a cow. Several construction trailers were parked near the highway, and a sign next to the trailer closest to the highway read, WELLS DEVELOPMENT COMPANY. SALES OFFICE.

The Priest stopped in front of the sign and stared.

After a moment, the door of the sales office opened. Quickly he hid himself behind one of the construction trailers, watched as a tall man with dark wavy hair, wearing a sheepskin coat, emerged from the sales office. A moment later a woman came out—a beautiful woman, an expensive woman in a fur coat, and a boy of about ten, a younger version of the man. The man began talking to the boy, pointing to the houses under construction, explaining something. A moment later the three of them got into the white Jaguar sedan parked next to the office; then they were gone.

The Priest watched, his hands clenched into fists, until the car disappeared down the highway. Then, walking quickly, he continued on until he came to a small Victorian house, a boxy structure with a large front porch, a flat roof, ornate white trim and lattice. It was very close to the road, but hidden behind an overgrown thicket of trees. The house was badly in need of repair, though

at one time not so long ago it had been immaculately kept and
carefully—lovingly—tended. The original pink paint was crack-
ing and peeling away in strips. The roof had shingles missing,
the side porch sagged, as did the front steps. There was an old
VW Bug parked out front, an even older station wagon in front
of that.

The rusted tin mailbox out front read s. SKITT.

The man they called the Priest stood in front of the mailbox
for a moment, then hid himself behind the trunk of a large oak
tree. Every so often he looked out from behind the tree, trying
to see movement inside. There was none. The windows were dark.

He began to walk around the house. There was an old ram-
shackle chicken coop on the side of the house, empty. About
twenty feet away was a grave. Fresh daisies lay on the snow in
front of the small tombstone. An odd sight, daisies in the snow.
The Priest bent down and read the words etched in the stone:

Laban Skitt
1949–1971
God has taken back His Gift

A wail—a scream—emerged from his mouth; then the Priest
picked up a rock and hurled it through one of the side windows,
shattering the silence with the sound of glass breaking. In seconds he was inside tearing the house apart.

9

When he heard the noises downstairs the following night, Woody Ames had just finished his once-a-weeker with his wife and rolled over. It used to be Woody couldn't get enough of his wife. Two or three times a day hadn't been unusual, and Woody would spend hours touching her, exploring her. That was way back in the beginning, back when he—when both of them—were nineteen and living high and fast and dangerous, two lifetimes ago. Before drugs took away his rather formidable sex drive the first time, and age and seventy-five extra pounds took it away a second time.

"Danny, there's someone downstairs," Kathy whispered. Sometimes—usually in bed—she forgot to call him Woody and called him by his real name.

Woody glared at her and brought his finger up to his lips. "Shhh."

He'd heard the sound of the back door opening too, the thud of the lock being broken, then footsteps across the floor of the back room where the pool table was. Whoever it was was in the bar right now.

Woody tried to remember if he'd removed the night's take from the cash register, then sighed with relief. He'd brought it upstairs with him in the brown leather sack, as he always did, for Kathy to haul over to the bank in the morning. There *was* the four thousand dollars he kept in the hidden safe, but no one would find that.

Naked except for his boxer shorts, his large belly pale in the dim light of the bedroom, Woody swung his feet onto the floor, then slid the night-table drawer open and took out the .44 Magnum revolver. He sat holding the weapon in his hands for a moment, taking a few deep breaths. Then he grabbed his worn terrycloth robe from the foot of the bed and, as quietly as his large frame would move, walked across the apartment floor, holding the gun down by his hip, thinking about the twelve years he and Kathy had spent building this life. The apartment wasn't anything spectacular—five rooms over a bar—but he owned the bar fair and square, even if it was mostly with drug money, and it was a good life, even if they would have laughed at it in the old days. He and Kathy had taken what money they'd managed to save from the hundreds of thousands that had passed through their hands during their drug days—including Wiz Jackman's nine thousand for a deal that never went down—and answered the ad in the business section of the *New York Times*. Saloon for sale. Upstate New York.

No way was anybody going to take what was his, what he'd worked and sweated for. Woody had taken care of his share of fuckers in his day. He would take care of this one.

He moved across the room and into the hallway, the floor creaking with every step he took. He'd have to go down the back steps by the kitchen. Kathy had forgotten to turn the kitchen light off when she came to bed, though Woody saw right away that she hadn't forgotten to do their dinner dishes. The kitchen was spotless, as always.

No. No one was going to take what was his. He could catch the guy by surprise from behind as he went back out the door.

As quietly as he could, Woody slid the locks open and went out onto the landing. There he stopped and listened. The noises suddenly stopped too, and there was a moment where he and the intruder were aware of each other's presence, he was certain of it. The thought crossed his mind that maybe it was Wiz Jackman downstairs, though he would later find out that Wiz had been killed in a shootout with police only a year after he and Kathy split.

Woody never had a chance to ponder this thought further then, though, because suddenly the intruder was loping across the floor downstairs. Woody started down the stairs himself and caught a glimpse of the man as he raced by. It was the same man who'd come into the bar yesterday afternoon, he was certain of it. The weirdo. The one who was looking where he shouldn't have been looking.

Woody rushed to the landing, aimed, squeezed the trigger. He heard the crack of a single shot. He thought he might have hit the man but he wasn't sure because the guy just kept on running, exiting through the open back door. By the time Woody emerged

from the back door himself, all he could see was a shadowy figure crossing over the back fence.

Woody stood for a moment in the cold night air, thinking. He
could try to chase the guy, who had by now disappeared into the
woods behind the bar. Maybe he could get off a better shot. But
the guy was long gone, and Woody Ames was fifty years old and
weighed two hundred and forty-nine pounds. His chasing days
were over.

Woody glanced down at his slippers. Last night it had rained,
washed away some of the snow. He was standing in a patch of
icy mud, the only place on the lawn that was bare of grass, the
place where no matter what he did the grass refused to grow.
His next-door neighbor, Mrs. Riccardelli, had told him some years
ago that once the Palukas—the former owners of Woody's back
when it was called Adley's—had built a bonfire in the backyard
on just that spot.

Why anyone would have had a bonfire in his backyard, Woody
wasn't prepared to guess. Mrs. Riccardelli didn't know why either, or wouldn't say. John Paluka had seemed like a right enough
guy, though his wife was completely smashed the day they signed
the papers. Woody supposed it was because of the bonfire that
the grass would never grow there.

"Woody, are you all right?" Kathy was standing in the doorway in her bare feet and her robe.

Woody started back inside. "Yeah, I'm all right. I hit him."

"You sure?"

"Well, it might have just grazed his arm. I got a look at him,
though. He was in here yesterday."

"Could you identify him?"

Woody nodded.

"Call the police," she said.

"Wait a minute, Kath, let's just see if anything's missing first."

She nodded.

The first thing Woody checked was the cash register. He rang
up a "no sale": the twenty-five dollars he habitually left inside at
night was still there. His eye scanned the length of the bar. Nothing was amiss; everything was where it had been when he'd
cleaned up a few hours ago. The television was still there on its
shelf in back of the bar.

So what the hell did the guy take?

"Maybe he was looking for a drink," Kathy said. "Or a place
to sleep."

Woody shrugged; then suddenly his eyes shifted downward to
the small cabinet next to the sink, where the man had been looking. He switched on the lights over the bar, walked to the sink,

placed his slippered foot on top of a floorboard just to the left and pressed firmly.

"Come on, Woody, no one would have found the safe. It's too well hidden."

"Doesn't hurt to check."

The cabinet door popped open. Woody knelt down. The safe behind the door didn't appear to have been tampered with. He placed his fingertips on the lock. Right 25. Left 41. Right 6. The tumblers slid into place, the safe popped open; he reached inside, withdrew a stack of papers along with a small leather case.

He zipped the case open and looked inside. Four thousand dollars. In hundred-dollar bills. Still there.

"Well, thank God," Kathy said. "Looks like he didn't take anything. You must have interrupted him."

Woody zipped the case closed, then peered inside the safe again. It was completely empty.

"Well, he did take something," Woody said.

"What?"

"My gun."

The goddamned gun, something else he'd taken from Wiz Jackman, had been there since he bought the place. He'd put it there the very night he and Kathy had moved in. Jesus Christ! The fucking guy broke in and stole his gun. And it was a beauty, too. A Walther 9 mm. semi-automatic, worth maybe fifteen hundred dollars.

"Call the police," Kathy said.

Woody nodded, then stood up and began walking over to the phone. Fifteen years ago, he would have no sooner thought of calling the police than he would have jumped off one of those cliffs at the east end of town. But that was then.

Just as he was about to pick up the receiver, he stopped. Woody Ames may have turned his life around, but the gun was the same one he'd stolen from a drug dealer out in Hollywood. What the hell was he going to tell the police? That his gun, for which he had no license or registration—which before he got his hands on it had an extremely violent history, including one murder that Woody had witnessed himself—had been stolen? No way. Not unless he absolutely had to.

Woody took his hand off the phone.

"I can't call 'em, Kath. That gun is illegal as hell. Remember where I got it?"

"But someone must have heard the shot. They'll report it."

"Not necessarily, Kath. Let's just wait a few days and see what happens."

"All right, I guess you're right . . . Woody, look at your slippers."

He looked down. His slippers were covered with mud.

"Yeah, I know."

"I'll see what I can do with them in the morning," she said. "Come on. Let's go to bed."

Woody switched off the lights, then put his arm around his wife and kissed her.

"Probably shouldn't have kept the gun anyway," he said as they headed back up the stairs. But he couldn't help wondering who the hell the guy was, and how he knew about the safe inside the cabinet. He must have known exactly what he was looking for. After all, it had only taken Woody a few minutes to get down here, if that. The guy could have been in the bar for a minute or two. It was as if he'd walked in, headed straight for the cabinet, opened it, reeled off the combination to the safe, took the gun, and left. Only someone who knew his way around this bar would have known all that, which meant it must have been someone who knew his way around before Woody's time, when Paluka owned the bar.

And why had he left four thousand dollars cash in a safe he'd just taken the trouble to break into?

Oh, well. No use in trying to figure it out. There was nothing to be done. Hopefully, it would be just one of those unfortunate losses, something to be chalked up to Woody Ames's past, like dealing drugs, like his former sex drive or his real name, like his lost youth.

10

Randy Slessenger got back from his Narcotics Anonymous meeting at eight-thirty on the evening of December 16, 1982, with an attack of the creepy-crawlies. A guy Randy knew, whose name was D. T. Cox, had warned him weeks ago about the creepy-crawlies. Cox had said the creepy-crawlies were even worse than the initial symptoms of coke withdrawal—the chills, the fevers, the runs, the cramps—which could be pretty bad, especially if you were coming off freebasing. At the time, Randy was only a day into detox and quite certain nothing could be worse. But now, as he climbed the stairs to his fourth-floor apartment, he decided D. T. may have been right.

Creepy-crawlies. It was a good name for the feeling. Crawlies outside—his skin tingling with the feel of thousands of little crawling bugs. Creepies within—his insides felt like a small animal was inching its way along his stomach, gnawing away at pieces of tissue, releasing something hot and foul.

Randy stopped to rest at the third-floor landing and stood on the shabby rug listening to the incessant beat of heavy metal music in 3B. They never listened to anything else in there.

Angelo Maraccini popped his head out of 3A.

"Turn that goddamned fuckin' radio down," he yelled over the music in a voice loud enough to wake the dead. He glared at Randy for a moment as if Randy were responsible, then said, "What the fuck is the matter with *you*, goonhead?" And slammed the door.

The music kept blaring away.

Randy took a deep breath and climbed up to the fourth floor. Damn. The lightbulb in the corridor was out again. He felt his way along the railing in the gloom. There was a smell in the hallway, stale cabbage, sweat, urine, something indefinable. It had never bothered him when he was using.

Something soft on the railing squished beneath his fingers. He jerked his hand back, almost glad the light wasn't on so he wouldn't have to see what it was. He fumbled for his key in the dark, then realized he'd left the door unlocked. His goddamned memory was completely shot.

Before going in, he turned on the lamp by the doorway and peered into his apartment for a moment. Still the same stink-hole—one room and a bathroom—he'd been living in for over three years now, but somehow it always looked worse after a few weeks clean. He threw his key next to the pile of mail he'd picked up that morning and left unopened on the kitchen counter. A few bills he had no money to pay. A few catalogues from some-one with a sick sense of humor or a bad address list.

Suddenly Randy had the feeling he was being watched. It wasn't so much that there was someone there, more that some-one had been there. He spun around. Nothing was out of place; the bowl and cup from his dinner of canned spaghetti and coffee were still on the table; none of the drawers or closets were open. Everything seemed the same, but the space had somehow been violated, he was sure of it. Someone had been there, recently, rifling around in his things, someone smart, someone careful to leave everything as it was.

He looked around. At his unmade bed. At the chest of drawers in the corner. It was the same bureau he'd had at home, back in Comity. His parents had given him all the old furniture from his room when he got his first apartment, a hovel near Columbia University in Manhattan that was a palace compared to this place. That was about a year after the trial. He'd been staying at home before that, getting really heavy into the drugs. They'd finally kicked him out but helped him get set up in a series of shitholes ever since, which was their way of being tough on him.

He began opening the drawers, one by one. Everything was there: his clothes, such as they were, in the top three drawers. And in the bottom drawer, a pile of yellowed newspaper clip-pings about the trial, old letters and old catalogues and pie-in-the-sky travel brochures for things and places he'd always wanted to buy or to do but never had the will or strength for, not to mention the money. A brochure for a military-style detox camp in Utah where you had to do a hundred pushups every morning and march around in formation saluting everyone. Guaranteed to come out "Drug Free." Vacation from Hell in Hell.

Everything was there. Maybe he was wrong.

He glanced over at the letters he'd dropped back on the kitchen table and decided he was just experiencing a case of creepy-crawly paranoia.

What would anyone want with him? No one knew what he was; there was nothing here to find.

Just the resident junkie.

And this time he was going to stay straight. He'd even written his mother and told her.

He decided to open the mail. There was a notice from the telephone company, who would turn off his phone next week if he didn't pay the bill. Let them. His mother had sent some money, but he'd promised her he'd buy himself some decent clothes and go out and look for a job—this through a long tear-filled conversation on the phone a few weeks ago. She said if he had a job he'd have his self-respect back. She didn't know it wasn't quite that simple.

The next envelope was an offer to open a charge account at J. C. Penney, which was pretty fucking funny when you thought about it.

He threw the whole pile in the trashcan, sat down. A cockroach scurried across the table.

The creepy-crawlies were back.

Damn. Someone was at the door, he could hear the knocking. Who the hell could it be? No one ever came to see him. Why would they?

"Who is it?"

No answer.

He asked again, but all he heard was more knocking. Finally, he opened the door.

"Hello, Randy."

Randy Slessenger shrank back into the room, felt his knees crumbling.

"Thirteen years," the man whispered.

"God help me," Randy said, slumping down on the couch.

But it wasn't God who was standing there, towering over him, aiming a gun at his head. It was a man for whom time had ceased to have meaning, a man for whom thirteen years wasn't a whole lifetime but merely a blink.

Part Three

The Scene
of the Crime

11

When my brother, Alan, called me with the news of Randy's suicide, I flew in from Akron. No one knew that the police suspected a homicide all along. Randy had been shot at point-blank range in the side of the head. A three-line note was found beside the body:

Dear Mom and Dad,

I can't go on living this way. You should have written me off years ago. I'm sorry.
You deserved better than I ever was.

Love Randy

A suicide made perfect sense. Randy had made a mess of his life. Even though we had all lost touch after Ethan Skitt's trial, even before that, I had been aware of Randy's increasingly serious drug problem. His addiction had apparently started in junior high with the marijuana we all smoked, then escalated to amphetamines and finally to cocaine and heroin.

I remember there were about fifty people already sitting in the pews when Alan and I got to the funeral home, but it wasn't until later, when we all rose to go to the cemetery, that I got a look at their faces and realized they were all old. Everyone who came to Randy's funeral was a friend of the elder Slessengers, and each of them, I knew, was silently thanking God that it hadn't been his or her son that had messed up his life so completely, at the same time as they offered their sympathy. There were no contemporaries, no friends, except Alan and myself—and we weren't really Randy's friends—not anymore. I was there because of my memories. And maybe my guilt.

I didn't cry, not until after the minister's eulogy, when Randy's sister, Susie, got up and made her way to stand next to the gleaming mahogany casket covered in white roses. I wondered what relation this poised, stylish woman in a black-checked suit, black pumps, and veiled hat dipped over one eyebrow had to that little girl I remembered, Randy's kid sister, who was always pestering us to let her join the gang.

In a voice choked with emotion, Susie said she had loved her brother, had tried to help him all his life, but that there was something inside Randy that haunted him. "He was on self-destruct for a long, long time," she said. She'd first noticed it when he was about fourteen and he began spending more and more time in his room, playing his guitar, as if the outside world was too much for him.

"Drugs were what ruined my brother. If he could have gotten through adolescence without them, maybe he would have been okay ..." She looked up from the notecards in front of her, shrugged. "But maybe if it hadn't been drugs it would have been something else. I tried to ask him why he was so sad all the time, and later I tried to help him break his addiction. I had him picked up once and forcibly taken to a drug rehab center. He told me to stay out of his life. I did. My brother lived his life alone—that was the way he wanted it. I don't know ... I want to remember him as a young boy, when he used to laugh, and clown around, and make me laugh. I won't remember what he became."

Randy's mother started weeping uncontrollably at the cemetery. We stood on a knoll overlooking a sea of graves, about twenty of us. The ground was still wet from a morning rain, but the sun had come out over the landscape of white stones and green lawn. It was as they began to lower the casket into the ground that Estelle Slessenger began to wail. It reminded me of the sound Donna made in the delivery room when she gave birth to Craig and Chris—an animal sound, guttural, primitive. After a few moments, she seemed to collapse, and her husband—a large bulky man whose interests ran to sports and hunting—and her daughter propped her up between them like a rag doll.

About a week later, a man named Woody Ames identified Ethan Skitt as having stolen a gun from his safe two nights after he was released from prison.

Though I didn't really follow Ethan Skitt's second trial, I did know that he pled guilty to first-degree murder and was given a life sentence.

* * *

I turned into the Drummond Rehabilitation Center just as the sun was setting, a lavish orange orb in a haze of pink clouds. Drummond is a sprawling complex of low white buildings at one end of a muddy lake. A labyrinth of roads leading to each of the buildings snakes off from the main drive. The lawn, expansive and lush, is dotted here and there with stands of trees under which benches and striped lawn chairs are clustered.

Riding in semi-darkness, I passed a croquet lawn, a tennis court, a basketball court, a pool. I wondered how Lana Paluka had ended up in a mental hospital that seemed more like a country club. Her parents hadn't been exactly rich; her father owned Adley's Bar.

Following a series of small, strategically placed signs, I found the visitors' parking lot just to the right of the largest of the buildings, the only one graced by a portico and white doric columns. There were very few cars in the lot.

Inside, at the front desk, I flashed my press ID at a middle-aged redhead who looked like she lived on Hostess Twinkies.

"Jack Wells. Westchester *Herald.*"

"A reporter?"

I nodded. "You have a patient here named Lana Paluka. I'd like to talk with her."

The receptionist looked at me for a moment. "Well, you could talk to her," she said. "But I don't think she'll be doing much talking back, sir. She hasn't spoken in years."

"I was told she had . . . snapped out of it. That she woke up."

"Woke up?" The receptionist smiled. "I'm afraid catatonic patients don't just wake up, Mr. Wells. You must be—"

"Look, if you'd just call. Please?"

The woman shrugged, then dialed a four-digit number on the console.

"Doctor, this is Edith Sammonetti, out at reception. There's a man here, a reporter. Says he has information that Miss Paluka suddenly—well, woke up. I told him . . ." She listened for a moment, then looked up at me. "Where did you get this information?"

I didn't want to get Ann in trouble. "We have stringers," I said, idiotically.

She repeated that into the receiver, said, "All right, doctor, I'll tell him," then hung up. "I'm sorry, Mr. Wells. I didn't know about Lana's recovery. I just got back today, I've been out for a week." She pointed to the blank lines in the visitor's registry.

"If you'll just sign here, the doctor will be out in a few minutes."

"No problem." I signed my name and the date, August 24, in the space at the bottom of the page, handed the book back to her.

"Does Lana have visitors?"

"Almost no one. Even her parents hardly ever come. Real low-class people, if you ask . . . Oh, shit, I forgot I was talking to a reporter. You won't quote me, will you?"

I smiled. "Strictly off the record."

"Once in a while a doctor from somewhere else will come to see her."

"Thanks for the help."

I plopped myself down on the leather couch in the waiting lobby and picked up the copy of yesterday's New York *Post* that was sitting on the table. I skimmed Don Able's piece on Elmond Dixon and had almost finished the rest of the paper when I heard a man's voice.

"Are you Mr. Wells?" The tall doctor standing over me had brown bushy hair, a matching mustache, and a name tag on his white coat: JONATHAN BALDWIN, CHIEF OF PSYCHIATRY.

I stood up. "Yes, I am."

"You want to see Lana Paluka?"

"These are visiting hours, aren't they?"

Baldwin nodded.

"Is there a problem, doctor?"

"My patient is in a highly vulnerable state right now, Mr. Wells. She has just awakened from an extended ordeal. A *very* extended ordeal. There are special circumstances—"

"Dr. Baldwin," I said, "I understand perfectly. But in addition to being a reporter, I happen to be a close friend of Lana's. I've known her since we were children." That last statement, at least, was true.

"I'm looking out for my patient's best interests, Mr. Wells. I know how reporters can be."

"I work for a reputable paper, doctor. The Westchester *Herald.*"

"That isn't what I meant. I just want to make sure your visit will be in her best interest, that's all. I know there was some . . . ugliness in the past."

An interesting euphemism.

"Does Lana know about the trial?"

"She's been made aware of what happened. She has no memory of it."

"Doctor," I said, "it was my brother who testified against Ethan Skitt. He was one of the witnesses. We were on *her* side."

"Were you?"

"Look," I said, "don't you think it would help Lana to have some contact with her past?"

He paused for a long moment before answering. "You may be right."

"Would you mind answering a few questions yourself first, doctor?"

"One or two."

We sat back down on the sofa and I conducted a brief interview with the man, got the details of Lana's present condition.

"Why do you think she suddenly came out of it?" I asked finally.

"I honestly don't know. I don't know why she came back to life—or why she survived the fall in the first place, for that matter."

"Do you have a theory?"

"I guess if you insist on a theory, I'd have to say it's a miracle— a double miracle. Hardly a theory."

A few minutes later Baldwin led me out of the reception area, down several long corridors and finally into what appeared to be an older part of the same building. Stylized scenic murals painted in primary colors ran continuously along the walls. Most of the doors in the corridors were closed.

Baldwin opened one into a large, well-lit room furnished with clusters of bright print sofas. In one corner, five or six patients were gathered around a large-screen television, one of them tied into a wheelchair, all of them mesmerized by an old episode of "All in the Family"; others were sitting around staring off into space. One woman in a large wingback chair kept mumbling to herself and pulling at a thread in her pants. Despite the obvious attempt to make the place comfortable, the nice furnishings, the spotless, cheery surroundings, I couldn't help but feel the same sense of hopelessness here that I'd felt in a filthy state-run institution I once went into for a story. The patients themselves were dazed, unresponsive, unreachable, no matter how clean and well-cared for they appeared.

I spotted Lana right away: I would have known that yellow pearl-colored hair anywhere, though it looked like someone had taken an ax to it. She was standing near the far wall, looking out a window. I couldn't see her face.

I recognized the elderly man and woman standing with her. Twenty years older than when I last saw them, but unmistakably John and Ellie Paluka. John's hair was completely gray, and he seemed to have shrunk about six inches. And Ellie! Alan always used to say Ellie Paluka was the best-looking woman in Comity, even if she was half-drunk and spoiling for one of their spectacular domestic brawls, which were legendary in town. Ellie's spectacular body was only a memory now, of course, but she was wearing a flamboyant leopard print dress that would have been too much on a woman half her age. Her hair was dyed a harsh blond in pathetic imitation of the truly beautiful natural color that had seemed the only physical attribute Ellie had in common with her daughter.

I was perhaps ten feet away when Lana suddenly turned and saw me. I stopped walking.

What *was* this? Catatonia kept a person from aging?

If anything Lana seemed younger, healthier. Certainly slimmer. She'd always been on the heavy side; now her features seemed to have been sculpted from somewhere within the flesh I remembered. In fact, she looked a lot like her mother used to look, the same carved features, prominent nose, blond-lashed blue eyes. But she was bonier than her mother had been, more angular. And taller. She looked quite beautiful.

She was staring at me with no expression whatsoever on her face. For the first time since I got the call from Ann, it crossed my mind that Lana might be less than happy to see me. And at the same time, though this was several days before the publisher's phone call, the thought crossed my mind that there might be a book in Lana's story.

"Lana?"

She took so long to respond that for a moment I wondered if she recognized me.

Finally, she said, "Jack Wells."

"How are you, Lana?"

"Fine. How are you?"

"Fine."

Which seemed to exhaust *that* subject.

"I'm a reporter now," I said. "I wanted to find out how you were. My brother and I—"

"I thought I recognized you," John Paluka said. "You're Alan Wells's brother, aren't you?"

I nodded, held out my hand. John Paluka had a firm handshake for someone his age.

"We never got a chance to properly thank your brother for all he did at the trial for Lana," he said. "It's a goddamned disgrace they let Skitt out at all. Your friend Randy would still be alive if they'd kept that man behind bars."

"He was a menace," Ellie said. "I always said he was no good."

"He was worse than no good," Paluka said. "He took my baby

and corrupted her. Made her take all those drugs." He turned to Lana. "You were a good girl until you started in with that Skitt."

How could the man be so incredibly naive? Alan had fucked her long before Ethan Skitt ever came near her. So had I, for that matter.

Paluka glanced at his daughter, who looked young enough to be his granddaughter. He seemed bewildered.

"You know he came back to get Lana after he killed your friend Randy Slessenger," he said. "I caught him myself. It's a good thing I happened to be here that day. At least now he's behind bars forever."

I nodded.

"We're just glad to have our daughter back." He patted Lana on the shoulder.

"But we'll never forgive Ethan," Ellie said. "Never."

"How do *you* feel, Lana?" I said.

"Weird, Jack. Really weird."

"It's like we've been without her for twenty years," John Paluka said, "and now suddenly she's been restored to us."

"Do you remember what happened with Ethan that day up on Devil's Meadow, Lana?"

"I remember some of it. Not much."

"Do you remember why Ethan pushed you?"

"What reason does there have to be for a murdering son of a bitch?" Ellie said.

"Lana?"

"We were arguing about something." She stared at me, owl-eyed, then shook her head. "I just can't remember."

"Lana's memory will return in due course," Baldwin put in. "Some memory gaps are to be expected."

There was a silence.

"We're not in Comity anymore," Ellie said. "We live in Connecticut. Danbury."

I nodded. "I'm glad you're better, Lana. Can I come talk to you again sometime?"

"Sure, Jack. If you want."

"Good. For now, can I ask you one more thing? High Exposure is a two-hundred-foot cliff. How did you survive? Do you know?"

"I broke my legs."

"You were very lucky."

"Luck had nothing to do with it," Lana said. "I just didn't land right."

People will turn each other on.
Only good vibes. But no demands.

—Jerry Rubin, Do It

12

When the call came in that someone had gone down at High Exposure, Michael Timothy Morino was out at Opatcho's. He'd just finished checking the barn and was heading back to the house to reassure Barbara Opatcho—for the third time in less than a year—that there was no one prowling around her farm. He really did feel sorry for the woman, losing her husband after forty years of marriage. Jim Opatcho had left Barb with a few chickens, a few more cows, and a pair of useless kids who'd scattered to the four winds years ago. He'd also left her with a hundred acres of fairly decent farmland and a pile of bad debts. The debts were gone now, along with the cows and the acreage. Barb Opatcho, now down to the house and the chickens and a small vegetable garden, lived in constant dread that someone might invade what little territory she had left.

Morino took the radio call in the patrol car.

"One of the climbers?" he asked Harry Larson, who was working dispatch that afternoon.

"No. One of the local kids."

Damn. Those kids were always hanging around up there. Everyone always said something tragic would happen if something wasn't done. There'd even been a town meeting about it last spring, but nothing ever came of it. Morino himself had broken up a pot party or two up on Devil's Meadow. Technically it wasn't the town's responsibility to police the area, since it was a private preserve.

"Mike, you'd better check it out right away. I think we've got a homicide up there."

"What?" Mike Morino was already turning on the ignition, pulling out of the driveway, turning on the siren.

"Call came in at four-ten. Two witnesses. The one who made the call said his name is Alan Wells."

One of Kevin Wells's boys. Fine family. Alan was the tall one Morino's daughter mooned over all the time. All Mike Morino knew was that the Wells kids seemed to be the only ones left who wore their hair a respectable length. Of course, Alan Wells was a swimmer and swimmers had to.

"What'd he say?" Morino asked.

"He just said she was pushed."

"Who was pushed?" Morino was already out on Canyon Flats Road, siren blaring.

"Lana Paluka. You know. John Paluka's daughter."

Morino could hear the ambulance siren in stereo with his own. He parked the patrol car in a space at Lookout Point, the scenic overlook about a hundred feet below the summit at the High Exposure cliff. From there it would be a downward climb first through the woods, then to the rock ledge at the base of the cliff.

Lane and Murkowski pulled in behind his car just as he was heading into the woods. Morino knew these woods and these rocks like the back of his hand; he'd grown up in Comity, lived here all his life. The woods cleared about three hundred yards below; then it was down along the rocks, traversing the bottom half of the mountain to the face of the cliff, the landing below it. It was difficult going down that way, but at least it was manageable without all that climbing equipment you had to use for the section above the landing.

He motioned for Lane and Murkowski to follow him and began preparing himself for the sight of the girl's smashed body.

But the three cops stopped short about twenty yards away from the site. What the hell was going on? Who fell?

All they could see was a teenager Morino vaguely recognized as John Paluka's kid, sitting on the rocks below the cliff. Just sitting there staring into space, her arms extended straight out from her body, legs tucked up beneath her.

Alan Wells and a teenaged boy Morino didn't recognize were standing there too, as pale as if they'd been hand-dipped in flour.

Morino moved in closer. Definitely John Paluka's girl. About ten years ago, John had taken over Adley's Bar, where Morino sometimes stopped after work for a couple of beers. Place was a real dive, even worse since Adley sold it to Paluka. Of course the bar did have John's wife, Ellie, to look at, a fine-looking woman

even if she was a drunk. He'd never been able to figure what she
was doing with a guy like Paluka in the first place. And they were
always at each other's throats. Morino himself had gone to break
up their fights a couple of times. It was always Lana who answered the door. Then either Ellie or John would tell him who
hit whom, while he stood and took down a report. Then he'd
leave. It wasn't a cop's business if a man wanted to kick his wife
around, or if a woman wanted to kick her husband around, for
that matter. It had obviously gone both ways in that house.

Morino could hear the sound of the ambulance pulling in. It
would be a while before the paramedics made their way to the
scene.

"Lana?"

He went up to her, squatted down, and looked her straight in
the eye. She stared right past him as if he wasn't there.

Morino checked for her pulse, then looked around him at the
gray jagged rocks, his eye moving up to the ledge high above. He
looked back down again at the two boys standing there, and at
her.

"Okay, what the hell's going on here?"

The two boys looked at each other, the cliff, then back at him.

"We know what we saw," Alan Wells said. "He pushed her."

"Who pushed her? Where?"

"Ethan Skitt. Over the cliff." He pointed up to the ledge.

A cool breeze stirred the fine hair on the back of Morino's neck.

"Come on, kids. No one would survive a fall from up there."

"We know what we saw," Alan Wells said.

"Who are you?" he asked the other boy. He was a slight kid
with frizzy brown hair that fell across his forehead and reached
the tips of his shoulders.

"Randy Slessenger." The boy's voice was barely audible.

The two paramedics were on the scene now, taking the girl's
blood pressure, looking into her eyes. She didn't respond, didn't
move from that odd position.

"You see this happen, Randy?"

The boy nodded, eyes wide. "He pushed her."

Morino glanced over at Lane and Murkowski, who shrugged.
It was hard to believe that even Sarah Skitt's kid would try to
kill someone. But he *was* always getting into fights, from what
Morino had heard. Had a violent temper.

He motioned for the paramedics to take her. Carefully, awkwardly, they picked up the immobile body, set it on the stretcher
and headed back.

"All right, kids, come with me," Morino said.

* * *

"There he is."

Alan Wells pointed out the window of the patrol car at a lone figure walking fast along Canyon Flats Road, heading back to town. Running, really.

Morino pulled up alongside the boy, who kept walking, head down. It was definitely one of the Skitts—all of the Skitt kids had a lanky, long-armed, stoop-shouldered carriage and that poker-straight black, black hair. Good-looking, like their mother, with straight proud noses and intense dark eyes.

This one seemed lost in thought, but stopped and turned around when the parade of vehicles pulled up alongside him.

"What's the matter?" His eyes shifted to the ambulance speeding past. "What happened?"

When he got out of the car, Morino could see that Skitt's eyes were red, as if he'd been crying.

"You know Lana Paluka?"

The boy glanced at the other two boys in the back seat of the patrol car, then looked back at Morino.

"What's wrong? Is it Lana? Is it Lana?"

"She's had . . . an accident, Mr. Skitt."

Now his eyes followed the ambulance receding in the distance. "Oh, man," he said, "I should have turned back. Something happened to her. I *knew* something happened to her. I felt it, man. I feel everything with Lana. Oh, my God, I shouldn't have yelled at her—"

"What did you yell at her about, Ethan?"

Ethan Skitt stared at him for a moment, then said, "She went off the cliff, didn't she?"

The kid was spilling everything.

"You have the right to remain silent, Ethan."

The boy stared at him. "Why?"

"Anything you say now can be used against you later."

"What do you mean?"

"You have the right to have a lawyer present if you speak to me. Do you understand?"

"What the fuck are you—"

"Do you waive that right?"

"Yeah, man, I waive it."

"Why'd you try to kill her, Ethan?"

The boy looked at him, wide-eyed, pale as a ghost.

"I didn't try to kill her. I love her. She's my life, man."

"Then how'd you know she went down?"

"Because I felt it. Here." He touched his chest. "I feel everything she feels. That's the way it is when you find your soulmate. It's like, you don't even have to talk to know what she's thinking." Tears were spilling down his cheeks. "I felt that she was falling. See, we had this argument, and I left her there, but I never thought she'd . . . I knew I should have turned back to help her. See, man, it might as well have been me falling."

Morino looked at him, at the wide glassy eyes, the dilated pupils, the mud-covered clothes. The kid was on some kind of drug. Yeah, sure, it might as well have been him falling. Only it was her.

He put a hand on the boy's shoulder.

"You'd better come with me."

"I want to see her." Ethan Skitt put his face in his hands and began to sob. "Oh my God, oh my God, we had an argument, but I never thought she'd . . . oh my God."

Mike Morino glanced over at the two boys in the back seat of the patrol car. "They say you pushed her, Ethan."

For a very long moment the kid just stared at him.

Finally he said, "They are fucking lying."

"Why would they do that?" Morino asked him.

Ethan Skitt stared at Morino for a moment, then glanced over at the other two, then back again. Finally, calmer, he said, "I don't know. You have to ask them."

13

In the lexicon of my childhood, the Skitts were so notorious that we had a game called "Skitt." The idea was this: there had to be at least four kids, one of whom—the "Skitt"—had to tag everyone else in the game within ten minutes. The first one he touched would have to be Skitt in the next round, and whoever he touched after that would have to act crazy—which generally involved falling down on the ground, butting around, screaming obscenities, doing whatever we imagined crazy people did. Sometimes the game was played in the field next to the Skitt house. Once in a while Sarah would come out, hair flying, usually in one of the floor-length peasant dresses she wore years before other women began wearing them. There she'd be in those crazy Mexican dresses, screaming, "Go away and leave us alone!" but since the rules didn't allow a player to step on Skitt property, she could never catch us.

As we got older, there was another game we played up at Devil's Meadow. Each player would mount his bicycle at the far side of the meadow, then ride as close to the edge of the cliff as he dared. The one who stopped farthest from the edge became the Skitt and had to lie down on the ground and act crazy. Of course, the game was really just a glorified version of chicken, developed by Alan after we all saw *Rebel Without a Cause*. But when we were kids, "Skitt" was a general term for anything from craziness to cowardliness to thickheadedness to ugliness—despite the fact that by almost any standards the Skitts were a handsome clan.

Approaching Comity from the west after my visit with Lana, I was struck by how little the town resembled the place in which

I'd grown up. Of course, the transformation had occurred over many years, but the culmination of it was that the cliffs looming high above town in the distance were the only landmark that seemed familiar. Or maybe I was just more aware of the changes this time. A huge modern high school had recently been built on a new road just off Route 6, three miles from what used to be considered Comity's western outskirts. There were new developments everywhere. And shopping centers. And motels too, all advertising climbers specials.

The changes in the center of town were older, and I remembered them from previous visits. The old red-brick school on Mason Street was now a Pergament and a McDonald's. Bromfield Square, which used to be a hodgepodge of row houses and separate structures built in different eras and bearing no apparent relation to one another, was now something else entirely, something "cute," something staged. All the buildings in the square— the triplex movie theater; Adley's Bar, which had been called Woody's for years; Dad's and Alan's medical offices, the Wells Medical Arts Building, complete with a pharmacy on the ground floor—were uniformly painted white and decorated with white-and-pink awnings. Along one side of the square a group of little craft shops occupied the site of the row houses where the town's poor had lived.

I glanced at my watch as I drove out of the square. I had time to go over to Shawangunk Hospital, which was two blocks in from the square, assuming it hadn't been moved. It hadn't.

I showed my press card to the admissions clerk and asked if she knew of any nurse or doctor now on staff who had been working at the hospital twenty years ago. She told me that Rowina C. Burn had been head nurse for almost ten years and on staff for years before her promotion.

"When is Nurse Burn here?"

"She has day shifts. She usually gets in about eight A.M."

I thanked her and headed over to my parents' house.

Alan's wife, Jocelyn, was the first person I saw when I pulled into the driveway and parked next to my brother's latest Jaguar sedan. She had the front passenger door open and seemed to be stooping to retrieve something from the floor in front of the seat. As I turned off the ignition and stepped out of my car, I noticed that the house seemed somehow too large for its one-acre lot, then realized that an addition had been built off the kitchen, a two-story structure with a peaked roof that dwarfed the peak on the other side of the original tract split-level. I remembered my mother mentioning something on the phone about building an addition. There was a new porte cochere at the front, too, making the whole house look like some lost baronial estate, somehow picked up from its more probable setting and dropped in the middle of a neighborhood of modest homes.

Jocelyn emerged from the car holding a large box wrapped in silver paper. She gave me a tight little smile and a peck on the cheek. She was wearing too much perfume.

"How are you, Jack?"

"Fine." I stepped back and took a look at her. Jocelyn had been a spectacular beauty: bountiful red hair, creamy white skin, full lips, and what Alan had called "a great pair"—the reason, he once jokingly told me, that he'd married her in the first place. Now, fourteen years and three children later, Jocelyn didn't look quite so spectacular. There were dark circles under her not so creamy skin, and beneath her expensive green-and-yellow linen outfit and carefully made-up face she just looked worn out.

She handed me the box.

"For you, Jack." She smiled and, for a moment, still looked spectacular. "When we heard you were coming for dinner, Alan insisted we get you a present. I told him he would know better what you might like, but he's been so busy with this new project he's been working on."

No doubt, at my brother's instructions, she'd chosen something outrageously expensive. "What's the project?"

"Florida real estate."

"I'm glad you picked it out, Jocelyn."

We walked together up the front lawn and into my parents' house. I stopped dead in the doorway.

The whole place seemed to have been redecorated in a single nightmarish act. By a stoned decorator with an animal fetish. There wasn't a single piece of furniture I recognized, except for a small antique gold pendulum clock that Alan and I broke once while throwing a football in the house, and a small art deco lamp that had been our grandmother's. Who lived here amidst the plush black sofas and the angular white laminate coffee tables, laid over a zebra-skin rug?

What had happened to my mother's Shaker furniture and collection of Early American crafts? Mom had always been a homey person, with her church social committee, her crafts, her flower club, and her PTA presidency. This looked more alien than homey.

"Like it?" Jocelyn asked.

"It doesn't seem like my parents," I said.

"Wait till you get a look at the new family room."

I had the feeling Jocelyn didn't think much of it either. After a moment, she said she wanted to go check on Douglas and Alan, Jr., who were in the den playing Nintendo. I headed into the kitchen, where I did find one of my mother's projects, one involving arrangements of dried weeds and flowers. These were piled into one corner of the kitchen, which bore no resemblance whatsoever to the one I remembered.

I stood for a moment in the doorway watching my mother slide a casserole dish into the oven, next to a roast turkey that smelled delicious. Casseroles and turkey, like my mother, somehow seemed out of place in this gleaming high-tech kitchen. She had lost some weight, and it didn't sit well on her. My mother had always taken great pride in her appearance and been rail thin. Now she looked like a bony and frail old woman. It was amazing to me though that she was still wearing her hair in the shoulder-length flip she'd been wearing for as long as I could remember, no doubt dyeing what had to be surely all gray by now.

I could hear Alan and Dad enjoying a baseball game from somewhere in the house, Alan whooping and hollering. Alan had always whooped and hollered.

Mom closed the oven door, turned, and saw me.

"Darling, you look wonderful." She kissed me, then glanced around as if she were just seeing the place for the first time. "How do you like it?"

"Did you pick everything out?"

"Alan did it," she said gaily. "I mean, Jocelyn found the decorator. He came all the way from Manhattan. Alan insisted that we get the best."

Which didn't surprise me; Alan had always been very generous. He once offered to buy me a sixty-thousand-dollar Porsche.

"Do you want to see the addition?"

"I think I've already seen it."

She waved me off, completely missing my meaning. "No, I mean the *inside.*"

She led me toward the sounds of the baseball game. There, in the middle of a huge two-story room with a cathedral ceiling, big enough for three separate groupings of furniture, a bar, *and* a pool table, were my brother and father and Alan's oldest son, Keith, all watching the Mets beat Cincinnati on a TV screen so large it was scary.

Dad had undergone bypass surgery a few years ago but was completely recovered—at least, he was again like the tall vigorous man I remembered, though his hair was pure white. Alan looked more like him than ever. Mom had to yell to get their attention, but I was heartily welcomed and given Dad's then

Alan's robust handshakes, which quickly evolved into backslapping embraces.

Alan stepped back, gave me a long look, and flashed one of his big infectious smiles, the dimple smile.

"Well, well, well, how you doin', kid?"

"A little less hair, otherwise about the same."

Alan touched his own still splendid head of dark hair, which was only now beginning to go gray, and only at the temples.

"If I could give you some of mine, kid, I would."

I laughed. Actually I was the older twin, by ten minutes, but it had somehow evolved that Alan called me "kid."

"No," Jocelyn said, coming into the room, "he wouldn't give any of his hair to you, Jack, don't let him kid you. He's far too vain for that."

Alan laughed. A silence followed, punctuated only by the sounds of the game.

"Why didn't you just move, instead of doing all this work, Dad?" I asked.

He frowned, glanced over at my mother. "It was your mother's idea. I told her putting money into this house was a bad investment, but you know how stubborn she is." He shrugged, laughed. "But *she's* the boss, as you know."

Actually, I had never thought of my mother as either stubborn, or as the boss. Possibly it was true when we were children: we always sought out the comfort of her arms for our scraped knees, or our hurt feelings, but as the years went on, it seemed to me that our house became a predominantly male domain.

Mom had sat down on one of the chairs in the corner of the room farthest away from the rest of us. It was an oversized chair in some kind of splashy print, and she looked lost in it.

"This is our home, Kevin," she said. "Why should we move?"

My other two nephews, Alan, Jr., now eleven, and Douglas, six, arrived then. The two older boys, Keith and Alan, Jr., were both like Alan, tall and athletic and energetic and smart. The younger, Douglas, was only energetic and smart.

The boys asked how their cousins were. I told them Craig and Chris had spent the month of July with me and were now back with their mother in Akron.

"So, what's new in the crusader business?" Alan asked. "Read your piece last week about Dixon. That guy comes off like a Number One pervert—or am I reading between the lines?"

I told them I'd been working that morning on a new installment in my series about Dixon, and about Georgina White, leaving out the part about the bribe. Both Alan and Dad seemed impressed.

"So. Are you all ready for the opening Sunday?" I asked. "I didn't get a chance to drive by the mall on the way in."

"If we're not ready now, we'll never be."

"Don't you still see patients?" I asked.

Alan shrugged. "About fifteen hours a week, at this point. Real estate is where the money is, Jack."

"Alan still didn't get to the most important thing, Jack," Dad said.

"What? Tell me?"

Alan said, "I'm going to run for Congress next year."

"Congress? You?"

"Dan Sheritan's been representing our district for almost ten years now," he said. "I think it's about time for some new blood."

I had never known politics to particularly interest my brother. I had always been the political animal in the family, at least since I began college. I remember I used to come home for weekends, heady with the idealism of the student protest movement, eager to argue politics with anyone who was fool enough to argue with me. Dad occasionally expressed opinions, such as his early support of the antiwar movement, but I always thought they were based less on any longstanding beliefs than on the fear that his two sons might be killed in Vietnam. There wasn't much chance of that; we were assigned number 289 in the lottery, and we had student deferments, anyway.

In any case, I could never engage Alan in any kind of political discussion at all. He kept quiet about politics. It was almost the only time he *did* keep quiet. I assumed he had no political opinions, or very few, anyway. Of course, my own opinions have changed over the years, softened a bit, I would say, although my basic left-wing sensibilities remain. But Alan's interests always seemed more personal, more about personal power and wealth.

I guess I must have been sitting there with my mouth hanging open, because Dad finally said, "Well, Jack, what do you think?"

I looked back and forth from my brother to my father and finally managed to ask what party.

"I've always been a Republican, Jack, you know that."

"I do?"

"Actually, kid, I was going to call you," Alan said. "I really think you'd be the perfect one to head up my campaign."

"Me?"

My brother laughed and looked around—for allies, I suppose. "Well?"

"Alan, I'm flattered but I have no experience whatsoever in running a political campaign."

"What does that matter, Jack?" Dad boomed. "You're smart, you know how to get things done. That's all that counts."

I remembered the time about fifteen years ago, just before the market became saturated with diet fads, when Dad and Alan had tried to talk me into working with them on a diet book idea they were kicking around. I refused; they never went ahead with the idea and ever since then never failed to remind me that we had all missed out on a real moneymaker.

"It would be a good opportunity for you," Alan said.

"I already have a career." I waited for Dad to comment about my working for peanuts for a second-string newspaper. He didn't.

Alan said, "It was only a thought."

Over dinner Alan regaled us with the details of his political plans. He'd already spoken to some consultants to test out the waters, and he was having a meeting in a few weeks to get the ball rolling. Everyone made encouraging comments; then, in the fast and exuberant manner I was so familiar with, Alan described his latest deal, a condominium complex in Florida that had not only netted him nearly a million dollars in two years but also provided a new kind of mixed-age living arrangement for the elderly who didn't want to live out their lives surrounded only by other old people. "It's a new idea, more natural this way," Alan said.

I found myself spacing out, barely able to listen. From the time I was young, I had been my brother's confidant, listener, sounding board, foil. Sometimes it had seemed to me that I was just there to catch the spillover of Alan's energy, which was considerable, astounding, exhausting. Sometimes at night, in the room we shared, he would keep me up for hours whispering across the beds, describing in the minutest detail his female conquests, his plans for the future, his opinions of people. Sometimes it seemed that my brother never slept.

I decided I would be glad for my brother that he was so successful, so happy. That he'd found a productive outlet for all that energy. That his three boys seemed to hang on his every word.

I noticed during dinner that my mother barely ate anything. She never did, really. She would always prepare dinner, then sit down with the family to eat, but mostly what she did was push the food around on the plate, only occasionally taking bird-size bites. I used to kid her about it. "You can never be too rich or too thin, right, Mom?" I would say, to which she would reply that we weren't rich. Now we *were* rich (or at least my brother was rich) and my mother had taken her thinness obsession to new heights, now barely making even the pretense of pushing the food around on the plate.

During dessert, after the kids excused themselves and left the table, the conversation turned to the pharmacy. A CVS had moved into town. Alan said the low prices were killing the Wells pharmacy business, even though the pharmacy was located right in the building with the medical offices.

"Obviously people care more about other kinds of convenience nowadays," he said. "I say we open a big place in the mall, not just for pharmaceuticals but hard goods, cosmetics. Everything. That way we'll get the old patients plus the new customers who come to the mall. They'll be coming from two counties, maybe three. And the pharmacy space won't go to waste. We can use the empty space to open, I don't know, maybe a blood-giving clinic, or a walk-in surgery clinic."

"Even in the mall we still can't compete with the national chains, Alan," Dad said.

"Sure we can. It isn't all about price, Dad. If we merchandise it right . . . we could call it something more modern, like SuperX, or how about Wells ValueRight? Something like that."

Dad was shaking his head. "I don't know . . ."

I looked over at my father, then back at my brother. It was just as it had always been, Alan offering his opinions to everyone, almost as if he were trying to get rid of some of them because he had an excess. Usually Dad was a good place to offer, since he thought his two sons could do no wrong.

"Maybe," Dad said. "Maybe that's what we'll do."

Alan smiled. "Hey, kid, how about opening your present?"

It turned out to be a Ralph Lauren silk robe, or maybe it was supposed to be a smoking jacket. What the hell was I supposed to do with a silk smoking jacket?

When I started to get up to help clear the table, Alan stopped me.

"Mom, I keep telling you that if you'd get help in the house, you wouldn't have to do all the work," he said. "You know I'll be glad to pay."

She laughed. "I've lived for sixty-one years without help in the house, I can live a few more years without it."

Alan parroted the last part of the sentence along with her. Obviously he'd made the offer before. Jocelyn joined Mom in the kitchen, leaving us alone with Dad. That was how it always was. Kevin Wells and his two boys.

"Guess who I saw today?" I took a sip of my coffee. "Lana Paluka."

"Lana? No kidding?" Alan said.

"She's at a place called the Drummond Rehabilitation Center. Long-term psychiatric care."

"I heard she's still a zombie," Dad said.

Mom called from the kitchen. "The Palukas don't live in Comity anymore."

"I know," I called back. "I saw them, too."

"So," Alan said, "how'd you happen to be at Drummond? Working on a story?"

"As a matter of fact, Lana *is* the story. Her legs eventually healed, but she's been in a catatonic state all these years. Then, apparently she just suddenly recovered. Came out of it."

There was a long silence. Alan was staring at me.

"What do you mean, came out of it?"

"Well, she seemed perfectly rational to me. Well, almost perfectly."

He glanced at Dad, then said, "When did this happen?"

"Last Saturday, they tell me."

"No one ever recovers completely from that kind of thing, Jack. For one thing, the memory is shot."

"Apparently that's true in Lana's case—at least, she doesn't remember what happened with Ethan that day. But her doctor said she would regain her memory at some point."

"Oh, they always say that kind of thing," Dad said. "To give hope."

"No, I think he's right," I said. "After all, she did survive a fall from High Exposure. If she could do that—"

"A *fall* from High Exposure?" Jocelyn was standing in the kitchen doorway. "My God, I've been up there. How could anyone survive that?"

"Well, survive she did," I said. "No one knows just how. And not just a fall, a push."

"Who pushed her?"

"A bastard named Ethan Skitt."

There was another long silence.

Finally, Alan said, "What a trip! Can you imagine, waking up like that after twenty years?"

"Imagine it?" Jocelyn said. "I can't believe it. No one could survive a fall like that—it's impossible."

"She broke both her legs."

"She should have broken every bone in her body, and some that weren't in her body."

"I did ask her this afternoon how she survived the fall," I said. "And?"

"She said she landed wrong."

"What in the world is that supposed to mean?"

"I'm not sure what it means," I said. "It shows she's not all there, I guess."

14

Only five hours into a twelve-hour shift and Nurse Rowina C. Burn felt like she was back at her old job at the Boston Memorial ER. At Comity Hospital someone might come in with a badly cut finger, you might see a case of heat prostration, or, more likely, lacerations or broken bones from an accident involving one of the climbers. Once there was a suicide, a plunge from one of the cliffs, but that one had gone straight to the morgue.

Already that day the emergency team had treated four victims of an accident involving a truck and two cars over on Route 6A; a fairly serious knife wound following an altercation at Adley's Bar and Grill, even an accidental gunshot wound. The team had also seen three kids—two drug overdoses and a concussion— brought all the way down from Bethel, overflow from Woodstock.

It had been a busy, bloody day. And this one would be more of the same. The paramedics had radioed ahead: a jumper.

Nurse Burn rushed through the double doors just as the ambulance pulled up, followed by two police cars. The last burst of siren sound drowned out the loud screech made by the three vehicles.

Damn, it was hot. The hot weather was an aftermath of the torrential rains that had turned that weekend's music festival some fifty miles north into an overpopulated mud bath.

Two paramedics bolted from the blue-and-white van, unlocked the double doors at the back.

Rowina nodded at the cop getting out of the police car behind the ambulance. She had gone out with Mike Morino for a few months last year after he lost his wife. And one of the two teenaged boys sitting in the back of the car was Alan Wells, who before graduation last June had swum on the varsity swimming team with Rowina's son.

She turned her attention to the ambulance as the two paramedics wrenched the stretcher carrying the stiff body of a young girl down onto the walkway.

It was the most bizarre ER admission she'd ever seen. The patient wasn't even lying down on the stretcher, she was sitting up. Her legs weren't visible beneath the sheeting, but her chest and head were thrust outward and upward, both arms extended at about a 50-degree angle from her body. She looked as if someone had arranged her, then frozen her stiff. Her eyes were open and she was staring straight in front of her.

"What's this?" Rowina said. "Some kind of joke?"

"No joke," one of the paramedics said as he adjusted the gurney height. "Kid's in some kind of stupor."

"I thought you said she was a jumper." There wasn't a drop of blood on her, or anywhere on the pristine sheeting of the gurney.

"I think her legs may be broken," the paramedic said. "But I can't really tell. The legs are, like, *welded* in that position. The arms, too."

Rowina lifted the sheet from the patient's lower body. The girl didn't move, didn't speak, didn't change position. Her legs were tucked up underneath her. Oddly angled, possibly broken. Still, a jump from that height . . .

"She jumped. I don't care what they say."

The voice had come from inside the second police car. Rowina C. Burn bent down to peer into the back seat. A young boy was sitting there, about the same age as the two boys in the other car and the girl on the stretcher. His eyes seemed to blaze out at her.

"Lana's gone." The boy got out of the car.

There was something about him that bothered Rowina—something about his expression, his manner. His eyes glistened as if he'd been crying, yet in his eyes there was almost a look of triumph, or at least defiance. She was reminded of a dog she once had, a lovable beast named George who had the unlovable habit of stealing her underwear. When she scolded him, he hung his head in abject remorse, yet there was something in his eyes that told you he was thinking, Ha, ha, I got away with it, and I'm going to do it again.

"Rowina?"

Nurse Judith Orlanski and Dr. Evan McNeil, the surgical resident, were already following the gurney bearing the oddly positioned young woman through the doors. Rowina followed.

Dr. Edmond Reinman, the chief resident, met the group just as the paramedics were wheeling the gurney up to an examining table, clanging one steel edge against the other.

Reinman stopped in the doorway. "What the hell's this?"

"Lana Paluka," the paramedic said. The pair of them awkwardly transferred the stiff body onto the table. "Local girl, eighteen years old. Found sitting on the rocks at the bottom of High Exposure—"

"Sitting *where?*"

"The bottom—"

"I heard you," Reinman said, "but I don't follow you."

"I mean she was pushed. At least, that's what the two witnesses say." The paramedic shook his head. "Looks like her legs may be broken, but other than that I can't find anything physically wrong with her at all. She's one lucky kid."

Edmond Reinman watched Nurse Burn slap a blood pressure cuff on the girl's extended right arm, which remained extended even under the weight of the cuff. Now he could get a good look at her. Blond, a bit heavy, but pretty features—completely slack. She was staring upward, pupils fixed and dilated in watery blue irises. She was wearing mud-soaked sandals, bellbottomed blue-jeans, and a T-shirt that said LOVE in a big square block on the front.

"Lana?" Reinman waved his hand in front of her face. No response.

"Lana, can you hear me?"

Nothing. Not even a flicker.

"Stuporous," Reinman said. "What's her BP?" He shined a light into the girl's eyes. No response. Pupils remained fixed and dilated.

"BP one-twenty over eighty. Pulse one-forty."

"Good."

Vital signs were good. Blood pressure normal. Good respiration. She was pale but not cyanotic, her pulse fairly rapid, but no more than it would have been after a few laps around a track. Extremities warm, even her fingertips and toes. All of which meant there didn't appear to be any internal hemorrhaging. No heart attack. No stroke.

So what the hell was the stupor?

"Okay, let's get these clothes off."

Nurse Orlanski took a pair of scissors and cut through the jeans in a single motion, removed the remains. Both Reinman and McNeil began examining the legs.

"I'd say a fairly serious break in the left fibula and a less serious one in the right tibia and patella," Reinman said.

He sat her up further. Like a piece of soft clay, she allowed him to position her without resistance, then remained there, still holding both arms out while he examined her spinal column. It appeared to be intact. Lucky? It was a miracle.

Reinman turned back to the paramedics. "You sure she went down from High Exposure?"

"There were two witnesses."

Reinman turned back to the girl. She reminded him of something, sitting there that way with both arms extended. Some new way of meditating he'd seen on television? A Hare Krishna? The position was almost . . . Christlike. No, that wasn't it, the hands weren't right. The palms were turned toward the floor, the arms thrust upward. In fact, the whole position gave him a feeling of great movement. Yet the girl was completely motionless.

Edmond Reinman could see Nurse Burn staring at him.

"Someone get the witnesses in here," he said. "I want to talk to them."

Nurse Orlanski left the room.

"Lana?" Reinman said again. "Can you hear me?"

Nothing.

"Lana?"

Reinman clapped his hands in front of the girl's face.

Not a blink.

"Lana?"

"She won't answer. She's gone."

Looking up, Reinman saw a boy standing in the doorway, his face dead-white, a policeman at his side. Handsome young man, even with the shoulder-length hair and the mud-soaked bellbottomed jeans that looked like he hadn't changed them in a year. His T-shirt was orange tie-dye.

"You a witness?"

"No. I'm her . . . boyfriend. Ethan."

"What's her name?"

"Lana. Lana Paluka."

"Do you know what happened, Ethan?"

Softly. "We did some Purple Haze at Woodstock—"

"LSD?"

He nodded.

Edmond Reinman had seen the pictures of the Woodstock disaster on television. Miles and miles of kids. A twelve-mile-long traffic jam. No sanitation, acres of mud, hundreds of bad trips and OD's. Damned stupid kids—what the hell did they think they were playing with?

"Do you know when you took the drug, Ethan?"

"Sunday morning. Yeah, Sunday morning."

"Where'd you get it?"

He shrugged. "I don't know, some guy."

"You wouldn't happen to have one of these pills you took?"

"No, man—I told you we got it from some guy. There was this brown acid going around that wasn't good, everyone said. But this guy said the Purple Haze was good stuff, best there is. He was right. It was incredible, man, except . . ."

"What?"

The boy shrugged. "Nothing." Then he looked over at the girl on the table, shook his head, mumbled. "Stupid. Stupid."

"What's stupid?"

"Acid. It makes you do things. Crazy—"

"What does it make you do?"

The boy hesitated a moment, then said, "It makes you think things, man."

"What?"

"She was talking about flying." He looked from the doctor to the policeman, then let out a long deep breath. "I'd already crashed pretty bad, but she still seemed tripped out on the Haze when we got a ride back to Comity this morning. They let us out over on 6A, and we decided to go over to High Exposure. It was where we met. And we had some things to talk about, to work out. And then she started saying she could fly—you know, like be on a different plane of reality, like a bird's reality—and then . . . well, we had an argument. And then I left."

"Sooner or later, Ethan," the policeman said, "you're going to have to tell us the truth."

There were tears in his eyes. "I wouldn't have hurt her. She was my love. My soulmate . . ."

"Hey, wait a minute," Reinman said. "I've got a girl in there I've got to find out what's wrong with. Now, that cliff is over two hundred feet high. Did something break her fall?"

"I already told you I didn't see it," Ethan Skitt said. "Anyway, High Exposure is a fucking cliff. Nothing broke her fall."

The policeman shrugged. "We've got two witnesses, doctor."

Reinman looked at him, then over at the girl sitting frozen on the examining table in ER One. So there had been a fall. Reinman didn't believe it was possible, but there it was.

"Okay, if you say so," Reinman said. She was one lucky kid, all right. But a couple of broken bones were easily fixed; an LSD-induced psychosis was something else again. If only he knew what was in the drugs they'd taken.

Reinman went back to his patient. Better not risk giving her a phenothiazine, in case the stuff they'd taken had been cut with PCP.

"Okay," he said, "let's get some diazepam into her before we get her up to X ray. Fifty milligrams in saline. Stat."

While Nurse Burn prepared the injection, Reinman took hold of the girl's extended arms and moved them five inches downward into a new position. They remained where he placed them, stiff like boards. He moved both arms back up again. Again they stayed there.

"Shit," he said. "And we'd better get Don Clayfield down here from psychiatry."

It was so dark. Dark and still and cold. Lana could sense the presence of others nearby, other figures, other forms. Were they shadows? No. She could hear their voices, a low droning hum. Why couldn't she see them? Was she imprisoned here? Where was Ethan?

Now she could see the others, the humans, there on the other side. She could see them moving around, trying to help her, moving her wings up and down.

Don't show you're alive.

She could see them all so clearly in the bright white light—the gleaming instruments, the white uniforms, the pinkish-white flesh. Maybe everything was so clear because she had a different type of eyesight now. There was one nurse with graying hair wrapping something around her arm. She wanted to speak to the gray-haired lady. Open her mouth and speak.

Shhh. *Don't talk to her. She may be the enemy.* But who was the enemy? Ethan? No! It was so dark and cold here. She didn't want to be here. She wanted to take it all back, take it all back. She wanted to go back to standing on the edge with Ethan.

Now there was a man in a white coat bending over her. Her doctor? That must be it. She was in a hospital, the wrong place for her, and this must be her doctor. He was trying to help her, touching her, moving her, talking to her in a low voice. What would her own voice sound like?

Don't speak. Don't give yourself away. How could she be there and not there at the same time? How she could look like them and not be like them?

She strained to hear what the man in the white coat was saying. *Keep still. Do what they say. Let them put you whatever way they want.*

"Okay, let's get the X ray."

Did he say they would take an X ray? Look inside her? See inside her bones. See her blood, her organs.

They couldn't do that. If they did that, they would know. She had to get away.

No! No! No, no, no, no, nonononononono . . .

Dr. Donald Clayfield was already in the hospital the day Lana Paluka was brought in. As the only practicing psychiatrist in a nearly thirty-mile radius, he was on call most of the time and even had a small office in the hospital. He'd seen an emergency admission—an acute schizophrenic who'd gone off his medication—around lunchtime. And he'd just finished up a final session with Gilda Lowman, a depressive about to be transferred out to a long-term facility down in Westchester County. Comity General wasn't equipped to handle long-term patients.

Clayfield was in the doctors' lounge having a cigarette when he heard his name over the PA system. "Dr. Clayfield to emergency. Dr. Clayfield, emergency."

He pushed the elevator button for the ground floor. He would have to walk clear over to the other side of the hospital.

"Dr. Clayfield to emergency. Stat. Dr. Clayfield, stat."

Doctor Donald Clayfield broke into a run.

Before he was off the elevator, Clayfield could hear the screams. Female screams: "No, no, let me make it up to you. I'm sorry, Ethan, I'm sorry."

Sorry for what?

There was a young man standing next to one of the local cops in front of the door to ER One. As Clayfield approached he realized he knew the boy. Ethan Skitt. He'd come in with his mother and other brother about three months ago. The younger boy was severely psychotic; Clayfield had hospitalized him for a month, trying various courses of drug therapy that didn't help, then sent him to Edgewater, a state-run mental hospital down in Putnam County.

Clayfield stood in the doorway next to the boy. Obviously he knew the young woman inside doing the screaming; yet he didn't seem to be reacting. He didn't even turn to acknowledge Clayfield's presence.

Inside was a scene of complete bedlam. The patient was standing in a corner of the room with her back against the wall, stabbing out wildly with a pair of scissors. Her hair, long and tangled and blond, hung about her face. She was wearing only underpants and a LOVE T-shirt. With each stab of the scissors she stamped a foot on the floor and made clicking noises with her tongue.

She began to scream again—a feral, low-pitched sound, the words coming so fast that Clayfield could barely make them out.

"Stay away from me. Stay away, stay away I'm sorry I want to be dead be dead . . ."

"Her name is Lana Paluka," Dr. Reinman called out, not taking his eyes off the girl. "Just admitted. Boyfriend says she took some LSD. Until a minute ago, she was in some kind of a stupor."

"Catatonic?"

"Looked like it to me. Waxy flex, limbs like clay. She was holding her arms out like some kind of statue for almost ten minutes that I saw."

"And another fifteen in the van," one of the paramedics said. He was holding a straitjacket.

"I gave her diazepam, about seven minutes ago," Reinman said. "Nothing. And there's something else, Don."

"What?"

"Her legs are broken. I don't know how the hell she's standing on them."

Reinman looked completely freaked, which didn't surprise Clayfield. The catatonic stupor was one of the rarest and most bizarre conditions a psychiatrist ever encountered, and *this* was worse. It looked like excited catatonia, in which the patient goes completely out of control, as if the circuits are running amok. Which was why the girl was moving continuously. Tapping her foot and screaming. Stabbing. A patient in such a state of excitement might chew paper, stick out her tongue, roll her eyes, turn circles, anything, just to keep moving. Catatonic excitement might even explain the fact that she was standing up—*stamping*—on two broken legs.

They had to get her under control immediately—a patient in such a state was like a windup toy. She'd scream and move around, and run around, and rant and scream some more until that broken bone ripped right through the skin or she collapsed from exhaustion. Unless she had a heart attack first.

She was screaming, "I'm sorry, Ethan! Forgive me, forgive me, forgive me . . ."

Clayfield glanced over at the boy. The policeman grabbed the boy's arm and began leading him away.

"Hey, man, I didn't do anything," Skitt was saying. "Alan and Randy are lying, they are fucking lying!" He began to resist, and his screams got even louder and more obscene as the policeman led him away.

Clayfield took a deep breath and went inside ER One.

The patient had stopped screaming now and was standing immobile, still holding the scissors. Her head was cocked to one side, as if she were listening to something. But her eyes were empty.

"Lana?"

No response. Pupils fixed.

"Lana?"

He went over to where Reinman was standing. The patient's eyes didn't follow him. That was good. Good for them, bad for her.

Clayfield returned to the girl, removed the scissors from her hand; her fingers released their hold on them easily, but suddenly her legs buckled beneath her and she collapsed onto the floor, and just as suddenly her arms rose outward from her body, her head tilted upward.

Clayfield leaned down and looked into her eyes. Fixed and dilated.

For a moment, no one moved.

Then Ed Reinman went out into the hallway and got a wheelchair. Clayfield helped him lift her into it, grabbing her underneath the armpits and supporting her beneath the butt. It was like lifting a statue.

"Okay," Reinman said, "let's get her to X ray."

Clayfield went along as Reinman wheeled her still form out of the room. As a matter of fact, she reminded him of a statue he'd actually seen once in a museum. An ancient Greek statue? Head and chest thrust proudly upward. Wings at the back, extended to their full breadth. The statue of an angel. Or a winged goddess.

It looked to him like Lana Pakula was poised for flight.

15

Lana's parents bought Adley's Bar and Grill and moved into the apartment above it when we were all about nine. It seems to me that someone in school—I don't remember who—hung the name Paluka Bazooka on her the very first day. In fourth grade, everyone got called names like that, but Lana's nickname stuck for some reason, and soon no one called her anything but Paluka Bazooka. It just seemed like the perfect name for a fat girl. And the fire was further fueled a few years later when someone caught a glimpse of her full name on a school form. Lana Turner Paluka. We all got a good laugh out of that one. But no one really knew her, or spoke to her; she was just a girl in school.

One summer evening when we were about eleven, looking for something to do, we rode our bikes over to the small duck pond in the middle of Bromfield Square. At about ten o'clock we suddenly heard loud noises coming from the apartment above the bar, which lies at the southeast corner of the square. We all stopped, stood very still, and listened to the sounds drifting out of an open window, a lot of yelling and cursing. Then there was a loud crash, like something had been broken. At one point we could hear someone yelling, "Stop it, stop it!" It sounded like Lana's voice. Then there was a siren. We watched a squad car pull up in front of the bar.

Teddy Morino's father got out, mounted the outside steps. Lana herself answered his knock. By this time we had grown bolder and were standing next to the stairs, spellbound by the domestic drama unfolding in front of our eyes. Lana shrank back into the shadows when she saw us. We couldn't hear what was happening, because Teddy's father disappeared inside and closed the door behind him. A few minutes later he came out shaking his head, muttering to himself. But it was quiet now, so he must have done something. He saw us as he came down the steps.

"You kids get out of here. This is none of your business."

It seemed like the first exciting thing that had happened in Comity in years, but we scattered.

Late into the night Alan and I discussed what had happened at the Palukas' that night. Alan's theory was that they were arguing because Lana's mother was a boozer. He'd heard Dad call her that. Teddy's father, Alan said, had shown up to stop it before he killed her. I'm not sure I had my own theory, but I disagreed with Alan, anyway.

The next day was the first time I really talked to Lana. Mom asked me to ride my bike over to Dad's office to deliver something to him, and I had to go by the bar to get there. Lana was sitting on the front steps when I rode by. The first thing I said to her was, "Hey, Paluka Bazooka, how come the cops showed up at your house last night?"

Alan had insisted I spend the night at his place. I'd agreed, mostly because I could use his home office to write my story in the morning. It was all set up for the modern executive, with a computer, a modem, and a fax machine.

The house, on four acres just outside of town, had a tennis court, and pools, indoor and outdoor. It was surrounded by lush green lawns, strategically lit. Beyond the lawn on all four sides the woods were dense and untamed, and I could see the mountains looming above the treetops.

The house had obviously been decorated by the same decorator who did our parents' house. The animal motif here seemed to be leopard. Jocelyn and the boys had gone to bed, and Alan and I took a late-night swim.

When I got out of the pool, the moisture evaporated quickly on my skin, leaving me chilled and uncomfortable in the damp night air. I wrapped myself tighter in the towel and settled back on the chaise nearest to the pool. The sky was inky black, dotted with stars, silent, and the pool, lit by three powerful pool lights, was a speck of luminous blue under the vast night sky.

Alan was still bobbing around in the water, occasionally taking a lap across the length of the pool with his fine, strong crawl. His stroke was still powerful, his fluidity in the water and his technique almost as spectacular as when he won the state high school championships, though his pace was more leisurely, of course. From the chaise, I watched him do a flip-turn at the far end of the pool, then a strong butterfly toward me, his face set with concentration. I could see every muscle on his body, working, moving, shimmering and pale in the water.

I sat back and watched him, looking out over the pool and patio area, and beyond that, at the lawns and the surrounding woods, all swathed in darkness and the silence of the night.

It was then that I heard the noise. It came from the woods to my left, about twenty-five yards away. I sat for a moment, very still, listening. There it was again. A crunching of leaves on the forest floor.

"Shhh, Alan," I said. "I heard something."

He stopped moving around in the water, and stayed still, looking at me, droplets of water beading up on his face.

Now there was nothing, only the night silence and the gurgle of water. Perhaps it had been the rustle of trees, or squirrels, or a night animal foraging for food.

"Probably just a deer," he said. "We get them a lot out here."

"No," I said, "I don't know, it was heavier than a deer, it was more like . . . rhythmic. Like footsteps."

He shrugged and hoisted himself out of the pool at my end, grabbed a towel, and wrapped it around his waist. Then he lit up a cigarette, and plopped down on the chaise next to me.

Alan had taken up smoking relatively recently, just when everyone else was quitting, though well after his swimming career ended. He inhaled deeply, blew the smoke out in a perfect ring that floated up in the air and hung suspended for a moment just above his head.

"What did she look like?" He stared into the center of the smoke ring.

"Who?"

"Lana."

"Well, someone had chopped up her hair. I guess even in a place like that—"

"What kind of place is it?"

"It seemed pretty nice—no, really nice, considering what kind of place it is."

I suddenly remembered sitting around another pool once, talking about Lana with my brother. The junior high school pool, twenty-three years ago. Alan had swum in a meet that day, won a blue ribbon for the butterfly. The bleachers surrounding us were emptying out when Alan suddenly said, "I got Lana last night."

"You had sex with her? Didn't her parents care?"

"They were working at the bar, we were up on Devil's Meadow. She wanted it, bad. And you better believe I wasn't the first one in there."

"What was it like?"

Alan made a noise, a kind of snorting in his nose and throat.

"You really want to know, kid? It was like fucking an elephant . . ."

Alan had now finished his cigarette and was putting it out in the ashtray.

"So, besides the hair," he said, "what does she look like now?"

"Exactly the way she looked then, only thinner. It was damned strange."

"Oh, come on. She has to have—"

"She hasn't. She didn't look a day over eighteen, as a matter of fact. Slimmed down quite a bit. Actually she looks like her mother used to look."

"Well, that's an improvement. That Ellie was one sexy woman, if memory serves. Still, once a cunt, always a cunt."

I looked at my brother, mildly disgusted. It was one thing to talk about a girl that way when you were a kid. But we were adults.

Alan picked up the cigarette pack, crumpled it up and tossed it back in the ashtray, then jumped up.

"Gotta go for smokes. Back in a few."

"I'll go with you," I said, then felt his hand pushing down on my shoulder. "What's this, I can't come?"

He took his hand off my shoulder, dropped the towel.

"Sure, sure, you can come. Of course you can come."

We put our clothes on and headed back to the house. We had walked only a few steps before I heard the noise again. This time he heard it too.

We stopped and stood very still, but then there was nothing. He started to walk again but I held back.

"Alan, there's something out there. Someone's watching us."

"Hey, kiddo," he said, motioning me to come along, "you're getting paranoid in your old age. It's only an animal."

"No."

I pulled away from him and began to walk toward the woods. The forest spread out in front of me in all directions, dark and thick. About twenty-five feet away from the edge, I started to run. But whoever was watching us—definitely no animal—was already running away, fast. I could hear the receding footfall, the crunch of leaves, and I knew it would be impossible to overtake him, running blind through the dark of the forest.

"Come on, kiddo. Nothing there," Alan said.

I decided not to argue. The two of us walked toward the car, Alan's arm around my shoulder.

I settled myself into the leather seat and closed my eyes; Alan eased the Jag out onto Kennelson Road, then followed it up to Route 6, where the four-lane highway gave him an opportunity to show off the way the car handled. He pointed out the mall on the way, a sprawling dark hulk.

About two miles past it he pulled into an all-night convenience store, but parked the car beside the telephone booth near the road instead of taking one of the empty spaces by the store.

"Have to make a phone call," he said.

"Now? At a phone booth?"

"You know how wives are," he said. "They don't appreciate you calling your girlfriends from home."

"Why not use the car phone?"

Alan looked down at the phone on the console between us.

"Well, to tell you the truth, I need some privacy for this particular conversation. And besides, the goddamned phone sounds like it's at the bottom of a well when it's working, and at the moment, it's not."

"How long has this been going on?"

My brother looked at me for a moment, then laughed and said, "Hey, give me a break, bro. You had someone on the side, too. Remember?"

Which was true. It was only one—well, two, if you counted my one-night stand. But I had at least felt guilty about it, guilty enough to confess. It was what had broken up my marriage.

Alan slapped me on the shoulder, then got out of the car. I watched him go up to the brightly lit store. After a moment I looked down at the phone. Without even thinking about it, I pushed the power button. Nothing happened. I turned the key halfway in the ignition, pushed the button again. The fluorescent lights on the phone lit up immediately. I picked the phone up, got a dial tone, and punched in my own phone number. Might as well check my messages. There was only one, from my son Craig, who wanted to know my decision about the earring.

Alan reappeared with a pile of change in one hand and a pack of cigarettes in the other. The cigarettes went into his pocket, the change on the metal shelf under the phone. He closed the phone booth door.

The light went on. I watched him push buttons. Definitely a long distance call, with an area code.

He dropped a bunch of quarters into the slot, talked for barely a minute into the receiver, slammed it back into its cradle, and got back into the car.

I laughed. "What, was she with another guy?"

Alan eased the car out of the lot and back onto Route 6.

"No, she was with *two* other guys."

"The car phone seems to work perfectly," I said.

"You checking up on me, kid?"

"No, Alan," I said. "I just called for my messages."

Just before dawn on Saturday morning, an electrical storm rolled in from the southeast and stalled over the mountains. I awakened to the sound of booming thunder, heavy rain drumming along the roof, flashes of white light pulsating through the darkened room.

I lay very still in bed while gusts of wind whipped the curtains into drifting ghosts at the open window. I looked over at Alan's bed—

Alan's bed?

I wasn't in my parents' home, I was in my brother's. And we weren't kids anymore, not by a long shot.

For the first time since my divorce, I found myself remembering the times I'd awakened in bed next to Donna during a thunderstorm in the night and lay there watching her sleep, listening to the boomers and the sound of the rain pelting the screened windows, the sheet lightly draped over us, waiting for the boys to awaken and come scampering into the bedroom.

Why were those the only times in my life that I could remember ever feeling completely safe?

I got out of bed. I could hear morning sounds; everyone in the house was already up. Jocelyn had a full breakfast on the table by the time I sat down. She sat with Alan and me while we put away huge helpings of pancakes. It reminded me of all the Sunday mornings that Dad made pancakes for us when Mom went to church.

"I'm gonna go and see Sarah Skitt," I said.

"For the article?" Alan asked.

"Really what I want is to go and talk to Ethan. She'll know what prison he's in."

He nodded.

"Where are the rest of the Skitts?" I asked.

"I'm not sure," he said. "I know Nathan's still institutionalized. Seems to me I heard Laban was killed in Vietnam. I also heard he changed his name to Brent before he went over. Can you believe it? Brent? Anyway, God knows where the rest of them have scattered."

"But Sarah's still there, is she?"

"Yep. Still in her house out on Route 6. When we were building the West Farm Acres development back in '82, we offered her a lot for it, but she refused to sell. I couldn't figure out why, since she'd really let the place go to hell at that point, though she's fixed it up again over the last few years. From what I hear, she's still a religious nut, Jack. Now it's a bunch of holy rollers over in Kingston."

"I still want to see her," I said. "Mind if I use your office when I get back?"

"Sure, make yourself at home. But how about a game of tennis before you get down to work? I promised Keith we could have a set or two, but I'll make it one, to have room left for you."

"Why not?" I said. "I'll whip your ass." It was a comfortable routine for us.

"You probably will, kid."

After breakfast, I called my sons.

"Hello?" Donna's voice, low and full-bodied.

"Donna, it's Jack."

"Hello, Jack." Her voice always took on an edge when I was at the other end of the line, though it had been three years since we split. I could barely remember the name of the girl who had triggered our breakup. At least now we could have a civil conversation. Sometimes I missed her tremendously.

"I'm in Comity," I said, "visiting my parents and my brother."

"Good."

"I thought you never liked my parents and brother."

"I never said I didn't like them, Jack. I only said that every time you saw them you got crazy for a week before, and took another week to recover."

There was a silence. Then, "Can I talk to the boys?"

"Sure. What's the verdict about the earring?"

"I think we should let him do it, Donna. He could be asking a lot worse. But let *me* tell him, okay?"

"He's over at his girlfriend's house."

Girlfriend?

"Then I'll talk to Chris. Is he there?"

"I'll get him."

A few seconds later, I heard Chris's voice.

"Hi, Dad, how's it going?"

"I'm visiting Grandma and Grandpa."

"How's Uncle Alan?"

"He's fine. Very prosperous. Unlike your underpaid reporter father. I sure do miss you two since you left."

"Us too." He hesitated. "You still with Elaine?"

"We broke up."

"Well, I won't tell Mom."

"Why not?"

"I don't know, I just won't."

"How is she, Chris?"

"Oh, she's okay. She's seeing a new guy, a teacher. He's pretty nice."

Whereupon Chris launched into a blow-by-blow account of his victory in some local tennis tournament, then a rundown of his plans for the upcoming senior year. He ended this monologue with a description of his girlfriend, Samantha, "who made Craig's girl look like a contestant at the Akron dog show." The whole discourse reminded me of the way Alan used to talk sometimes when we were in high school.

I decided it was just the age.

I spent most of the morning interviewing Nurse Rowina C. Burn, who had actually been in the emergency room at Comity Hospital the day Lana was brought in twenty years ago. She was very cooperative and blessed with an excellent memory. That admission, she said, was one she would never forget as long as she lived. Once she'd described it, I could see why.

Then I headed over to Mike Morino's. He was retired from the Comity Police now and living in the Palmetto Townhouses on the east end of town. I interviewed him from a lawnchair on the tiny patch of grass out in back of his house while he tended a huge steak on a barbecue. I disappeared after some awkward hellos when a fat and balding Teddy—whom I had never really liked and hadn't seen since high school—showed up for lunch with his wife and two kids.

I headed out to Sarah's, driving past what used to be the Opatcho farm, now the subdivision my brother mentioned—West Farm Acres. It was huge, with street after street of colonial splits, a guardhouse out front, and an enormous red-lettered sign with a huge drawing of a farmer and a cow.

Before my brother and others like him got their hands on it, Comity had been a small rural town built around the surrounding farmland and a now-defunct textile mill. There was one movie theater on Main Street, Kevin Wells was the doctor, the women all bought their meats from Mr. Antwerp. Now there were three sprawling supermarkets, including the one I had just passed next to the mall, and nearly all the farmland was subdivided. Where did all the people who lived in these developments work? There wasn't a new factory, and they certainly weren't farmers. It seemed more like a suburb than the little village it had been. But what was it a suburb of ?

Sarah's house, at least, was exactly as I remembered it. A neatly tended Victorian, painted pink. There was an old VW Bug in the driveway.

A state police car was sitting in front of the house. I could see the two men sitting inside, watching me as I pulled in. I wondered what they were doing there but didn't approach them. I walked up to the door.

Sarah Skitt answered the door on the first knock. In her fifties now, she was still a striking woman. Her hair, still worn very long and parted down the middle, was now completely gray. A large cross hung around her neck.

"Mrs. Skitt," I said, "I'm Jack Wells."

She glanced over at the police car, then looked at me without expression.

"What do you want here?"

"What's the police car doing here?"

She shrugged. "You'll have to ask them." She started to close the door.

I put my foot in to stop it. "I came to talk to you about Ethan. I'm a reporter now, and I'm doing a story on Lana."

She peered out at me from behind the half-closed door, her expression softening a bit. Then she touched the cross around her neck, closed her eyes for a moment and whispered, "Praise the Lord for His miracles."

"Then you *know* Lana's come out of her . . . coma?"

Her eyes narrowed. "I have nothing to say to you, Jack."

"Do you know where Ethan is, Mrs. Skitt?"

"No." She started to press the door closed again. "I said I have nothing to say to you."

"Wait a minute—"

She stopped. "I've got some advice for you, though. My advice is maybe you should leave the whole thing alone."

"Why?" I said. "I'm a reporter."

She started to laugh. "A reporter?"

"You disapprove?"

"In this case," she said, "let's just say that when you go digging up graves, you sometimes find spooks."

Spooks? She was crazy, just like everyone said.

I retreated from her front porch. By this time, both of the cops were out of their car and standing next to mine. I walked up to them.

"What's going on?"

"Who are you?" one of them asked.

I introduced myself, told them I was a reporter.

The man glanced at his partner, then shrugged. "Nothing doing here," he said.

"What d'you mean—"

"I mean he's still at large—"

"*Who's* still at large?"

"Isn't that why you came here?"

"I don't know what you're talking about."

He glanced at his partner again. "We figured you were here after the story. Didn't you know? Ethan Skitt escaped from the Green Haven Correctional Facility between four and six o'clock last night."

"*What?*"

"What kind of reporter are you? There's been an all-points bulletin out on him for nearly twenty-two hours now."

*I am not so foolish as to equate what happens under
the influence of mescaline or of any other drug, with
the realization of the end and ultimate purpose of
human life: Enlightenment, the Beatific Vision. All I
am suggesting is that the mescaline experience is what
Catholic theologians call "a gratuitous grace,"
not necessary to salvation but potentially helpful
and to be accepted thankfully.*

—*Aldous Huxley*, The Doors of Perception

16

NOVEMBER 1970
COUNTY COURTHOUSE
KINGSTON, NEW YORK

Sometimes it seemed to attorney Eugene T. Shanagan that he'd never had a guilty client. Shanagan had once represented a man who insisted he hadn't known the female victim in the case, even though his sperm and pubic hairs were found inside her and his size fourteen triple-E bootprint was found near the scene of the crime. And *this* boy—this Ethan Skitt—was no better. Two eyewitnesses and still he denied the crime.

Shanagan hurried up the steps of the courthouse, a crowd of reporters at his back, mostly the same ones who had dogged him earlier when he came out for lunch. At least they'd left him alone while he grabbed a sandwich in the deli across the street. Now they were back, more of them than ever, following him up the steps, shouting questions at him.

"Mr. Shanagan, what were they arguing about?"

"What kind of drugs were they on?"

"What's her condition now?"

Shanagan continued to climb the steps.

"Why not plead temporary insanity?"

Damn, he was tired. After three years in the public defender's office, he could count on both hands the number of defendants who actually admitted their guilt. Most people thought courtrooms were run like the ones on TV, where Perry Mason saves the day with dramatic new evidence or courtroom theatrics. Most of Shanagan's cases were a matter of defending the indefensible.

Not that he didn't still have a little of the idealism that had drawn him to the public defender's office in the first place. But the scales of justice weren't always even, and little things—often very unfair things—could tip the balance one way or the other. So much had to do with the way the witnesses presented themselves and the way the defendant did. Here, it wasn't even a contest. Skitt was one angry, sullen, messed-up kid. With a mother who kept saying only, "The Lord will provide for Ethan."

Well, Eugene Shanagan wasn't the Lord, and the kid was guilty.

The district attorney, David Bonsall, had been very strong in his opening statement that morning. Shanagan could still see the jurors' faces, rapt with attention: *This young man, ladies and gentlemen, who sits now before you is a cold-blooded killer. Heartless, remorseless, brutal. It does not matter that his victim— an innocent young girl—somehow miraculously survived and at this moment lies in her hospital bed. It is the intent that matters. And of that there can be no doubt. Attempted murder is the appropriate term here. He tried to snuff out the life of this young woman, by pushing her from the top of a two-hundred-foot cliff. And this boy—Ethan Skitt, the defendant—sits here before you, healthy and whole, with not one shred of remorse for what he has done. On the contrary, he denies having done it. Two witnesses to his crime and still he denies it . . .*

"Mr. Shanagan, is she dead yet?"

Shanagan glared at the female reporter who'd asked the question.

"No comment."

It was nearly two. He was late. He hurried up the steps and through the huge double doors. Then he fairly ran to the courtroom on the second floor. The room was jammed by the time he got there.

He took his seat at the table and began emptying papers out of his case, then stood up a moment later when they brought Ethan Skitt in. It was a courtesy to the attorney-client relationship, not to the boy himself. The boy didn't even acknowledge his mother, who was sitting directly behind the defense table, where she'd been throughout the trial. No wonder the kid was a mess. The mother was as queer as a three dollar bill. She wore her hair waist-length, and every day she came in wearing some kind of dress that reached the floor, carrying a crucifix and clutching it to her breast.

"How are you doing today, Ethan?"

Skitt shrugged, sat down, picked up a pen, and began doodling on the pad of paper on the table. At least he'd agreed to cut his hair before the trial started. He looked a lot better now than when Shanagan had interviewed him in the holding tank at the Comity jail, hair past his shoulders and covered with mud. But no amount of fixing up could hide his sullen expression or make him look you in the eye.

If the kid would just admit his guilt, Shanagan might get him off with a temporary insanity defense. He could argue that it was an act of passion, or plea-bargain the charge down to assault. But Skitt kept insisting that he'd left Lana Paluka up on top of the cliff before anything happened. No matter what the witnesses said. When Shanagan asked him why the witnesses would lie about it, all he would say was, "They've always hated me." It was hopeless. The kid admitted he'd been up there, even that they'd been arguing, but flatly refused to say what it was about. And he insisted he would do the same on the stand.

Shanagan had never seen a more stubborn boy, or an angrier one.

Now his only course was to try to impugn the witnesses' characters, get one or both of them to look like he was lying. Which was unlikely, since they weren't.

The judge was coming in now. Shanagan looked up from his papers, everyone in the courtroom rose—except Ethan Skitt, who had his head down on the table. Shanagan had to tap him on the back to get him to stand up.

Dave Bonsall called Alan Wells, and a tall, handsome young man took the stand. The bailiff swore him in.

"State your name," Bonsall said, rising from his seat.

"Alan Sterling Wells."

Bonsall approached the stand.

"Objection," Shanagan said. "The prosecuting attorney has blocked my view of this witness."

Judge Suskind snorted. Bonsall made a slight bow and with a nod moved over to one side.

"Mr. Wells," Bonsall said, "how long have you known the defendant, Ethan Skitt?"

"All my life," Wells said. "He was in our classes all through school."

"Who does 'our' refer to?"

"I'm sorry, sir. I always think of myself as a 'we.' My brother, Jack, and I. We're fraternal twins." He pointed at a young red-headed man sitting at the back of the courtroom who looked nothing like him.

"I see. Now, can you tell us what happened on the afternoon of August eighteenth of last year?"

"Well, it was the day after Woodstock. I went up to the festival with our friend Randy Slessenger and got back on Monday morning, about five A.M. I slept until noon Monday—I got almost no sleep while we were there—then I woke up and called this girl I knew, Ally Wilson. She had a friend with her, Susan McGill. She suggested I call one of my friends and maybe the four of us could do something together. Like have a picnic up on Devil's Meadow."

"Did you do that often? Invite girls up there?"

"She invited me, Mr. Bonsall. It's a beautiful place."

"I see. And what happened?"

"Well, I thought it was a good idea, so I called Randy. My brother, Jack, was already up at school. You see, we all used to hang out together a lot—there was a group of us, ever since elementary school—and since we were all going our separate ways, Randy and I wanted to spend as much time together as possible. It was sort of a sad time for us."

"I see. And what happened then?"

"Well, as it turned out, the girls canceled, but Randy and I decided to spend the afternoon together anyway. I picked him up about two o'clock in my car, we drove over to Banshaw Park and left the car there. Then we walked up through the woods—that was the way we all used to go up to Devil's Meadow when we were kids. And we were just coming into the meadow when we saw them."

"Who?"

He pointed. "Ethan Skitt and Lana Paluka."

"Let the record note that the witness has pointed to the defendant," Bonsall said. "Go on, Mr. Wells."

"They were standing near the edge, at the far end of the meadow. Arguing."

"How could you tell that?"

"Gestures. Like, the way they were talking. You can tell when people are mad from the way they stand, move."

"Could you hear what they were saying?"

"No, we were too far away. But Ethan was definitely mad at her about something. He was yelling at her, we could see that."

"Did you try to stop the argument?"

"It wasn't our business. Ethan and Lana were, you know, like, boyfriend and girlfriend. They went together all through high school. It seemed like a personal thing."

"Now, we've been made aware that both of them were high on drugs. LSD, commonly known as acid. Did it seem to you that Mr. Skitt was out of control, perhaps because of drugs?"

"Objection," Shanagan said. "Calls for a supposition."

"Sustained."

"I withdraw the question," Bonsall said. "Okay, so you're there watching the two of them arguing about something near the edge of the cliff. What happened then?"

"Well, we were about to turn around—like, leave them to settle their differences alone—go back to the park for a while, when suddenly, before either of us could do anything, Ethan pushed her. He deliberately pushed her. We couldn't believe it. And she was standing very close to the edge, so she lost her balance . . ."

"What happened then?"

The witness hesitated only a moment, then said, "She went down. We saw her go over the edge."

The prosecutor kept the witness on the stand for nearly two hours, spending a lot of time on a complicated map he drew on an easel at the front of the courtroom, describing the different ways to get to the site of the crime, showing the meadow, the park, the wooded areas and paths, the road that skirted around the eastern side of the cliff, Lookout Point.

Now it was Gene Shanagan's turn. He positioned himself in front of the witness.

"Now, Mr. Wells," he said, "you said that when you and Mr. Slessenger came into the clearing at Devil's Meadow, you saw the defendant arguing with Lana Paluka. Is that correct?"

"Yes, that's right."

"And then suddenly you saw Mr. Skitt push her?"

"Yes."

Ethan Skitt stood up. "You fuck. You are fucking lying, Alan."

"Request a five-minute recess, your honor." Shanagan rushed to his client's side.

"Denied," Judge Suskind said. "Control yourself, young man, or I'll have you out of my courtroom and your trial will proceed without you."

"I don't recognize your right to try me, I don't recognize your—"

"SHUT UP!"

Skitt glared at the judge for a moment, then slumped back into his seat. It was the second outburst that day. What the hell did he think he was? One of the Chicago Seven?

Judge Suskind had the bailiff read back what had come before the interruption; then Shanagan asked the witness, "What did you do after you saw him push her?"

"Well, we just stood there in shock. We didn't know what to do. Then, like, we just started running."

"Where?"

"Back down through the woods, toward the park. Where we'd left the car."

"Was Ethan Skitt aware that you saw what happened?"

"No. He had no idea we were there. As you can see on the map, Mr. Shanagan, there are several approaches to Devil's Meadow. Ethan and Lana must have gone up Canyon Road, through Lookout Point, and come up that way. We—Randy and I—approached from the west, through the woods. We left that way, too."

"And after you left?"

"We drove to the phone at the gas station on Canyon Flats Road and called the police."

"Mr. Wells, didn't it ever occur to you to go and help Miss Paluka, who was sure to have major injuries after such a fall?"

Bonsall stood up. "Your honor, what might or might not have occurred to the witness is irrelevant."

"I'd like to answer that," Alan Wells said before the judge could rule. "We were scared. We just froze. Going for the cops seemed like the right thing to do. Maybe it was a mistake."

"A mistake?" Shanagan said. "Surely it must have crossed your mind that maybe you could help her."

"Your honor," Bonsall said, "what the witness did or didn't do to help the victim has no bearing here. What he saw is the only thing that matters."

"Look, maybe leaving was a mistake," Alan Wells said. "I don't know. The truth is, it never occurred to either of us that there would be, like, anything left to help. Have you ever *been* to High Exposure, Mr. Shanagan? It's a sheer drop; there's nothing to stop a fall. I guess neither of us was in any mood to see someone we knew smashed like that. We went back later, to meet the police."

Silence.

"All right, Mr. Wells, let's move on to another point. What were you and Mr. Slessenger going to do when you got up to the meadow?"

Alan Wells stared at Shanagan for a moment, then said, "Hang out."

Shanagan glanced over at Bonsall. "What exactly does that mean, hang out? Maybe smoke some pot?"

A wave of titters ran through the courtroom.

"I object," Bonsall said.

"I'm trying to establish the credibility—or lack thereof—of this witness," Shanagan said.

"My objection stands."

"I'll allow the witness to answer."

Shanagan turned back to the witness. "Remember, you're under oath, Mr. Wells."

Alan Wells smiled. "What was the question?"

More titters.

"I asked if you smoke marijuana, Mr. Wells."

"No. I do not."

"Oh, come on, son. You'd just gotten back from a weekend at Woodstock, where, according to all reports *I've* seen, both the drugs and the sex were flowing."

"Badgering the witness, your honor," Bonsall said. "He has already answered."

Shanagan smiled and bowed. "I withdraw it." He turned back to the witness. "You had a relationship with the victim at one time, didn't you, Mr. Wells?"

"Yes, but that was years ago. We went out a few times. I was fifteen at the time. Ethan and Lana went together all through high school."

"Your honor," Bonsall jumped up again, "I simply don't understand the relevance of these questions."

Judge Suskind said, "Nor do I, Mr. Shanagan. Are you suggesting that this witness is lying, because of some past relationship with the victim?"

"Yes, I'm suggesting the witnesses are lying. My client flatly denies their story."

"Both of them?" Bonsall said. "For what conceivable reason?"

"I don't know. Mr. Wells, how do *you* account for the fact that the defendant flatly denies your and Mr. Slessenger's account of the events that transpired on August eighteenth?"

"It's obvious. He's trying to save his skin."

Shanagan looked at his client. Finally he said, "I have no further questions." And sat down.

Bonsall stood up for redirect.

"Mr. Wells, what university did you begin last fall?"

"Objection," Shanagan said. "What does it—"

"Your honor," Bonsall said, "Mr. Shanagan has tried to undermine the character and credibility of this witness, despite the fact that there are two witnesses here, not just one. I think that gives me the right to point out a few things in Mr. Wells's behalf."

"Overruled. The witness may answer the question."

"I'm beginning my sophomore year at Harvard."

"And with what class ranking did you graduate from Comity High School?"

"Fourth in the class."

"And what offices did you hold in high school?"

"I was president of the student body. Captain of the varsity swim team. And valedictorian of my class."

"What line of study are you pursuing, Mr. Wells?"

"Premed. I want to be a doctor. Like my father."

"That's all. Thank you, Mr. Wells."

"The witness may step down."

"The prosecution calls Mr. Randall Slessenger to the stand."

Eugene Shanagan watched as Alan Wells walked to the back of the courtroom. He'd blown it, but he still had another chance with the witness now moving toward the stand. Randall Slessenger, a waiflike boy, skinny as a rail, with a long frizzy ponytail hanging halfway down his back. Next to Alan Wells, he looked like a scared little rabbit.

But he corroborated the whole damned thing. And Skitt got up on the stand and did just what he'd said he would do. He admitted he and Lana Paluka had been arguing but refused to say what they'd argued about. "It's no one else's business," was all he would say.

The jury brought in a guilty verdict in less than an hour.

17

I remember Ethan was always touching her. Every time I would see them in the halls, he had his hand on some part of Lana's body. His arm would be around her waist, or draped over her shoulder, the hand almost brushing her breast. Or he would be holding her hand, touching her hair, the top of her arm. Once I saw him kissing her, out in back of the bleachers on the football field. It was a long kiss and I stood there watching for almost a minute. He was touching her even then; he had his hands on her face.

The two state policemen at Sarah's wouldn't give me much detail. Apparently Skitt had been assigned the job of loading the trucks that took the garbage out of the prison every day. He left in the back of a truck, then jumped out before it reached the dump. How he managed to get by the guards on the garbage detail, they wouldn't say, or didn't know.

I didn't want to waste time asking too many questions, anyway. I sped back to Alan's. Jocelyn was in the kitchen.

"Where's Alan?" Though I was trying, I couldn't control the hysteria in my voice.

"Playing tennis out back with Keith. Jim Harling phoned, Jack. Your parents gave him the number. What's the matter?"

I didn't stop to tell her. I ran out to the back of the house, found Alan and his son sitting on the bench, toweling off their faces.

"I'm afraid I can't keep up with him anymore," Alan said.

Keith laughed. "It's only because you're smoking, Dad."

Alan, red-faced, shook his head and laughed. "It's because I'm an old man."

I looked at him, aware for the first time of the visible signs of aging in my brother, too, the network of lines around his eyes and mouth.

"Alan, Ethan Skitt escaped," I said.

"*What?*"

"Yesterday. They haven't caught him yet. I think it was him in the woods last night."

"What are you talking about, Uncle Jack?" Keith said.

Alan shrugged. "It doesn't matter, Keith."

"What do you mean, it doesn't matter?" I said. "For God's sake, Alan, the bastard killed Randy. What makes you think he's not coming after you?"

Alan sighed. "Twenty years is a long time—"

"Will one of you please tell me what's going on?" Keith said.

By this time Jocelyn had come onto the court. "Yes, I want to know, too."

Alan wiped his face off again, stood up. "You remember that girl we were talking about last night, the one who was pushed off High Exposure? Well, our friend Randy and I saw him do it. Unfortunately, we had to testify against him. He's out for revenge. At least Jack thinks so, anyway."

"Alan, you're making it seem like I pulled this out of the air." I turned to his wife and son. "When Skitt got out of jail the last time, the first thing he did was murder Randy. Just went to his place and gunned him down."

"Just for testifying against him?"

"That's right. Just for revenge. This is a really *bad* guy we're talking about, Jocelyn. He tried to make it look like a suicide. But they caught him—"

"Oh, my God," Jocelyn said. "But why didn't the police let us know he was out?"

"Damned bureaucrats," Keith said.

Alan smiled, patted his son on the back.

"I think it was him last night, Alan," I said.

"*What* was him?" Jocelyn said.

"We heard some noises in the woods."

"You mean you think he was *here*? At our home?" Her eyes scanned the surrounding woods for a moment. "For Heaven's sake, Alan, let's go inside. You've got to hire bodyguards. Round the clock. We've got to call the police. I'm going to give them a piece of my—"

"All right, all right." Alan put one arm around his wife, the other around his son. "I guess I should be careful."

* * *

The local police were sympathetic on the phone, but unhelpful. They were aware that the man had escaped and was considered dangerous, but it wasn't their problem. They told Alan to call the state police or the FBI or the state corrections department.

Corrections said it wasn't their policy to inform specific people of a prison break, but when Alan told them that he thought Skitt might have been at his home last night, they said they'd consider sending a couple of men out to the house.

"Oh great, while they're considering, you could be dead," Jocelyn said.

It turned out Harling wanted to tell me about Skitt's escape.

"I'm running the AP piece on it today," Harling said. "Weird fluke, though, his escaping only a few days after she woke up."

I told him about the potential threat to my brother.

"And to her, too," he said. "What do the police say?"

"They say it isn't their policy to inform potential victims."

"All right, why don't you do the story on her, and we can run it as a sidebar tomorrow with whatever the developments are on his escape."

I called the corrections department and the state police myself and got statements from them. The manhunt had been expanded to cover New York, New Jersey, and Connecticut. I asked if someone had alerted Lana. They said they hadn't, so I phoned Drummond security and informed them of the potential danger.

They assured me that security was tight at Drummond but promised to post a guard at Lana's room.

Just as I was getting off the phone with Dr. Evelyn Bronteman, a nationally known criminal psychiatrist I had worked with on a number of previous stories, two state police cars and a van pulled up at my brother's house. There was a police dog in the van, a huge German shepherd. The man holding the dog introduced himself as Sergeant Watson. The dog was called Buster.

Watson took what appeared to be a green piece of cloth— perhaps a shirt—from the bag he was carrying and brought it up to the dog's nose. Immediately the dog began straining forward, sniffing along the ground, then, nose to the ground, led him and the three other men on a thorough search of the property and surrounding woods. Keith and Alan, Jr., followed the search party around, asking questions, which one of the state policemen answered paternally.

"If he was here last night," Watson said when they'd finished, "he's long gone. Buster didn't pick up anything. We'll find him, though."

"I don't want to hear that," Jocelyn said. 'I want some protection—"

"Calm down, Jocelyn." Alan put his hand on her shoulder. "They know what they're doing."

"We'll catch him, ma'am," Watson said. "We've set up a surveillance at his mother's house—"

"What good is that going to do?"

"Nine times out of ten they contact a relative for help. We'll catch him."

"Aren't you going to stay and watch our house?" she said. I had never seen her this forceful.

"Dewey and Parsons will be staying," Watson said. "We're posting a twenty-four-hour guard on the house."

"Hey, I'm not sitting in this house like a scared little rabbit," Alan said. "I've got a mall to open tomorrow. I'm about to undertake a campaign for Congress."

"Wherever you go, Mr. Wells, we'll be right behind you."

Half an hour later I was sitting in my brother's office, staring at a computer screen, rereading the opening graphs of my story:

WOMAN WHO SURVIVED PLUNGE FROM CLIFF EMERGES FROM 20-YEAR CATATONIA

Doctor Calls It a Double Miracle

Dutchess County, NEW YORK, August 23, 1989—A woman who miraculously survived being pushed from a 200-foot cliff twenty years ago emerged this week from the catatonic state in which the fall left her. The fall occurred on August 18, 1969. According to two witnesses, the woman, Lana Paluka, who was 18 years old at the time, had been pushed from the top of a cliff in the Shawangunk Mountains just outside the town of Comity, New York, by her then boyfriend, Ethan Skitt, following a lovers' quarrel. The physical injuries Ms. Pakula sustained in the fall were not serious or life-threatening and have long since healed.

In an unrelated development, Ethan Skitt, who served thirteen years in prison for attempted murder and was released seven years ago, escaped yesterday from the Green Haven Correctional Facility. He was serving a life sentence for a 1982 revenge murder in which he shot one of the men who testified against him in the original trial. He was captured several weeks after that killing on the grounds of the Drummond Rehabilitation Center, where Ms. Paluka had recently been transferred. Security has been beefed up at the Drummond Rehabilitation facility to counter a potential threat to Ms. Paluka. Authorities have also posted a twenty-four-hour guard on the remaining witness to the original crime.

"I wouldn't be at all surprised if this man was still seeking revenge, even after so long," Dr. Evelyn Bronteman of the Creedmore Institute said. "The sociopathic personality has a long memory." Dr. Bronteman is considered an expert in the field of criminal psychology.

Meanwhile, Ethan Skitt remains at large. (See facing story.)

"There must be a guardian angel watching over Lana," Dr. Jonathan Baldwin of the Drummond Rehabilitation Center in Kingston said. "First she survived that fall, a miracle in itself, and then she suddenly emerged from a long-term catatonic state in a way I've never seen before in my entire professional career."

Baldwin, who has been Ms. Paluka's doctor for the past year at the long-term psychiatric facility, described Ms. Paluka's current psychological state as "free of major psychiatric disorder."

"Her memory is spotty, but it should improve with time," Baldwin said. He defined a catatonic state as "a condition in which the patient tends to remain motionless in a stereotyped position or posture for long periods of time."

Ms. Paluka has no memory of the events leading up to the argument or of being pushed, except that she and Ethan Skitt, her then boyfriend, had attended the Woodstock Festival over the previous weekend. It was on their return to Comity, their hometown, sixty miles south of the festival site, that the argument between them took place. No one knows how she survived the fall, sustaining only a few broken bones.

"We are very glad to have our daughter back," John and Ellie Paluka of Danbury, Connecticut, formerly of Comity, said, "though we'll never forgive Ethan Skitt for taking her away from us. It's like we've been without her for twenty years and now suddenly she's been restored."

The cliff on which the incident occurred, known to locals and to mountain climbers as High Exposure, is the highest peak in the Shawangunk range, rating a 5.6 on the internationally recognized scale of mountaineering. . . .

I typed in a few more paragraphs using the Burn and Morino interviews, then reread the whole piece. Not bad. I glanced over at my notepad. I had so much material from the very helpful Nurse Burn and from Mike Morino that I couldn't possibly use it all or the story would run forty graphs.

Setting the machine to print out the story, I stood up to stretch, then sat back down again and looked out the huge picture window, which afforded an idyllic view of the side lawn and garden. The office itself had deep mahogany paneling, mahogany appointments, a leather-topped partners' desk, a red oriental rug. The far wall of the office was covered with framed photographs: several of Alan in his swim trunks, obviously taken after meets; a couple of Alan and me together, our arms around each other. One of Dad and Alan and me together. I remembered when that one was taken, right before I left for BU. There were also more recent photographs of Alan's boys and his wife. And a wedding picture. Jocelyn really had been gorgeous. In the upper corner, there was a small photograph of the gang.

The machine had stopped printing. I took my pages out, wrote a cover note to Jim Harling in longhand, then faxed the whole pile down to my office.

Then I went up to the photo wall again to examine the photograph more closely. None of us could have been more than thirteen in the photo. I couldn't even remember when or where it'd been taken, but we all had our arms around each other. All smiling, happy, ready to conquer the world—Alan and I, Greg, and Denny Hartigan—and Randy.

"Hey, Jack, you ever coming out of there?" Alan was standing in the doorway. He glanced over at the photograph I was standing in front of. "Remember when it was taken?"

"No, I really can't."

"It was just before the eighth-grade class trip down to Washington. Mom took it right after she warned us to behave ourselves." He laughed. "But did we listen to her?"

"No way," I said. "We left messages on the bathroom doors of the Smithsonian. We dropped water balloons from the balcony of the hotel. We were up until four A.M. discussing Patty Marchand's tits."

"Which were minimal at best."

Patty had been my first love, though that was several years later.

"Sounds pretty juvenile now, doesn't it?" Alan said.

I nodded, looked back at the picture. Randy Slessenger. Alan's best friend, my best friend.

Poor Randy. He never really survived the sixties.

Still, Ethan Skitt had murdered him in cold blood.

The phone was ringing in Alan's office. I was closer to it, so I picked up the receiver.

"Hello?"

"Alan Wells, please."

"Who's calling?"

"Douglas Enworth. I'm returning his call of late last night."
Enworth? He'd said it was a girlfriend.

"Hello? Is Mr. Wells there?"

"Just a moment." I held out the phone. "It's Mr. Enworth."
Alan took the receiver.

"Hello . . . Yes, that's right. Why wasn't I informed? . . . You were called out of town? Is that an excuse? . . . How the hell did you find out? . . . You've studied the situation, then . . . I see . . . Fine. I want a complete update on a daily basis. That's what I pay you for." He hung up.

"Who's Douglas Enworth?"

"My stockbroker."

"But it's Saturday."

Alan picked up the pile of papers I had put on his desk and handed them to me.

"Jack," he said, "there's no rest for the weary or the rich."

Part Four

The Meadow

"Fools!" said I "You do not know
Silence like a cancer grows
Hear my words that I might teach you
Take my arms that I might reach you"
But my words like silent raindrops fell
And echoed
In the wells of silence.

—Paul Simon, *"The Sound of Silence"*

18

It was just after nine o'clock in the morning when Sarah Alexandra Skitt charged into the newly built Comity Town Hall, a neoclassic structure of which the townspeople were quite proud.

"Maude, I have to see the mayor. Right now."

Maude Bates, the mayor's secretary, looked up from her typewriter to find Sarah standing in front of her desk. She was wearing a floor-length peasant dress made of a white gauzy material with embroidery at the bodice, two armloads of noisy bracelets, and sandals. Through the dress it was plain to see the woman was braless.

"Morning, Sarah," Maude said. "I'm afraid Mayor Johnstone is busy right now. Can I help you?"

"I've had a vision up in the mountains this morning, Maude. At Devil's Meadow. Did you hear me, Maude, I've spoken to God this morning."

"Sarah—"

"I always take a long walk every morning, Maude. It's good for the constitution. And this morning I was taking my walk and I was drawn to the meadow. I went up through the forest. It was very cool in the woods, and when I got up to the top there was a storm. I lay up there in the rain, thinking how clear everything was . . ."

Maude stared at the woman in front of her. How fervent she looked, how intense. It was true that many people believed God's presence was particularly strong in high places, which was why people so often went to mountaintops to commune with Him. And it was true that as high places went, the large grassy field called Devil's Meadow was very impressive. But visions of the sort Sarah Skitt seemed to be describing, if not uncommon in biblical times, were surely the sign of a diseased mind in ours.

"Sarah," Maude said, "how could you have been up to the mountains? It's been pouring all morning and you're as dry as a bone."

"Dry?" Sarah Skitt looked down at her clothes, as if she were seeing them for the first time. "So I am. Well, miraculous things happen in holy places."

"Sarah, it could be dangerous up there during a storm like that."

Sarah shrugged. "And God spoke to me—"

"He spoke to you?" All of a sudden, Maude felt sorry for the Skitt children, who probably had to get themselves ready for school each morning while their mother took a brisk walk and talked to God in the middle of electrical storms. Anyway, for all her talk of cozy chats with God, she had the morals of a rabbit.

"God let me know that Devil's Meadow is a holy place."

"Sarah," Maude said, "this is New York State. There are no holy places around here."

"Any place can be a holy place if the forces of nature are in balance there. It's a wondrous place, Maude. It can make all wrong things right. I know God spoke to me there . . ."

Maude sighed. Sarah Skitt had moved into Ethel Mason's house a few years ago, and since then Maude had thought the woman was peculiar, but this was the worst Maude had ever seen her, or anyone for that matter. Even when her boy Ethan and Maude's Adam got into that fight at school last month and Sarah called Maude screaming about how everyone was always calling her crazy and her children bastards and how she was sick and tired of it, and how she didn't blame her son Ethan for popping Adam in the face one bit—even then, she hadn't been as irrational as this.

When people said she was nuts, Maude always tended to say Sarah was just a little "different," even if it *was* true that the father of her fourth son, Nathan, was Carolyn McKennie's husband. She'd gotten paid back for that, hadn't she? The kid was practically an imbecile. But this, now, this was something entirely new, and Maude decided right then and there to speak to the mayor and see if anything could be done, maybe have the woman locked up or something. Of course, that would leave her children motherless as well as fatherless . . .

"It wasn't like God spoke in words to me," Sarah was saying. "It was more like I felt His presence up there. You know?"

"There *is* God's beauty in nature," Maude said.

"Don't patronize me, Maude. Do you think I want this happening to me? Do you think Jesus wanted the fate He was assigned?"

It was probably blasphemy, but there was no point in getting into an argument with the woman.

"I'm not patronizing you, Sarah."

"God must have His purpose for revealing Himself to me," Sarah said. "I wouldn't presume to know what that purpose is unless He tells me, which He hasn't. But I do think the place should be renamed God's Meadow. Devil's Meadow doesn't seem right for a holy place." With that, she opened her clenched fist and piled a handful of grass into a small green mound on Maude's desk.

"Do you think we give a hoot what you think?" This from Ellen Speter, whose desk was across the reception room from Maude's.

Maude believed that each and every soul deserved respect, no matter how odd. But before she could call Ellen off, Ellen had stood up.

"Do you think Carolyn McKennie cares what you think, Sarah?"

Sarah drew herself up with dignity. "You're a petty woman, Ellen," she said.

"Petty? I don't think Carolyn would call it petty."

"You know, Ellen, it would serve Carolyn McKennie right if her husband did cheat on her. She's a dried-up old prune."

Ellen Speter, shocked into silence, sat back down.

Sarah looked around the room, drew her arms out in a wide sweeping motion, and turned back to Maude.

"Do you know how strong God is, Maude? I felt as if He were inside me up there. As if, up there, I could in some small way understand His purpose, even perform His tasks. I felt so full of God I couldn't hold it all in . . ."

During these ravings, Maude Bates—who believed that God was to be found every Sunday in church and also in her love for her children—managed to keep a quiet face until Sarah Skitt began to describe the precise angle with which a brilliant light had shone down on her as the sun rose that dawn after the storm, and the way it had gathered from behind the clouds into a cone of filtered light, and how that cone of light followed her like the fiery cloud that led the Children of Israel toward the Promised Land. Which, of course, proved beyond a shadow of a doubt that God was up there.

"You'd better go home, Sarah."

"But don't you see, Maude? We could rename it, just like the Indians used to name things. We could call it the Church of the High Vision. Or, the Church of the Shawangunk Vision. Or the Church of God's Truth. The place just needs a few benches and a roof, something simple and beautiful, where people can go to worship, to experience God within themselves."

At which point, Maude was unable to restrain herself.

"What about Grace Baptist, over on Main, Sarah? What about United Methodist? What about Union Lutheran, out on Route Six?"

Sarah smiled and jangled her bracelets. "They all mean well, I'm sure."

There was a long silence. Ellen Speter began to snicker but stopped when Maude glared at her.

"Sarah, the town fathers can't do anything at all up on Devil's Meadow," Maude said.

"They could if they wanted to. They could if they understood."

"No, Sarah, they couldn't. You know the mountains don't belong to Comity; they belong to Shawangunk Corporation. It's a privately owned preserve. You have to petition them."

Sarah started to push her way past the gate. "I have to see the mayor."

Maude stood up and positioned her impressive bulk in front of Sarah, blocking her way. The mayor was too busy for this nonsense.

To Maude's surprise, Sarah stopped dead in her tracks. There was a long moment's silence while the two women stood staring at each other, Maude with her light gray eyes and Sarah with her blazing dark ones.

"Why don't you go and see Dr. Wells, Sarah?" Maude said, softly. "Maybe he can help you."

Sarah Skitt stared at Maude for a few seconds longer. Then she said, "Lightning struck the meadow this morning, Maude. It struck right at the edge, right on the point. You know how the ledge used to come to a point at the top? Well, a big chunk of rock came away from the wall. And now it doesn't come to a point at all."

She turned and went back out the door, the way she'd come in. Maude exchanged a glance with Ellen but waited until Sarah had closed the front door behind her before she said, "How many children does she have now?"

"Four or five," Ellen said. "Every time I turn around that woman is in Comity Hospital giving birth to another one. And I hear she's pregnant again."

"Doesn't look it, Ellen."

"Well, Dr. Wells told Bernice she was definitely pregnant again, and Bernice told Eileen Masterson. So it's the truth. Don't these men, whoever they are, realize what the hell they're in bed with?"

Maude Bates shrugged, then looked back down at her type-writer and began typing where she'd left off. "Dear Mr. Dubling: Pursuant to our conversation . . ." After a moment, she looked up again. Through the window near her desk she saw Sarah Skitt picking her way down the main street of Comity. She looked like she was crying.

Maude sighed. It was a damned shame, especially for those kids. A loony like that, they should have tied her tubes.

19

Not long after Sarah showed up at town hall saying she'd had a vision on Devil's Meadow, my mother called a meeting to see what could be done about her. We were nine at the time, and Sarah had started taking her children up to Devil's Meadow each morning to pray, which for some reason was particularly offensive to my mother, who had been born and raised in Comity and went to Holy Name Catholic Church on Bromfield Road her entire life.

At the meeting my mother served tea and little coffee cakes, the women swapped Sarah Skitt stories, and Alan and I listened at the top of the stairs. "Did you hear that she told Maude Bates she was like Jesus?" "Did you hear she's pregnant again?" "Did you know that that Ethan beat up my Jimmy?"

I remember there was one woman, Mrs. Masterson, who said at one point that she thought Sarah Skitt was some kind of a devil.

"Maude Bates told me Sarah *had* to have been up there that morning because she knew that lightning had taken away a chunk of the rock," Mrs. Masterson said. "If she wasn't up there, how did she know?"

"We *all* heard the thunderstorm that morning," my mother said.

Mrs. Masterson shrugged. "Well, Maude said Sarah described the rock exactly the way it looks now, but she came back from the mountain as dry as a bone."

The other ladies in the room looked at Eileen Masterson as if she were as demented as Sarah.

But you couldn't have someone committed or arrested for having babies out of wedlock, or for being peculiar either, and in the end the ladies just went home. The fact that Sarah Skitt danced to her own drummer was just one of the things everyone in Comity lived with. You knew it. It was part of your vocabulary, a point of reference, like the mountains.

Around noon on Sunday I set out on Route 6 for the mall, which took me past the Skitt house again. The police car was still out front.

The mall itself was an endless gray structure anchored on one side by a J. C. Penney, on the other by a Sears, and encircled by a huge parking lot already jammed with cars. Over the entrance was a GRAND OPENING banner. Streamers draped with red, white, and blue triangular flags encircled the perimeter of the parking lot.

I pulled into the west entrance and let a man in an orange suit that looked vaguely military direct me to a space in parking Section B. From there I walked. I found my brother in his shirtsleeves, supervising the setup from a platform stage at the center of the mall. He looked like a sitting duck up there on that platform. I imagined Ethan Skitt crouching behind one of the cars, aiming a rifle at Alan's head, positioning the scope.

Behind the platform was a huge statue of Atlas holding up the earth. Water spouted—gushed—from the top of Atlas's head. The two cops, my brother's protection, were standing between Atlas and the platform, each at one corner of the stage.

Alan waved, then bounded off the stage and over to me, smiling, greeting, shaking hands as he passed through the gathering crowd.

"Looks to me like you're *already* running for Congress," I said.

He waved an arm to take in the whole plaza. "So, what do you think?"

"Pretty impressive. What's on the agenda?"

"Well," he said, whispering, "first we've got the dogs. The Comity High School Band—remember that?—and a group of dancers from over in Kingston. Angela Allwin is supposed to show up around two, the lieutenant governor at three. The RX—that's a local rock band—is supposed to come at one, since the Sha Na Na's canceled. Sue—that's my assistant—is trying to line some other groups up."

"Where are Mom and Dad?"

He didn't answer. Actually, it was a stupid question. I don't think I can remember a single Sunday that our mother missed church, though Dad often did.

All around me, kids were getting helium balloons or having

their faces painted. A fortune teller was setting up her booth right in front of the mall entrance. Alan excused himself and went over to move her, leaving me alone in the crowd.

"Jack!"

"Patty? Patty Marchand?"

She had two children in tow and had gained some weight. Her hair, which used to be dark brown, was dyed red. A pretty shade, though.

I gave her a kiss, aware that her kids were watching with interest, then stepped back.

"Billy, Chip, go have your faces painted. Look for Daddy . . . So how are you, Jack?"

"I'm fine. Really good."

"I heard you're a reporter."

"So they tell me. How about you? Are you working?"

She glanced over at her kids and laughed. "You mean other than raising two kids?"

I laughed too. I'd been caught in that trap before. "Yes, other than that."

"I was into real estate until the market went soft; now I'm thinking of going into interior decorating." She looked over at the face-painting booth. "Billy! Stop hitting your brother."

We both laughed.

"I saw Greg Horan about three months ago," she said.

"Really? What's he doing?"

"He lives in—where was it?—Virginia, I think. Does something for the government. You ever see Denny?"

"He moved out west."

"I heard about Randy. That Ethan Skitt should have been strung up by his balls."

"One time where even *I* would have voted for the death penalty," I said. "Did you hear he escaped from prison? Last night."

"Oh, my God!" She glanced over at my brother, who was standing near the face-painting booth, talking to some people. "Alan should be—"

"I know."

"Well, I hope they catch him soon."

"They will, I'm sure. They've got Sarah's house staked out. I guess they think he'll contact her."

She nodded. "Wouldn't he know that'd be the first place they'd look?"

"He might be desperate if he's got no other resources—no money, no transportation . . . So, Patty, did you marry a nice guy?" Did I expect she would tell me if she hadn't?

She smiled. "A *great* guy, Jack. You'd like him. He's around here somewhere." Then, after a pause, "Remember that time your parents went away to the medical convention and we spent the weekend in their bed?"

I remembered, though I was surprised she'd brought it up. It had taken almost a year for Patty finally to "go all the way," as we called it, and even then our lovemaking had consisted of a half-dressed frenzy in the back seat of my VW. It had become very important to me to see Patty completely naked. That medical convention weekend was the first time. I couldn't get enough— we *had* spent the weekend in bed.

"And my brother kept yelling through the door 'When are you two going to come up for air?' "

She laughed, touched my arm.

"You'd really like my husband, Jack. He's a contractor."

"I'm sure I would."

"As a matter of fact," she said, "Alan has been wonderful to Bill. Did you know he hired him to build the subdivision just west of here? West Farm Acres."

"No, I didn't." I glanced over at my brother, who was up on the platform at the microphone introducing the high school dancers from Kingston, who were dressed in hot pink tights and tiny purple skirts.

"Alan's a fine man," Patty said. "I hear he's planning to run for Congress."

"So he says." The dancers had begun a comically uneven high-kicking dance to "One," from *A Chorus Line*.

"He's a shoo-in, I think." She turned to take the arm of the tall, husky, gray-haired man suddenly standing next to us. "Bill, this is Jack Wells, an old . . . friend of mine. Alan's brother."

"Ah," he said, smiling, "the old boyfriend." He shook my hand.

"Very old," I said. "A long time ago."

A few pleasantries later I spotted Joette Larson taking notes, said goodbye to my brother, told him to take care of himself, then slipped through the noisy crowd and got in my car.

"Nice piece on Lana Paluka, Jack."

The following Tuesday I was working on a follow-up to the Dixon article. I looked up and saw Joette Larson standing over me.

"Thanks, Joette."

I went back to the computer screen. WOMAN WHO SURVIVED PLUNGE wasn't a particularly good piece, but it had been picked up by the wire services. That was what impressed Joette. I was also covering Ethan Skitt's continued evasion of an ever-widening manhunt.

The phone rang.

"Wells. *Herald.*"

"Jack? It's Marvin Saferstein, Jarvis Publishing."

"How are you, Marv?" I'd met the man once, when I'd interviewed him on a story about the changes in the publishing industry.

"Fine, Jack. I read your piece on the Paluka woman. Really good stuff. Mysterious stuff—miraculous, even. I really think this one's got all the makings."

"Of a book?"

"Absolutely. Especially now that Ethan Skitt's escaped from prison. It could be a true-life blockbuster, Jack, a really classy one. Not all murder and mayhem and dismembered corpses and sexual perversions. Although it does have *some* of that, too. Just enough."

I didn't remind him that it had been Jarvis who'd published a book last year documenting, in every gory detail, the weird and occasionally fatal sexual practices of a certain pagan cult out in Flagstaff, Arizona.

"The story really has a certain magic about it, don't you think, Jack? The woman seems to lead a charmed life."

"Unless Skitt's planning to finish what he started twenty years ago."

"Planning it and actually doing it are two different things," Saferstein said.

"You know, Marv, she does seem to lead a charmed life. And you wouldn't believe the way she looks. Strong. Healthy. And young. She looks eighteen and she's nearly forty. It's damned spooky. The doctor says that after so long in that condition, her muscles should have atrophied."

"Can you imagine waking up to the world as it is now from the world as it was then—without everything that came in between?"

"You know, the story does have possibilities, doesn't it? An old murder, or what should have been a murder. The sixties, drugs, hippies. Woodstock. Plus there's Lana's adjustment back to the world as it is now. And Ethan Skitt's taking revenge on the people who testified against him. And his second trial. And his escape. I guess you don't know this, Marv, but I knew all the players in this drama from back when we were kids. My brother was one of the witnesses. He's got a twenty-four-hour guard right now."

"Do they think Skitt's coming after him?"

"*I* think so."

"You may be right. How about her?"

"They've put a guard on Lana, too."

"That's not what I meant. I mean, can she tell you her story?"

"She doesn't remember what happened up on the cliff that day, though her doctor says she will at some point. She also seems a little bit confused."

"How so?"

I told him what she'd said about not landing right.

Saferstein laughed. "Doesn't matter why she thinks she survived, it's still a miracle. And look, Jack, there's all this nostalgia over the Woodstock anniversary. You could do a real retrospective of the era. Find out where everyone connected with the case is now. You already know what happened to the two witnesses. But how about Skitt's lawyer, the cops who found her, her doctors?"

"It *might* make a good book . . ."

"Draw up a proposal, Jack. If we like it, we'll offer you a twenty-five-thousand-dollar advance."

Well, it wasn't peanuts, but it wasn't particularly generous. On the other hand, *I* wasn't Joe McGinniss, at least not yet, but I didn't have to be a sap.

"I can really do this story right, Marv. I'm the only one who can."

"I know twenty-five is on the low side, but we're probably going to have to offer her something too. Maybe we can do something for you at the back end."

"I might be able to get her to give me an exclusive," I said. "Since she knows me."

"Offer her twenty-five."

"That's low compared to what the television people will offer."

"Tell her you can really do her story right in a book, Jack. Real depth. Anyway, these are all just starting points. Feel her out, see if she's interested. Maybe she'll do it for you for less because she knows you."

"Maybe."

"The thing is, you've got to get to her before the tabloids and the television vultures get to her, if they haven't already."

"Let me think about it and I'll get back to you."

Just after I hung up, it occurred to me that even if the deal with Saferstein didn't work out, I could still get the rights to the story from Lana and sell them to the highest bidder.

The phone was ringing when I came into my house around six that evening.

"Hello, Jack?" It was Lana. Even on the phone, she sounded young.

"Lana! I was going to call *you*."

"Why?"

"Because I've been approached by a publishing company to tell your story."

"That's what I wanted to talk to you about, Jack. There were three reporters here today."

Damn. "Did you talk to them?"

"I told the receptionist I didn't want to. But one of them snuck onto the grounds when I was outside this afternoon—"

"Outside? Lana, do you know about Ethan?"

"Yeah, they told me."

"I'd stay inside if I were you."

She was silent. Then, "Hey, I've been inside long enough."

I decided not to argue. "So what happened with the reporter?"

"He wouldn't leave me alone. He offered me money to talk to him. I had to get someone to kick him out."

"They're vultures, Lana."

"I don't know why they all want to hear my story. I'm not all that strong yet, Jack. I don't want to talk to strangers."

I took a deep breath. "You don't have to, Lana. Give me exclusive rights to your story—*I'll* be able to pay you too. The publisher offered twenty-five thousand dollars."

"Wow! Really?"

"Is your memory any better?"

"As a matter of fact, it's, like, starting to fill in a little bit now."

"Do you remember why Ethan pushed you?"

"No, but I'm starting to remember why I wouldn't speak. Why I thought I had to stay so still."

"Good."

"Twenty-five thousand is more than the other guy offered," she said.

"There could be others who'll offer more. But this way, you won't have to talk to anyone but me."

"I'd be more comfortable with that, I think. What would telling you my story involve?"

"Well, the world is a very different place now than it was then. A lot less . . . idealistic. What we all felt then just seems sort of naive nowadays. Of course, there was the war then, but it wasn't just that. There were the drugs we were all into, the politics, the attitudes toward sex. Peace, love, and all that. The changes that have taken place—in attitudes, in the world, in technology—have been incredible."

"I can see that just from walking around here. There are, like, all these *computers*. They're all over the place."

"That's right, Lana. And your story could dramatize—personalize—the changes. And I'd interview everyone connected with the murder trial, my brother, the nurse who first attended you, the lawyers . . ."

"Ethan?"

"Yes. Do you want to see Ethan?"

"I loved Ethan, Jack. He always said we were soulmates."

Soulmates? I hadn't heard that word in twenty years.

"He tried to kill you, Lana. He killed Randy. You don't know what you're dealing with—"

"I can take care of myself, I always have."

"Just be careful, that's all."

She was silent for a moment, then said, "I'll be out of here soon. I *will* need some bread . . ."

"I might be able to get you more than twenty-five. In any case, the best way to go about this is for me to come and talk to you, see what we have, then I'll go back and try to get as much as I can from the publisher who called me. Or another one."

"No, I'd feel more comfortable if it was all settled," she said. "See if you can get more, but I'll take the twenty-five thousand. Then, I could, like, tell all these other reporters I've already sold the rights and they would leave me alone. You bring, like, legal papers up here the next time you come. And we can start."

"I'll be there on Friday evening."

"Okay. See you then. Jack, are you sure they'll give me that much bread just to talk to you?"

"I'm sure."

"But what will I talk about?"

"You just have to answer my questions, Lana," I said. "Just tell the truth."

"About what?"

"Well, how about if we start with your background."

"But you know all about my background, Jack," she said. "My mother was the town drunk."

Hare Krishna, Hare Krishna
Krishna Krishna, Hare Hare
Hare Rama, Hare Rama
Rama Rama, Hare Hare

—*Hindu Chant*

20

Lana had decided at a very early age that John and Ellie Paluka weren't her real parents. Her *real* parents lived in a house with a garage and a patio and a lawn in front, not some dingy apartment with walls so thin that all day and night you could hear the noise from the bar downstairs. Her real parents didn't hit each other and scream things too awful to repeat.

Lana's real mother didn't always have a bottle of vodka beside her, and didn't live more in the movies then she did in real life. And Lana's mother wasn't too drunk to make her kid dinner. Lana was certain of that.

One steamy summer evening when Lana was eleven, she told her friend Angie Riccardelli her theory. Angie lived next door to the bar. It was a Sunday, just a few days after school let out for the year, although the oppressive heat made it seem more like August than June. Sundays were the worst time, because the bar was closed and Ellie and John had nothing to do but fight. They were already at each other by noon.

The two girls spent the day together, as they did most every other day, mainly at Angie's house playing jacks on the floor in front of the big window air conditioner in Angie's living room, except for a few hours when they went over to the lake near Opatcho's farm and took a swim. Angie's mother said Lana couldn't eat dinner with the Riccardellis since she'd had dinner there three nights that week, so at five Lana went home and tried not to listen to Ellie and John bickering as she made herself a hamburger; then she went back to Angie's at six-thirty.

It was just dusk when the two girls came down the steps in front of Angie's house. Lana noticed some of the boys from school hanging out in the square: Randy Slessenger, Denny Hartigan, the Wells twins. Jack Wells had been in her class that year but they weren't really friends.

She hated Denny because he was the one who first called her Paluka Bazooka. That was three years ago, when they first moved here from Kingston. Now everyone called her that. She had hoped it would stop this year but it hadn't. Such a stupid name—Paluka. So Polish. So conspicuous.

"There's Alan Wells," Angie whispered.

Lana began to walk faster. Alan Wells was the most popular boy in the whole school. As the first pubescent fantasies began to churn, he was already one of the primary objects of desire among the sixth-grade girls. A startlingly handsome boy with bold but patrician looks, he was a study in contrasts. Though his skin was more swarthy than fair and he had dark wavy hair, his features were small and his eyes were light in color, like two aquamarines, the color of a South Sea island lagoon. And it was those eyes, along with a pair of disarming dimples, natural charm, athletic ability, and obvious intelligence, that made Alan Wells a natural leader, a boy with everything going for him. All the girls were always talking about him.

Lana began to walk faster. She didn't want Alan—or any of them—to see her. Not for the first time she found herself wishing they hadn't ever moved here to Comity. Things were so much better in Kingston, even if this apartment was bigger. No one made fun of her there. Here, Lana had only one friend, Angie. Even Ellie was better before they moved.

"Hey, what are you walking so fast for?" Angie said.

Lana shrugged, glanced back. The boys hadn't noticed the two girls passing by; they were pitching stones into the duck pond in the middle of the square, and the ducks were making an astonishing racket. She slowed down her pace.

"Want to hear a secret?" she said casually as they turned the corner off Bromfield Square and headed down Mason Street.

"What?" Angie looked delighted.

"My parents aren't my real parents," she said.

"They're not?"

"Nope." Lana pulled her pack of Marlboros out of the pocket of her jeans. "They took me from my real parents just after I was born."

"You better watch it, Lana," Angie said with a glance back. "They'll catch you."

Lana laughed, and stopped for a moment to light up, then re-sumed walking beside her friend. "Aw, they don't care what I do."

"My mom would kill me if I smoked," Angie said, peering at Lana through the thick glasses she wore.

"Yeah, but since Ellie isn't my real mother, she doesn't give a shit."

"How do you know she isn't your real mother?" Angie said.

Angie had to be stupid if she didn't know.

"No real mother would name her kid Lana Turner Paluka," Lana said, "after some broken-down old movie star whose daugh-ter shot her mother's boyfriend."

"But that hadn't happened yet when she named you," Angie said. "My mother says Lana Turner was one of the most beautiful women ever. Maybe your mom wanted you to be beautiful, like her."

Lana laughed again, took a drag on the cigarette. "No way. She doesn't want anyone to be beautiful. Except her."

Angie was silent. Her mother had told her more than once that Ellie Paluka was a cheap woman. Angie wasn't certain exactly what that meant, only that there was disgust in her mother's voice when she said it. Even though she herself thought Ellie Paluka *was* beautiful, and she was certain her father did too be-cause of the way he looked at her, like his eyes might pop out of his head, she decided it would be best to say nothing. One time Angie had caught her father looking at Ellie Paluka that way. It was just last year and they were standing on the sidewalk in front of the house when Ellie came out in a pair of short shorts and a halter top that left little to the imagination. Angie would never forget the look on her father's face when he became aware that Angie had seen him staring at Lana's mother's chest. It was almost as if Ellie's beauty was somehow shameful.

"I know exactly what happened," Lana was saying. "See, my real mother has brown hair, and she wears it in a flip on her shoulders, and she has blue eyes, and she wears those little flat shoes—Pappagallo shoes—and she has them in all different col-ors, pink and green and blue and purple, to match all her outfits. And when she was in the hospital having me, Ellie snuck in and took me. Right out of my crib. The nurses all went crazy, looking for me, but they couldn't find me because Ellie took me away and hid me. And she never told anyone what she did. Even my dad doesn't know."

Angie stared at her, but kept walking. "You should try to find her. Your real mother."

"I would if I knew her name. You see, she still cries for me, every day. I know she does."

They were passing by the school now. There were some kids playing kickball on the field. Lana plopped down on the grass next to the sidewalk and lay flat on her back, looked up at the sky. Angie lay down next to her.

For the better part of an hour, as the sun set behind the mountains, Angie asked Lana about her real parents. It was a well-developed fantasy, and Lana had an easy time describing them, though certain embellishments came to mind in response to Angie's questions. Lana described everything: how rich her real parents were, and how proper, and how nice their house was. And how she had brothers and sisters, maybe four of them. And, of course, how her real family wasn't Polish.

"They have a nice short name," Lana said. "Maybe Smith, or even Winston."

"Hmmm," Angie said, "Lana Winston. That's funny."

Lana sat up. "No, not Lana. Maybe Hope. Yes. They would have named me Hope. Or Susan. Yes, Susan Winston. That would be good."

"What do you think *my* name would be?" Angie said. "How about Debbie? Debbie Stewart."

"Hey," Lana said, jumping up, "let's get out of here. We just finished this place."

"Yeah, I gotta get back, anyway. My mom says I gotta be in by nine. Boy it's hot. I'm gonna sit in front of the air conditioner for about three years when I get back."

"Oh, can I come sit with you? It's so hot at my house."

"Mom said you should stay at your place tonight, 'cause you're always at ours."

Lana shrugged, and tossed her fourth cigarette onto the sidewalk, ground the heel of her sneaker into it. The two girls turned and began walking home.

"Turn that goddamned television off, Ellie."

Even before Lana mounted the stairs next to the neon *Adley's* sign, she could hear her father's voice through the open window, above the sound of the blaring television.

"I said turn that damned thing off. I gotta have some peace and quiet around here."

They were beyond bickering now. When she left earlier they were like two animals, scratching and clawing from opposite ends of the cage. Now they were on the verge of an explosion; she could tell by the volume and pitch of their voices. Her dread was reflexive, instinctive, and she could feel the flush of shame burning into her face. Quickly, she said goodbye to Angie and hurried up the stairs. If only she had been here, if only she hadn't gone out with Angie, maybe she could have done something, stopped the escalation somehow.

Ellie had a movie on. She was sitting atop the coffee table in her peach-colored silk robe, a robe so short that you could almost see the bottom of her buttocks above the pale white flesh of her long legs. She was sitting so close to the portable television in the living room that she could touch the screen, a glass of vodka in her hand. Her blond hair was wet, slicked back off her face as if she had just taken a shower, but she had a smudge of frosted pink lipstick on her mouth. Her eyes were bleary, half-closed, and she was very drunk. Her feet were bare; the high-heeled mules with the fuzzy white trim were sitting on the floor next to the table. The stale odor of the greasy hamburger Lana had cooked for dinner still hung in the apartment, clinging to the walls, the furniture, the very air of the place.

John Paluka was heading toward the television set as Lana came in. He glanced at her for a moment before snapping off the set.

"Goddammit, I was watching that." Ellie took a swig from her glass, leaned over, and turned the set on again.

John whirled around and knocked the glass out of Ellie's hand. It fell to the floor with a dull thud. Ice scattered onto the carpet.

"You son of a bitch!" Ellie stood up and lunged at him; he blocked her attack with his forearm, set her spinning backward. She fell back onto the couch. The peach robe fell open, revealing a white lace bra beneath it.

"Stop it," Lana pleaded. "Stop it!" Lana moved to the couch in front of Ellie, trying not to look at the way her mother's breasts bulged out above the bra, trying to prevent her from getting up again. If she didn't get up again, it would pass. John would go downstairs and—

"Get the hell out of my way," Ellie screamed. "I'm gonna kill him."

She threw Lana aside and lunged at John again. He blocked her attack again, then stepped back. He looked at her for a moment and there was a long silence. Then, he began to laugh.

"Go clean yourself up, Ellie. Your lipstick's smeared." Slowly he turned and began to walk toward the kitchen.

"You son of a bitch!" Ellie picked up the glass from the floor. She was weaving, barely able to stand up.

"No! Mom. Don't!"

Lana tried to grab the glass out of her mother's hand as she drew it back, but she was too late. Ellie had already hurled it at his back. It hit him on the shoulder and bounced back to the floor, shattering this time into a thousand pieces.

John Paluka turned around now, his face swollen with rage. He pushed her up against the wall next to the television. Ellie's eyes rolled back in her head; she seemed so small next to him. Lana could see her father's face glistening with sweat and fury as he smacked her across the mouth with the back of his hand. Ellie drew her hand to the side of her face and collapsed onto the floor as if she were a rag doll.

"You son of a bitch," she said, but it was a whisper now, a whimper.

John Paluka stood over her. "Don't make me do it again, Ellie. Don't—"

"No, no, please!" Lana grabbed him by the shoulder. Her voice sounded so small, so useless. If only she could make her voice louder—

He shoved her aside. "Get out of my way, Lana. You want a drunken slut for a mother?"

Lana began to cry. She couldn't help it; she always told herself that she wouldn't, but when they started screaming the tears began to slide down her cheeks without her permission.

She ran; the broken glass cracked and crackled beneath her feet. In her room, she got into her bed and pulled the covers over her head, but it didn't help. She could still hear them screaming and cursing at each other, her mother's drunken whining voice, and her father's deep, enraged one.

"That's it, Ellie, tell me to shut up—tell me. Tell me again. This time I'll make you pay."

Lana pictured her father standing over Ellie, his hands clamped on her shoulders, forcing her to kneel in front of him, she so drunk by this time she could barely stand up. Once, she'd actually seen her father make Ellie beg, like a dog. She didn't feel sorry for her mother, though. She *was* drunk all the time. And she threw plenty of punches herself, had even threatened him with a knife one time. When Lana asked Ellie once why they were always screaming at each other, hitting each other, her mother smiled and said, "Oh, that's just our way." Lana said it was scary; then Ellie just said, "Tell it to *him*, why don't you?" But Ellie wasn't Lana's real mother, so it didn't much matter what she said.

"Get away from me, get the fuck away from me—"

"Why should I?"

Lana threw off the cover, got up, and closed the window in her bedroom. Did they think she couldn't hear? She got back into her bed, huddled under her sheet, chilled by the truth: they didn't care if she heard or not.

Sometimes she wished there was such a thing as a big cork, like the kind on an expensive wine bottle, only big enough to cork up this place so no one, not even Angie or Mr. or Mrs. Riccardelli, or Mr. Kirk next door, would ever hear.

"I'm telling you, John, one more year of this." Ellie was sobbing now. "One more year, and I'm gone. You hear me? Gone."

"Where you gonna go, Ellie, a drunk like you?"

"I got friends."

"What friends? You ain't got no friends anymore, Ellie. Who'd be a friend to the likes of you? Fine example you set for your kid—"

"Kid? You got some nerve. If you weren't too goddamned selfish to use a—"

"And if you weren't walking around drunk in the middle of the day all the time with your tits hanging out . . ."

And then, finally, silence.

Lana held her breath, prayed that it wouldn't start up again. She could hear her father's footsteps. He was going downstairs.

Slowly she got out of bed and opened her bedroom door, peered out into the hallway, then tiptoed as quietly as she could down the hall and into the living room. It was empty. She could hear her mother rustling around in the kitchen. She began to pick up the broken glass from the floor. Ellie would cut herself in her bare feet when she came back in. And she probably wouldn't even notice that she had. Yes. She had to clean up the glass before her mother came back in. She pulled the ashtray over from the other side of the coffee table and began to pick up the pieces of glass from the floor—

But there was another sound now. From somewhere outside. It was getting closer, louder.

A siren. A police siren.

Holding a small piece of glass in her hand, Lana sat down on the couch and stayed very still, listened as a car pulled up in front of the bar, listened as someone climbed the stairs. Then, loud knocking.

"Everything all right in there?"

Ellie was still in the kitchen and John had disappeared downstairs. Lana had no choice but to answer the door. It was getting dark; the street light just in front of the bar illuminated the policeman's face.

Teddy Morino's father was standing there in his uniform. Great. Tomorrow it would be all over, all the kids would know, she'd never hear the end of it when they started school in September. Paluka Bazooka, Paluka Bazooka . . .

"Everything okay in here?"

She started to speak, then stopped when she heard some noises from the street. She looked down at the bottom of the stairs. The group of boys she'd seen when she and Angie were out walking were standing on the sidewalk just next to the stairs. She'd completely forgotten about them. Alan and Jack Wells, Denny, Randy . . . What were they *doing* down there? She felt her face burn, shrank back into the shadows. It was bad enough to have parents who were the laughingstock of Comity without having the Wells twins actually see what went on.

"Everything okay?" Mr. Morino said.

Ellie staggered in from the kitchen, holding a new glass with one hand and an icepack over her eye with the other. The robe was closed now, but the bruise on the side of her face was yellow and purple.

"Can I help you, Mike?" There was that sweet voice, that voice she used when men were around.

Lana moved further back into the room.

"Mrs. Riccardelli, next door, reported a disturbance," Mike Morino said, coming in, closing the door behind him.

"Tell her to mind her own business." Ellie slammed the drink down on the table near the door.

"You've got to stop this, Ellie. You and John got to find some way to get along."

"I don't know what you're talking about, Mike. We were just having a little disagreement."

He moved in closer. "Oh, yeah? So what's with the icepack?"

Ellie giggled. "Bumped right into a door this morning, Mike. Clumsy old me."

"Ellie. The Riccardelli woman said it sounded like you two were killing each other." He glanced over at the pile of broken glass on the floor.

Ellie wiped her forehead with the back of her hand. "Oh, my goodness, can't a person have a little disagreement in her own home with her own husband?"

"Just making sure no one gets hurt. I'm here for your protection, Ellie. John's a big man."

Ellie shrugged, put her hand on her hip, moved closer to him. "I can take care of myself fine. Don't you think, Mike?"

Lana shrank back further into the shadows. She could see what was going on. Her mother was flirting with Mr. Morino, just like she'd flirted with Mr. Battleman, her history teacher, right in front of Lana. Probably the most humiliating moment of her life.

"Where's John?" Morino said.

Ellie shrugged.

"Ellie, I'm just trying to help."

Lana felt her fists clench. She wasn't sure whether they clenched because she wanted her mother to say she needed Mike Morino's help, or because she wanted Mike Morino to disappear from the face of the earth so he could never tell anyone what happened.

"Well, thanks, Mike," Ellie said. "But I'll whistle for you when I need your help." She giggled. "I'll put my lips together and blow. You recognize that one, don't you, Mike?"

"Good night, Ellie."

The next day, Lana left early in the morning during the afterfight. That was what she called the fight the next morning, in which each of them blamed the other one for the first fight. John and Ellie were already into it. She went over to the lake by herself and swam, managed to stay there until about noon. Ellie was already drunk by the time Lana got home. She found her mother's movie magazines spread out on the kitchen table, the small television tuned to an Edward G. Robinson movie. A cigarette was burning in the ashtray, the long ash evidence that it had been lit but she'd forgotten about it. Ellie's finger was bleeding badly, and there were shards of glass strewn across the counter.

"Dammit, Mom, you cut yourself."

Ellie looked down at her finger as if it belonged to someone else. "You fix it for me, honey."

Lana got paper towels and a Band-Aid. She rinsed off the wound in the kitchen sink, watched the red blood mix with the water on the white enamel, then drain out.

Her mother had begun to kiss her on her forehead.

From the way Ellie smelled and the way she pronounced her words—very, very carefully—Lana could tell she'd been drinking heavy for maybe two hours. This was the sloppy stage, almost worse than what came after it. She held her breath.

"I love you so much, honey," Ellie was saying. "I just wouldn't know what to do without you. You see the way he treats me, Lana. You see?"

"He doesn't like it when you drink," she said.

"He's full of shit, Lana. Don't you forget that. I can hold my liquor fine. Look at me. See?" She stood up straight, as if to prove she could hold her liquor fine. "I can stop any time I want."

"Why don't you?"

"Who are you to tell me what to do?"

Lana put the Band-Aid down on the counter and began to back away.

"Hey, I'm sorry, Lana . . . it's just that . . ." Ellie held out her hand

and cocked her head to one side, held out her finger, beseeching. Lana came back to her and began to unwrap the Band-Aid.

Ellie was mumbling now, more to herself than to Lana. "If I had any brains, I'd walk right out of here. I'd walk out tomorrow. Today. You'd come with me, honey, wouldn't you?"

"Why don't you?" Lana said.

Ellie Paluka looked at her. Lana could see the small crease lines on the pale skin around her mother's eyes. The eyes were moist, teary.

"Why don't I what?"

"Walk out."

Ellie hesitated a moment, then said, "Where would I go? See, my parents disowned me, honey, when I became a—" She stopped. Then, "See I've got no one to take care of me, like you do. So where would I go?"

Lana didn't know. All she knew was that she felt like she might vomit standing so close to Ellie, who reeked of liquor and cigarettes. She finished cleaning her mother up as fast as she could, then went into her room to change out of her wet bathing suit. Then she went outside.

She sat down on the steps next to the bar and was about to light up a cigarette when Jack Wells passed by on his bicycle. He was wearing blue jeans and a baseball cap and riding a shiny three-speed. He stopped in front of the steps and put one foot down on the sidewalk.

"Hey, Paluka Bazooka, how come the cops showed up at your house last night?"

She shrugged. "What were you doing, Jack? Spying?"

"We were just hanging out in the square. Hot night and all. And then your mother came out, took a walk. We watched her."

"Lucky you. You got a glimpse of Miss Radio City Music Hall."

"Why do you call her that?"

Lana took out her pack of Marlboros and lit one up.

"Because she says she was a Rockette. But I think it's bull-shit." She took the smoke deep into her lungs, the way she'd been practicing, then relaxed her mouth and let the stream of smoke rise up into her nose. Jack looked impressed.

"How long have you been smoking?"

"A few months."

"Why'd the cops come?"

"Oh, they're always fighting. My house is a regular prize fight."

"Really?"

"Oh sure."

"So what do they fight about?"

She pitched the barely smoked cigarette onto the sidewalk next to the bottom step. "None of your business." She got up and started back up the stairs.

"Hey, I'm sorry, Lana."

She stopped, turned back. "Where are you going?"

"Banshaw. There's a ball game with some of the kids."

"Who? Your brother?"

"Yeah. And Greg. And Randy. And Denny."

"Denny's your cousin, isn't he?"

"Yeah. Oh, well, gotta go."

"Hey," Lana said, "can I come?"

"I don't know."

"I'm a good hitter, Jack. Really."

"Well, sure—I saw you play once. But we gotta ask the rest of them."

She got her old bike out from under the steps, pulled it up alongside Jack's sleek shiny one. It was pathetic next to his, with its thick frame, fat tires, and rusted spokes. And it had only one speed.

"My real bike got stolen last week," she said.

"That's too bad," Jack said. "Won't your parents buy you another one?"

"Yeah, but they didn't get around to it yet."

She couldn't tell if he knew it was a lie. Well, it wasn't completely a lie. Her bike *had* been stolen a few years ago, and that one *had* been much better than this one.

When they rode up to Banshaw together, Lana could see Denny, Greg, Alan, and Randy already on the field along with some other boys from school. For a moment, Lana thought of turning and running. What if one of them said something about last night, in front of everyone?

Randy was pitching to Alan, who made a solid hit past left field just as they rode up. Lana decided to stay, stand her ground.

"Lana wants to play." Jack hopped off his bike and laid it on the dusty dry dirt next to the wire fence. Lana put hers right next to it.

"Hey, Paluka, where'd you get that antique?" Alan said.

"Her other bike was stolen," Jack said.

"Too bad, Paluka Bazooka."

"I saw her play at school, Alan," Jack said. "She can hit. Really."

The others had come in from the outfield now.

"Paluka Bazooka wants to play," Alan said.

Nobody said anything.

"Sure, okay," Alan said finally. "You can play outfield."

And that was it. She was in.

Sometimes Lana wondered how it felt to have such power over people. Not power like her father had over Ellie, but easy power, natural power. Like Alan's power.

21

Everyone in Comity knew the story of Sarah Skitt's encounter with God the morning the rock point at Devil's Meadow disappeared back in 1960. That story had flourished into a local legend. In fact, Louise Marchand, whose abstracts are now featured regularly in Soho galleries, even did an oil painting of Sarah Skitt in Devil's Meadow as a senior class project. The painting, hung in the hallway near the gym, showed a stormy sky and a small figure virtually rising off the edge of the precipice at the top of High Exposure, hair flying, lightning at her fingertips. Louise never said the figure was Sarah Skitt, but everyone called the painting "Sarah's Folly"—except the artist, who called it "The Moment of Flight."

I wrote a followup to the Paluka piece using a telephone interview with Lana's doctor and some of the leftovers from the Rowina Burn material. The story appeared in the *Herald* on Thursday and was picked up by the wires. Reporters from all over the country were starting to telephone—apparently, Lana was telling them to call me for information.

On Friday morning, I brought a copy of the proposal I'd worked on most of Wednesday night to a meeting in Marvin Saferstein's office on Third Avenue. In addition to Saferstein there were two editors and a lawyer.

My proposal had gone by messenger Thursday morning, so Saferstein had already had a chance to go over it. In it I outlined the way I intended to organize the book: like a novel, each section told from the point of view of the people who been there at key points, including Lana herself.

I also provided a partial list of the people I intended to interview: Lana's doctors, her parents, Alan, Randy's mother, the prosecuting attorney in the case, Ethan's defense lawyer, Ethan, when they caught him. I already had an address for the physician who had admitted Lana to Comity Hospital twenty years before. For a sample chapter, I'd written up material I had from my interview with Nurse Burn. I'd really labored over the chapter, trying for an account that would read like fiction, a style that was new to me. The result was a mixed success.

After a round of handshakes and introductions, we all sat down.

"Jack, we're all very impressed with what you've done here," Saferstein said.

"Well, it's a rough draft, but I think you can see where I'm going with it. They haven't caught Skitt yet."

"Maybe you can find him first," one of the editors said. She looked about twenty-three.

I decided not to comment on that and went on. "Each chapter will have an epigraph, a thematic quote from the era. Hermann Hesse. Huxley. I remember reading Huxley's *Doors of Perception* as if it were some Bible authorizing our use of hallucinogenic drugs. Or how about songs? Dylan, Moody Blues, Simon and Garfunkel, Jefferson Airplane."

"You have to get licenses to use song lyrics, Jack," the lawyer said. "It's generally a hassle."

I shrugged. "Well, I'll see who I can get a response from, and how much it's gonna cost, and then we can talk about it further."

Saferstein said it all sounded great; the two editors agreed.

"What would you say the theme of the book is, Jack?"

"Well," I said, puffing out my cheeks like the fool I was, "there are a lot of themes. Here you've got this naive girl who believes she and her boyfriend are soulmates, lovers in the cosmic sense. They do acid together. They hitch up to Woodstock. They believe in the era's causes. They practically *live* for each other, or she thinks they do, anyway. And then he betrays her. And look what kind of guy he turns out to be. Violence in the Year of Love, the Age of Aquarius. As a symbol of the death of the era."

Saferstein was smiling.

"I like it," he said. "I really like it, Jack."

We kicked around some possible titles: *Second Chance, The Age of Aquarius Murder, The Lana Paluka Story, Miracle, Cheating Death.* None of them was strong enough. But a title would come.

All that was left was to negotiate price.

"The best way to go is to get some preliminary material from her," Saferstein said. "See what she's selling—"

"I tried that, Marv. She wants to settle price before she talks to me."

"Good. Fortunately she doesn't have anyone advising her."

After a lengthy discussion, it became clear that Saferstein's top figure for both Lana and me combined was sixty thousand, half on signing, half on acceptance. He also offered me a royalty jump to fifteen percent after the first ten thousand copies, which could amount to big money if the book became a bestseller. And sixty percent of the paperback sale, which was generous for a first-time author.

Saferstein leaned back in his chair. "If she really wants to do it before we know what we're buying, sixty thousand is as high as I can go."

Oh, well. She'd said she would do it for twenty-five. I could take the remaining thirty-five as my own advance. No, I couldn't— I'd split the advance with Lana. The money really wasn't the issue, was it? I was doing it to establish myself. Next time I'd get myself an agent and name my price.

A check for Lana, and two contracts—one for Lana, one for me—arrived from Jarvis by messenger on Friday afternoon. I read the contracts carefully, had a few questions, which Saferstein answered over the phone; then I signed and sent back my contract. My own check would arrive once the contract was executed, contingent on Lana's signing hers. We would get the remaining thirty thousand on acceptance of the completed manuscript.

I went into the office and asked Harling for a leave of absence.

"Take as much time as you need, Jack," he said. "I owe you vacation time anyway. And good luck."

The Hostess Twinkie lady wasn't sitting at the front desk when I arrived just after six on Friday evening. This receptionist was young and very pretty.

I showed her my ID. "I'd like to see Lana Paluka."

"You're the third reporter today," she said, "but you're the only one she says she'll see. She's out on the south lawn right now." She pointed to the entrance. "Just go straight back out to the patio and take a left; follow the sidewalk next to the road. The south lawn is right next to the lake."

I found Lana seated on one of the striped lawn chairs, about twenty feet away from the shade of a large tree. She seemed very exposed, sitting there on the lawn. A woman was seated in a chair next to her. They didn't seem to be talking. It was a hot day, the sun dazzling, the sky flawlessly blue. In the sunlight, Lana's hair looked almost white. It was pulled back with a barrette, but here and there pieces too short to fit curled in random tendrils.

"Lana?"

The woman sitting next to her looked at me and stood up.

"Someone's here to see you."

Lana didn't turn around. She was following the passage of a flock of geese flying in formation overhead, her head moving in an arc.

I went around the chair and stood in front of her. She had an open Bible on her lap, parts of the text highlighted in yellow.

"Hi, Lana," I said.

"Hi." She turned to the woman sitting with her. "This is Elizabeth Norton. Did you bring the papers?"

I took them out of my briefcase.

She leafed through them without actually reading them. "Where do I sign?"

"You really should read it before you sign, Lana."

"I've been telling her she ought to talk to a lawyer before she signs anything," Elizabeth Norton said. "Or Dr. Baldwin. Or her parents."

"My parents?" Lana laughed. "Now, there's a really good one, best I've heard in twenty years. You know what Ellie said when I told them you were coming? She said I should let her handle it for me. She'd probably steal my money. Do you have a pen, Jack?"

I showed her where to sign. She handed the papers back and I gave her the check, which she handed to Elizabeth Norton.

"Do me a favor, Liz. Would you take this back to my room? I don't want to lose it."

"Sure, Lana. I'll leave you two alone."

Lana watched her walk away, then said, "You look old, Jack."

"Thanks a lot. You look fine—no, great."

"Because I'm thin, right?"

"Partly. But also because you look so young."

"It's almost like I didn't age." She said this with a sigh, not to me but to herself.

"It almost seems that way." Neither of us spoke for a moment. Then I asked, "Lana, when you said last Friday that you hadn't landed right, what did you mean?"

"Well," she said, "like, you're supposed to twist backward on the downstroke to slow down, then use the muscles of the talons to bend the legs and create a cushion for the landing. Otherwise, like, it's one hard surface against another." She slapped one palm against the other. "Now can you dig why I broke my legs?"

I hadn't heard "dig" in that context for so long that I almost laughed.

"No, Lana, I don't understand."

"Of course, my legs are all healed now. They tell me I was in traction for almost a year."

She was staring down at her legs. She straightened the knees, twisted them this way and that, first one, then the other.

She giggled. "You don't dig because you think I'm human."

I was getting more uncomfortable by the minute. It was like talking to a different person from the rational one I'd talked to on the phone. Granted, she'd been a little confused last Friday, but now it was as if she'd passed from one mentally deranged state into another. First catatonic, now just plain nuts.

"Aren't you human?"

"If I were I would have, like, died in that fall, wouldn't I?"

"Apparently not," I said. The thought crossed my mind that I should just leave her alone.

"Cut me a break, Jack," she said. "You've been to High Exposure. *We've* been there together. We're not talking about a little fucking hill here. There's nothing to grab onto, nothing to stop a free fall. I should be dead."

Now she sounded like the tough teenager I had known at fourteen.

"Why not just thank God that you somehow survived? Chalk it up to . . . a miracle."

"Could be. Or maybe, like, I *am* dead and you only think you're talking to me. Like I'm a ghost. BOO!" She burst out laughing.

"Lana—"

"Now, I could be a cat. You know what they say, a cat always lands on her feet. If she landed on her back, she would break it and die. Right?" She was speaking very quickly, breathlessly, all the while thumbing the pages of the Bible front to back, then back to front. "But a cat falling from that height would have enough time to right herself and land on her feet. She might break her legs but she'd probably survive."

What in the world was I supposed to say to someone as crazy as this? The only thing I could think of was Professor Galworthy, who taught my one and only psychology course, standing in front of the class yelling, "How can we find the unconscious mind when we aren't given a map?"

Finally I said, "You're sitting here talking to me. That makes you human. Cats can't talk." No one would believe this conversation. And I had just given her fifteen thousand dollars to collaborate on a book.

She giggled again.

"I never said I was a cat." She looked out across the lake, then back at me. "But I could be an angel. Angels have wings. I could have flown on angel wings down from that cliff."

"Lana—"

"Never mind, I'm not an angel. I'm just, like, kidding around with you. I've got it all figured out. I'm a bird. To land, you have to hover first, then bend. I looked it up."

I glanced over at the building—no sign of the woman who could rescue me.

"There's one more reason I know I'm not human, Jack. The most obvious one, really. By observation. I don't have the characteristics of being human anymore." She pointed at her chest. "Inside. Here. I remember I used to hurt. Now, I don't. I don't feel hurt anymore. The thing is, I don't feel much of anything."

"Lana, give yourself some time. You've been through a lot."

"Are you recording this conversation?" With her foot she nudged the briefcase I'd set on the ground. There was a tape recorder inside. It wasn't on.

"Why? Does it make you uncomfortable?"

"No, no. I want you to record everything I say."

I opened my case and turned on the recorder, set it on my lap.

She looked at me. "Why did you come here, Jack?"

"To talk to you. To write your story."

"You sure?"

I nodded.

She glanced down at the Bible on her lap and said, "All right, so let's get going. What do you want to know?"

22

Sex had become the main topic of conversation among the girls at school. Lana and Angie couldn't stop talking about it; there seemed to be no limit to the amount of time they could spend on the subject. Angie had lost her virginity at the beginning of the eighth grade, to a boy named Joel Pashmar, whom she and Lana had met when they hitchhiked over to Kingston. He was a tenth grader, but even so, Lana didn't think he was that cute and he had talked to both of them, not just to Angie. Still, Angie had his name written all over her notebooks, even though she'd only seen him a few times after that. "Mrs. Joel Pashmar," the front of her science bookcover proclaimed. "Mrs. Angie Pashmar." "Angie Pashmar." "Angela Riccardelli Pashmar." And various other permutations.

All Angie could talk about was how great sex was, describing it, demonstrating it with her fingers. Lana just *had* to do it too.

Angie told her about an orgasm one day on the way home from school, said it was the reason everyone made such a fuss about sex. But when Lana wanted her to describe what an orgasm felt like, Angie couldn't, though she spent a lot of time describing everything else.

Lana didn't want to admit to Angie that she was afraid of doing it, what she knew of it anyway. Angie kept saying it was the only way to express your love for someone, but what Lana's parents did at night didn't seem like love to her. Still, she wondered about it, about something so mysterious, so compelling that her parents did it even though they hated each other.

"Now, let's see," Angie said one day just after the start of the school year, "who should you do it with first?"

Lana didn't know, so she said nothing. None of the boys liked her. All the girls had someone who liked them, except Lana.

"Jack Wells is cute," Angie said.

Lana laughed. "Too short. What about Randy Slessenger? He's kind of cute."

Angie looked at her as if she were nuts. "Oh, come on. There are so many possibilities. What about Dave Dillon, or Lee Tranter, or Barry Carlson?"

They both laughed when she said Barry. He was cute, like a big funny teddy bear.

"What about Alan?"

"Hmmm," she said. Alan was the only boy she ever thought about, and Angie knew it.

But Alan Wells would never look at someone like her. Playing baseball with her when she was a kid was one thing. This was something else.

Still, she often came home from school and dreamed about him. She would sprawl across her bed and close her eyes and pretend he was kissing her. But her fantasies never got any further than that. She just couldn't imagine anything else. And anyway, Angie said you had to be naked and she'd grown fat over the last few years. Well, not fat, exactly, but big. Bigger than Ellie, who was small-boned, petite. Lana was built like John, sturdy, almost burly. Still, she liked the time when she came home from school and the bar was open and her parents were downstairs working. She could lie there and dream about Alan.

That's what she was doing the day he came over. Thinking about how tall he'd grown over the last few years, not like a boy anymore, more like a man. At school that day, he'd looked at her in science class. Or had he?

Mr. Marley had been talking about the periodic table, or some such thing; Lana hadn't really been listening. She'd been looking out the window, bored with the doodles she'd been making on her notebook. And then suddenly she'd turned back and caught Alan staring at her. He smiled.

She wondered if she had smiled back at him, or had she just sat there like a lump, too dumbstruck to respond. Anyway, he didn't say anything to her after class, so maybe she imagined it.

She got up, looked at herself in the mirror above her bureau. Come on. Who was she kidding? Alan Wells could have any girl he wanted. Why would he even look at her? She touched her hair. Why in the world had she ever cut her hair so short a few years ago? Now, it looked like a giant blond frizzy ball around her head. When would it ever grow? Angie had told her that when your hair was long enough you could iron it so that it would be straight. Or you could take a toilet paper roll and wrap your hair around your head. There were so many ways to straighten it out. If only it would grow.

"Lana, are you home?" It was Ellie. She was on one of her sobriety kicks that never lasted longer than a few days.

"In my room."

Ellie knocked at the door, then opened it, stood in the doorway. "Hi, honey, how was school today?"

She sounded sober. Maybe she really was going to stop drinking so much, like she'd promised Lana last week. She and John had had a particularly bad fight, and afterward John had said she was a drunk, and that if she didn't stop drinking he was going to kick her out. Ellie said—again—that she could stop any time she wanted. John dared her to stop. And every night since that, Ellie had pointed out loudly how many days it had been since she'd had a drink, and how she could handle her liquor just fine, thank you.

"School was okay," Lana said.

"Want something to eat?" Ellie looked pale, and both her voice and her hands were trembling. This was even worse than when she was drunk, this fussing over Lana.

"Not hungry," Lana said.

"Take that stuff off your eyes, Lana."

"I like it," Lana said.

"Yeah, well, it looks slutty." Ellie turned and backed out of the door.

Lana sighed. It didn't matter if her mother hadn't had a drink in five days. One of these days she would.

She lay down on her bed and opened her history book.

"Lana, someone's here to see you."

Lana opened her eyes. She was lying on her stomach on her bed, her cheek on her history text. She had fallen asleep.

"Who?"

"I don't know, Lana. A boy. He's a nice-looking boy. Fix yourself up."

Lana jumped up and looked in the mirror. Her makeup was smeared; there were two black half moons under her eyes. She rubbed some cold cream on it, tissued it off, then tried to push her hair down, but decided it was useless. She went out into the living room. She felt her heart take a leap when she saw Alan Wells standing there.

"Hi, Lana." He smiled.

"Hi, Alan."

"Want to go for a walk?"

"Sure," she said, and was out the door in a moment.

They walked up to the woods near Lookout Point. Most of the time he talked. She couldn't really concentrate on what he said, only on the sound of his voice, and on trying to keep her heart from pounding right out of her chest.

When they got to the woods, he took a joint out of his pocket. She and Angie had already tried marijuana a few months ago. Angie had gotten some from her brother. Lana had liked it; it made you feel happy, not like drinking, which made you mad and angry and crazy. She and Angie had giggled for an hour.

Alan lit up and handed her the joint.

"Where'd you get it?"

He shrugged. "Greg's cousin. Did you ever try it?"

"Yeah, me and Angie do it all the time." She took the joint and held it to her mouth, inhaled.

"Hold it in as long as you can," he said.

She tried again, this time inhaling more deeply. Then it was his turn, then hers.

After a few moments, she started to giggle, but was cut off when he leaned over and kissed her, spread her mouth open with his tongue. He had only been kissing her a moment when his hands sought her breasts.

She froze.

He stopped for a moment, looked at her. "You've done this before, haven't you?"

"Sure." She felt light-headed, giddy.

He laid her back in the grass and started kissing her again. She liked the kisses but stopped him when he touched her breasts again.

"Come on, Lana, you're going to love it." He seemed annoyed.

She opened her eyes; she could feel the leaves pressing on her back.

"Everyone's doing it, Lana. Sex is a natural part of love," he said.

Did that mean he loved her?

It couldn't mean that, but still, she closed her eyes and didn't do anything when his hands touched her breasts again, then reached around her back to unhook her bra. She helped him take off her bra; he rubbed her breasts. His hands felt heavy on her skin; her nipples stood up when he touched them. He reached between her legs. She was going to do it.

She lay there quietly, expectantly, drifting, stoned; then he took out his penis and she saw it pale and hard and ready to enter her. It hurt at first as he pumped inside her, but very soon the pain became a different sensation, pleasant but not exquisite enough for her to understand what all the fuss was about. It was pleasant enough, though, to hold out the possibility that she might soon discover this mysterious secret. She knew it would be wonderful when she did. It was already wonderful to be held, touched. And wouldn't all the girls be so jealous of her, that he had chosen her—

She could feel Alan's penis suddenly soft and squishy inside her. He pulled out and sat up.

"Was it all right?" she asked.

"Sure," he said. "It was great." He didn't ask her how it had been for her. He must know she had liked it. Or maybe she had done something wrong and he didn't care if she liked it or not.

For the first few weeks Alan came by almost every day, and it wasn't long before she found out what all the fuss was about. He lasted a lot longer, and it didn't hurt anymore. Instead it produced a sensation that started in her toes and raced wildly through her body to her fingertips, leaving her momentarily floating, euphoric, happy. Only, it was never long enough, never full enough, even when they smoked a joint first. She always wanted the feeling to last longer, or maybe it was that she wanted something more, something she couldn't put her finger on, or even explain to Alan, even if he *had* asked. Still, she couldn't get enough of it, of him, and began to sit in her room waiting for him to come by or to call, though he did so less and less often. For the first time in her life she felt needed, wanted. She wanted that feeling to last, too.

Especially now with things getting really bad at home. Ellie was worse than ever. Her five-day sobriety had ended on the sixth day and, twice that winter, Lana came home from school and found her passed out on the living room floor.

She cried a lot in her room during those months. Maybe she'd made a mistake, maybe she should have made Alan take her out first. Maybe she was too fat. Too ugly. Too awful. Her mother had told her enough times how awful she was. Still, she couldn't have been that awful if he wanted to be with her in the first place. It was all so confusing.

One evening when Alan hadn't called or come by in almost two months, he rode up on his bicycle when Lana and Angie were smoking a cigarette together on the steps in front of the bar.

"What are you doing, Lana?" He didn't even look at Angie.

"Nothing much. Where've you been?" She tried to keep her voice steady. She knew perfectly well where he'd been. She saw him at school every day, usually with a girl.

"Want to go for a walk?" he said.

God, he was so beautiful.

"Not tonight, Alan. I have a test to study for."

Without a word, he turned and rode away.

"Maybe I should go with him," Lana whispered to Angie.

"He's using you, Lana," Angie said. It wasn't the first time she'd said that.

Angie was bitter because Joel had stopped calling her.

"Oh, yeah?" Lana said. "Well, maybe I'm using him, too."

Lana stood up. "Alan, wait a minute. I'll go with you." She ran to catch up with him.

Angie was just jealous. Why make such a big deal about it? This was a new age, a new generation, with different values. They were going to make their own rules, get rid of all their parents' hang-ups. And "using" wasn't part of that. Sex was a natural part of love.

Alan had taken her to a dance. He was holding her very close; she could feel the muscles across his back. There were very bright lights all around them, and people dancing, admiring them. He said he loved her . . .

She awoke to the sound of voices. They were fighting again. She glanced at the clock next to her bed. One-thirty. It was the summer of 1966 and it was only a dream.

"I'm not putting up with this shit much longer, John. You said we'd be in entertainment, now I'm stuck with a fuckin' kid around my neck. I tell you, I'm not putting up with this much longer. I got places to go, John. Places to go."

It was the anthem of Lana Paluka's childhood. Ellie Shonovich Paluka thought, breathed, screamed, probably even dreamed it: "I got places to go."

By this time the bar would be closed and her father would have thrown the last customer out. He should have been cleaning up, wiping down the mahogany bartop, checking his inventory, wiping the tables. And Ellie should have been collecting the glasses, washing down the grill in the back. Instead they were shouting at each other, their voices wafting up the back stairs into the apartment above, where Lana was supposed to be asleep.

Lana already knew what tonight's argument was about. She'd come downstairs earlier and looked through the beads that hung between the back room and the bar. She wasn't allowed to set foot in the bar itself; it was one of her father's rules. (Did he think she didn't know what was going on because she never actually came inside?) From her vantage point behind the beads, she could see Ellie parading around in high heels and one of those tight black skirts she wore, serving drinks from the small cork-topped tray, a cigarette hanging out of her mouth, dangling there, as if it were glued to the lower lip. Lana usually recognized the men who came in. They were regulars and they were trash, as her mother put it.

That night she had watched Ellie serve a drink to Mr. LaPeter, who worked as a carpenter. Lana knew that because once she saw him repairing the front steps of the Presbyterian Church on Mason Street. Ellie stood a very long time talking to him, leaning over him when she served him the drink. Lana watched the man's hand graze her mother's thigh. Her father, using the electric mixer in back of the bar, was watching too. The whir of the machine seemed to get louder and louder. But John Paluka, a tall barrel-chested man with powerful arms, didn't say anything; he just watched. Nothing ever happened until John Paluka closed the door.

"Christ's sake, Ellie, if you throw your tits in a guy's face, what the hell do you expect?"

"Aw, shut up."

Sometimes Lana thought she preferred the sound of their fighting to the sounds that came from their bedroom at night. She had heard them fucking more times than she could count, moaning and whispering and giggling. She could never understand it. They passed each other like two strangers during bar hours, screamed at each other the minute the bar closed. And then, sometimes right after that, she would hear them fucking.

Parents were weird. No, *her* parents were weird. If she had Alan's parents, things would be different. She'd only met Mrs. Wells once, one time when she came over to talk to Alan. Mrs. Wells had offered Lana some cookies and milk, but Alan told her they had to go. They hadn't really had to go. The only thing they did after they left was go up to Devil's Meadow, smoke a joint, and have sex. And all through it Lana kept thinking how beautiful Alan's mother was, so tall and elegant and well dressed, with her glossy brown hair so perfectly styled in a flip.

That was how Lana wanted to be, just like Bernice Wells. Only with her own blond hair. But straight blond, not curly and frizzy. And Alan's father was so distinguished-looking, with that gray at the temples. Everyone, even her mother, looked up to Kevin Wells. Her mother said his name almost with reverence.

"Leave me the hell alone," Ellie was screaming. "I have to have some fun in this life."

"Get your cunt over here and I'll give you plenty of fun . . ."

Giggling. "You think you can just snap your fingers and I'll come running. I ain't your slave. I got places to go, John . . . places to go."

But there was no place to go for a fortyish alcoholic former chorus girl whose looks were fading as fast as her wits. And there was no place for her daughter to go either, because her daughter hadn't gotten her period in three months.

Lana sat up in bed, shivering, trying not to listen to the noises from downstairs. It didn't matter what they did. She had her own reality to face. And she had to face facts. She'd had sex with Alan Wells exactly sixteen times (she'd been keeping count), the last time nearly two months ago now, and every day since then, she'd run to the bathroom maybe ten times a day, hoping to see the familiar red stain in her underpants, each time overcome with a vague sensation of nausea when she didn't. She'd called Alan a few times when her parents were downstairs and couldn't hear, but he always got off the phone right away, said he couldn't talk to her, that he was busy. Well, he *was* busy. He was captain of the swim team and president of the student council . . .

Lana got back under the covers. Tomorrow, she would call him and tell him she was pregnant. Maybe that would make him like her again. She couldn't wait any longer.

Alan would know what to do.

23

All but one of the five boys who went up to Devil's Meadow that afternoon in 1966 were virgins. None of us cared that Ethan Skitt's mother said she had talked to God up there one day back in 1960. None of us gave a hoot about the ravings of Ethan Skitt's crazy mother. None of us even cared much about the spectacular beauty of the place. We were all fifteen, except Randy, whose birthday wasn't until October, and we had other things on our minds. In fact, the only thing that might have interested us about Devil's Meadow was the fact that, before we left it that afternoon, we would no longer be virgins.

I spent nearly three hours with Lana that Friday evening and came to see her every day for the next week. I took a room in a boarding house near the hospital and would arrive at Drummond about ten. We would talk for several hours each time, always out on the lawn in the same spot except once when it was raining and we met in the dayroom. She still spoke in that sixties vernacular that sounded so dated to my ears, and her voice still held the bitter quality I'd heard that first day, a bitterness that only disappeared when she talked about Ethan. She was holding onto a fantasy about him.

The oddest thing about these interviews was that she sounded perfectly sane so long as we didn't talk about why she thought she had survived.

She insisted that I tape everything, but it was she who directed the conversation, saying I had to know everything to tell the truth. I never intended to use a lot of the material she gave me, since it had no direct bearing on my project, but she was so candid, her perspective on Comity so different from mine, that I found myself fascinated. I had known that her parents fought and her mother drank—everyone knew that. But it was an unsettling and humbling experience to hear this child-woman talk so many years later about her humiliation and her confusion and her fear in the face of alcoholism and domestic violence, particularly when I had given her situation so very little thought at the time and when my own upbringing seemed so perfect and loving by comparison. Lana said she was surprised that Ellie and John were still together—even that her mother was still alive. Ellie had apparently quit drinking now, but that didn't make up for anything she had done or not done to her child. She had never been a mother. Now, suddenly, Ellie was trying to be Lana's friend.

"I took this money," Lana told me, "so I wouldn't ever have to depend on them again."

I too began to hate her mother and father for the damage they had caused.

"No one ever loved me, Jack," Lana said. "Until Ethan. If it hadn't been for Ethan I wouldn't have made it. We planned our lives together, away from Comity."

I never asked her why she was revealing so much to me, why she would recount the details of her relationship with my brother, and of course I didn't tell her how often I had already heard these things from Alan. Yet, as uncomfortable as I felt upon hearing the details from *her* point of view, discomfort somehow wouldn't begin to define the way I felt when she began to describe her relationship with Ethan Skitt, the intensity with which she grew to love Ethan, his unfailing kindness to her. And although I had assumed I would write about Lana's background and, certainly, her relationship with Ethan, I never intended to include the day we all went up to Devil's Meadow with her . . .

At the end of the first week, Alan, Jr., my brother's middle child, called me and asked me to help him with a story he was working on for the middle school newspaper. I left my stale little room at the boarding house that Friday and stayed at Alan's house, so I could help him Saturday morning. He didn't need all that much help, actually. He'd written a pretty damned good story for an eleven-year-old.

I set out for Drummond again at about noon. On the way out of Comity, I had to pass by Canyon Lane, the narrow road that takes you up to Lookout Point, which is about halfway up the big cliff called High Exposure, just beside the western face. I made the turnoff.

The road twists and winds its way up and across the mountain, always steep and sometimes precariously so. It had seemed much more threatening when I was a kid on my bike.

I parked the car but sat for a moment with the engine on, watching a pair of teenagers making out in an old Buick parked in one of the far spaces. To the town kids, Lookout Point had always been the local makeout spot. To tourists en route to the Catskills it was a scenic overlook, a place to take pictures only a short detour off the highway. Of course the tourists didn't know about Devil's Meadow, almost a hundred feet higher but accessible only by a hidden path in the woods.

I shut off the engine. The teenagers came up for air long enough to take a look at me, then went back to their embrace. I wondered if they'd spent the night there.

The clouds had thickened noticeably by the time I got out of the car and walked to the path. The woods were still dense and lush in late summer, and the leaves crunched beneath my feet. I made my way through the brush and, finally, out into the meadow at the top. Devil's Meadow.

The vista hadn't changed in the twenty years since I'd been up there. On a clear day you can see seven counties, everyone says, although I've been up there on many a clear day and could never tell where one county ended and another began. And this day wasn't that clear, though the vista was still spectacular.

I peered over the ledge for a moment, then quickly stepped right back, dizzied by the sheerness of the drop. Sometimes as kids we would sit at the edge and actually dangle our feet. Now, just standing there for a moment gave me vertigo.

I moved back further, sat down on the grass and looked up. Scenes from an adolescence spent in this place shifted like visions before me.

I remembered the way the clouds looked that afternoon, shifting in the distance, rising from the far horizon, darkening the sky overhead by degrees much the way they were now; I could feel the ground beneath me, the scrapes on my knees from the dirt; see Lana standing near the edge, naked but in a way strangely dignified. I remembered the color of her nipples.

It was Alan who invited Lana along that day. She called him in the morning while we were eating breakfast. I remember I was very tired. That night Alan had kept me up half the night with his whispering. A few weeks before, we'd seen a show on television about the richest men in the world, and Alan had decided he was going to be on that list someday. "Gotta get out of this two-horse town, Jack," he kept saying; then he would begin out-

lining how he intended to do that, where he wanted to go, how
large a house he would have, how many people he would have
working for him, what a knockout his wife would be. And that
would usually lead to a diatribe on Lana. Sometimes it seemed
to me that my brother never rested. How many hours, on how
many nights, had I listened to Alan's descriptions of their fucking? Sometimes, lying in bed, we would share a joint and Alan
would launch into detailed reports on the things Lana did for
him, to him, with him. If I said I didn't want to hear any more,
Alan either appointed me Skitt for the next few days or accused
me of not wanting to hear because I was jealous that Alan was
having sex and I wasn't.

Alan's end of the phone conversation consisted mainly of one-
word answers to whatever Lana was saying. "Yeah ... sure ...
if you want ... We're going over at ten."

After Alan got off the phone he sat down across from me, rolled
his eyes, and mouthed the word "cunt" with his hand cupped
over his mouth so that our mother wouldn't hear.

Mom, who was turning pancakes at the stove, said, "If that girl
had any breeding, she wouldn't be calling you all the time, Alan."

"Yeah, that's right, Mom. You tell 'em." He glanced over at me
with a familiar conspiratorial twinkle in his eyes.

I took a gulp of my orange juice, hoping he hadn't invited Lana.
The day had already been arranged. We were going to play some
baseball in the park—a real game with some guys from school—
then head up to the Devil to smoke some hash Greg had gotten
from his cousin.

"Did you tell her she could come?" I asked.

"Yeah, I told her."

Lana was sitting on the bleachers at Banshaw when we got
there. About ten guys had already arrived for the game and were
warming up on the field.

"Hey, Paluka Bazooka," Denny said as we rode up and laid our
bikes down next to the rest of the bikes piled there.

"I need to talk to you, Alan," Lana said.

Alan shrugged and started walking away from the group; Lana
followed him. They walked about twenty-five yards and stopped
near the trees behind the bleachers.

I watched Lana put her hand on my brother's shoulder and say
something to him. Alan looked at the ground while she spoke
and, after a few moments, took a step back. They talked for a
few minutes more; then Alan came back, leaving Lana standing
there, facing away from the field. She stood there by herself for
what seemed to me a very long time before coming back to the
bleachers.

"What's her problem?" Greg yelled from second base.

Alan took his place on the pitcher's mound. "You know what a pain in the neck girls can be."

Which none of us did, of course.

After the game, which we lost, Alan and I, Randy, Denny, and Greg hiked through the woods up to the Devil, planning to smoke a few bowls of Greg's hash up there, which would effectively end physical activity for the day. Lana trailed behind.

When we came out into the meadow, I noticed the sky had changed. Great dark clouds were rolling in over the mountains. It looked like a whopper of a thunderstorm was coming.

"Maybe we should go back," I said.

"You Skitt, kid?" Alan said. "Scared of a little rain?"

"Get fucked, Alan."

"Maybe he's afraid we'll be swallowed up by Sarah Skitt's mountain god," Greg said.

"Well, shit," Lana said, "I think it'd be great to be up here in the rain." It was the first time she'd said anything since her pregame talk with Alan. She turned to Greg. "Now where's that Afghani you promised?"

"Hey, man, give me a minute." Greg pulled a small foil-wrapped packet out of his pocket.

Everyone moved in closer to watch him unwrap it. He broke off a small piece from the reddish-black chunk, placed it in the hash pipe he carried everywhere in the pocket of his jeans, packed it in tightly with his fingertip.

"Anyone got a match?"

Alan had a pack in his pocket.

We each took a turn with the pipe, passing it around, lighting a new match every time the bowl went out. After about three hits, the familiar high settled over me, and I lay back on the cool fragrant grass and floated beneath the shifting clouds. Everyone was silent for a long time. Greg rewrapped the hash, put it in his pocket. He looked over at Alan, then lay back and stared up at the sky too.

"Hey, man, these clouds are far out," Randy said.

Everyone looked up and said something dumb about the clouds. Then Alan sat up.

"Let's play Skitt."

"Too ambitious," I said.

"Come on, kid, this is a new version. Lana's first."

We all groaned, but everyone except Randy and me stood up.

"We need a blindfold." Alan looked around and finally focused on Denny, who was wearing a cotton scarf around his forehead. Denny pulled it off over his head; Alan unfolded it, readjusted it, and tied it around Lana's face so that her eyes were completely covered. All the while he kept talking.

"Now, the idea is to see who has the most guts. First, we put on the blindfold. Then we turn you in circles." He put both hands on her shoulders and began to twirl her around.

"Shit," she said, "this is just like blindman's bluff."

"Yeah, only it's a real bluff. And the loser has to do what we say."

Everyone had their hands on Lana now, turning her around while she laughed that loud full laugh. After what seemed like about five minutes, Alan took his hands off of her. Everyone else did too; she stood swaying for a moment, shifting her weight from foot to foot. Alan motioned for them to back away.

"Okay, Lana," he said, "you have to pick a direction and walk thirty paces in that direction without stopping."

The words hung in the air. We were standing less than twenty paces from the edge of the cliff.

It almost seemed to me that Lana got visibly smaller standing there, as if the air had been sucked out of her. There was a rumbling in the sky; the storm was getting close.

"And what if I don't?" Lana said. I couldn't see her eyes, but her mouth had a defiant set.

"Then you lose."

"And?"

"And you have to do what I say. No matter what it is."

There was a long silence. It was as if, suddenly, everyone understood what the outcome of this game was going to be. Still nobody said anything.

"And if I do it, Alan?"

"You get what you asked me for."

Jack could see that if Lana were to walk thirty paces straight ahead of her, she'd be walking almost parallel to the edge of the cliff. She didn't. Instead, she turned about thirty degrees and began walking in that direction.

I held my breath, wondering, not for the first time, why she was going along with it. Why, for that matter, did she put up with the way Alan treated her? She could have refused to play, taken off the blindfold, gone home. She didn't.

One, two, three, four . . . Lana was taking long slow strides, right toward the edge of the cliff.

Nine, ten . . . she was only a few yards from the edge.

She stopped.

"No stopping," Alan said.

"Alan—"

"Shut up, Jack."

"This isn't fair, Alan," Lana said softly.

Alan's laugh was loud and mean.

"Paluka, I ask you, is life fair? Ask the Biafrans if life is fair. Walk forward or you lose."

She hesitated.

"You can change direction if you want."

Very slowly, Lana turned about ninety degrees and began walking. Twelve, thirteen, fourteen . . . away from the cliff. She stopped and turned again. I felt myself exhale a breath of relief. She had figured out that if she turned and walked a few paces in one direction, then in another, she'd be walking in a circle and could walk out the thirty paces without going over the cliff. Alan figured the same thing out at the same time.

"No more directional change."

I began to pray that she would simply stop and refuse to play. She didn't. She did what Alan told her to do—she always did. There were beads of sweat on her forehead above the blindfold. She was now less than ten feet from the edge of the cliff and heading straight for it. Twenty, twenty-one . . .

"Anyone who says anything loses before she does," Alan said.

I bit my lip hard to keep from crying out. Blood rushed into my mouth, and I wiped it away with my forearm. It smeared along the skin.

Twenty-seven, twenty-eight . . . Lana was no more than three feet from the edge when she stopped. I looked out at the open sky beyond the precipice, then down at the rocks below, the taste of blood from my lip still metallic in my mouth.

Finally, Lana took off her blindfold and stood for a moment staring out at the drop in front of her. I saw the look on her face; it wasn't one I recognized.

Alan began to laugh. "You lose, Paluka."

She shrugged, started backing away from the edge.

"So I lose."

"Now you have to do what we say."

Lana lay down on the ground and began to wriggle around the way we all did when elected Skitt.

"I said the loser has to do what we say."

Lana opened her eyes and stood up, hands on her hips.

"Okay, Alan, what do I have to do?"

A long silence. Then, "First you have to take off your clothes."

"What?"

"You heard me."

"You don't mean this."

Alan just stood there staring at her.

"And if I do it?" she said finally.

"I told you."

She stared at him for a very long time, her heavily lined eyes wide and fierce. Then, still looking right at Alan, she slowly pulled her T-shirt over her head. There was that expression of defiance on her face, and something else I couldn't read. She didn't have a bra on. Her breasts were large; they stood full and firm, at attention. Her nipples were the color of the coffee Mom drank every morning after she mixed it with cream.

The five of us formed a circle around her.

"Now the pants," Alan said.

Head down, Lana stepped out of her jeans, then pulled her white cotton underpants down and kicked them away with her foot. They landed near the edge of the cliff.

She stood there, naked. Her body was muscular, her hips and stomach full and round, like her breasts. A body more like a woman's than a young girl's.

My erection was painful. I had never seen a girl naked before.

"You want me to ball them, don't you, Alan?"

Alan just looked at her.

"Is that it?"

Alan smiled.

"Share and share alike, isn't that what you're always saying? We reject the morals of our parents. Right, guys?" He looked around for approval.

"He's right," Greg said. "It's like this pipe here. I give you my Afghani, you give me what you have."

"Is that it, Alan?" Lana looked at none of us except him.

"Damned straight."

Alan lay back down on the ground, propped himself up on one elbow to watch. After a moment, Lana lay down on the ground, bent her knees, and spread her legs. Everyone stood there for a moment.

I could feel my heart beating so hard I was afraid everyone would hear it. And now, incredibly, I felt completely straight. It was as if the high had washed out of me. I thought my knees would buckle, but instead I stood there staring at the place between Lana Paluka's thighs, the place my brother had described so often.

"Well, go ahead," Alan said to no one in particular, a king granting favor to his subjects. "I think I'll pass. I've already had this snatch."

Lana made a noise in her mouth, an intake of breath.

Greg was first. He was finished in a minute. Denny took forever. Randy tried to mount her but didn't have an erection and had to get up. And through all of it, Lana just lay there silently, her head turned to one side, her eyes closed.

When my turn came, I pumped inside her for a few moments, then quickly pulled up my pants and rolled away and lay there on the ground near the edge of Devil's Meadow, smelling the sex-sweat smell on myself and the clean smell of the approaching thunderstorm.

Suddenly, as I lay there, I became aware of someone standing over me, a tall lanky form that seemed to have emerged from nowhere. Ethan Skitt. I could see the pores in Ethan's dark skin, the dark eyes, the glossy black hair that fell onto his forehead.

I realized that Ethan must have been watching the whole thing from the woods, and I wondered if he knew the origin of the games we played, if he had ever seen us act Skitt, writhing around on the ground and screaming.

I couldn't move; I just lay there in the dirt.

"Go for it, Skitt," Alan said.

My brother's voice sounded very far away, but his meaning couldn't have been clearer. Lana was now the lowest of the low, no longer a person. She was a snatch. Even Ethan Skitt could take his turn with her.

Lana turned her head in Ethan's direction.

Ethan never said a word. He bent down and started picking up Lana's clothes. Lana sat up, then crossed her arms over her breasts.

Alan laughed.

Ethan looked at him, then knelt down and put his hand lightly on her cheek, looked into her eyes. She looked away, then took her T-shirt from him, quickly slipped it over her head. She pulled her underpants over her ankles, stood up, drew her jeans back on, and walked away with him. The five of us watched the two of them disappear into the woods together, Lana leaning against him, Ethan with his arm wrapped around her shoulder.

And that was the way I always saw them after that, all through high school, always together. He was always touching her.

*The nature of outer life is activity. Inner life is all
silent and quiet. At this quiet end is absolute being,
non-changing, transcendental bliss.*

—*Maharishi Mahesh Yogi*

24

On the day Ethan brought Lana home the first time, Sarah had
worked in her garden all morning, trying unsuccessfully to take
her mind off her troubles, which over the last year had taken root
and flourished like the weeds in the daffodil bed. Perhaps Sarah
could have borne her problems better if she still had Ethel to
talk to, but Ethel had died two years ago. Sarah missed her ter-
ribly, even though Ethel had become somewhat cantankerous in
her last few years, particularly as the old woman was confined
to bed. As a young girl, though, Sarah had recognized a kindred
spirit among the conventional Newcastle clan in her father's sister Ethel, with her flaming red hair and her tarot cards and her
direct manner. When Sarah was a little girl and the family got
together, Sarah used to enjoy her long talks with Ethel. They
would sit out on the porch together, swinging on the swing, and
Ethel would tell Sarah about her travels to South America and
the Far East. Sarah heard what everyone in the family said about
Ethel, that it was a disgrace for a young woman to marry an old
man like Jimmy Mason. She could still hear the way her mother
said that, with such loathing in her voice: "Old man." Sarah
thought Ethel's husband, Jimmy, was a nice man, even if he was
nearly sixty when Ethel married him. She missed Ethel's open-
minded council and supportive friendship. But losing her only
adult companion was the least of it. Although Ethel—good and
kind woman that she was—had left everything she had to Sarah,
including this fine sturdy old house that she loved, the money she
left was nearly gone. Sarah had exactly four hundred dollars left.
She'd counted it last night.

It took Sarah a week to embroider each peasant blouse she

made, and she only made five dollars profit from each of them, when you took out the cost of the blouses and the thread and her needles. She had to work months making enough of them to sell at the crafts market over in Kingston, and it cost fifty dollars just to get a booth there.

Still, even money was the least of it. The Lord always seemed to find a way. They wouldn't starve, not while she had a breath left in her body. No. Sarah's troubles were more serious than poverty.

Ethan. And Nathan.

Laban had left early with one of his friends that morning, and Ethan had disappeared too. Sarah needed her two oldest boys because Nathan was having one of his bad spells that day. When Nathan got up he'd seemed fine, ate his breakfast, said he would help Sarah and Adam and Rose weed the garden, but as the morning wore on he began to withdraw. By noon, he was sitting on the ground next to the garden with his eyes shut, his hands clapped over his ears. Somehow Sarah had always known what was coming for Nathan, and as she watched him withdraw from life, each day a little more, each time a little longer, she knew there was nothing she could do. Except pray. That's what she was doing now, as she pulled weeds from the daffodil bed, praying for her son, trying to hold back her tears, and wishing Laban hadn't gone off in Brad Banks's car that morning. Laban was her pillar, her rock, always had been, but he had been going off with his friends more and more.

She didn't like that Banks boy; he seemed too slick, too polite. She was glad, though, that Laban seemed to have friends. Ethan was always by himself. On Saturdays he always disappeared early in the morning and didn't return until almost dark. Sometimes Sarah wondered if he were meeting a girl, but she suspected he just went walking up in the mountains, because he occasionally brought a bunch of wildflowers back to her. But he worried her, even more than Nathan did. In the last month he'd gotten into three fights at school, and Sarah had to go down to the principal's office. She tried to tell him not to fight, but his eyes would glaze over when she said it, and the only thing he would ever say in response was that he had to defend himself— and her, too.

Sometimes, even now, she wished that Ethan and Laban's father were here to help her. She had left her parents' house with Miles Skitt at seventeen. They didn't approve of Miles because he was nearly thirty and because he had no steady job. But Sarah had loved him with every fiber of her soul; it was almost a hunger. When he made love to her it was as if she had never lived until that moment. When she tried to explain it to her parents, they had smacked her across the mouth. Even now, when she looked at Ethan sometimes, a hot flush came to her face and she had to turn away in shame, for Ethan had grown to look just like Miles, so tall and handsome and proud. Too proud.

No. Sarah could never have abided by her parents' refusal to let her see Miles, which left her no choice but to leave. Deliriously happy, she married Miles Skitt right away, listing her age on the marriage license as twenty-one. They moved to New York City and rented a tiny, roach-infested apartment on Ninth Street. Miles got occasional work as a carpenter. As she looked back on their years together now, she tried to remember the good times, but she knew, even looking back, that it had always been a struggle, and that there had been many bad times too, times when Miles didn't have work and there was no money even to buy food for the babies. Once, when she was pregnant with Ethan, Miles hit her. But he swore to her that he would never do it again and he hadn't, right up to the day he was killed by a hit-and-run driver just outside their apartment.

He lingered on for two days, and Sarah had no place to leave her babies as she maintained her vigil at the hospital. And afterward, she had no place to go. She couldn't go to her parents—they had never spoken to her again, had never even seen their grandchildren. How was she going to support herself and two small children? If it hadn't been for her father's sister Ethel, who owned this house, she *wouldn't* have survived. And wouldn't have had the joy of Joshua, or Adam, or Rose, or even Nathan. *Their* fathers didn't matter. All of Sarah's babies were a gift from God, though sometimes she wondered if her troubles with Nathan and Ethan weren't also her punishment, too, for having physical needs that drew her to strangers she didn't love.

"What do you hear, Nathan?"

Little Rose was standing near Nathan, watching him, her head cocked to one side as if she were trying to hear what he heard. But Nathan kept rocking back and forth, eyes closed, hands clasped over his ears.

Nathan opened his eyes. "Nathan hears a sound. Like bees."

"Bees?"

Sarah stood up from the bed of daffodils, which she had cleared now of weeds, pulling each up individually from the soil, roots and all. They lay in a pile at her feet. The pain on her son's face was too much to bear. She stripped the gloves from her hands.

"Rose, honey, Nathan's just listening to something."

"But I don't hear it," Rose said.

"Neither do I."

Rose looked back at her brother, then touched him on the shoulder.

"Nathan, what do you hear?"

Nathan turned slowly to his sister.

"Nathan?"

Suddenly Nathan smiled, and Rose began to laugh and clap. "See, Mommy? Look!"

"Yes, baby, I see."

Nathan looked over at Sarah; then he allowed Rose to lead him by the hand over to the swing. Rose was very gentle with him. Sarah was proud of her.

It seemed to Sarah that she had been holding her breath all day; now, finally, she could let it go. It was over for now. She turned and began to gather up the weeds. She had to hurry; there was a thunderstorm coming.

25

JACK'S STORY

In the beginning of my junior year, the student council sponsored a fiction-writing contest that was judged by a panel of three English teachers, two parents, the school principal, and two students. As editor of the school paper, I was appointed one of the student judges. Ben Mateland, the editor of *The Rag*, the school literary magazine, was the other judge. I remember I was shocked to find a story by Ethan Skitt in the pile of submissions.

It was a beautifully written fairy tale about a certain king who ruled in a dreary kingdom in a far corner of the earth. The kingdom was completely cut off from the rest of the world by a huge range of mountains, and it rained almost continually there. From time immemorial, the people in the kingdom had followed a rigid code of behavior that prescribed their every thought and deed. For instance, one of the rules was that a blue-eyed woman couldn't marry a green-eyed man. Because everything was spelled out in rules, the people didn't have to think, so everyone went about their business in a state of numbed dutifulness, unaware of any life beyond their rain-soaked territory, making no progress, unaware even that there was progress to be made. There was no joy in their lives, and they did not know enough to miss it.

The king had two sons, whom he loved dearly. The older boy, next in line to ascend the throne according to the rules, spent all his time sitting up on the mountaintop, gazing out at the flat landscape that stretched as far as the eye could see, wondering what was out there. How, the king wondered, would the boy be able to make decisions and grant judgments when all he wanted to do was sit on the mountaintop and dream? The younger boy had a much more kinglike turn of mind: stern, serious, analytical, good with figures and money and dates. But the rule dictated that the throne pass to the oldest of the king's progeny. And rather than change the rule, the king tried to change his son.

Again and again the king would tell the boy that there was nothing beyond the kingdom, that only a fool would think there was. The boy, a dutiful son, would try to content himself with the business of the kingdom for a day or a week—until he was drawn to the mountaintop again. He believed there was something wonderful beyond the kingdom, a world of unimagined grandeur and unlimited achievement. And so he found it more and more difficult as the years went on to obey his father, with whom he was more and more often at odds.

One warm spring day when he was twenty or so, the boy set out on foot to find out what lay beyond the mountains, taking only a backpack and a bag of sweet rolls. The whole kingdom gathered to ridicule the young man as he began his journey, a small lone figure in that vast landscape, convinced that he would find what he was looking for.

The king, of course, would have lost his older son to his dreams in any case. But because the father refused to acknowledge his son's right to follow his own heart, he lost the boy to bitterness rather than only to his dreams. He never knew whether his son found a land beyond the horizon, because the boy never set foot in the kingdom again.

Ethan's story won. Everyone on the panel voted for it except Ben, who chose a story by Alice Macadoo about a girl whose brother had come home from a tour in Vietnam.

Lana told me it was she who talked Ethan into submitting the story. It was really Sarah's story, she said. Sarah used to tell it—and others like it—to her children at night while the rest of Comity was watching television.

During my third week on the project, I decided I had to find Ethan. The department of corrections and the FBI couldn't find him; I don't know why I thought I could. I certainly needed some information on him, though, and to that end I went to the Green Haven Correctional Facility and talked to a guy named Arnold Scoggins, a lifer. He was a huge red-headed man who had known Ethan during his first incarceration and again during his second. We spoke through a glass partition.

"I understand you were a friend of Ethan Skitt's when he was inside," I said.

He smirked. "A friend? Wouldn't say I was a friend. No one's a friend of the Priestman."

"The *what?*"

"Priestman. Name he went by."

"What's it mean?"

He shrugged, sat back in his chair, folded his arms. "Why should I tell you? I already had all the screws askin' me 'bout him."

"You want me to go talk to your lawyer about your case?"

"No, man, my lawyer's a worthless shit. Why do you think I'm here?"

"You mean you didn't do it?" I said.

He laughed. "I ain't sayin' I never did nothing this side of the law. I'm just sayin' I didn't do what I'm in here for."

I nodded.

After a moment, he said, "You asking about the Priest? I'll tell you something about him. Priestman was a strange cat, man, strangest I ever seen."

"Why's that?"

"I mean he had that way about him. Know how some guys just look at you and they spook you? He was one of those. Not the first time he was here, though. He was always getting beat up then. He was a skinny guy, people figure he's ripe meat, if you know what I mean?"

I said I did.

"But he never let no one near him. Stabbed a guy for it. I always known he was goin' after revenge when he got out. Said so the day he got out the first time. I could of told 'em, then, if they ask me."

"No one asked?"

"He maxed out, they had to let him out. And it was different when he came back. He just had somethin' about him then that made people stand back. He was always preachin' and prayin'. Some of the guys used to listen to him, too. And in his cell at night, there'd be these sounds. Like flappin'. And humming. Personally, I think the Priest had some kind of powers, man. One time I seen a guy in here, a real big guy who had a big rep, name of Ice, and four other guys, try to get on him in the yard one day, and I swear, that guy got one look from the Priest and he just backed off. Five guys just backed off. People just left the Priest alone."

The next day I drove up to Kingston, found and interviewed Ethan's court-appointed lawyer for the first trial. The lawyer in the second trial had moved to Idaho. I put that on the back burner.

That weekend I went back to Comity, planning to visit with my brother before starting the interviews again on Monday. The police car, I noticed, was gone. I got out of my car and followed the sound of teenage laughter to the pool.

"Hi, kid," Alan said when he saw me standing on the edge of the patio. "Come and join the party."

"Hey, Uncle Jack," Keith yelled from the water. He had a beautiful young girl in a tiny pink bikini on his shoulders and was playing chicken with another boy, who had a beautiful young girl on *his* shoulders, this one wearing one of those one-piece suits cut up to the hipbone and down to the waist. Keith stopped playing long enough to point to each of the other teenagers and yell out their names: "Felice. Danny. Christine. My Uncle Jack."

I said hello to the kids and sat down on the chaise next to Alan, who had some paperwork on his lap.

"She's some looker, Keith's girlfriend," he said softly, watching the girl. "What do you think?"

I nodded, feeling a little like a dirty old man. "The other one's not bad, either. What happened to your protection?"

"I sent them home."

"Why?"

"I say if he hasn't shown up yet, he's not going to. He's probably out of the country by now. Besides, this would be the last place he would show up. He has bigger problems on his mind than me."

"I suppose you're right," I said, though I couldn't shake a nagging sense of danger.

"So," Alan said, "have you had a chance to think about my proposition?"

"What proposition?"

"About being my campaign manager."

"Alan," I said, "don't you think it might come out that you used to smoke pot? Look what happened to that Supreme Court justice nominee."

"Who's going to say anything about that, kid? It wasn't like we advertised it—everyone in school thought you and I were completely straight. Just the gang knew, really. And I gave it up when I was at Harvard."

"Didn't Ethan's lawyer say something about it when he cross-examined you?"

He looked at me. "I denied it, kid. Remember?"

I sighed. "I have my own career, Alan. As a matter of fact I have a *new* career. Jarvis Publishing gave me an advance to write a book about the Paluka case after reading my story in the paper."

"Why?"

"They think her survival is some kind of a miracle, something people might want to read about. The publisher thinks it could really be a nonfiction blockbuster. A real retrospective of the era."

"What era?"

"The sixties."

"What the hell were the sixties?"

I laughed. Those times really did seem far away.

"Well, I don't get it," he said. "Seems like an awfully thin story compared to what they're doing nowadays. I mean, there's not even any good perverted sex."

The kids were toweling off now.

"We're going to the mall, Dad," Keith said.

"Thanks for letting us use your pool, Dr. Wells," Felice said.

"Yes, Dr. Wells, thanks so much." Christine smiled at Alan in a way that could only be construed as flirtatious. Not an uncommon female response to my brother, even for the teenage girlfriend of his son's friend.

Alan responded with his own flashy smile. "My pleasure, Christine."

"Anyway," I said after we waved goodbye to the kids, "the publisher seems to think there's some merit to it."

"Well, well," Alan said. "A new career as an author. What about the newspaper?"

"I took a leave of absence."

"Then you have time to consider my proposition too. I've been putting together a staff for my campaign and I agree with Dad that you'd be great at the job. Of course, he just wants to see his two boys together again. How much are they paying you for the book?"

"Sixty thousand. Thirty for Lana, thirty for me."

"Thirty thousand? Kid, I'd pay you four times that much."

Why the hell was he so intent on this? When he mentioned it a few weeks ago, I'd thought he was half-kidding.

"I'm a reporter, Alan. I don't have any experience running a political campaign."

"What's that matter? Like Dad said, you're smart. All the big PR men started as journalists. What's the big deal?"

"To tell you the truth, Alan, it sort of bothers me that you don't have any experience, either. You're a doctor and a real estate developer. Since when are you interested in politics?"

"I'm pretty well liked around here, kid, believe it or not. I've brought in jobs, the mall . . . Look, will you at least give it some more thought? I'm having a meeting here next Thursday night. Would you at least come?"

I told him I'd think about it, then changed the subject. "I've spent the last few weeks talking to Lana."

"That must be absolutely thrilling, kid." He walked over to the table on the deck, took a cigarette out of a pack of Marlboros, lit up. "So has she started to regain her memory?"

"Not yet. I'm still hoping. She really thinks she survived by flying."

He laughed. "Like she turned into a bird?"

"I guess so."

"It's a shame she survived all this time and she still ends up a cuckoo."

I shrugged. "Actually, except on that one point, she's pretty rational. I wouldn't call her a cuckoo."

He took a drag on his cigarette. "So if she doesn't remember what happened, what do you talk about?"

"About her parents, about her relationship with Ethan, that sort of thing."

"Who else are you planning to interview?"

I ran down the list for him. "And of course, I'd most like to get an interview with Ethan."

He laughed. "Get in line."

"I want to interview you, too, Alan."

"Sure, kid, anytime." He stubbed his cigarette out in the ashtray on the table. "But not now. I told Mrs. Abrams I'd meet her at the office this afternoon on an emergency basis." He laughed. "She's got an earache."

I arrived at Drummond that Monday morning around nine, having awakened just before dawn and not been able to get back to sleep. I signed the visitors' register, then headed out to the south lawn.

At first I thought the woman sitting with Lana was Elizabeth Norton, but as I approached I realized it was Sarah Skitt. She had her arm around Lana's shoulder and was talking to her. I could hear her soft singsong voice, but not what she was saying.

"Hi, Lana. Sarah." I walked around to the front of their chairs.

"Hi, Jack," Lana said.

Sarah nodded at me. "Sit down, Jack. Lana told me you two have been talking."

I nodded. "You didn't tell me Ethan had escaped, Sarah."

"They won't find him," she said. "It's a very large planet."

I sat down on the chair facing them. "Do you know where he is?"

She stared at me for a moment, then got up. "Goodbye, dear."
She leaned over, kissed Lana on the forehead, and whispered
something in her ear.

Lana closed her eyes for a moment, and when she opened them
I could see tears.

We watched Sarah walk away.

"You think Sarah knows where he is?" I asked.

"She says she doesn't. Me, I don't really know. Sometimes
Sarah has her own reasons for doing things, or not doing
them." She looked away. "Sarah was like a mother to me,
Jack."

I nodded.

"She believes Devil's Meadow is a special place, a holy place,"
Lana said. "She believes that the naturally harmonious forces of
the universe are very powerful up there, that the place has good
karma. That's why she used to take her children there."

"You believe that?"

She shrugged. "It didn't have good karma for me, that's for
sure." She clasped her hands on her lap. "What should we talk
about today, Jack?"

"Do *you* know where Ethan is?"

"No. I want you to find him for me."

"Me? How am *I* going to find him if the FBI and the police
can't? Believe me, Lana, I want to. But so far—"

"You can find him, Jack," she said. "And when you find him,
would you tell him that I *know* he wouldn't have tried to kill
me?"

"You were arguing about something."

"Yes. I remember that. I can't remember what it was about,
though. Still, he wouldn't have hurt me. Ethan loved me."

Very naive, she was. In her mind, she was still eighteen and in
love.

She squeezed her eyes closed. "I remember we were arguing. I
can sort of picture us there at the meadow. And I was tripping,
my tongue felt all, like, swollen . . . He was yelling at me. I felt
terrible about something—he was right to be mad at me, I think,
whatever it was about. And the next thing I always remember is
flying down the mountainside. I have to flap my wings very hard
to stop myself from falling. I keep thinking that if I can move
them fast enough I'll be able to soar." She opened her eyes. "But
I know Ethan wouldn't have pushed me."

"Lana, my brother *saw* what happened."

"Your brother must have lied."

"Why would he?"

"I don't know . . . Shit, Jack, don't look so horrified. You think

Alan wouldn't be capable of lying? Alan is an animal. Don't you know that?"

"A *what?*" My mind shifted back to that day on the meadow. She was obviously holding a grudge against my brother, perhaps against me, too. Then why was she talking to me?

"That's what Ethan always used to call Alan. An animal."

I had to keep from laughing. The pot calling the kettle black. "Look, Lana, I know we—Alan—didn't behave particularly well toward you when we were kids. We—"

"You don't know shit."

"It was twenty-three years ago—"

"Not to me."

"But in reality, it is."

"Whose reality?"

I started pacing. "Lana, no one has these kinds of tripped-out conversations about reality anymore. The world's a very different place. And as you grow up you mature, mellow." As soon as I made this little speech, I realized that I hadn't grown up, that I still saw that day with a teenage boy's eyes. I'd never examined it from any other angle than the one from which I'd experienced it.

She laughed.

"For God's sake, Lana, you *let* Alan use you. You let all of us use you."

"Did I?"

"We didn't force you," I said, but I could picture the streaks of dirt and tear-smeared makeup on Lana's face as she stood up that day. I remembered thinking at the time that her tears didn't make sense, since she could have refused if she hadn't wanted to do it. We wouldn't have raped her, I'd been very sure of that.

Her eyes were filling up with tears now. "That's true, you didn't force me."

"Then why did you do it?"

She was crying now; I could see the little girl beneath the apparently confident exterior.

"Let you all fuck me?"

"Yes."

She wiped her eyes. "Why do you think I did it?"

"I don't know, Lana. Because you liked sex? Just for kicks? To prove how liberated you were? To get back at your mother?"

"Why should I talk about it to you, Jack?"

"You said you would tell me everything." This was a stretch, but suddenly, desperately, I needed to know.

"You think I should just automatically tell you about the most fucked-up day of my whole fucked-up life?"

"No, I—"

"I can't talk about this, Jack. Just this one thing. Really. Please don't ask me about it."

It was then that my perception changed. For the first time I felt what it must have been like to be her. I even thought I understood what might have motivated her to do what she did that day, let my brother treat her the way he did. And, for the first time, I felt genuinely sorry for her, and for my part in taking advantage of her. Still, I didn't want to be a party to her paranoid imaginings regarding my brother.

"Alan testified on your behalf at Ethan's trial," I said. "Doesn't that make up for anything?"

"It might. But since I know Ethan would never have tried to kill me, Alan has to have lied."

"I know you hate Alan, Lana. I can even understand that. But what about Randy? He saw what happened too."

She was silent.

"Lana, what you're suggesting is monstrous. Ethan went to jail, for Christ's sake. Why the hell would they both have lied about what happened?"

"I have no idea. You're the reporter, Jack. You find out."

"That's crazy," I said.

"Don't you want to know?"

"I already *do* know."

"You're a very thick-headed man, Jack."

"What does that mean?"

"It means that I've sat here all this time and opened myself up to you. I've told you what it was like between Ethan and me. And all you can do is try to shake my faith in Ethan. You haven't gotten anything I've said."

"That's not true, Lana. I believe you."

"You just don't think I know what's going on in the world because I've been out of it for so long? I'm being, like, naive about Ethan because I don't want to face the truth. But you, older and wiser, know it isn't that way. Is that it?"

"People lose their tempers, Lana."

She nodded and stood up.

"Yeah, Jack, they sure do."

Part Five

Jack

26

JACK'S STORY

I was the editor of the Comity High *Tattler* for two years. One chilly fall day in our junior year, after I'd been going with Patty Marchand for about nine months, Alan came to the newspaper office to pick me up after swimming practice. I had stayed late, rewriting a story about Jody Walingford's science project and the award it won at the district science fair.

"Hey, kid," Alan said, "all work and no play . . ."

He was standing in the doorway, his dark hair still wet. I jerked my rewrite out of the typewriter, stood up, and stretched.

"Want to do a few laps?" I said.

"Sure."

We raced down the steps and out onto the football field, dumped our books and coats on the bleachers. We began the first lap, jogging in tandem, keeping a constant rhythm. Except for two boys tossing a football around on the field and a couple huddled together in the bleachers, the field was deserted. I could hear our sneakers grinding in the dirt as we ran, see the double white puffs of our breath in the approaching darkness.

Alan broke the pace at the beginning of the third lap and headed for the stands. I followed him.

"I broke two minutes on the two-hundred-meter freestyle today." He was sprawled out on the bleachers, panting.

"That's great, Alan." I leaned over and put my hands on my knees, struggling for my own breath, filling my lungs to capacity with the crisp air. The sunlight had disappeared now from this end of the field and it was that hour of neither darkness nor light just before the moon rises in which everything has a ghostly, golden cast.

I suddenly became aware that Alan was staring at me intently, his eyes shining in the intensifying shadows. I couldn't recall ever having seen Alan look at me like that.

"What is it?" I said.

"Do you love Patty, Jack?"

"Yeah, I think I do."

I could hear the cars passing by out on Route 6, a giggle from the female half of the couple on the top row of the bleachers.

"What's it like?" he said.

"What's *what* like?"

"Loving someone."

I sat down beside him, flattered—and confused. One minute we'd been having a routine run around the track and the next Alan was asking me to describe love. I didn't think I could *describe* it. Even now I don't think I could.

"I mean it, Jack," he said softly. "I want you to tell me what it feels like."

"Christ, Alan, you've had more girls than—"

"I'm not talking about fucking."

"How about Cindy? Don't you love her?"

Alan shrugged. "She's all right."

"How about Dana?" I said. "Or Ellen?"

"I didn't even like them, particularly. Any of them."

"Then why did you go out with them?"

"You have to go out with someone."

"You mean there's no one in the whole school that you want to go out with because you like her?"

"I don't know how to answer that, Jack. Mostly I take girls out for sex. I used to think everyone did, but since you've been going with Patty . . ."

"Come on, Alan." I felt oddly embarrassed. "You must have cared about one of the girls you've been with."

Alan looked at me with the most serious expression I had ever seen on his face.

"No. I really didn't. It scares me sometimes."

"You'll meet someone, Alan. In college, or somewhere. And then you'll know what it's like."

"Maybe, Jack," he said. "But I don't think so."

He got up and started running toward the school parking lot. I started after him, still thinking about our strange conversation and the fact that he hadn't once called me "kid."

I became desperate to find Ethan. The day after my discussion with Lana about people losing their tempers, I went to see Bernie Palittski in his office above a seedy bar in Portchester called the

Blue Horse Tavern. Palittski was the private detective who'd gotten me the list of former Dixon employees from which I'd dug up Georgina White. The guy smoked foul-smelling cigars and called me "Wells" like we were in a B movie, but he did get results.

Palittski was on the phone when I got there. He motioned me into a chair and then kept me waiting nearly ten minutes while he talked and puffed on his cigar. I looked around. His desk was piled high with papers, some of which were underneath a glass paperweight with a tiny plastic statue of a naked woman embedded in it.

"So, Wells," he said when he finally hung up, "I see you made good use of my info on that Dixon creep."

"I did at that," I said. "Appreciate it."

"Hey, maybe I should be the newspaper reporter and you should be the detective. Or better yet, maybe you should put me on retainer. Like full time." He laughed.

I laughed.

"So, what can I do for you now?"

I explained the situation. He puffed on his cigar.

"You want me to find this guy, when the cops can't?"

"I thought you were a genius," I said. "You told me so yourself."

He put his cigar down in the ashtray, leaned back in his chair.

"So, do you think you might be able to find him?"

Palittski hesitated only a moment before saying, "The best thing to do is put a tap on the mother's phone. Everyone calls his mother, eventually."

"Maybe," I said.

He frowned. "The only thing is, the cops probably did it already."

"They were watching her house."

"Exactly."

"But I don't think they're there anymore."

He picked up his cigar again. "Hmmm. If they were watching her house, they probably did tap her phone. But if they tapped her phone, that means they think she's cooperating with them. Right? So they probably would figure if she's cooperating, she wouldn't do anything behind their backs. Like find some other way to contact him. Which means they might not be following her. Which means I could."

"Sounds good to me."

He laughed. "Hey, don't get yourself in an uproar, Wells. I'm only sayin' I might get lucky."

"It's worth a shot, though."

"I could also lose my license."

He was silent for a moment, then made a whistling sound between his teeth. "It's gonna cost you."

"I figured."

"All right," he said. "I like a challenge. First, I'm gonna check out the phone, that is, if there's no one around. And while I'm in there, I'll take a look around. Maybe we'll get lucky and there'll be a phone bill."

Which was what I'd had in mind in the first place.

He went over his fees with me. Two thousand dollars to break in, look around and set up the equipment, plus five hundred dollars a day for every day he had to stake out the place. Plus expenses.

"Sounds high to me," I said.

"Hey, my van cost me thirty thou," he said. "You think this equipment is cheap?"

"No, I—"

"I'm taking all the risk here, Wells. They're watching the house and they catch me, I lose my license. You get what you pay for." He puffed on his cigar.

I considered my alternatives—or, rather, my lack of alternatives—and told him to go ahead.

He then wheedled another eight hundred dollars out of me and told me he'd call me when he had something.

He called that night.

"Wells? Palittski."

"You have something already?"

"It was just like I figured, Wells. There was a tap on the phone, but the cops, they were gone. She went out at about three. I went through her house. There was a bunch of papers and stuff on the desk. Found two letters, looked like from two of her kids. One named Adam, one named Rose Petal. *Rose Petal?*"

"That was the youngest kid's name."

"If you say so, Wells. Anyway, there wasn't anything about a brother named Ethan in either of the letters, but one of them mentioned a brother named Laban—another winner of a moniker—who apparently was killed in Vietnam. Which doesn't necessarily mean they don't know where the one we're looking for is. How many kids did this broad have, anyway?"

"Six. Was there a phone bill?"

"Yeah. A few local calls. A couple of calls to Oregon to a phone in the name of Rose Skitt, and one to Adam Skitt, in Maine. I could fly out to tap them if you want, but that'll be expensive and I still think our best bet is the mother. Like I said, everyone contacts their mother eventually. You just gotta hope he finds some other way than the phone."

I told Alan—reluctantly—that I would attend his "Campaign Analysis" meeting that Thursday night. Only that I would come to the meeting, not that I would get involved.

"That's all I can ask, kid," he said, but I knew he intended to lay on the hard-sell again. Even if I couldn't figure out why.

Palittski called me again Thursday morning.

"You know, Wells, it's just damned fortunate you hired yourself a genius."

"Who's arguing?"

"Yesterday morning, she gets up bright and early. Eight A.M. she gets in her car, an old VW Beetle, can you believe it? And the first thing she does is drive to this little church in Kingston—the Divine Light Church of God. Sits in the third pew from the front. Wells, there was a note from him under the seat. She reads it right there, then leaves right away. I followed her."

"And the cops didn't follow you?"

"Nowhere in sight. Free and clear. She drives down to Poughkeepsie, parks her car at the train station, then waits for the train. I almost missed it while I was finding a place to park. Then she takes the train into Manhattan and gets on a bus. Goes uptown. The long and the short of it is, I followed her to an apartment at Ninety-sixth and Third. Right on the corner. Pisshole of a building. Apartment 4B. Name of E. Percelli on the door. She stayed about an hour; then she left."

I thanked the man and hung up.

There were six other people at my brother's meeting: an elegantly attired PR man from New York named Reggie Hughes; a mustached professional pollster named Maxwell Eck, who looked like a member of a barbershop quartet; an economics expert from one of the conservative think tanks; Bill Wilson, Patty's husband; Arnold Krass, a local lawyer. And Jocelyn.

I got there late. Jocelyn answered the door and led me into the living room.

"I'm glad you could make it," Alan said when he saw me. He introduced me to the group as his brother, whom he hoped would be his campaign manager, and gave them a quick bio on my background. I felt like I was at a job interview for a job I didn't want.

Everyone nodded; no one seemed impressed.

I sat back and listened to a wide-ranging discussion of the political situation in the state, the chance for conservatives to make inroads in Congress in the face of Cuomo's waning popularity and the voting record of Dan Sheritan. Everyone agreed that the mall opening had been good exposure for Alan, and that it was important to get him in front of the public as soon and as often as possible—at school board meetings, church functions, environmental rallies, tax proposal hearings. Bill Wilson and Arnold Krass said they would start talking to some of the people they knew about holding meetings in private homes, both to raise money and to build support.

This was followed by Maxwell Eck's detailed presentation of polling methods and statistical analysis of voter attitudes. Then Alan talked for a little while about Dan Sheritan's voting record—pitiful, he said, when it came to the tough issues. I started to ask what *his* position was on the issues, but Eck interrupted me.

"That's good, Al. Definitely take a firm stand about Sheritan's voting record. But I wouldn't go into specifics until we see what we're up against."

"What's that mean?" I asked.

"Well," he said, actually twirling his mustache, "your brother and I have been working on a questionnaire about the issues—gun control, abortion, state taxes, some of the local issues. Our plan is to distribute it to a statistically significant portion of the district, then analyze where the majority stand on the various issues."

"And then that's where we take *our* stand," Alan said. "You see, Jack, it's *because* no one knows where I stand politically that I have the advantage over Sheritan. I can get in with my positions—positions the public already supports—before Sheritan even turns on his motor. And *he's* stuck with the same old positions he's always had. Get it?"

"I get it."

The plan wasn't outlandish. In fact, this kind of thing was being done all over the country, at every political level. I'd written an article on it back in Akron two years ago, calling such polls a cynical debasement of the American political system. But to hear my brother describe the process so blatantly seemed somehow worse than cynical. It was sinister.

"Well, Jack?"

"It just seems to me that political beliefs ought to be deeply held from the outset, and not subject to alteration according to what's found popular by a poll." I heard a snicker from both the PR man and the pollster.

"Political realities, Jack." Alan didn't even look chagrined at my verbal castigation.

And, indeed, why should he? Modern politics was *exactly* what Alan was suited for. He was a born leader: attractive, quick on his feet, even charismatic. He could talk rings around anyone, and he had the stomach for modern political realities. I never doubted for a moment that my brother might actually be able to win the seat for the district, perhaps even a senatorial seat, were he so inclined. Anything he wanted. As usual. Indeed, it suddenly seemed surprising to me that this hadn't come up before.

I nodded at him, then sat back and listened while Alan asked Eck and Hughes to prepare an analysis of his potential base of support.

After everyone else left, Alan, Jocelyn, and I went back into the living room to finish our coffee.

"So what'd you think of the meeting, kid? Real pros, don't you think?"

"Definitely pros," I said.

"Of course, this is all just preliminary. The election isn't for two years yet. So are you with me or not?"

"I'm sorry, Alan, I just can't."

Keith came downstairs with his girlfriend, Felice, who looked even more beautiful dressed than she had in her bikini. I was embarrassed. The girl's face was flushed, and her lips had that slightly bruised post-sex look.

"We're going to a party," Keith yelled from the front hall.

"Keith?" Jocelyn said. "Come here."

He left Felice standing in the hallway and came over to his mother.

"I told you I didn't want you two upstairs alone," Jocelyn whispered.

Keith looked at Alan, then back at his mother. "Ah, Mom, would you rather we did it up at the Lookout?"

Alan laughed. "He does have a point, Jocelyn."

"It makes me uncomfortable in your bedroom, Keith. What would her parents think of us?"

"My guess is, they'd rather we did it in the safety of my bedroom."

"I don't think a boy your age understands the responsibility having sex brings with it," Jocelyn said.

Keith rolled his eyes and began to back out of the room.

"Talk to her, Dad," he said.

After he and Felice left, Alan said, "Come on, Jocelyn, what do you want the kid to do?"

"I think we should finish this discussion after Jack leaves, Alan."

He shrugged and turned back to me.

"So, are you reluctant to come around because of the business about the survey?"

"For God's sake, Alan," Jocelyn said. "He said he doesn't want to do it. Let it be."

He ignored her. "*Is* it because you feel uncomfortable with the survey?"

Jocelyn got up and left the room. Alan watched her go, then said, "This is 1989, kid. You can't accomplish a damned thing unless you get elected first."

"You're absolutely right, Alan."

"That's a pretty self-righteous attitude you've got there, kid."

"I just have other things I want to do," I said. "I'm sorry, but that's it."

Alan shrugged, then put his arm around my shoulder. "Well, you can't blame a brother for trying—right, kid? If you change your mind there'll always be a place for you . . . Now tell me, how's *your* project going?"

"I actually think I have a lead on Ethan Skitt," I said, grateful for the change of subject.

"How'd you manage that?"

"I hired a private detective."

"I didn't think you had it in you, kid."

"The guy's a jerk but he produces. He followed Sarah to some building in Manhattan."

"Where?"

"Ninety-sixth and Third. Corner building, he said."

"His name wasn't on the door, was it?"

"She went into an apartment with the name E. Percelli on the door."

"Did you call the cops?"

"No."

"Why not?"

I laughed. "Can't hurt to go check it out first, right? After all, I think it's Ethan, but I don't really know. I'm going to check it out in the morning. *Then* I'll call the cops."

"You could be arrested for something like this," he said seriously.

"Let me worry about that, okay?" I sounded more confident than I felt.

He shrugged. "It's your life."

I nodded, waited a moment before saying, "You know, Alan, Lana really holds a grudge against you."

"What for?"

"Because of the way you treated her."

He shrugged again. "I never did anything to Lana Paluka that she wasn't asking for."

The next morning I decided to go to see Lana one more time before I drove down to Manhattan to see if E. Percelli and Ethan Skitt really were one and the same.

I arrived just before nine and signed my name in the guest register as usual, then noticed the name neatly printed at the top of the page. Douglas Enworth. Same name as the man who had phoned my brother that first Saturday. Lana's name was neatly printed in the "Person Visited" column. The date noted was September 19. I turned back to the previous few pages and scanned them. Three visits by Lana's parents, four by Sarah. There it was again. Douglas Enworth, September 1. And again, Douglas Enworth, August 20.

Today was September 21. I'd first come to see Lana on August 24, then gone to stay at my brother's house that night. He made that bizarre phone call to Enworth from the phone booth in the middle of the night; I accidentally intercepted Enworth's return of his call the next day, August 25. Unless the name was a coincidence, which wasn't likely. So who the hell was Enworth?

I looked backward a few more pages. Enworth wasn't listed again. I closed the book and headed out to the south lawn, which was flooded in morning sunshine. Lana was sitting crosslegged on the grass, reading a handwritten letter.

"Lana?"

She squinted up at me.

"Who's the letter from?"

She folded it up. "A friend of mine."

I wondered what friend she had but didn't pursue it. I sat down beside her on the grass.

"Do you know a man named Douglas Enworth?"

"Enworth has come to see me a few times. Asked me a whole bunch of questions about how I was feeling and what I remembered. Shit like that. He's the head of the Miracle Foundation."

"The *what?*"

"They've, like, been paying for my care here for all these years."

I had wondered where the money came from.

"Why?"

"You know, it's like a charity. They do good works for people who need their help. I needed their help, don't you think?"

"Yes, I guess you did. But what's the Miracle Foundation?"

"Sarah thinks it's a miracle that I survived. So do you, at least that's what you said."

I nodded.

"What's the matter, Jack?"

"Alan seems to know a man named Douglas Enworth too. I was wondering if it's the same guy."

She shrugged. "Why would Alan have any connection with someone who's, like, helping me? He wouldn't help me if I was the last person on earth."

"Why do you hate him so much?"

"He *deserves* my hate, Jack. The funny thing is that I didn't always hate him. It took a long time for me to hate him."

"I don't understand."

"I mean even after that day in the meadow with all of you, I still didn't hate Alan."

"We all did it, Lana. If you were going to hate someone, it should have been all of us."

She sighed. "Jack, if you're going to tell my story, you have to tell the truth."

"I never intended not to."

"Don't be so sure. Sometimes the truth isn't what you want it to be."

"I don't have any preconceived notions," I said, after a moment.

"That's good, Jack. Because you've paid me for the rights to my story and you've got them. I've already cashed the check." She laughed. "Cheer up, Jack. This is going to be the best story you'll ever work on. Lots of surprises for you. And it can make you rich if you have the guts to tell it right."

What the hell was going on?

"You still *want* to tell my story?"

"Of course."

"Okay, then, I'm gonna answer your question."

"What question?"

"I'll tell you why I let you all fuck me that day. And then you'll learn something, Jack. Something about your brother."

"All right, Lana, tell me."

She was staring at me. "You really *don't* know why I did it, do you?"

"No, I really don't. Why did you?"

"I did it because Alan told me he would help me, but only if I did whatever he said."

"Help you do what?"

She uncrossed her legs and stretched them out, leaned back on her hands.

"I was three months pregnant, Jack. I was fifteen years old, and I was desperate, and your father was a doctor. Alan didn't give me a choice."

I pulled into Nazareth,
was feeling 'bout half past dead.
I just need some place
where I can lay my head.
Hey, Mister, can you tell me
where a man might find a bed.
He just grinned and shook my hand,
and "no" was all he said.

—J. Robbie Robertson, "The Weight"

27

JULY 1966
COMITY, NEW YORK

By the time they got to the clearing next to the park, Lana couldn't think of anything except the pain that was spreading upward from her groin, radiating out in hot waves through her body. The image of everything else—the way she had stood naked in front of those boys; the weight of each one on top of her, one after the other; the thing Alan had called her, the way he looked at her—had receded in the face of the pain. Even this boy, Ethan Skitt, who was holding her up, helping her to walk, seemed somehow distant from her. It was as if all of it had happened to someone else, *was* happening to someone else. The pain felt like a knife cutting her in two pieces from between her legs, a blazing fire in her gut. She could think only of that. That, and her father's face when he found out.

"Lana?"

She tried to turn her head to look at the boy, but her field of vision faltered and she couldn't focus on his face. Why would Ethan Skitt help her? She had never even spoken to him; she had even made fun of him sometimes, along with the Wells gang. She didn't need anyone's help, anyway. She was alone, she could stand the pain alone. She started to speak—to tell him to leave her alone, leave her to die—but no words came out. Through her haze and disorientation, she had a vague notion that it was raining, that she was getting wet, but her body was so clammy and filthy and sweat-soaked that she wasn't sure.

She knew she was crying, though; she heard the sobs.

She walked a few more steps. The pain seemed different now. Like a subtle twisting inside her, a turning and twisting, round and round. It seemed so desperate, so purposeful. Yet curiously it seemed to have nothing to do with her. But she felt nauseated, dizzy. And there was something seeping out of her, a hot liquid between her legs. She looked down. There was a dark, reddish brown stain spreading down the leg of her jeans. She shuddered, looked over at Ethan Skitt.

His eyes were wide, fearful. "Lana, we have to get you to a doctor—"

"No, please—" Was that her voice?

She tried to pull away, but her legs wouldn't hold her up.

The last thing she remembered before she lost consciousness was that he had his hands under her armpits and was trying to get her to stand.

"I want to do a rain dance, Mommy."

Sarah Skitt had managed to get the children into the house just before the clouds opened and it began to pour. All except Rose.

"Come on, now, Rose, we'll get all wet. See, it's—"

"Remember how you told us about the rain dance?"

Rose, her reddish brown hair quickly getting soaked, her face filled with delight, took Sarah's hands and began to dance her around in a circle, singing "Rain, rain, go away, come again another day."

Sarah couldn't help it. She began to laugh, despite her troubles.

"No, Rose, the Indians did the rain dance to pray *for* rain, not so it would go away."

The child stopped dancing, turned her moon-shaped face up to Sarah's. "But why would they do that?"

"So that the crops would grow, honey. They can't grow without the rain."

The rain was pelting into the ground now, driving at Sarah's head and back, soaking her. Her dress was sticking to her body. Sarah looked up. The clouds were moving in, low and dark and threatening. Where was Ethan? Walking up in the mountains in a thunderstorm? It was so dark now, it seemed like night.

"Come on, honey."

"No, Mommy, let's—"

The sky was eerily ablaze again with the crackle of lightning.

Rose looked up at the sky, now suddenly fearful. She took Sarah's hand and began to lead her inside just as a deafening clap of thunder exploded directly overhead.

"Sarah, she needs help."

Sarah turned around. Ethan was standing there. He was carrying someone in his arms. A blond-headed girl Sarah didn't recognize. The two of them were completely soaked. The girl looked very pale and she was limp, her head lolling back, her eyes closed. She seemed to be unconscious. There was a dark reddish-brown stain on her jeans.

"Ethan—"

"Her name is Lana. She needs help. I brought her from the meadow. She was—she had an . . . accident."

She stared at her son. From the meadow? Had he carried her all the way?

"What's the matter with her? Is she sleeping?" Rose had a frown on her face.

Sarah didn't answer her. She touched the girl's cheek. Her flesh was wet from the rain, cold and clammy.

"Mommy!" Rose had started to cry. Rivulets of rain and tears were streaming down her face. She wrapped her arms around Sarah's legs. "Mommy! What's the matter with her?"

"She needs to be in a hospital, Ethan."

The girl's eyes flew open. "No, please, no! Don't take me to a hospital. Please don't take me to a hospital." She kept whispering it, over and over.

Ethan looked down at her. "We won't, Lana. We won't, I promise. I'll help you." He turned to Sarah. "Please help her."

"But I don't know what to—"

"Please, please. They'll kill me," the girl kept saying. She was struggling now.

"Who will kill you, Lana?" Ethan said.

"My mother. My father." Her voice was a raspy whisper.

"No, they won't kill you, Lana," Ethan said.

"You don't know them," Lana said softly, weakly. "You don't know. I always . . . had to act so . . . tough . . ."

"Not with me, Lana," Ethan said, holding on to her, looking down at her.

"Alan said he'd help me. He said his father would give me an—"

"I'll kill that Alan Wells," Ethan said.

"No, no! He'll help me, he'll help me . . . I know I can't I can't I can't . . ."

The girl was raving. She kept repeating "I can't, I can't." Over and over.

Sarah didn't know what she was talking about. All she knew was that the girl was making catlike sounds now, weeping sounds, cries of despair. And she was getting weaker. Any moment she would lapse into unconsciousness again.

"I'll take care of you," Ethan said softly to her. "I'll always take care of you."

Sarah looked at her son. It was what Miles had told her the first night they made love.

"All right," Sarah said wearily. "Bring her inside. Let's get out of this storm."

28

Dad wanted to be our buddy.

I remember one Sunday morning after Mom had gone to church, Dad was standing at the stove, mixing up a batch of pancake batter for the three of us. Alan and I were at the kitchen table.

"Hey Dad, you know what I think?" Alan suddenly said. "I think you should try getting high with us."

I glared at him. How could he say a thing like that without so much as mentioning the idea to me?

There was a moment of silence. Then Dad turned around and said, "Sure. Why not? When?"

Alan laughed. "How about now?"

"You have marijuana *here?*"

For a moment I thought Dad was going to act like a father. I had visions of him going nuts on us, of the police swooping down on our house. But he acted as if he had known all along that we smoked pot. I still don't know if it was a surprise to him or not.

"Sure," Alan said. "I'll get it."

And so the three of us sat down at the kitchen table that Sunday morning and passed around a joint Alan brought down from the stash in our room. Alan demonstrated how to hold it, inhale deeply, hold the smoke in. I felt incredibly uncomfortable but took the joint when my turn came.

Dad coughed on the first few hits and kept saying he didn't feel anything.

"It's very subtle," Alan said. "Not like getting drunk."

Finally, after about eight or ten hits, Dad said he thought we should put it away because Mom would be home soon.

212

"You don't feel anything?" Alan said. By this time the two of us were completely wrecked.

Dad stood up, his eyes glistening. He laughed.

"I guess I'm just one of those over-thirties you can't trust."

"Come on, Dad, try some more." Alan held out the red-tipped joint.

Dad put out his hand. "No, I've had enough." He went back to the stove, and before long we heard pancakes crackling on the hot griddle.

We were on our third helping when he finally said, "These are the best pancakes I've ever tasted. They taste like ... heaven."

Alan and I thought this was hysterically funny. He looked at the two of us laughing, then broke out in his own booming laugh, which set us off again. When Mom came in, we were still laughing uncontrollably, holding our sides, by this time in pain from laughing so hard. Mom took off her dainty pink hat and laid it on the counter.

"What's so funny?"

"Nothing, Bernice," Dad sputtered.

She picked up the ashtray full of ashes and matches that we'd neglected to put away, and then, still silent, put it down and went upstairs. This was the pattern in our house. Mom never raised her voice, never argued with him in front of us, but she would freeze him out. At night we would hear them after we all went to bed. We couldn't hear what they were saying, but the tone of Mom's voice was harsh and bitter.

About two weeks later, Alan and I were lying in our beds across from each other in the dark. They were arguing again, and this time we could hear Mom say, "I'm sick of it, Kevin. I'm just sick of it."

The bedroom door slammed; then the front door slammed.

"Guess Dad's still in the doghouse," Alan said. He giggled. "Still no pussy for him."

"Alan, for God's sake!"

He shrugged. "Well, shit, don't blame me—that's what *he* said."

"Dad wouldn't say that."

He shrugged. "Believe what you want, kid, but he said it." Then he rolled over and promptly fell asleep.

I still don't know if he was lying.

I had planned to check out the address Palittski had given me, but what Lana had told me seemed to change everything.

The front door of my brother's house was unlocked and I let

myself in. I found him in his mahogany-paneled office, a spreadsheet up on the computer screen.

"What are you doing back here, kid? We don't see you for years and now you've practically moved in."

"I need to talk to you, Alan."

"Well, sure, kid. I was just running some stock numbers. Sit down." He swiveled around in the chair.

"I'm back because ... because I'm doing my retrospective on the Paluka case. On the sixties, Alan. You remember the sixties? When we all talked about peace and free love? Lana gave us some free love up in the meadow that day."

"Jack, what the—"

"Only it wasn't free," I said. "She just told me you blackmailed her into it."

Alan stared at me for a moment, then suddenly burst out laughing.

"Oh, Christ, Jack!"

"Alan, Lana says she was three months pregnant and you told her you'd get Dad to give her an abortion if she did what you said."

"Oh, I just figured it was time for me to introduce my brother and my friends to the joys of sex. Even if it was with a pig like her."

I tried to keep my voice steady.

"You mean you did it to show off?"

"Of course not. I did it ... Oh, I don't know why I did it, I never stopped to think about it. What's the difference?"

"Alan, she's a *human being*. What you did is ... it's so twisted I can't even begin to—"

"Oh, for Christ's sake, I was a kid. What the hell did I know? It seemed like a good idea at the time."

"A *good idea?* Alan, what you did is ... it means we all *raped* her. Can't you see—"

"I see you're getting carried away over something that happened over twenty years ago. I admit it was a pretty dumb thing to do. But you can't call it rape—rape is a whole different thing. Lana loved sex."

"You still don't get it, do you?" I said. "She loved *you*. She loved sex with *you*. Not with four boys when she was three months pregnant with your baby."

"How the hell did I know it was my baby? I told you she screwed lots of guys before me."

"That's what you said." I realized I had tears in my eyes. Any second they'd be rolling down my cheeks. I had nothing else to do with the incredible loathing I felt at that moment, not only toward my brother but toward myself.

"Alan, did you and Randy lie about what you saw?"

"For Christ's sake, why would we?"

"I can only think of one reason."

"What the hell are you suggesting, Jack?"

"I don't know what I'm suggesting. Until this morning I never even thought about it."

"Well, stop thinking about it."

"Alan, was it you who tried to kill Lana?"

He got up and walked over to the wall of pictures, then turned around to face me.

"Of course not. Randy and I went up there that day, and we saw the two of them arguing—"

"No, please, I was there in the courtroom. I heard the whole thing. I even heard Ethan's defense lawyer accuse you and Randy of lying."

"The guy was desperate. He had to say we were lying. They always do that, when two stories are contradictory. They have no other legal recourse."

"Fuck, Alan, tell me the truth. I need you to tell the truth."

"I did. Randy saw it—"

"Randy isn't here, Alan. Randy's been gone for seven years."

He came over to me and put his hand on my shoulder. Good God! Was *he* crying?

"Jack, please. Christ, I can't believe you'd think I would do that. Sure, I did a dumb thing with Lana that day. Worse than dumb. But that doesn't mean I'm a murderer."

I wanted to believe him. I wanted so much to believe him. I wondered if he really didn't understand that what he'd done with Lana wasn't just dumb, it was *revolting*. Maybe it could be excused as a young man's lapse in judgment. But Alan was about to have his thirty-ninth birthday, and he *still* didn't seem to see how revolting it was.

He really was crying now. I couldn't remember the last time I'd seen him lose his composure.

"What happened to the baby?" I said finally.

"I don't know. She never mentioned it to me again."

"I have to go, Alan."

Alan came toward me, eyes red, glassy. I felt myself cringe with revulsion.

"Jack, please."

"Please what?"

"You've got to believe me."

I looked at my brother standing there, crying.

"I want to," I said.

The two of us stared at each other for a moment; then I said, "Did you really think Dad would perform an abortion?"

"I . . . I don't know. I never asked him."

Without saying another word, I turned away from him and rushed out by the front door, only stopping once, to wave to my brother's three boys, who were tossing a football on the front lawn.

The development of Comity hadn't yet reached Cold Canyon Road. It was exactly as I remembered it, a winding country road set at the base of the mountains, a few houses hidden within the still dense woods. I passed by the turnoff to Canyon Road, the road that took you up to High Exposure, and continued along Cold Canyon until I came to the familiar green mailbox.

Randy's parents' house had been repainted in a peculiar mustard color, but otherwise it was the same low-slung ranch where I'd spent maybe a third of my childhood. As I drove up, I could see Randy's mother sitting on the front lawn, reading. For a moment, I thought of turning around and pulling out again. I wasn't even sure what I was doing there.

She looked up as I parked. Her hair was pure white, and at the part I could see her pink scalp. She seemed even smaller than I remembered her.

I got out of the car. "Mrs. Slessenger, it's been a long time. I'm Jack Wells."

It took her a minute to register the name; then she smiled.

"Well, Jack, it's nice to see you."

"You too, Mrs. Slessenger."

"I lost my husband last year," she said. "He was never the same, after Randy . . ."

"I'm very sorry."

"How are you doing, Jack?"

"Oh, all right. I'm doing a story on Lana Paluka. I'm a reporter, do you remember?"

"Lana? That Ethan Skitt destroyed her too. Just like my Randy. When I think of what he did to my boy, I . . ."

"I just wanted to stop by to see how you were doing."

She shrugged. "How should I be doing? My husband's gone, my son murdered. He was a good boy, Jack. He just needed to straighten out . . . and he was going to, too. If they hadn't let that Skitt out of jail, where he always belonged—I said so from the very beginning—my Randy would have been all right. I know he would have." She sighed, shook her head. "You know, sometimes

I think about going over to that Sarah Skitt's house. How she could stay here after what her son did, I don't know. I'll never know. She'll rot in hell along with him."

I just stood there. All I could think of to say was, "I'm sorry," but I didn't want to say that again, so I kept quiet.

"My Randy was such a good boy. Do you know that, Jack? He always made us laugh. And he loved his sister, Susie, too. I remember once you boys had all gone out somewhere and Randy came back really late and I was sitting up waiting for him in the living room, sewing a Halloween costume for Susie. Of course at the time I didn't know what was going on with you boys—that you were all up there on Devil's Meadow smoking marijuana. But even then Randy came in and apologized to me for being late, then sat down and helped me put the sequins on Susie's costume. Just sat there and pasted sequins on while we talked. That was the night Randy told me he'd decided to be a music teacher." She looked up at me. "He would have made a good one, too."

"He would have been a fine teacher, Mrs. Slessenger."

"And then, that summer, everything just seemed to go to pieces. My Susie—I mean Sue, that's what everyone calls her now—she'd argue with me about that. She says Randy changed much earlier, and maybe he did. All I know is, he never went back to college again after he came home to testify at that trial. He never went back, never laughed or made jokes anymore. He never even played his guitar anymore."

I nodded. Randy had had a beautiful singing voice, not as powerful as my brother's tenor but more memorable, sweet, and melodious, the kind of voice that accompanies an acoustic guitar perfectly. Randy often used to bring his guitar with him wherever we went, and accompany himself in a Donovan song, or Simon and Garfunkel, or Dylan, but he *had* changed over the last few years of high school. He began to retreat into his own world, only occasionally hanging out with us, and when he did, he was quiet, withdrawn, even grim.

"I'll never understand it," Estelle Slessenger was saying. "Every time we saw him he looked worse. You think you get over it but you never do. Just before . . . it happened, he wrote to us that he was going to straighten himself out—I'll bet you didn't know that. And then when I think of what happened . . . that Skitt, what he did to my Randy, I just . . ." She was crying now. "Why did you come here, Jack?"

"I was back in town, and I started to think about him," I lied. "I don't know, I was just thinking about him."

"You too?"

I nodded.

"I have a whole box of his things saved. Would you want to see it?"

She was already heading into the house. I followed her into her bedroom, where she opened a closet and pulled out an album with a shoebox on top of it.

"Look at these pictures, Jack. He was such a beautiful boy."

I began looking through the photographs of Randy at ascending ages, all labeled. A few baby pictures, at six with his mother and father, at nine on his bicycle, at ten with his sister in costume, at eleven with Alan and me in front of the Slessenger house, at thirteen with his guitar, at fifteen in a school play, at sixteen with the whole gang at Banshaw Park.

One of the last photographs in the book was one of Randy and Barry Carlson, a tall kid I recognized from school though he hadn't been part of our gang. I hadn't really known Randy and Barry were friends, though I had a vague recollection of seeing them together a few times in the school parking lot.

The picture wasn't labeled, but I knew it had been taken when we were seniors, because in our senior year Randy had started tying a bandanna around his forehead.

I began to leaf through the letters. She had saved everything: birthday cards he'd made for her; letters from Camp MacAdoo, "Your fun camp in the sun," the camp we all went to the summer we were ten; a postcard from Washington, the time we were almost arrested for water-balloon throwing.

Dear Mom and Dad,

Wish you were here! Only kidding. We're having a great time. The hotel is far-out! We all loved the tour of the FBI.

See you soon.

> Love,
>
> Randy
> And hugs to Susie.

And finally, I picked up another letter. This one on plain white paper, dated the first of September 1970.

Dear Mom and Dad,

Today I got the subpoena to appear at Ethan Skitt's trial on November 14th. Please, please see if you can talk to Mr. Bonsall. He's the prosecuting attorney, the one we talked to before. They don't need me. Alan Wells's testimony will be enough. You've got to get me out of testifying. I'll write out one of those depositions instead. I'll freak out in that courtroom. I know I will. Please help me.

Love,

Randy

P.S. Love to Susie and a big hug.

I held my breath. "Do you know why Randy didn't want to testify?"

"My husband thought he was afraid of getting up in front of all those people," she said. "I don't know. Maybe with all those drugs he was using he was scared of the whole thing, with all the police and the judges and lawyers around. That's what I told Detective Wu when I showed him the letters."

"Who's Detective Wu?"

"The policeman who investigated his murder."

I nodded. The trial *was* intense. Even I thought so, and I hadn't had to get up there on the stand.

"May I see the album again."

She looked at me, puzzled, but handed me the book. I leafed through the pages of photographs, stopping again when I got to the one of Randy and Barry.

"That's Barry . . . I can't remember his name."

"Barry Carlson. Were he and Randy friends?"

She shrugged. "He and Barry became friends after . . . after you and Alan dropped him."

"Dropped him? We thought he dropped us."

"Doesn't matter now," she said.

I looked back at the picture for a moment, closed the book, apologized for not being more helpful (then or now) and made a quick exit.

I called directory assistance from a phone booth for the number of Barry Carlson's parents. A woman answered the phone.

"Hello, Mrs. Carlson? This is Jack Wells. I'm an old friend of Barry's. From back in high school."

"Yes?" The woman sounded wary.

"I wanted to get in touch with Barry. I was wondering if you could tell me where he might be?"

There was a long silence. I could hear her breathing into the phone.

Finally she said, "He's in New York."

"Do you have an address?"

"Well, I . . . why do you want to see him?"

"I just want to visit."

Another long pause, but she gave me an address in Greenwich
Village.

I got to Greenwich Village around four. Amazingly, I found a
space just in front of the building on Christopher Street.

The building looked as dilapidated and unremarkable as the
rest of the buildings on the street. Inside, there was a strong
medicinal smell, and something else I couldn't identify. A woman
was sitting at a desk in the front foyer. When I told her I had
come to see Barry Carlson, she nodded and held out a hospital
mask.

"Put this on. He's in room three."

I looked around. "Why do I have to—"

"This is the Good Samaritan Hospice, Mr. Wells. We have AIDS
patients here."

"My God. His mother didn't tell me."

She shrugged. "Not unusual, believe me."

I put the mask on—not so I wouldn't catch AIDS, she said, but
so the patients wouldn't catch anything from me. I followed her
to a room at the far end of the hall. There were four beds in the
room, each with its own skeleton beneath the sheet.

"Barry's there." She pointed to the one on the right by the
window.

I stood for a moment in the doorway, then slowly made my
way to the bed.

The first thing I thought was that someone had removed this
man's skin, taken everything out beneath it and then draped the
skin loosely back in place, leaving it to hang there on the bare
bones. He was covered with horrible red sores and had only a
few gray tufts of hair on his head.

I knew it was Barry only by his wristband. His wrist was no
bigger than a child's. But his eyes were open and aware.

I stood over the bed, unable to speak.

"The Angel of Mercy has other deaths to attend." Barry glanced
toward the doorway. A rattling sound came from his chest, as if
it were hollow.

I was about to ask him what he meant, then realized he was
referring to the woman who showed me in. She seemed to be the
only nonpatient in the place. The Angel of Mercy.

The two of us stared at each other—I could barely look at those
bright but glazed eyes in the skeletal face—until I realized that
he didn't recognize me. Why should he?

"Barry," I said, "I'm Jack Wells." I found myself speaking very
softly. My voice sounded muffled behind the mask.

No reaction.

"From high school," I said, speaking a little louder. "I had a twin brother. Alan." Surely he'd remember the Wells twins.

A glimmer of recognition.

"How are you?" I said, idiotically.

"It'll happen any time," he said. "What do you want, Jack? Come to see the faggot get his just rewards?"

"I . . . My God, Barry, when I called your mother she didn't even tell me."

"My mother is very good at denial. Always has been. So why are you here?"

"I, ah, came to ask you something, Barry. Is it okay?"

"Sure. We don't get many visitors here."

"It's about Randy Slessenger," I said.

"Randy? Where is he?"

"You didn't know?"

"Are you going to tell me he's dead too?"

"Seven years ago. He was murdered."

"Murdered? God, I didn't know. Well, at least it was quick. At least he was spared this." He wiped a dribble of spit from the corner of his mouth with the back of his hand. I watched the tube connected to the vein move up and down with his hand.

"I'm sorry," Barry said. "I have very little sympathy left. What about Randy?"

"I . . ."

A weak smile. "What is it you want, Jack? You want to know if Randy and I had a thing? Can't even bring yourself to say it, can you?"

I stood there, my mouth as dry as dust. Randy? A homosexual? All the impromptu baseball games, all the Saturday afternoons bike-riding, all the football games, and playing chicken up on High Exposure, horsing around in the locker rooms . . . And Randy had always been smack in the middle of the group boasting sessions with me and Alan and Denny and Greg, the ones covering girls we'd done it with, girls we'd tried to do it with, girls we'd wanted to do it with . . .

"The answer is yes," the man in the bed said. "Right toward the end of high school, Randy and I . . . found each other. Kind of ironic, when you think about it. What I thought was going to save me was really the beginning of the end."

How the hell could Alan and I have missed something so basic about our best friend? Or maybe Alan didn't miss it. No. He would have said something if he'd known. Wouldn't he?

I realized that I could no longer say what my brother would or wouldn't do.

"You had no idea he was gay, did you?" Barry said.

"I . . . no idea."

He shrugged. "It was always very important for Randy to keep it a secret. And to me too, then. This was before gay pride and all that." He laughed feebly, bitterly.

But I wasn't even listening. I was thinking how devastating it must have been for Randy to realize that he was homosexual. It must have been an incredible, never-ending struggle for him not only to have to keep it a secret from his best friends (could I really still call him a best friend?), but to have to fake an entire set of desires about girls that he probably didn't feel. He couldn't tell us, of course. I wasn't sure how I would have reacted, but Alan would have been merciless.

And Alan could be merciless.

"I . . . was . . . could anyone have gotten any proof that Randy was a homosexual, Barry?"

His chest was heaving; I could see it rising and falling beneath the thin blanket.

"I don't know what you're talking about, Jack."

"You know. Something that would have proven he was gay."

"Like what? What for?"

"I don't know. A letter?"

His expression was fierce. "We never wrote letters."

"Or a picture? Did you take pictures?"

"Of course not. What for?"

"I don't know. Some sexual reason, maybe."

"Not likely. For God's sake, Randy was obsessed with not letting anyone know about us. Why would we photograph it?"

He struggled to sit up. I propped a few pillows up behind his head. He looked a little better sitting up.

I just stood there.

"You know," Barry said, "when you're gay you know it early. Real early. It's not like something you learn or are taught. You just know you're different. Randy was the first time for me. I was for him, too. It was sort of like a release, finding him. After living with it for so long, thinking you're the only one, hoping that if you just find the right girl it will all go away, blaming yourself. All that shit. And then we found each other. It was . . . healing. For both of us."

"How long were you together?" I asked, struggling for control.

"Just a few months, senior year."

"What happened?"

"Randy suddenly just cut it off. I never understood why. It wasn't like anything happened between us. But he just stopped it, said it was all a mistake, that he really wasn't gay. And that it was perverted and disgusting. It devastated me. I couldn't be with anyone for years after that. I even tried a woman once, which was a goddamned disaster. And then, for Christ's sake, I couldn't get enough of men. I began to go to the bathhouses down here—shit, I did that for years until I found Steve. Steven and I were together four years. Oh, what's the difference. Steve died. And now . . . well, you see the rest."

"Then you were never with Randy again after high school?"

"I left for Berkeley in September and never saw him again." He stopped. "What do you want, Jack? Why dredge it all up now?"

I couldn't answer, but he didn't seem to expect an answer.

"When Randy suddenly stopped it, we'd been making plans to see each other when we were in college," Barry said. "And then, suddenly, he refused to even talk to me."

I wiped my eyes.

Barry reached over and touched my arm with his bony fingers. "What's wrong, Jack?"

I felt like I was in a surrealist play, receiving compassion from a dying man.

"When did Randy stop seeing you, Barry?"

"When? It was right around the time of Woodstock," he said. "Right after that thing with Lana Paluka. The day after, in fact."

*The capacity for self-delusion is the principal
accomplishment of the soul.*

—*Aldous Huxley,* The Doors of Perception

29

Rain was already pelting the ground by the time Randy Slessenger turned the corner on his street; the air was filled with the crackle of thunder. Randy had fled from the meadow and ridden down from the mountain dangerously fast, heart pounding, tears blurring his vision as he pedaled. He was crying uncontrollably by the time he approached his house.

He couldn't go home like this, with tears streaming down his face. He got off his bike and laid it down by the side of the road, then ran into the woods. He wanted the forest to consume him, envelop him in its coolness, in the scent of pine. It was waiting for him, expectant. He lay down on a bed of pine needles, turned his face to the sky, and allowed his tears to flow free and mingle with the rain.

Randy Slessenger had known since he was ten years old that there was something wrong with him. He could pretend to feel what the other boys felt, and sometimes the fear would go away. But nothing could have prepared him for the pulse-pounding terror he felt when Lana took off her clothes in Devil's Meadow. He looked at the faces of the other boys, flushed, restless, ready; then he looked down and saw his penis as limp as an old rag.

He could tell himself now, lying here in a soaking rain, that if he hadn't been so chickenshit scared, he could have done it. Or he could tell himself that just because he couldn't get it up for Lana didn't mean he couldn't get it up for some other girl. What about Judy Cannon? She was always teasing him in school; she liked him. If it had been Judy, he would have been able to do it. Lana had those wide hips and big boobs. Judy was more his type. Slim. Almost no boobs at all. He just liked girls skinny, that's all.

He could tell himself that, but he would know it wasn't true. He knew it wasn't true because when he lay on his bed at night he thought about the way Alan Wells looked when he swam, the muscles along his back, the bronze skin glistening in the water. Sometimes he would count when he had these thoughts, try to concentrate on the numbers. One . . . two . . . three . . . but nothing he did could stop the thoughts, the feelings he had. Once he got hold of a *Playboy* magazine and tried masturbating with the centerfold open on his bed, but it didn't work. Nothing worked. He was like a broken dam; the thoughts just kept coming, welling up, pressing on him, driving themselves through.

And now, lying here, all he could think was that the guys *knew*. They knew how disgusting he was, the repulsive things he thought about at night. They had seen the fear in his face; they had seen everything. Why hadn't he just walked away when Lana started to take off her clothes? He could have said he didn't think it was right, or that he was too stoned, or that he didn't want to, but instead he stood there like the rest of them, and when his turn came he even lay down on top of her. And they *saw* it all. They—

"Randy? What in God's name is wrong?"

He opened his eyes. No. It was a dream. A nightmare. His father was standing there in the rain, looming over him.

Randy tried to sit up, but his body wouldn't move.

"Randy, what the hell are you doing? It's pouring."

He rolled over, pushed himself up onto his knees.

"Randy!"

He managed to stand, wiped his eyes, turned. "Dad, I—"

"Why the hell are you lying in the middle of the woods? Are you hurt?"

"No, I . . ." He started to move away, but his father caught him by the shoulder and whirled him around.

"Randy!"

A fresh flood of tears came, then anger.

"Why are you following me?"

"I wasn't following you. I saw your bike by the side of the road. I thought maybe you were hurt."

Randy wiped his eyes and his nose with the back of his hand.

"Well, I'm not. I'm fine." He tried to wriggle out of his father's grasp.

"Oh, yes, you look fine, son. Now tell me what's wrong."

Sometimes Randy thought about telling his father. But he could never imagine saying the actual words, because his father's fury and disgust would rise up and swallow him whole. No. He would have to keep it a secret; he would have to hope and pray that the guys didn't know, or hadn't guessed. And he would have to carry around his secret for the rest of his life, like a burden he could never lay down.

"Randy, *what is wrong with you?*"

Randy Slessenger looked into his father's eyes. Sometimes it seemed to him that his father had figured it out already and that that was why he looked at him that way.

Randy knew what Jerry Slessenger wanted. He wanted a red-blooded American boy, a boy who would, if given half a chance, fuck anything in skirts, a boy who would eventually marry, and have children, and give him grandchildren in his old age.

But Randy Slessenger would never do any of those things. Deep in his heart, no matter how many excuses he made, no matter what he did to distract himself, no matter how stoned he got, Randy had known he was gay since he was ten years old.

30

The night after Alan testified at Ethan's trial, Dad and Alan and I went to a bar in Kingston. Drinking with my father was a lark for me; I was heavily into drugs by the end of freshman year.

The place was dingy, almost as sleazy as Adley's, and there were about six or seven other men there, working-class types, nursing a beer or a drink after work.

I remember Dad kept toasting Alan as if he had done something very special and brave.

"I was proud of you up there on the stand," Dad said again and again, raising his glass.

"Yeah," Alan said, "I was something, wasn't I?"

I remember there was a woman at the bar, not unattractive but wearing a minidress that was about two sizes too small. She was the only woman in the place and she kept getting up from the bar and playing the same song on the jukebox, over and over. I remember the song: it was the Jefferson Airplane's "Somebody to Love." She would drop another quarter into the slot, then sit down again at the bar, close her eyes, and mouth the words to the song with a pained expression on her face, as if she were performing on a stage.

She was about to play the song for maybe the tenth time when Dad said, "Hey, lady, you play that song one more time and we're going to get ugly. My two boys and I are going to get real ugly."

"Dad!" I said.

Alan started to laugh; then Dad began to laugh, too. I stayed very quiet after that, and their laughter went on for what seemed a very long time. Soon everyone in the bar was laughing at her.

She glared at the three of us, then gulped the rest of her drink down and walked out.

Everyone in the bar, including the bartender, began to clap.

It took me over an hour to drive uptown in the rush hour gridlock. The outer door of the tenement at the corner of Ninety-Sixth and Third was open. I stood under a dim lightbulb in a lobby that smelled of cooking and urine, scanning the names on the roster. Most of the slots were empty, the ones listed were mostly Spanish names: Rodriguez in 2B; Pina in 3A; Mirabelles in 5C. There it was: E. Percelli, 4B. I buzzed and waited.

Nothing happened.

I buzzed again.

Nothing.

I buzzed Pina. The door opened, and I climbed the steps to the fourth floor. I stood for a moment on the landing listening to the sounds of a thin-walled tenement building—a baby crying, a radio blasting, a couple screaming at each other above the din of the music.

I knocked on the door of 4B, then tried the knob. Locked.

I sat down on the steps, trying to figure out what to do. It took me nearly fifteen minutes to get up the nerve to throw my weight against the flimsy door until it gave way.

Inside, I found myself standing in a small single-room apartment with one very dirty window, wide open. There was a battered chest of drawers and an unmade bed in one corner, and a kitchen of sorts along one wall, a pile of dirty dishes in the sink. A bowl of soggy-looking cereal and a glass of milk were sitting on the counter across from the sink. Whoever lived here had left in a hurry, right in the middle of breakfast.

There was no desk, no telephone. I checked the dresser but there didn't seem to be any personal papers. No photographs. A transient apartment for someone who moved around a lot.

I went into the bathroom, found nothing of interest, then walked around back of the kitchenette counter.

It was then that I noticed the blood. It was splattered on the back of the cabinet and in a pool on the floor. At first I wasn't sure what it was. It looked so dark against the wood floor and cabinet, and there was so much of it.

I bent down, touched the stain with my fingertip. It came up red, shockingly red. Fresh. And there were some skid marks, as if something heavy had been dragged across the floor.

I knelt there for a moment, my heart pounding in my chest. Then, I ran.

* * *

I checked myself into a hotel in midtown, and, once inside my room, I lay down on the bed, trying to think of a single other interpretation for what I had seen. I stared at the ceiling, but all I could see was that scene: the uneaten meal, the blood all over the place. Someone had been murdered there, the body removed. Ethan Skitt's body. It had to be.

No. It just wasn't possible. My brother hadn't killed anyone. I was jumping to conclusions.

I thought back to the day Alan asked me what it was like to love someone. Had his concern been something more than adolescent insecurity? Could that question have been the truest thing my brother had ever said to me?

No. Alan was not—could not be—capable of what I was thinking. If he had somehow blackmailed Randy into testifying to a lie, why hadn't Ethan said so at his trial?

And yet, as I lay there, Ethan's reason for killing Randy became suddenly, painfully, clear. I could even justify this revenge in my own heart. But if there had been some form of blackmail, why hadn't Ethan killed my brother first? Alan was the *reason* it had all started. Alan was the one who forced Randy into it. And why would Alan have killed Ethan now, when Ethan was the outlaw, when Ethan was the one everyone was looking for?

It suddenly seemed to me that everything I had believed my whole life was a lie. Before Donna threw me out, she told me that I would never be able to be truly intimate with anyone until I was willing to be intimate with myself. It sounded to me like a quote from one of the pop psychology books she was always reading, and maybe it was, but now it seemed that she was more right than wrong. I'd filled my life with diversions of one sort or another, with endless activities, even with women, in an effort to avoid being alone with myself. The fact that I'd chosen a career that proposed to discover the "truth" may, too, have been a way to keep busy discovering other people's truth in an effort to keep from discovering my own.

Even as I thought all this, another part of me was posing my journalist's questions: What relation did my brother have to Douglas Enworth and to the Miracle Foundation? What *was* the Miracle Foundation? How was the foundation related to whatever had happened between Alan and Ethan and Lana so many years ago? Why had Ethan kept quiet about what happened all these years—allowing himself to be convicted of attempted murder? So that he could execute his *own* revenge when the time came?

As I lay there I became more and more convinced that the Miracle Foundation was both the link and the key. I got the phone book out of the night table drawer and looked up first the Miracle

Foundation, then Douglas Enworth. It was a shot in the dark—I didn't even know if they were Manhattan-based. Neither was listed.

I picked up the phone and called Drummond. The receptionist tried to give me the runaround, but I insisted and, after a long wait, got Jonathan Baldwin on the phone.

"This is Jack Wells, Dr. Baldwin. We talked a few weeks back?"

"Yes, I remember," Baldwin said. "You quoted me out of context in the newspaper, Mr. Wells. You said I called Lana's survival a double miracle. What I said was that if I were *pressed* for a theory, I might say that."

Oh, brother. "I tried my best to be accurate, doctor."

"I suppose it is a nitpick," he said. "What can I do for you now?"

"I was wondering if you could tell me something about Douglas Enworth and the Miracle Foundation?"

He hesitated, then, "How did you find out about that?"

"Lana told me."

"I'm afraid I can't help you. The donations for Lana's care have been made anonymously."

"Can you at least tell me what city—or state, or country—they come from?"

"No. I'm afraid I can't tell you anything at all. The fact is, I don't know much about the Miracle Foundation myself."

"I understand," I said. But suddenly it didn't matter anymore whether I understood or not.

I had suddenly realized that I was the one who had given Alan Ethan Skitt's address.

Sleep was impossible. I needed to keep moving, keep busy, keep going. Keep hoping that it was all a mistake. I tried to think it all through. I could continue in the direction I was going and hope for the best, or I could stop where I was, forget the whole thing. To do that, I would have to get the money back from Lana and tell Saferstein there was no book in this.

Saferstein, the book. It all seemed a million miles away. The thing was, if I told Saferstein I couldn't do it, he would probably get someone else. Someone who might not discover what I had discovered. Or who might, which was worse.

Desperately needing to do something ordinary, I called my house for messages. The phone rang twice, then the machine answered. I listened to my voice on the machine: "Hi, this is Jack Wells and you know the bit . . . Wait for the beep."

"Jack, it's Marvin Saferstein. How's it going? Call me as soon as you get back. Let's talk."

There were four other messages. From Jim Harling. From my son Craig. A second message, less friendly, from Saferstein.

The last message was from Alan. "Hey, kiddo, call me back as soon as you can."

I hung up.

At about three A.M., in a state of torpor that felt like the prelude to complete hysteria, I went into the bathroom to take a shower. I felt filthy, as if I had been touched by something unclean.

When I stepped out of the shower, I caught a glimpse of myself in the steamy bathroom mirror. My face looked puffy, my eyes bloodshot. I reached up to wipe the steam from the mirror; it was then that I realized my fingerprints were all over that apartment: I had broken the door down, touched everything, left my mark everywhere. The police were probably there right now, taking *my* prints.

No. They couldn't be. The police would only be taking prints if they decided there'd been a murder, and since there was no body . . . But they'd find the body, eventually. And when they did they'd have physical evidence linking me to the crime—my brother had set it up to look that way. He knew I was planning to go there, so he got there first. He'd framed Ethan, now he was trying to frame me.

But why would he *kill* Ethan? Why not kill Lana? Now that she had awakened, she was the real danger to him. She was the only one left, except Alan, who could tell what really happened. Ethan had probably been telling the truth when he said he didn't know.

How, I thought feverishly as I tossed and turned all night, could I have lived with Alan, grown up beside him, shared his thoughts, listened to his schemes and his ideas, felt his charged energy like a pulse that never stopped, and not known what he was, what he was capable of? Was I blind, stupid, dull? Was he? Did he think I would let him get away with framing me?

I finally fell asleep just before dawn, awakening only a few hours later. I needed to find out what was going on—the whole thing, not just bits and pieces of it. I dressed, walked over to the library to get a copy of the *Foundation Directory*. There it was. The Miracle Foundation. Box Number 9847. Main Post Office. New York City.

The main post office in Manhattan is a neoclassic beauty of a building, graced inside with astonishingly intricate frescos painted on its high ceilings, and resounding with echoing clanks and booms. Most of the private boxes line the wall at the front, rows and rows of them, each numbered with a three- or four-digit

number. I scanned the rows but didn't come to number 9847 until I turned a corner and found another huge section of boxes
along one side of the building. I peered inside the tiny glass window. It was empty.

I stepped back and leaned against the wall near the corner,
where I could watch the box without being too conspicuous. I
decided to break up the day into three shifts, with a fifteen-minute
break at ten, another at eleven-forty-five, and a half-hour break
for lunch at around two-thirty. If I stood there ninety-five percent
of the time I would eventually catch anyone coming in.

I took my first break early, out of sheer boredom. My feet and
legs were starting to cramp up by two o'clock, but just before
my lunch break, someone slid mail into the box from behind. I
walked up and peered inside, turned my head this way and that,
but it was hopeless. I was unable to read anything on the envelope through the small glass.

I decided to stay put, skip lunch.

When four o'clock came, I realized I might have to keep watch
a long time. I didn't think it would be more than a week—no one
would rent a box and wait longer than a week to claim their mail.
On the other hand, I probably wouldn't have a job to go back to
after that long, or a book to write, either.

At about eight I went back to my hotel, went out for something
to eat around nine, then came back to my hotel and went to sleep.
I called no one. I saw no one.

The next morning I was back at the box by eight o'clock, going
through the same routine. I had a lot of time to think as I
watched. One moment I was filled with rage, the next on the verge
of tears. I was mortified at having attended that meeting in Alan's
home. How could he think that he could hold a high political
office? Did my parents have any idea of who their other son was,
of what he had done? Could they have known about it all these
years and done nothing? And what about Jocelyn? And Alan's
sons? And me? Like a fool, I had raced over to Alan's house and
insisted he get protection from Ethan, when it was Ethan who
needed protection from him.

On the third morning of my vigil at the post office, a completely
bald, impeccably dressed middle-aged man approached the box,
opened it, and took out the letter. I followed him outside, east
on 38th, north on Fifth. When he went into a men's shop a few
blocks up, I waited at the corner, watched the door until he came
out a few minutes later, then followed him to a small office building on East 45th.

I took the elevator with him to the fourth floor. He stopped in front of Suite 400. The sign on the door read "Strother Brill, Attorney at Law." Which explained why Douglas Enworth wasn't listed in the Manhattan directory.

Strother Brill, Attorney at Law, practiced alone in a small but beautifully appointed suite. Plush plaid sofas in the reception area over an oriental rug, fruitwood desks, a spectacular secretary in front of the latest in high-speed computer equipment.

"May I help you, sir?" The receptionist had a British accent, of course.

"I'd like to see Mr. Brill, please."

"Do you have an appointment?"

"No, I don't. My name is Jack Wells."

"I'm sorry, Mr. Wells, Mr. Brill won't be able to see you without an appointment."

"Look, if you'd just buzz him, I'm sure he'll see me."

She pushed the intercom buzzer. "Mr. Brill, there's a Mr. Wells here to . . . that's right, Wells."

"Tell him it's about the Miracle—"

She hung up the phone. "He'll see you." Then she rose and guided me down a small hallway.

Strother Brill stood up behind a gleaming red rosewood desk, held out his hand. "Mr. Wells. It's nice to finally meet you."

I simply stood there, obviously confused; Brill withdrew his hand. "Pardon me, but didn't you inform my secretary that you were Alan Wells?"

I reached out to shake his hand. "Yes. Of course."

"Yes, well, won't you sit down, Mr. Wells?"

I sat.

"May I ask why you've come in person?" he said. "Haven't my reports been satisfactory? Do you wish to change the arrangements?"

"No."

"I'm sure you are heartened that your generosity has been rewarded. Miss Paluka is most grateful for everything you've done for her. Of course, I have continued to protect your anonymity, but she asked me to convey her appreciation anyway." He hesitated. "Now that she'll be getting out of the hospital, do you wish me to continue the foundation's work?"

"Yes, I do."

"Will you be choosing another recipient?"

"You mean there's only been *one?*"

He stared at me for a moment, then dropped his eyes and the formal manner. "Who the hell are you?"

"My name is Jack Wells."

"*Jack* Wells?"

"Alan Wells's brother. I followed you here from the post office."

"You *what?*"

"I followed you."

The man sank down in his seat behind the desk.

"How can I help you, Mr. Wells?"

I'd had enough. I reached across the rosewood desk, grabbed his tie, and pulled him to his feet.

"Now look, Brill, I want to know what the hell is going on." I shoved him back into his chair.

He looked as if he'd never been touched before and found it completely distasteful. He straightened his tie, cleared his throat.

"I don't know what you're talking—"

"But you do, Mr. Brill. I'm a reporter for a paper up in Westchester. In the course of my preliminary work on a book about the Lana Paluka case, I discovered that Lana had an anonymous benefactor called the Miracle Foundation."

"She does. So what?"

"You tell me."

"I'm a reputable attorney," he said. "I set up a foundation for a Mr. Alan Wells to pay for the upkeep of a patient who was then in a state mental hospital."

"Did he tell you *why* he wanted you to do this?"

"He only said he was interested in this particular woman. He wanted her to have the best care, in the best facility—"

"How much does the best cost, Brill?"

"Three hundred thousand per year. All of it goes directly to the Drummond Center. Less my fee."

"What's that?"

"Look, Wells, I don't have to divulge my personal finances to you. This is all perfectly legitimate, completely—"

"Then why the box number? Why all the secrecy? Why use a fake name?"

He shrugged. "I was following my instructions. Your brother has a perfect right to give his money away in whatever manner he chooses. It's not against the law to make a charitable contribution anonymously."

"Maybe not," I said. "But there's *something* illegal going on here. And I want to know what the hell it is."

Strother Brill hesitated only a moment before saying, "I have no fucking idea." Then he pushed the intercom on his desk and said, "We are finished now, Sylvia. Would you please show Mr. Wells out?"

31

AUGUST 1969
COMITY, NEW YORK

What woke Lana that morning was the oppressive August heat
and the tinny intermittent rattle of the fan in the window. The
fan didn't help; her nightgown, her sheets, her skin were all damp.
She might have been dreaming, but she wouldn't remember the
dream because the moment she opened her eyes she was over-
taken by a single thought: This would be the last time she would
wake up in this bed above the bar. Lana had wanted to leave ever
since graduation two months ago, but it had only been last night
that Ethan had finally agreed.

Sarah always let them use Ethan's bedroom to have sex, but
last night they had spread out a blanket in a clearing in the woods
next to Lookout Point. It was a clear, starless night. There was
no longer awkwardness between them as there had been at the
beginning; they took off their clothes even before they kissed. She
had taken him in her mouth. She loved to do that, even with Alan
she had loved it. She loved the energy of the organ, the power.
There was something miraculous about the feel of it when it was
hard, something that couldn't be experienced fully, except with
the mouth. She had learned to bring Ethan to the edge, then pull
away so that he could pleasure her. He would always touch every
part of her body with his hands or his lips or his tongue before
he entered her.

There had been a moment of decision: she opened her eyes as
Ethan pumped inside her, catching sight of white thighs, a lean
shoulder, his face in the moonlight. Such a fine, sad face, so at
peace when he was making love to her. He opened his eyes, as if
he knew she was watching him.

He smiled. "We'll leave tomorrow."

235

They were leaving Comity for good; they had saved over a thousand dollars this summer between them, Ethan with his job at Sherber's Plant Nursery and Lana with her cashier job at Woolworth's. And Ethan had nearly a thousand dollars more saved, from all his other jobs. At one point last year he'd had two jobs, one after school at Sherber's, and one on Saturday at the dump.

With two thousand dollars they would never need to come back to this town. Except maybe to visit Sarah.

Lana looked at her alarm clock. It was nearly nine. She had promised to meet Ethan at eleven. She was to pack her backpack with everything she would need, then meet Ethan at Devil's Meadow for the ceremony. They didn't need some minister to marry them, some piece of paper. They would marry themselves with their own words; then they were going to hitch a ride up to Bethel for the rock festival. She'd heard people were coming from all over the country, had been gathering for days. And after that they would go wherever their hearts and the wind took them. All she needed was Ethan, to fill up the empty place inside her.

She didn't blame Ethan for hesitating to leave. Sarah had been in a terrible state these last few months. It had been less than a year ago that Laban had called the Skitt family together and announced that he had changed his name, legally, to Brent. Lana had been there that afternoon.

"*Brent?*" Rose started to laugh when Laban said it.

Adam, Lana, and Ethan looked over at Sarah, who just sat there and stared at her oldest son.

Laban stood up and began pacing around the room. "I told you I was going to change my name, Mom. Laban is a peculiar name. I'm sick and tired of being peculiar everywhere I go."

" 'Brent' is peculiar, Laban," Sarah said.

"It's not. It's American," Laban/Brent said.

"What's so great about America?" Ethan said.

Laban stopped pacing long enough to glare at Ethan.

"You know, I'm sick and tired of you saying stuff like that. Try going to some other country and see if the people are so free to smoke pot and call the government imperialist pigs." He looked back at his mother. "I'm sorry. I don't mean any disrespect to you. Really I don't."

There were tears in Sarah's eyes. She got up silently, wearily, and went upstairs to her bedroom. Laban walked out of the house, closing the door softly behind him. The next day he sent word that he had joined the army. He was shipped off to Vietnam only a few months later, to some place called Hue. The name—so far away, so alien, so incomprehensible—was on the TV news every night. Sometimes Ethan would come over to the Palukas' to watch it. Lana would watch him watch, sitting there on the edge of his seat with his hands clenched, listening intently to every word as the announcer recited the casualties of the day. Ethan kept saying he thought his brother was out of his mind to join the army. What for? Nixon had already announced his Vietnamization policy; the U.S. was already starting to withdraw forces.

Then, in June, Nathan had to be sent away. Since Laban left, he had grown more and more withdrawn and would often sit rocking, mute, back and forth on the front steps of the house, hands clamped over his ears, eyes closed, his face in a grimace of pain. Sarah and Ethan had taken him to a doctor at Comity Hospital, but nothing made any difference, and Sarah finally agreed to send Nathan to Edgewater. Ethan had supported her decision; she—none of them—could deal with Nathan or with whatever it was that tormented him any longer.

It had all been hard on Sarah, and Ethan hated to leave her. But Lana and Ethan couldn't live their lives for Sarah, could they? They needed to find out what life, their life, was all about. Ethan was the one who'd always said that life wasn't about this town; life was about the two of them together.

Lana believed that. They could hitch across the country, they could be in Washington for the peace march planned in the fall, they could go to Europe—to Amsterdam, where the kids were all free and could smoke pot in the streets. Or maybe to Italy or Nepal. Or Bangladesh. Or they could go down south to New Hope City, that commune Ethan had heard about, where life and work and spirit were shared. They would be welcomed there.

Lately Ethan had been worried about the draft lottery everyone kept talking about. What if he were drafted? She couldn't bear that. There wasn't a chance he wouldn't be shipped out to Vietnam, even if they really were starting to withdraw the troops. You couldn't believe anything Nixon said. Maybe they should go to Canada.

She lay there in her bed turning these things over in her mind. It didn't matter where they went really, as long as they were together.

The last few days' clothes—her blue jeans, a couple of T-shirts, one of the floppy-brimmed hats she and Ethan had gotten when they hitched down to New York City—lay in a pile on the chair at the foot of her bed. The dress she planned to wear, the white one with the embroidered bodice Sarah had given her, was hanging on the closet door.

She could hear Ellie rustling around, getting ready for the day. There was something awful about the thought of meeting her mother in the hallway in her nightgown that morning, both of them seeking the same bathroom. Why couldn't Sarah have been her mother?

She lay still, listening now to her father's sounds, to the creak of the floorboards in the hallway, the sound of urine hitting the toilet bowl from a distance, the gush of tap water, the squirt of shaving cream, the scrape of a razor blade across a stubbled male face.

Now she could hear that her mother had gone to the kitchen. She got up, took a shower, and got dressed—carefully, more carefully than she ever did. She even put on lipstick, a new Mary Quant lipstick she'd bought on her lunch hour at Woolworth's. Alan Wells had been in there with Cindy Watson, but he pretended not to know her until she passed by them on the way back to her register. They were standing by the book rack, and he said, "Nice hat, Paluka Bazooka."

She could hear the two of them laughing as she rang up a sale, grateful they hadn't bought anything.

She brushed her hair, looked at herself in the mirror. The lipstick was iridescent pink and made her skin look very pale. Ellie always said she looked fat in the dress. But her hair was beautiful, so full, so long.

Ellie was at the kitchen table drinking coffee, a cigarette hanging out of her mouth. Her pink robe was partially open, just enough to reveal the peach-colored lace at the bodice of her nightgown, the white flesh beneath it. Her face was a smudge of yesterday's makeup. Ellie always wore her makeup to bed.

Ellie barely glanced up when Lana came into the kitchen. Her mouth was like a dark slash. She was staring, empty-eyed, at the small portable television she kept on the counter.

"Hey, Lana—look at this, they got your movie on. Your namesake." She laughed.

"What?"

"*Madame X.*"

Lana glanced at the set. She did indeed recognize Lana Turner on the screen. It was the part of the movie where she testifies in the courtroom.

"For God's sake, Ellie, you've seen this movie a hundred times."

Ellie didn't take her eyes from the screen. "Can't you call me Mom, like all the rest of the kids?"

"Maybe if you were like all the rest of the mothers."

"They got no dreams in this town, honey," Ellie said. "You just keep that in mind. Just remember why I named you Lana." She gestured toward the screen, as if a glance at *Madame X* would explain all.

"Shit, Ellie—"

"Watch your mouth, Lana." Finally, Ellie noticed the back-pack. "Where are you going?"

"Out."

"What are you wearing that for?"

"Because if I don't wear it I'll be naked."

"Very funny. It makes you look fat, you know."

"Leave me alone."

Ellie put on her hurt look. "I'm just trying to help you, Lana. If you don't want to listen to my advice, then don't, but you're only hurting yourself. Slutting around the way you do. And with that Skitt boy, too. You're always over there. Never here."

"Why the hell should I be here? All you ever fucking do is yell at me."

Her mother slapped her. "I told you to watch that mouth."

The slap stung her face, but she didn't draw her hand to it.

"What the hell were you doing last night until two in the morning?"

"I was with Ethan."

John Paluka came in then, wearing only pants and an undershirt. Hair, graying and abundant, spread along his back and shoulders like weeds.

"Jesus! Are you two fighting again? Leave the kid the hell alone, Ellie."

"Do you think for once I could talk to my own daughter without any help from you?"

John Paluka opened the refrigerator, took out the orange juice carton, and poured himself a glass.

"Good God, Ellie! She's gonna marry that kid; why can't you leave them alone?"

"Marry him? Over my dead body."

John Paluka gulped down the juice in one swig, then wiped his mouth with the back of his hand and walked out of the room.

"You think screwing that boy'll get you somewhere?" Ellie said.

Lana couldn't help the happy flush as she remembered what she and Ethan had done last night.

"Answer me, Lana! You think that'll get you somewhere? If you'd lose some goddamned weight, you'd be kinda pretty. Then you wouldn't have to take up with loonies."

"Shut up, shut up, Ellie."

Out the door Lana went, slamming it behind her. She hesitated at the bottom of the stairs to adjust the pack on her back.

"So where the hell are you going?"

Without turning around, Lana called, "Goodbye, Ellie. I'll see you in dreamland. Don't wait up for me."

And walked away to the sound of her mother's screaming,

"Don't you talk to me that way. I want to know where you're going."

To hell with her. Good riddance.

It took her fifteen minutes to walk to Ethan's. He was out in the garden in front of the house with his sister, Rose.

Rose started to jump up and down. "Lana, Lana!"

"What happened?" Ethan said. "How come you're here early?"

She shrugged. "Miss Radio City and I had a fight."

Ethan put his arms around her, kissed her. "Doesn't matter."

"Lana, did you bring macrame for me today?"

"No, Rose baby, but I've got a stick of gum." She pulled the gum from her backpack.

"Thanks." Rose took it as if it were the best present in the world, then scampered off.

Ethan laughed. "I think sometimes Rose is happier to see you than I am. But then I know she couldn't be."

Lana glanced over at Rose, swinging back and forth in the tree swing, contentedly chewing her gum. She smiled. She and ten-year-old Rose had grown close in the last few months ever since Rose admired Lana's handmade macrame shoulder bag, and Lana showed her how to do macrame herself.

"Hi, Lana." Sarah was standing in the doorway. "Ethan tells me you two plan to hitch up to Woodstock today."

Lana held her breath.

"I heard about it on the radio this morning," Sarah said. "Sounds like they're going to get a lot more people than they expected."

"I thought you were going to say we couldn't go," Lana said. It was so hard for her to get used to Sarah.

"It's not up to me, Lana. You two have to decide." She put her arm around Ethan's shoulder. "It's just that I wish you wouldn't take all that money with you. I'll keep the money. Then after the festival, come back. And then you can leave."

Ethan looked at her, then at Lana.

"She's probably right," Lana said.

Ethan nodded, took their money out of the pocket of his backpack and handed it to Sarah. She was still clutching all the bills when they walked away.

Ethan put his arm around her. "I've got something very special planned for our ceremony in Devil's Meadow today."

"What is it?"

"You'll see."

Lana smiled. It was the most important day of her life.

32

The first time I became consciously aware of just how vicious Alan could be was when we were about eleven. There was a boy who lived one street over from us named Jason Marwell, a skinny, clumsy kid who played sports as if he had two left feet. In gym, he was always picked dead last to a chorus of groans from whichever team got stuck with him.

One Saturday morning, Greg and Randy met us at our house; then we all set off looking for something to do. All the backyards of our street and Jason's abutted, with a small patch of woods in between. We cut through the brush and came out in Jason's backyard, where we found him playing catch with a softball. And Lucy Reynolds. Granted, we sometimes played with Lana, but that was different, more like charity. Jason playing with a girl was absolutely hilarious.

"Hey Marwell!" Alan yelled. "You found a team that wanted you!"

"Ha ha," Jason said. "Very funny." Jason Marwell wasn't too quick, either.

"Keep practicing and you could end up captain of the girls' team, Marwell," Alan said.

Greg: "They'll call it Marwell's Marauders, and I bet you'll cream every girl team from here to New Jersey."

Me: "Yeah, but watch out, the girls are tough in New Jersey."

"Aw, come on," Jason said. "I was just showing her how to throw the ball."

"Better you should let her show you."

"Don't be stupid, Greg," Alan said, "pin-dicks can't show anyone anything. Come on, Marwell, show us your pin-dick."

And that was when Jason started to cry and fled inside the house.

Of course, it was the kind of thing any boys—not just us—might say, but Alan had managed to pick the one thing that would completely crush Jason. It was true—I had noticed it in the locker room at school. Jason had an unusually small penis.

When I got to Drummond I headed straight for the south lawn, but Lana wasn't there. I found her in her room, reading in a chair by the window, the noonday sun streaming in around her, illuminating her pale skin. I noticed she was wearing a thin rawhide band around her forehead, flower-child style.

Standing in the doorway—a humbled man, a frightened man—I watched her for a few moments and tried to gather my thoughts. She had a peaceful expression on her face that didn't change when she looked up and saw me.

"I have to talk to you," I said.

She closed the book. "Come on in."

My resolve wavered. How was I going to find the words to tell her Ethan was dead?

"Jack? What's wrong?"

Haltingly, I walked into the room.

"I found out . . . I mean, I know about Alan now, Lana. You were right. I know Ethan didn't try to kill you. He loved you. Alan's . . . I think he blackmailed Randy into saying Ethan had done it."

"Blackmailed? With what?"

"I'm not sure. Maybe a photograph. I found out that Randy was a homosexual. He didn't want anyone to know. I think Alan blackmailed him. Alan must have been the one who tried to kill you."

"I know that, Jack."

I sank down on the chair next to the bed. "All this time you remembered?"

She sighed, stood up and walked over to the window, looked out. "No. I don't remember. I just can't remember."

"Then how did you know?"

"From the moment I woke up I knew in my heart that Ethan wouldn't have done it, Jack. I told you that. All I needed to do was start with what I knew and work backward. And besides, Ethan told me. You remember the letter I was reading that day, the one I said was from a friend. It was from Ethan. A lot of it was personal stuff, but mainly it was instructions. He didn't say anything about why Randy had, like, gone along with what Alan said. He only said that if I were to remember what happened that day, I shouldn't tell anyone. He said that my life wouldn't be worth spit if I remembered. Because Alan would kill me."

All the things we Wellses had done to her, and to Ethan, and to Sarah. How was I going to tell her that there was one more thing we had done? The most awful thing, the thing that would finally destroy her.

I just simply said it. "I think Alan killed Ethan."

Her expression didn't change.

"I found out where Ethan lived. I went there. There was blood all over the place . . . as if someone had been . . ."

She started to cry, a soft whimper at first; then she sat down in the chair and began to sob. I have never seen anyone weep like that, great wrenching sobs that made her whole body shudder. "Why didn't he come to me?" she kept saying. "I knew he didn't do it."

"He couldn't come, Lana. They were all looking for him. He was a fugitive."

Over and over I told her I was sorry, but of course it didn't matter what I said, and when I put my arms around her I think it was more to comfort me than her. She didn't protest; her body was limp and damp in my arms. I held her for a very long time.

"Come on," I said when her crying had finally subsided. "We'll go to the police and tell them the whole story."

She didn't move.

"Lana?"

"I'm sorry, Jack." She wiped her eyes. "I can't."

"What do you mean, you can't? There's no statute of limitations on something like this. With your testimony, Alan will be tried and he'll be convicted. Of both crimes."

"What testimony? I told you I don't remember."

I stared at her, unsure of what to do or say. "But you know what the truth is."

"So what if I do?"

"Then you've got to do something—"

"You want me to lie and say I remember when I don't? You want me to lie to the law?" Her eyes were wide and bright and cold.

"But you can't let Alan get away with this, Lana. He'll get away with it."

"He's been getting away with it for twenty years."

"He has to pay for what he's done." My voice sounded high-pitched, shrill, as if it belonged to someone else.

"You're right, Jack, he does. And don't think I don't want to be

the one to make him pay—you cannot imagine the hatred I feel
toward your brother. I really, completely, totally, loathe him. He
is subhuman. An animal, just like Ethan used to say."

"Then why won't you help?"

"Because Ethan said the most important thing was that no
matter what happened I wasn't to tell anyone. No matter what."

"But Ethan is dead, Lana."

"No matter what."

"But *why?*"

She didn't answer.

Finally, I said, "Well, I'm going," and started for the door again.

"I'll deny it, Jack," she said. "I'll say I remember it just the
way everyone thinks it happened. Ethan and I had an argument,
he pushed me, he served his time, and that's it. With Ethan dead,
I'm afraid they'll think you're, well, like some kind of a nut."

"But—"

"Believe me, Jack. It's not that I don't want to pay your brother
back. I do. I spend my nights planning what I'd like to do to him,
thinking up something really awful. Something fitting. Bloody.
Maybe with a knife." She paused. "And I want to pay your friend
Randy back, too. But then Randy has already paid, don't you
think?"

I stopped. "What do you mean?"

"What do you think I mean, Mr. Reporter?"

"I don't know."

"Well, maybe you should find out."

"About Randy? Ethan killed him. For revenge. I could testify
to it. It's understandable, they'll give him a pardon—"

"What good would that do?" She wiped her eyes.

"It would . . . it would clear his name. People would understand."

"You're wrong, Jack."

"What do you mean?"

"Ethan wouldn't have killed *anyone.*"

"Lana, he had spent thirteen years in jail. How do you know
what he would or wouldn't have done after that?"

"Hey, how do you know *I* didn't blow Randy's brains into next
week?"

"Because you were—"

"What? Locked up in here, right? A zombie, right?"

"Yes. That's right."

"Well, Jack," she said, "for a reporter, I'd say you're not too
fucking bright."

"Lana, Ethan stole the gun that killed Randy. A man saw him.
Identified him."

"I *know* Ethan didn't do it."

"But he pled guilty."

She was silent.

"You think Alan did it?" I said.

"I don't know. Maybe."

What was I going to say, that my brother wouldn't have done such a thing?

"Lana, if you have all this hatred in your heart, why won't you help me?"

She sat down on the chair again. "Because my faith in Ethan is stronger than my need for revenge."

My faith in Ethan is stronger than my need for revenge. Lana's words repeated over and over in my mind. They were still there, like a mantra, when I got to my parents' house.

My father was sitting outside on the back porch, his face hidden behind the newspaper he was reading, only the thick gray hair on top of his head visible. I stood for a moment watching him, wondering what I was doing there. Did I want him to help me convict his son? Did I want him to calm my panic and assure me that everything would be all right? The doctor says take two pills and call me in the morning.

Mostly, I think, I wanted him to be surprised. No, shocked. And even that wouldn't be enough. I needed my father to be horrified with an intensity that equaled my own. I wanted a moment when his face would crumble, drop, the color drain out of it. I wanted him to be as appalled as I was to think that his son would have committed such crimes, not mere white-collar crimes, but *murderous* crimes, killing crimes that spill flesh and blood.

And, too, I stood there not like a man but like a little boy, and I wanted him to make it somehow all go away.

"Jack!" He looked up from the paper. "Well, come on in and sit down, son. It's good to see you."

I dropped into the chair across from him.

"Your mother isn't here." He folded up the paper. "She went over to Mrs. Dymond's house. Some ladies' luncheon or something . . . Jack, what in hell is the matter?"

"Ethan Skitt didn't try to kill Lana, Dad," I said. "Alan did."

There was a long silence. I could hear the sounds of the cicadas out on the lawn, a hot frenzied buzzing surrounding us from everywhere.

Finally my father said, "I know that, Jack."

"You *know* it?" My voice sounded strangled, like someone had his hands on my throat. "How long have you known?"

He shrugged. "A long time."

"And you allowed him to get up there and—"

"I didn't *allow* him to do anything, Jack. He only told me afterward."

"When afterward?"

"A few years."

I stood up, moved to the other side of the porch. "And you didn't *do* anything?"

"Like what? Go to the police and tell them my son lied and put an innocent man in jail? Not on your life."

For a moment I stood there looking at my father, feeling hollow, unreal.

"Once the trial was over," he said, "there was nothing to be done."

I turned around and faced the lawn, leaned my hands against the railing for support. Suddenly, finally, it was all clear to me, like a picture on television where the character in the foreground suddenly comes into focus. My father was in the foreground.

And he wasn't going to fix this for me because *he* was what was broken.

"Yeah." I almost choked on the words. "Yeah, I guess there was nothing to be done." I turned to go, then stopped.

"Dad, did you perform an abortion on Lana back in junior high?"

"The Paluka girl?" he said. "No. Christ! He got her pregnant, too?"

"Too?" I said softly.

"A real lover, your brother. There was another one, though. Cindy something. But you were already in high school by then. She was four months along before she even told him she was pregnant. I sent her to Ellis Metcalf, practices obstetrics down in Ossining. I went to med school with him. You remember him. We had him and his wife to dinner a few times."

I nodded. "I remember."

Slowly, I turned and began to walk down the steps.

"Jack, wait a minute . . ."

I turned. "What for?"

He stood up and came over to me, put his hand on my shoulder. "You've got to understand my position. I love you and Alan more than anything . . . it would have killed your mother if I'd done anything—"

"This has nothing to do with Mom," I said. "You didn't do it for her; you did it for you."

Part Six

Ethan

And so he gathered in all his life forces, focused them,
directed them toward her. Even his roots
trembled with the effort. . . . Out of
a half he had become a whole.

—*Hermann Hesse, "Pictor's Metamorphosis"*

33

It was finding Laban's grave that shattered Ethan Skitt's façade,
unleashing a furnace of rage he had worked long and hard to control. Almost from the beginning, he had promised himself he
would survive, even as Lana had. When he said goodbye to Sarah
in the courtroom after the judge imposed sentence, he had told
her he didn't want to see her again. That was part of his survival.
Sarah had abandoned him, she believed he was guilty, and he
would not forgive her for that. He told her not to visit, or call,
or even write to him. And she hadn't. Now Laban was nearly
thirteen years dead, and Ethan hadn't even known.

Ethan took a knife from a kitchen drawer and slashed at the
old gray couch in the living room until the white stuffing burst
out. He touched the clock on the mantel, then threw it to the
floor. He went into his mother's bedroom on the second floor, to
her closet, pulled the dresses off their hangers, tossed them on
the floor until he had a heap of cloth in front of him. The whole
collection of antique dresses.

He yanked open every drawer of the vanity, pulling some of
them completely out, and dumped their contents onto his pile.
He should have found lipsticks and creams and jewelry, but
Sarah didn't hold with such things. When he was little, this didn't
matter. Sarah was everything. She gave them all comfort, and
safety, and contentment, and she wrapped it up for them like a
present. It was as if no one else existed but them. Yes, they all
went to school, but that was the "outside." Life was home, within
Sarah's walls.

On top of the dresser, there was a bottle of the purple oil Sarah

249

had always used on her skin. He opened it, passed the bottle under his nose, and stood for a moment, remembering the smell of her. Lilac. She was dark and beautiful, Ethan's mother, like a Nubian princess, a dark goddess. Her skin was flawless. It was almost sexual, the hold she had over Ethan, over all of them, even Rose. Yet she was not a sexual person, Ethan didn't think, not really. He had never had the sense that she needed the men who were their fathers, only that she kept them around so she could have babies. He could remember when Rose was born, she would sit for hours rocking her, looking into her baby eyes, singing a lullaby to her. Her singing voice was just like her speaking voice, lilting and musical.

Had he ever recovered from the shock of discovering his place in the world? He had been eleven the first time he'd spied on the Wells gang. He had taken to walking in the mountains when he was feeling bad—just to be alone. He liked to walk through the woods, picking up interesting leaves or rocks, staring up into the trees, occasionally sitting down on a stump to examine the city of insects it housed. Sometimes he would pick daisies for Sarah.

That's what he was doing when he saw them come out into the meadow that first time. He knew the boys from school—Randy Slessenger was in his class that year, a slip of a boy with slumped shoulders and frizzled hair; Greg Horan, bulky, loud, with a thick dumb neck; Jack Wells, a freckled redhead, shorter than his brother and not nearly as arrogant; and Alan Wells, clearly the leader of the group, taking long graceful strides, a tall, elegant boy, with wavy dark hair and dimples and a flashing smile. As Ethan watched, suddenly Alan lay down on the ground and began to writhe around, making strange noises, cackling like a witch. Then each of the others took turns doing the same thing. At first Ethan had no idea what they were doing or why they thought it was so funny. Then he heard Alan say, "That's not like Skitt, Greg, that's more like *retard*."

He saw them do their Crazy Skitt routine many times after that. Spying on those boys became an obsession. He was there for their chicken games, and their Skitt games, and even their ball games. He was there, watching, when they started bringing Lana with them and when they started smoking pot. And when Randy started bringing his guitar up to the meadow.

Once, a few years later, Ethan actually saw Alan having sex with Lana up on Devil's Meadow. He watched the whole thing, even when Alan rolled off her and stood up and said, "Come on, let's go." Ethan had been so close he felt he could touch her skin.

It was no accident that he'd been up there the day when they all raped her. He watched the whole thing, thinking she wanted them to do it, and it was only afterward when he saw the tears that he understood. And when she lost the baby.

And even then he didn't understand.

Slowly, he poured the oil out of the bottle, watched it soak into the pile of clothes. The air was now thick with the smell of her. He inhaled it, then picked up Sarah's brush, ran his fingers over the hard bristles, pulling out long strands of her hair. Some of them were gray. She used to brush her long black hair one hundred times every night, without fail, and while she was brushing her hair, she would tell them stories. She would gather the six of them together, light a fire in the fireplace, and they would sit warm and cozy in front of it and listen to her.

". . . And all the court laughed when they saw that the emperor really was naked."

It was her favorite story. She said it showed how each person has to believe in what *he* sees in the world, not what anyone else sees.

"Laban, what do you see?"

Laban would say, "I see that people are cruel."

Sarah would shake her head. "They're cruel because they're afraid. Ethan, what do you see?"

Ethan would repeat something she had told them, "I see that God is all around us."

But as they got older, they all turned away from Sarah, one by one, each in his own way.

How many times had he come to back to this house, pained and raging, because he had nowhere else to go, nowhere to escape the taunts at school? He could remember searching for comfort in his brothers and sister, only to find them suffering too, each in his own way. All except Nathan, who suffered nothing, who danced to his own tune and always had, a tune that didn't include football games or boy's talk or friendships. And didn't long for them, either.

Sometimes Ethan thought it would be better to have been like Nathan, or even like Sarah, with her Bible-spouting and her theories and her pronouncements. She didn't care what people thought.

The truth was, a lot of the things Sarah said made sense to him. Like the time she became incensed over the war. It was 1965 and there was Sarah, with her handpainted sign that said STOP THE KILLING, marching around town hall. In some ways Sarah was ahead of her time. He had great respect for her sometimes.

Yet he hated her, too. She stayed inside the house once for nearly seven months. She ate only macrobiotic foods and insisted they all eat them too. Ethan ate so much brown rice that summer and fall that he lost almost fifteen pounds, and the school counselor made a house call. He found Sarah barricaded inside the house and had to speak to her through the window.

"Mrs. Skitt, I'm worried about your children." Everyone called her "Mrs." Ethan, who was hiding under the porch listening and watching through the slats, was aware of the implied condemnation in the way everyone said it.

Sarah peered through the glass at Mr. Bevins.

"Nothing to worry about, Mr. Bevins."

"I, ah, was wondering if the children were eating properly at home."

"More properly than you, I'd say."

"What are they eating?"

"We're on a completely macrobiotic diet."

"What does that consist of exactly, Mrs. Skitt?"

"Brown rice, mostly."

"Mrs. Skitt . . . children can't subsist on brown rice."

The humiliation at that moment wasn't even the worst of it. Thereafter lunch was provided for Ethan and his brothers and sister in the cafeteria at school. Each bite was a trial, but Ethan ate. He ate because he was tired of brown rice, even though eating the macaroni and cheese or peanut butter sandwich was betraying his mother. Sometimes he wanted to just howl and scream.

Her condition was something called agoraphobia, he found out later. It went away.

But that was only one time. Mostly, Sarah *wasn't* crazy, like everyone said. She just had her own ideas about things, that was all. She had taken a turn for the worse when they had to put Nathan away, but that was a day to make any mother crazy. He'd had so much rage then.

He still did. He picked up the knife again, bent down, began to slash at the oil-soaked clothing on the floor.

"Ethan?"

He turned. His mother was standing there, her shawl over her head. Slowly, she took off the shawl, folded it, laid it on the bed. She had aged quite a bit, but still wore her hair long. Now it was more than liberally sprinkled with gray. She was wearing a dress he remembered. It reached the floor, as did most of her dresses. The air was full of ghosts.

She held out her arms to him.

He looked over at the pile of her things on the floor, then at the knife in his hand. Finally he looked back at her and began to cry.

She put her arms around him. It felt good to be in her arms again.

He allowed her to hold him for a moment, then pulled away, stepped back. There was a wall between them.

"Everyone's gone, Ethan," she said. "Joshua and Laban are dead. Rose is happy in Oregon. Adam is in Maine. After I lost Joshua, I always knew all my babies would leave me one day."

Her *babies?* "What happened to Laban?"

"He was killed, they wrote to me—he died defending his country." There were tears in her eyes.

"Defending his country?"

She nodded.

"Why didn't you write and tell me?"

"Ethan," she said, "you told me not to write to you. You said you couldn't get through if I wrote. I wanted to—"

"Never mind. It doesn't matter now."

"My heart is full of grief, Ethan, that your brother died knowing I had anger in my heart toward him. Do you remember? Laban changed his name—"

"I remember. He just wanted to fit in, Sarah." He began to pick up the dresses from the floor.

She put out her hand. "It's all right, Ethan. I'll clean it all up." She stroked his cheek. "What have they done to you?"

He drew back. He would not suffer her pity.

"What about Nathan?"

Her eyes had a faraway look. "I still have Nathan."

"Where is he?"

"He's still at Edgewater, Ethan."

"Where's Lana?"

"She's in Massachusetts. At the Brody Institute."

"Why there?"

She shrugged. "I don't know."

"How is she?"

"She's the same, Ethan. She has not spoken."

He stood there and looked at her. The shock he'd felt when he first realized what people thought of her was as real and as potent as it was when he was eleven. He could still remember standing there watching those boys make fun of everything he knew, wondering who they were talking about. And then he realized that there was this bad thing they were calling his mother, this thing called crazy. He'd asked her what it meant. "It's a false word, Ethan, that word *crazy.* The language contains a lot of false words."

"Let me give you something to eat," she said now.

He nodded, followed her into the kitchen, watched while she

made a plate of tuna and cut vegetables for him. She heated up a can of soup. She arranged everything carefully on the plate, ladled the soup into a bowl, then put it all in front of him at the table.

He began to eat, taking each bite slowly, carefully, savoring the taste of the food. She sat down and watched him. Neither of them said anything. When he was done, he pushed the plates away.

"You remember we always used to ask you who our fathers were? I want you to tell me now."

"What does it—"

"It matters to me, Sarah."

She sighed, stood. "Your father, and Laban's father, was a carpenter. I left my parents because of him. I loved him."

"And Nathan's father? And Adam's?"

"He was a teacher, he meant nothing." She looked away.

"And Joshua's?"

"Parker McGill. I met him in church."

Ethan remembered him. He was a tall, dark man who came around and stayed for a few months but left after Sarah announced she was pregnant again. Ethan was seven at the time.

"And Rose?"

Sarah had never said who Rose Petal's father was, though for a while when Ethan was about ten, for a few months she went out of the house at night more often than she had. They all suspected she was meeting a man. Ethan wanted to follow her to see who it was, but Laban stopped him. But after Rose Petal was born, there were no more men.

"He was nothing," Sarah said. "He meant nothing. I loved you all more than life itself."

He remembered the time he was brought home by the school principal in his car, suspended for fighting with Alan Wells. Lana told him she saw Alan the next day in school. And it was Alan who started it.

"Ethan," Sarah had said. "You must not get into these fights. What do you care what other people say about you?"

"They say it about you, too."

"If I don't care, then why should you? The Bible says we must turn the other cheek."

He hadn't wanted to turn the other cheek. He hadn't wanted to be dragged up to Devil's Meadow to pray. Or to have the kids at school whisper and giggle when they saw him. He didn't want to march on Main Street when he was nine years old, the six of them carrying Sarah's signs. He didn't want to listen to her stories. Or to hear the kids laughing. Crazy Skitt.

Ethan Skitt knew about crazy, he had always known it, first-hand. That's how he'd been able to turn himself into Priestman. Nathan always spoke of himself in the third person because he said the voices wouldn't know where he was if he pretended he wasn't Nathan. It was where Ethan had gotten the idea for Priestman. It had kept him alive in the joint—nothing else would have.

After some practice, after some time, he would go back to thinking of himself as Ethan Skitt.

"Where's Alan Wells?" he said.

She stared at him.

"Do you know?"

She sat down at the table again. "He's still in town." Then, "Stay away from him, Ethan."

He felt a fresh surge of rage. "He ruined my life, Sarah. He—"

"He did the right thing, Ethan. He told what happened."

Now Ethan stared at her, tears coming to his eyes again. "You still believe what they said?"

She hesitated a moment, then said, "You've paid for your crime, Ethan. Don't think about it anymore. Stay here, we'll heal together."

"I can't stay, Sarah. Not while you don't believe me."

"It doesn't matter what I think, Ethan. Only God makes judgments on man."

"Don't quote the Bible to me; I can quote it right back to you. Whatsoever a man soweth, that he shall also reap."

There was a long silence. Finally, she walked over to the cabinet atop the sink, took a small metal box down from the top shelf, opened it.

She held out a stack of bills. "Here, Ethan, take it. It's yours."

It was the two thousand dollars he and Lana had saved, which they left with her before Woodstock. His fingers closed around it.

"I can't stay, Sarah."

"Where will you go?"

"I don't know."

She looked up at him, tears in her eyes.

"I did the best I could, Ethan."

"Why did you have all of us? Didn't you *know?*"

She stood up. "Don't negate your life."

"Why?" he said. "I want to know."

She smiled. "My babies were a gift from God, Ethan. All babies are."

If he was looking for reasons, he wouldn't find them here.

He put the two thousand dollars into his bag, then walked out the door.

He got a ride with a long-distance trucker who took him north, to Kingston. He spent the first night in a Holiday Inn just off the highway. It cost him thirty-six dollars. The bed was soft and clean. He could have slept, but he spent the night lying on his back staring out through the open window at the stars. At daybreak, just as the sun was coming up over the horizon, he got up, gathered his things together, paid his bill, walked back to the road and stuck his thumb out. An hour later a young kid in a convertible picked him up, took him east, over the bridge across the Hudson, but let him out only a few miles later. Several more rides put him just inside the Massachusetts state line, where a man in a pickup truck stopped for him.

"Where you going, Mister?"

"Brody Institute," he said.

The man stared at him for a moment, then said, "Brody? Hop in. I'm going right near there."

Ethan opened the door of the cab and sat down.

"You got a relative there?" the man asked.

"An old friend."

"Sorry."

"Why?"

"Not a nice place," the man said, and spent the rest of the ride telling him horror stories about the way they treated the patients at the state mental hospital.

Still, he was unprepared for what he found. After all the state institutions he'd been in, he thought he could handle anything, but Brody Institute was even worse than a prison: a dark hulk of a building with huge towering spires and bars on every small dark window. As he approached the crumbling gothic structure, he decided he had to get Lana out of here, no matter what it cost.

The woman at the reception desk said he couldn't come in for an hour. He went outside again, walked around the perimeter of the building, then sat down on the ground until they let him in. Inside it was drafty and dark and dank. The smell was overpowering. He could hear sounds of moaning from somewhere, and crying. The sounds of pain.

They directed him to a dark cavernous room that stank of urine and sweat. The only light came from tiny windows near the ceiling. He noticed a catwalk along the top of the room in front of the windows. He began to search. It was like passing through a hall of shadows. Each shadow stood in a separate place on the floor, unaware of its surroundings, each in its own world, making its own noises. Several, he saw, were masturbating. One was slapping her own face, again and again and again. He moved among them, stopping in front of each shadow, searching its face.

He found Lana backed up against a far wall, as if someone was standing in front of her, crowding her. She was looking down at the floor, her arms outstretched. It was as if she hadn't moved since he left her. Except she looked frail, small. And her long beautiful hair was short, matted and dull, the color of dry straw.

"Lana?"

She didn't respond.

He reached out and touched her face. "Lana?"

She was a statue, as still and cold as stone.

He began to speak to her: "Do you remember the time we took Rose to the crafts fair down in Rhinebeck? I loved the way you were with Rose. You held the stained glass up to the sunlight, showed her the way the light shined through the flowers the man had made out of glass. I wanted you to be a part of us, a part of our family. You needed us."

He could feel tears coming to his eyes. He could pretend she was sleeping. Once she had slept with him all night, in his bed. In the middle of the night, he woke up and looked over at her. She was curled up in a tight ball in the corner of his bed. He wondered how she could sleep like that, wondered what she was protecting herself from. He wanted to protect her. He lay awake all night, watching her. As morning approached, she became restless, rolled over onto her back, her arm splaying out across the pillow, one knee across his thigh. His thigh was so long and bony next to hers. Her flesh was plump and lush and warm, pale-white as a bridal gown.

Would she wake now and be well and whole?

He struggled for control, touched her arm, stroked her skin, all the while talking to her.

"Do you think I could have saved myself, told them what we argued about? I would never have done that. It would have humiliated you, and me too."

He stroked her cheek, held her to him. Her body was hard, rigid. He talked to her.

"You told me you could never love me, not after what happened. And you said no one would ever love you, even I would never love you. I promised to take care of you. You said you didn't need taking care of. You said that you were so tainted no one would ever take care of you. I think you really believed it. But Lana, it was your mother who was tainted. She hurt you, Lana. I knew. You just wanted to be loved."

"Lana, please." His voice echoed.

She winced. He said her name again, louder, but she didn't respond. Her arms looked too small for her body.

His heart filled with sorrow. He wondered what it was that had made the bond between them so strong. The recognition that her mother—the luminous figure in *her* life, too—was beyond the pale, beyond the bounds of normal? The recognition that as damaged as he felt when he realized his place in the world, Lana was more damaged than he? His mother had wounded him, but not like Lana's had her. His wounds felt more like grief and anger, whereas hers felt more like pain.

The "why" didn't matter now. The only thing that mattered was that the bond still held. They *could* begin again, if only she would wake.

He began to massage her arms, rubbed the skin on her hands, her fingers, as if hoping it would suddenly bloom with life, but it didn't. She was in some limbo land, purgatory, never-never-land. Why didn't she come back to life? He had kept faith for thirteen years. She had betrayed him, yes. But he would forgive her, he had forgiven her.

They were meant to be together. But the karma was still wrong.

34

I remember once, in junior year, before our gang for all intents and purposes fell apart, we were standing around in the school parking lot after school waiting for Greg when Ethan and Lana came out of the building. Their arms were swung around each other's waists, their heads and bodies in perfect sync as they walked and laughed. Lana was wearing one of those gauzy peasant dresses she had taken to wearing since she started going with Ethan, like the ones Sarah wore. So intent the two of them were on each other that they didn't even notice Alan and Denny and I standing there as they passed by.

"Hey, Skitt," Alan yelled out, "got some cuntburger for dinner?"

I could see Ethan's arm stiffen around Lana's waist, as if to hold her up as she momentarily broke stride, but since the pair were already past us I couldn't see his expression, or hers.

"Or maybe it's cunt stew," Alan yelled.

"Shut up, Alan," I said.

Alan glared at me, but before he could say anything in response, Ethan had pulled away from Lana, whirled around, and planted a solid punch on the side of Alan's face. Then he jumped on top of him and the two scuffled on the ground for a few moments before Mr. Delsnor, the assistant principal, came running over.

"What's going on here?" He grabbed Ethan by the collar and yanked him to his feet like a cloth dummy.

Ethan wriggled out of Mr. Delsnor's grip, backed up a few steps and stood there, clenching and unclenching his fists.

Alan stood up, wiped his pants off, then winced and held his hand up to his eye. The whole right side of his face was already starting to swell up.

"Alan?" Mr. Delsnor said.

"He attacked me."

Mr. Delsnor turned to Ethan. "Ethan?"

Ethan glanced over at Lana, who was standing there with her hand over her mouth. Their eyes locked long enough for me to realize that some sort of understanding had passed between them. Ethan said nothing, not even that Alan had provoked the attack. It is only now that I realize he wanted to spare Lana the additional humiliation of repeating what had been said.

Mr. Delsnor suspended the two of them for three days.

Mom made a fuss over Alan when we came home that afternoon, made him sit with an icepack on the bruise, which was by then a particularly sallow yellow-green. The two of us sat around the kitchen table with our homework while Mom made dinner. We were still there when Dad got home.

"How are my best boys?" Dad said when he came in.

Alan took the icepack away from his eye. "Damned loony Ethan Skitt attacked me."

"Good God, will you look at that?" Dad said. "How many times have I told you to stay away from those Skitts?"

"I was coming out of swim practice and he was, like, waiting for me. I had to defend myself—right?"

"Oh, come on, Alan!" I said.

Alan glared at me.

There was a long silence.

"Well, let me take a look," Dad said finally. He held Alan's face up to the kitchen ceiling light, pressed his fingers around the bruise, which made Alan wince, then said, "Doesn't look too bad."

Alan stood up. "Not too bad? Goddamned Mr. Delsnor suspended me."

"*Suspended?*" Dad roared. "Why didn't you tell him that the Skitt kid started it?"

"I did, but he wouldn't listen to me. He suspended both of us."

"There must have been a reason why he suspended both of you, Alan," Mom said, coming over from the stove.

"Bernice, let me handle this."

I stood up. The chair made a screech when I pushed it back from the table.

"Alan started it, Dad. He called Lana a name. Ethan was defending her."

"What name?" Dad said.

"What's the difference? He called her a name." I wasn't going to say it in front of my mother.

"Well, I don't care what it was," Dad said. "It was no reason to start a fight. Those Skitts are all nuts."

"Kevin—"

"Dammit, Bernice, if the kid is suspended it ruins his chances to win the state championships this year."

Dad's voice was so loud and shrill that Mom took a step back.

"That's right, Mom." Alan put the icepack back over his eye. "Goddamned Ethan Skitt."

Dad sighed. "Well, we'll just see about all this in the morning."

"Thanks, Dad." Alan flashed Dad a smile, then got up and went up to our room, slamming the door behind him.

I don't know how, but the next day my father went in and fixed the whole thing, got it completely erased from Alan's record.

Alan didn't speak to me for days afterward, but I was already pulling away from him, and his silence and rage no longer had the effect on me they once might have had.

When I left my father that afternoon, all I wanted to do was go home and crawl into bed. How can I explain what I was feeling? It didn't take much to deduce what might have happened in Randy's apartment that night back in 1982, though, of course, at that point I couldn't be sure of the details. But what was I to do with my deduction? Hold on to my small remaining shred of belief that Lana was wrong, that my brother had nothing to do with Randy's death, that he'd set up the Miracle Foundation out of guilt? Try to forget the whole thing? Confront my brother? Go to the police?

I was so devastated by what my father had said, so numb with shock, so utterly exhausted from lack of sleep, that I couldn't think straight. Yet I had a decision to make, and I wanted to try and make the decision with as clear a mind as I could, knowing that there would be irreversible consequences to whatever I did, particularly if I contacted the police.

I drove straight home. Reggie was sitting on the front steps waiting for me. I bent down to pet the cat; he arched his back and purred as I stroked his fur, then followed me inside.

Having spent the weekend staked out at the post office in Manhattan, I hadn't been home in days. I noticed the smell as soon as I turned my key in the lock and threw open the door. An overpowering odor, something putrid and foul. I stood for a moment in the front hallway, overcome with nausea, reminded of the way it smelled in a slaughterhouse I once went into for a story. The rows of hanging carcasses all looked fresh but the smell was there anyway. A smell of rotting flesh, dead flesh.

I looked at the cat. He was posing for me on the tiles, sitting back on his rear haunches, his face implacable, aloof, without either guilt or interest.

It didn't take me long to find the squirrel. I followed the smell up to my attic. It had to be ninety-five degrees in there. Holding my hand over my nose and mouth, nearly overpowered with the stench, I moved closer. The thing was so badly decomposed that I wasn't sure if it was a newer kill or the same one Reggie had delivered to the front hall last month, retrieved from the woods where I'd dumped it and dragged back into the house. All I could see was a gray lump of flesh, slit open, something white on top of it. At first I thought it was some kind of mold, or perhaps a white piece of cloth, but then I saw that the whole milky white mass was moving.

The thing was crawling with maggots.

I stood there, unable to turn away from the sly writhing mound in front of me, the tiny creatures moving sightless, mindless, on my attic floor. At the same time, a profusion of solutions raced through my mind. How was I to get rid of the repulsive thing without having to touch it and walk down three flights of stairs holding it? My mind came up with all sorts of illogical plans. I thought of setting fire to the thing. Or pouring boiling water on it. Or maybe I could go get the fireplace shovel and toss the whole thing out the attic window. I probably sounded maniacal as I laughed aloud at that one, picturing myself watching the thing drop three floors, maggots flying through the air . . .

I did finally manage to dispose of it with the help of the shovel and a plastic garbage bag.

That done, I opened some windows to air out the house, poured myself a glass of brandy, put some music on the stereo, and sat down in the living room. I suppose I was trying to manufacture a sense of normalcy for myself, of doing ordinary things, so that I could begin to decide what to do logically. How does a man make a decision? I thought about calling Jim Harling, my ex-wife, anyone. Around nine o'clock, with several drinks in my stomach, I decided that I was so exhausted that I had to go to sleep first, and *then* in the morning I could make the decision. I moved to my bedroom, took a shower, got into bed. But it was hopeless, of course.

Around midnight that night I finally decided that I had no choice. I had to go to the police. But who? Where? I remembered that Estelle Slessenger had mentioned that a Sergeant Wu of the Pelham police had been in charge of Randy's case. I would go there.

Once the decision was made, I did manage to get to sleep for the first time in several days, though not without the help of a sleeping pill.

Sergeant Detective Frank P. Wu's office in the police station in Pelham was small and cluttered. Wu was a fiftyish Chinese with thick glasses and the blackest hair I've ever seen.

I introduced myself, showed him my press card.

"You're the one writing the articles in the *Herald* about that Paluka girl, and about Ethan Skitt. Right?" He took a sip of what looked like tea from a styrofoam cup.

I nodded.

"They didn't catch him yet. But they will. So, what can I do for you?"

"I was a friend of Randy Slessenger. The man Skitt was convicted of murdering."

"Yeah, I remember. Should have given him the chair. If it was up to me—"

"I wanted to ask you some questions about the case."

He looked at me warily. "Yeah, what do you want to know?"

"What the evidence was against him?"

"Why?"

"I didn't follow the trial. I was out of state at the time."

"Why don't I just get the file?" he said. "Then we'll know what we're talking about."

The man left the room for what seemed like a very long time and returned with a green folder marked SLESSENGER, R. He opened it and began turning over the pages, scanning some, reading others.

Finally, he looked up. "That's right, I remember now. It looked like a suicide at first. There was a note in his own handwriting. Kid was a junkie, a real degenerate. Killed himself. Seemed cut and dry."

"So what made you think it wasn't?"

"Well, technically, a suicide is a criminal act and you treat it as suspicious. You collect evidence, do a background check. And anyway, when you come on a scene like that, you don't know what you're looking at. You gotta treat it like a murder until you're sure it's not."

"Mind if I take a look at the file?"

He handed it over. "Why not?"

The folder was very thick. According to the report, Randy had been shot at point-blank range through the right temple with a Walther 9 mm. semi-automatic. The shell split the frontal lobe of his brain nearly in half. The report went on to describe in detail the number and location of collapsed veins all over his body, the estimated length of time he'd been mainlining, approximately eleven years. The body had been found in an advanced state of rigor mortis with the gun in the right hand and the victim's fingerprints all over it. According to the report, there were some other prints on the gun, unidentified.

Clipped to the report, in a plastic bag, was the suicide note. And several photographs of the death scene and Randy's body, the top of his head a mass of blood, all of them gruesome and dispassionate and professionally done. There were various other reports, giving measurements of angle of fire, fingerprint pressure.

"I don't understand this stuff," I said. "What's it mean?"

"Basically the ballistic reports were inconclusive."

"Meaning?"

"He might have held the gun in his hand, he might not have. The print angles were within a certain margin where it's difficult to say."

I nodded, then scanned the toxicology reports under the photographs. "This says there was no evidence of any drugs in the bloodstream when he died."

Wu took the file back, looked at the report himself. "Yeah, according to this, it had been at least a week since he shot up. I remember that it seemed kind of odd to me that he would commit suicide after he'd been straight for a week. That was another reason I was suspicious. That, and the so-called suicide note."

"It was in Randy's writing," I said.

"Yeah, but it wasn't his style. We compared it to other letters he'd written to his parents, and in every one he'd ever written— *every single one*—he gave his love to his sister. In the suicide note, he didn't. Sometimes an inconsistency in substance is just as telling as an inconsistency in handwriting. No, it was a pretty clever attempt, but he was *forced* to write this note."

"If you saw the letters," I said, "then you must have seen the one where Randy begged his mother to get him out of testifying at the original trial—"

"Yeah, I saw it. Guy was a junkie. No wonder he didn't want to get up there and testify."

"That's what his mother said." It seemed to me that Wu's paying attention to the inconsistency in the style of the letters, rather than to the substance, such as the fact that Randy had begged his parents desperately to get him out of testifying, was a case of attention to certain details, but not to others, but I didn't say that.

He turned a few more pages in the file, stopped and read one, then looked up. "Yeah, here it is. About a week later, this woman shows up in the Comity Police Department and says she heard a shot coming from next door the night before the murder. She lives next door to the bar there, Woody's."

"Why didn't she report it that night?"

He shrugged. "You know. People don't want to get involved. So we questioned Woody Ames, who owns the bar, and he says he shot at an intruder that night. Says he recognized the guy, he was in the bar the afternoon before. Says the guy stole a gun from his safe. Says the guy had to *know* the bar, know the combination. Says he can identify the guy if he saw him again." We had him do a composite for the artist. Want to see it?"

I nodded.

He thumbed through the pages again, held up a charcoal sketch of a man's face that, with some minor changes in the eyes, would have resembled my notion of how an older, thinner, and harder Ethan Skitt might have looked.

"I see."

He closed the file, set it in front of him on the desk. "We ran the sketch through the national files and came out with a name. Ethan Skitt. The murder occurred on the third night after he got out of prison. We put out an all-points bulletin for him. And you know where we caught Skitt? At the Drummond facility just about two weeks later. The girl had just been transferred there, and there he went. Her father happened to be visiting that day—"

"Did Skitt have a weapon on him?"

"What's the difference?"

"Did he?"

"As I remember, no. But so what? It was clear he was going after her. Why else would he be there? Paluka had them call us when he saw him; then Ames identified him in a lineup."

"He may have stolen the gun, but how did you know it was he who pulled the trigger?"

"Wells, if it walks like a duck and it quacks like a duck, it is a fucking duck."

"It seems pretty circumstantial to me—"

"Circumstantial? Wells, what the hell are you getting at?"

"Maybe someone else did it."

"*What?* Wells, there were two guards from Green Haven who testified that on the day he got out, Ethan Skitt said he had a score to settle. Check the court transcript—matter of public record. Now just what are you getting at?"

"Maybe Randy's death really was a suicide."

"A suicide? Ethan Skitt pled guilty to first-degree murder."

I hesitated. Then, "Did you know Randy Slessenger was a homosexual?"

"So?"

"Did you know?"

He opened the folder again, scanned through the initial report, then looked back at me, his face impassive.

"There was no evidence of homosexuality, according to this report."

"How would there be?"

"Recent activity is obvious, of course, but even prolonged can be established. Condition of the anal canal, that sort of thing. How do you know he was a homo?"

"I didn't until the other day. I talked to a guy who had a . . . thing with him . . . I feel pretty bad that I didn't know. He was my friend."

"People keep their secrets." Wu shrugged, took a sip of his tea, peered at me from behind the glasses. "Fifteen percent of the population is homosexual, at least that's what they tell me. Personally I think it's disgusting." He closed the file, placed his hands on top of it. "Just what is this all about, Wells?"

I told him my theory.

By the time I had finished, he was looking at me as if I had suddenly developed leprosy. He stood up.

"Let me see if I've got this straight. You think that somehow your brother blackmailed Randy Slessenger into testifying in the Paluka trial because it was really *your brother* who tried to kill Lana Paluka?"

"Well, I don't know it for sure. The only ones who were there were Randy, Lana, and my brother. Randy's dead. And my brother isn't going to speak up, obviously. Skitt always maintained that *he* wasn't on the scene. And Lana can't remember."

"With what does this 'blackmail' take place? A picture, a letter, something like that?"

"I don't know. Maybe. It would explain why Randy didn't want to testify."

"So where is it? This picture or whatever?"

"I don't know. Maybe it's gone."

He folded his arms over his chest, whistled. "That's some theory, Wells."

"You've got to admit it makes some sense."

"No, I don't admit that. And even if I did, Skitt was in prison this time for another crime. We're not talking about the Paluka case here; we're talking about the Slessenger case."

"But it's all related. Don't you see? Randy—"

"Now wait a minute. This is a pretty wild theory, and you've got no evidence to back it up ... You must really *hate* your brother, Wells."

"No, I . . . I love my brother—"

"Yeah, I can see that." He was smirking. "Maybe she'll get her memory back sometime."

"Maybe."

I decided not to mention Ethan's instructions to her, or the fact that I'd gone to his place. Then I might still have the option to go back and try to wipe away my fingerprints from all over that apartment before the police got there. No, I couldn't do that. If I did that, I could be accused of withholding information on a fugitive, or conspiracy, or who knew what else, even if I wasn't accused of murder.

"All right." Wu was still smiling. "Say I did buy your theory. What do you want me to do with this information?"

"I don't know. Call off the search." It was absurd, but I was desperate.

"*What?* Now look, Wells, this man escaped from a maximum security facility where he was serving a life sentence for first-degree murder. He was tried in a court of law. He pled guilty. And he was sentenced. I couldn't call off the search even if I wanted to."

"All right, then, reopen the investigation in the Paluka case. Then maybe the truth will come out."

"The truth?" Wu shook his head and moved toward the door, all the while looking me directly in the eye.

He held the door open. "No prosecutor in his right mind would take on a twenty-year-old case when the principal doesn't remember, when there's no new evidence, *and* when the sentence has been long served. Now will you please get out of here?"

Om Mani Padme Hum

—Mantra

35

Ethan Skitt arrived at Randy Slessenger's apartment that winter evening prepared to kill him. He'd barely missed being shot by the proprietor of Woody's last night, but it hadn't deterred him from his plan. A break-in at Randy's parents' house that morning had netted him an address; he'd spent the day getting ready, purchasing the things he would need. Yes, he was prepared to kill Randy, he was prepared to kill Alan Wells. They deserved to die for what they had done to him, and to Lana.

Ethan waited in the alley beside Randy's building for nearly two hours before he spotted Randy coming in. He might not have even recognized the man but for the frizzled reddish hair. He waited ten minutes more before he opened the front door and climbed up the three flights of stairs. Someone was playing very loud music in the building. It would drown out the sound of gunfire.

He took the gun out, knocked, waited. Then he knocked again, louder this time. Finally the door opened.

"Hello, Randy." Ethan held the gun in Randy's face and backed him into the room.

"Thirteen years," he whispered, gazing down at the man cowering on the grease-stained sofa, a network of raw, ulcerated needle tracks snaking along his arms. Between the collapsed veins and the tracks, the insides of his arms looked like rancid meat.

"God help me," Randy said.

Moving in closer, Ethan grazed Randy's cheek with the butt of the gun and noticed the web of tiny burst veins in the white part of his eyes, like red lace. It was hard to believe this was the same kid who used to play his guitar in the meadow. Almost as hard to believe as that he, Ethan Skitt, was the same person who used to crouch down in the woods, watching.

But that boy was gone. In his place was Priestman.

Thirteen years in a cell, surrounded by men like Alan Wells— brutal men, cruel men. It wasn't so much the time Ethan had spent there, the confinement, the endless routine, the screams of men in the night, the beatings. It was mostly that he wanted back the time he'd lost with Lana. Time Alan Wells had stolen from him, time that he and Lana could have grown up, traveled, loved, had children. They would have raised their children differently than he was raised. Than she was raised. They would have raised them with love, understanding, acceptance. But it was too late for that, now. It was Alan Wells who had lived, married, had children.

He wanted back the time, and it was already gone. Lana was unreachable, her skin was withering. He had seen it at that horrible place.

He took a deep breath. Now Ethan Skitt really *would* be the Priestman. Alan Wells and Randy Slessenger had played God with his life; now he would play God with theirs.

Randy Slessenger looked up at the man standing over him with the gun. Closing his eyes for a moment, he felt the raw metal touch his skin. He wanted to say he was sorry but couldn't bring himself to speak. Had it been only a week ago when he wrote his mother? Had he known somehow that Ethan Skitt would be getting out soon and would come for him?

"I was going to go to the police, Ethan—"

"Don't try to con me, Randy."

"No, Ethan, I—"

"The name is Priestman," Ethan Skitt shouted.

"Priestman," Randy whispered, suddenly realizing that he'd been prepared for death for a very long time. Thirteen years ago when Alan threatened to expose him, he'd thought that life after exposure would be unbearable. The funny thing was that he hadn't lived, anyway.

Randy closed his eyes and held his breath, trying to steel himself for the pain. At least death would come quickly this way. One shot.

But nothing happened. Ethan Skitt was still standing there pointing the gun at him when he opened his eyes.

"Why couldn't you leave us alone?" the man who called himself Priestman said. "Lana and I weren't hurting you."

Randy could see tears in his eyes. "It wasn't me, Ethan."

"But it *was* you, you see. It was you because you didn't stop it.

And then it was you because you were in it with him. You testified with him, Randy. And you knew it was a lie."

"Please, Ethan, please kill me."

"PRIESTMAN."

Ethan shifted the gun so that it came to rest in Randy's right
nostril. He had learned how to con, how to threaten, how to be
cruel—all part of learning how to survive. He had learned by
listening. By watching. By being there for thirteen years.

Yet it gave him no pleasure to torment the man.

He lowered the gun, stepped back.

"You want me to feel sorry for you?" Ethan said. "Pity you?"

Randy Slessenger looked up at him through a haze of tears. "I
want you to kill me."

This struck Ethan as very funny. He began to laugh, waves of
pure rage and hysteria ripping through him and coming out as
laughter. He *could* kill this man. He could turn up the radio, flip
through the dials, find something loud enough to drown out a
gunshot. Maybe it wouldn't even be necessary with the music
blasting from another apartment.

"You know, Randy, I *should* kill you. I really should."

He walked around behind the couch and held the weapon to
the back of Randy's head.

"I want you to tell me why, Randy."

Randy turned around and faced the barrel of Ethan's gun. He
was trying to speak, but nothing was coming out.

Tell me why!

Randy began to cry.

Ethan stood there and looked at him. He had to know the truth.

"WHY?"

"I was afraid, Ethan. I couldn't let anyone know."

"Know what?"

"Alan blackmailed me, he said he would tell everyone that
Barry and I . . . that I was . . ."

And suddenly Ethan Skitt understood. He had spent the past
thirteen years in prison, suffering and dying, because Randy Slessenger was a goddamned faggot. He'd always figured it was
something like this. He began to laugh again.

Randy Slessenger was begging for mercy, begging Priestman
to end his suffering, end his misery. Bang. It would be a moment
of jubilation, of suffering paid back, of righted wrong. Wouldn't
it?

"How did he do it, Randy?"

"He had some pictures. Polaroids." Randy's voice was quiver-
ing.

"Where are they now?"

"He gave them back to me, once he didn't need . . . I burned them. Years ago."

Ethan raised the gun, kept his finger on the trigger. "We have something in common, Randy."

Randy wiped his nose on his sleeve, looked up at him. "What?"

"He's ruined all three of us. Lana. And you. And me."

Randy nodded.

"And how is *he* doing?"

"He's a doctor."

"I'm impressed."

"He's become a rich man."

"Doing what?"

"I don't know. Real estate, I think. Investments. I don't know."

A fresh surge of rage flooded Ethan's mind.

"Why, Randy?" he said.

"I told you. Because I was afraid. Because I didn't want anyone to know. I didn't want my *father* to know." This last, he whispered.

Ethan shook his head. "But why did Alan do it? Why did he try to kill Lana?"

"After he found out about me and Barry, Alan kept saying all I had to do was have a girl and I wouldn't be gay anymore. He would say it over and over. I tried to stay away from him, but he kept it up. For months." Randy made a noise from deep in his throat that might have been a laugh. "Then, the day before Woodstock, he called me and asked if I wanted to go with him, for old times' sake. I was stupid, I went with him, but even when we were there he kept after me. Kept pointing out all the girls walking around, saying I should try that one and that one. It was like a joke to him.

"Finally I left him, hitched a ride back to Comity. I couldn't stand it anymore. But he called me when he got back the next day and I agreed to go up to the meadow with him." He shrugged. "I don't know why. I should have stayed away from him . . . When we got there we could see you two arguing. What were you arguing about? If you had said what you were arguing about back then, maybe this—"

"It's still none of your goddamned business. And what the hell does this have to do with his trying to kill Lana?"

"He wanted me to fuck her," Randy whimpered. "I tried to tell him I couldn't, it didn't matter which girl it was . . . And then Lana came at him, screaming, she really lost it—"

"But why did he pick on Lana?"

"She was just a—"

"What?"

"She was just a cunt to him."

Ethan smashed the gun into Randy's cheek, watched as he slumped over, his eyes rolling back in his head, watched as a deep dark bruise appeared on Randy's face, swelling the lid, the cheek, the eye.

Would he kill this man?

"Only God makes judgments on man, Ethan. You are not God." Sarah had said that.

He sat down on the table in front of the couch and closed his eyes, tried to find a shred of compassion in his heart for this man who, like him and Lana, had been destroyed by Alan Wells. He was still sitting there holding the gun when Randy came to again a few moments later. By then he knew what he had to do.

Priestman would play God, but he would do it to help Lana. He did have pity for Randy Slessenger. But Lana needed him now.

"All right, Randy, I want you to pick up the phone and I want you to call Alan Wells. I want you to get him down here—"

"He won't come, he won't take a call from me. He pretends I don't exist."

"Tell him you've decided to confess. That you've been living with the guilt about framing me for too long now—"

"He won't come."

"He will if you tell him you're going to the police."

"I was going to, Ethan. I swear. I swear it."

"Shut up," Ethan said. "There's only one way you can make it up to me, Randy. Only one way. Your death isn't enough. I have to have Alan Wells too."

"But you'll never—"

"You're wrong, man. You know, I figured it was something like this. Something he blackmailed you with. I've had firsthand experience with guys like him. I know how they *think*. And I've had thirteen years to learn how to outsmart them."

Everything was ready. The apartment was perfect for what Priestman needed. There was a fire escape out the kitchen window, which he had left open just a little bit, so that he could hear what was said. It was freezing outside, but he would stand there, concealed in darkness and in the blindness of Alan Wells's arrogance. He'd ripped a hole in the bottom of Randy's sofa, placed the tape recorder there, then pulled the wire out through the springs and concealed the microphone just below the cushion. He'd told Randy he had another gun in his bag; Randy believed him. The Walther he set on the table, where Alan Wells would see it. He could only hope Randy would play his part.

And just in case, he had Randy's signed confession.

When the knock came at the door, everything was ready. Now it was up to God.

He heard the door open. He backed up against the brick wall of the building so he wouldn't be seen. Nothing was said for a moment; then he heard the voice he remembered so well.

"What the fuck happened to your face?"

Ethan held his breath. Why didn't evil *sound* evil? Why wasn't there some clue in the tone, in the cadence, in the accent?

Randy's voice. "I fell."

A laugh. Footsteps. "This place is a dump."

Silence. Ethan began to pray: Do it right, Randy. Do it right. It's the only way to pay me back.

"Now what the fuck is all this about going to the police, Randy? You call me like this at ten o'clock at night, it was so long ago, why the hell do you want to bring it up again now?"

"I can't live with it anymore, Alan."

"Why the fuck not?"

"I just can't. We ruined Ethan's life, Alan. We framed him. He went to prison . . . I just can't go on anymore like this—"

"Shut up. Shut the fuck up."

More footsteps. Alan Wells pacing, walking around the sofa. Then the pacing stopped.

"You know I can't let you do this, Randy."

Silence.

"I said I can't let you do this."

There was some noise, someone rummaging through drawers.

"Where are the fucking pictures, Randy?"

"I burned them."

"Don't you see I can't let you do this?"

"I have to, Alan." Randy was crying.

More noise. "Damn! Don't you have a piece of paper around here?"

"What for?"

Silence.

Finally, the sound of a drawer shutting. "All right, Randy, here's a pen. I want you to write a little note."

"What?"

"Write 'Dear Mom and Dad.' Good way to start."

Silence. From his position on the fire escape, Priestman felt a rush of exhilaration. He had won. God was with him.

"Keep writing, goddammit. 'I can't go on living this way. You should have written me off years ago. I'm sorry. You deserved better than I ever was.' "

Silence.

"That's it. Now, 'Love, Randy.' Isn't that sweet? 'Love, Randy.' and so true, too. They did deserve better."

Footsteps crossing the room again. Suddenly the radio blared— Alan had turned up the volume as high as it would go.

But it didn't drown out the gunshot. Not quite.

He could hear Alan Wells walking around, opening drawers. Still looking for the pictures. This was the risky part. Would he look under the sofa, find the tape recorder?

Ethan held his breath again. What if someone heard the shot? No. No one had, or wanted to get involved if they did. He had to count on that.

It seemed like a very long time before Ethan finally heard the door close. He watched Alan Wells pass beneath him on the side-walk below the fire escape, rushing to get into his car. Not the white Jaguar he had seen him in at that construction site. Another car, an American car, less conspicuous. He watched the car pull away.

Ethan stood there for another minute or two, thinking of Lana, thinking back to the time when it didn't matter what Alan Wells or his brother or the rest of them said or did. Lana had rescued him; she was still rescuing him.

He opened the kitchen window all the way and climbed back into the apartment. He stood for a moment looking at the bloody corpse on the floor with the gun so carefully placed in its hand, then got the tape recorder and left by the front door.

Now he would rescue her.

36

I suppose I always knew how my brother's mind worked. Even when we were little kids, if I did something against our parents' rules, he was always threatening to tell Mom and Dad on me unless I did some favor for him, or played what he wanted, or did things his way.

On the Tuesday after Patty and I spent the weekend in our parents' bed that time, we had an advanced algebra test. Alan had a swim meet on Monday night, and hadn't had time to study. On Tuesday morning, as we were walking to school, he began cursing that he hadn't studied.

"Hey, how about I cheat off your paper, Jack?" he said.

"Come on, Alan. Kamiree will catch us. I can't."

He frowned. "Don't be such a chicken. Now look, I sit across the aisle from you, and one back. It's perfect. All you have to do is just hold your paper where I can see it. In the lower right-hand corner. That's not too much to ask. I've just gotta ace this test or it'll screw up my whole grade-point average."

I began to walk faster. "Then you should have studied."

He stepped up his own pace. "I mean it, Jack. I'm going to let them know what went on in their bed all fucking weekend."

I stopped and turned, horrified. "You wouldn't do that."

He smiled wide. "Oh, no? Did you wash the sheets?"

I shuddered at the thought of Mom getting a whiff of the sheets before she put them in the washing machine. I had changed them, put on a new set, but I hadn't washed them. I had simply put them in the hamper.

"Oh, for God's sake," I said, "go ahead. But don't blame me if we get caught."

"We won't get caught," he said.

So I did it. Most of the hour, I held my paper in the lower corner of my desk so that he could see my answers. Kamiree didn't even glance in our direction. He was grading papers at his desk through the whole test.

The funny thing was, Alan didn't *need* to cheat off my paper. I don't even think he did cheat. I got a B— on the test. He got an A.

After I left Wu's office, I drove straight home. I could hear the phone ringing as I fumbled with my keys. I pushed open the door, raced into the kitchen, and picked up the receiver.

"Jack? This is Sarah Skitt."

"Sarah?" Why was she calling me? Had Lana told her Ethan was dead?

"Yes, Jack, Sarah. I . . . I went over to visit Lana at Drummond this morning, and when I got there, they told me she was gone."

"Gone where?"

"I don't know. That's why I'm calling. She left a note, Jack. It's addressed to you."

"Me?" What in the world—

"Do you want me to read it to you?"

"Yes."

I listened for a moment to the crackling sound of an envelope being ripped open. Then I heard her voice again.

"It says, 'Dear Jack, I won't be seeing you anymore. I'm going with Ethan. I have no choice but to be with him. There is no God. Flying was all just a joke. Human bodies aren't suitable for flying. I hope you make a shitload of money on your book.' "

Sarah hesitated a moment, then said, "I don't understand, Jack. Why would she write this to you? And why wouldn't they tell me where they went?"

Where they went? What in the world did that mean? Ethan was dead.

"What's all this about flying, Jack?"

"I—I don't know," I said, certain that somewhere inside me I did know what it meant.

"All right. Well, if you do figure it out will you let me know?"

I told her I would, then hung up the phone, my hand visibly shaking as I replaced the receiver in its cradle. I stood there for a very long moment, trying to feel something except the numbness that was spreading through my body like ice. Obviously Sarah didn't know that Ethan was dead. The only people who knew it were Lana and I. Maybe Lana figured that what Sarah didn't know wouldn't hurt her. On the other hand, with Ethan gone, Lana might well feel she had nothing to live for—

That was it! It was a goddamned suicide note. And it even told me how she intended to do it. And where.

It was mid-afternoon when I got to Lookout Point. I parked my car, got out, and walked toward the path in the woods. I was running by the time I came out into the meadow. I stopped in the middle of the field, realizing that I was alone.

There was no one around.

Maybe I was wrong.

I looked around, out over the sweep of the meadow, to the sky and the horizon beyond. The sky was a clear blue, the sun directly overhead. High grasses swayed all around me in the cool breeze. Otherwise, there was no movement, no sound.

Was I too late?

Slowly I walked to the edge of the precipice, peered down at the rocks below me. I backed up, stood for a few moments gazing out into the sky; then suddenly I heard a movement behind me. I turned and saw someone approaching in the distance. As the lone figure came closer, I realized that it was my brother. He was carrying a small briefcase. He saw me at almost the same moment.

"What the hell are you doing here?" He was standing about ten feet away now, with a panicked expression on his face, an expression unfamiliar to me.

"I could say the same thing, Alan," I said.

We stood, staring at each other; then he glanced down at the briefcase he was holding as if he'd never seen it before.

"Was anyone else here?" he said.

"Who?"

"Anyone."

"Lana?"

"No, I—" He stopped, turned around, and started to walk away.

"What's in the briefcase, Alan?"

He continued to walk.

"The *briefcase*, Alan! What's in it?"

He halted in mid-stride, turned, and faced me. His forehead was moist with perspiration.

"You might as well tell me," I said. "I already know everything, anyway."

"What's that mean?" He glanced down again, almost imperceptibly, at the briefcase.

"It means I know everything."

"I don't know what you're—"

"What's in the briefcase?" I screamed. I had the sudden notion that inside it he had a gun, one he was about to pull out and aim at my head.

He didn't. Instead, he held the case out. "Look for yourself."

I took the briefcase from him. It was a brown case, of the finest quality leather, as was everything my brother owned. I set it down on the ground, tested the locks, snapped open the latches on each side and slowly raised the lid.

The whole briefcase was filled with money.

I knelt there for a very long time, staring at the stacks of bills. "Three hundred thousand dollars, Jack," Alan said.

I ran my fingers over the money, searching for something real I could cling to. Money, that was real.

I stood up, leaving the briefcase open between us, stacks and stacks of money.

"I came here to pay them off," Alan said. "Get them out of my life forever."

"Them?"

"Lana called me and told me to meet her up here with three hundred thousand dollars. She said she would be out of my life forever if I brought it. She said she wouldn't ever tell anyone what happened. I decided it was in my best interests to pay her off."

I stared at him. I'd been so certain of the suicide theory. But it didn't make sense if Lana also called Alan for blackmail money. And not for a minute did I believe my brother had planned to pay her off and let her go. Not after killing Ethan. A man like this would want everything nice and neat. No loose ends. He was going to show her the money, then kill her. Maybe talk her off the cliff. Or even push her again. Maybe *he* left the suicide note to divert attention from himself. No, that wasn't possible either. How would Sarah have gotten it?

"Did *you* write Lana's suicide note, Alan?"

"Lana's suicide note?"

I could see he was genuinely surprised by the question. "She left a note that said she was going to join Ethan," I said. "I assumed it meant she was going to join him in death."

"Death? Skitt is dead?"

"Shit!" I hissed at him. "Don't give me shit anymore, Alan. You know he's dead, you fuck. You killed him."

"Jack, Jack, wait a minute. I didn't kill him, I swear to God."

"Don't swear to God, Alan."

"Jack—"

"Don't insult my intelligence anymore. I've pretty much got it all figured out, anyway. The only thing I don't know is how you managed to force Randy to back up your story. What was it? A letter? A picture?"

"What's the difference?"

"The difference is that I want it. I want the picture negative. Or I want a copy of the letter that you kept. I want it."

"What the hell for?" He hesitated, then said, "It was Polaroids, Jack. There were no negatives."

"But where did you get them?"

"I took them, I didn't *intend* to use them to blackmail him, it was just that . . ." Alan let out a long sigh, closed his eyes for a moment. Then he opened them and said, "I didn't try to kill Lana, Jack. That's the truth."

"Alan, if you didn't try to kill her why are you up here twenty years later to pay her off?"

He groaned. "It was an accident. I didn't *mean* to push her—it all started as a joke, for Christ's sake."

"A joke?"

"Remember those couple of days you went up to Boston, just after Christmas of senior year?"

"To visit colleges?"

"Yeah. Well, one day while you were gone, I went over to Randy's. And when I got there, he . . . well, he made a pass at me. Fucking guy was a faggot. Can you believe all those years, the way we used to talk? And the fucking guy was a faggot."

My brother said this as if it justified murdering him. I said nothing.

"You probably didn't notice but I barely spoke to him after that," Alan said. "Every time I went near him all the rest of senior year, well, it was *creepy*. But then I figured we'd been friends and I owed it to him at least to try and understand it, not that I ever would understand. The whole thing just gives me the creeps. Anyway, about three months later, maybe in April or May—I remember it was the weekend you went away with the *Tattler* staff—I went over to his house again. I was going to talk to him about it. I knocked at the front door but no one answered. I don't know where his parents were. I walked around the house and that's when I saw him there with Barry Carlson. It was the most disgusting thing I'd ever seen. I swear to you, Jack, I have never felt so sick in my life."

"Alan, if you were so sick, why did you take pictures of it?"

He stared at me, as if he didn't have any concept of what I was talking about. Finally, he shrugged, and said, "Well, I was standing there at that window thinking 'Jesus Christ, Jack's never going to believe me when I tell him this' and then suddenly I remembered that we'd left the Polaroid camera in the car, the one we got for Christmas that year. Remember, we'd been taking pictures of everyone at that party after the senior play? The camera was still on the floor of the back seat. And, well, it was too good to pass up. I mean the camera was *in the car!* And I figured you'd never believe me if I didn't have proof—"

"Believe you? Alan, are you so goddamned warped you think I would have— Why the hell did you care so goddamned much that Randy was homosexual? I can see it might have been unsettling, but why take it personally? It had nothing to do with you."

"Jack, he'd told me he *loved* me, he wanted to do . . . well, what he was doing with Barry. When I think about him thinking of me that way all those years, I still get sick—"

"So why didn't you show me the pictures?" I said.

"I meant to. I stuck them in a drawer and then we got so busy with the end of school, I just forgot about them. And then in August when I heard about Woodstock, you'd already left for Boston, so I asked Randy if he wanted to go with me. It should have been you, Jack. Anyway we spent the whole two days together. Well, part of it, anyway. He left early, I don't know why. It was great. Free sex and free dope.

"When I got back Monday morning, I slept until noon. And that afternoon I called him again. I knew that if he just had the right opportunity he would change. I just knew it. And we went up to Devil's Meadow that day, and we saw Lana and Ethan there arguing—"

"What were they arguing about?"

He shrugged. "I don't know. What difference does it make?"

"No difference," I said. "But he left her there, Alan. They were arguing and he left her there."

"Yeah, that's right. And then she just stood there for a while. She was standing about there." He pointed to the edge of the precipice, where the lightning had struck back in 1960.

"We stood there and watched her for a while. She put her arms out, began moving them like a bird, like she thought she could fly. It was weird."

"She was tripping, Alan."

"So was I."

I sat down on the rock.

"And then suddenly," he said, "everything became clear to me. All of a sudden I knew how to cure Randy. So I went up to her. I said, 'Hey Lana, my friend Randy here needs a woman.' I told her she'd be doing him a good deed. I told her we needed to share the wealth. It was a joke, only she fucking came at me, Jack. She was, like, beating at me with her fists. I swear she was trying to kill me. And I couldn't get away from her. She was like a wild woman. I had to protect myself, right? Well, I guess I lost my temper, and before I knew what was happening I gave her a shove, and she stumbled at the edge and went down. Don't you see, Jack? Once she went down I didn't have a choice. I had no fucking choice.

"Because the next thing that happens is suddenly Randy abandons me. He says he's going to the police. Jesus! I couldn't let that happen—it would have ruined my whole fucking life. Right? You understand—right?"

"And what about seven years ago, Alan? Who killed Randy?"

He stared at me, then turned around and faced out to the open sky.

"All right, I did kill him. So what? Who the hell cared? He was a fucking junkie. And suddenly he decides to tell everyone. Thirteen years later. I had no fucking choice—"

"You never have any choice."

"Oh, and you do?"

"Ethan took the rap for you again, didn't he?"

Alan shrugged. "I'd say we're even, Ethan Skitt and I. You think he's any different than me? He set me up to kill Randy. He's been blackmailing *me* all these years. He, and his fucking mother. Two hundred fifty thousand a year."

I looked up at him. Now I knew. There were no more illusions. Alan hadn't set up the Miracle Foundation out of a sense of guilt. He didn't even have a concept of what the word *guilt* meant.

"So if you're even," I said, "why'd you kill him?"

He turned around. "What the fuck are you talking about?"

"I saw his apartment, Alan. Blood all over the place. And now it looks like *I* killed him. You set me up. And you were going to kill Lana too, try to make it look like another suicide. You're pretty clever, Alan—"

"I don't know what you're talking about. I never—"

"Don't lie to me. Don't fucking lie to me."

"I'm not, Jack. I really don't know what you're talking about. But listen to me. You've got to listen to me. All right, let's say I had gone to the police the day Lana . . . fell. My life would have been over."

"Your life is over anyway."

"What's that supposed to mean?"

"Do you honestly think I can just forget about all this?"

"Why not? It's not like I'm an ax murderer or something. What happened was just an . . . unfortunate combination of circumstances. And you're my brother, for Christ's sake."

"I know. That's what scares me the most."

"Jack, what you don't seem to realize is that if you don't look out for yourself in this world you might as well go through your life in the sewer. Look at you. What do you make, forty thousand, maybe forty-five? You think I should have let some two-bit faggot junkie ruin my life?"

"Alan, you shot Randy Slessenger in cold blood."

"He was going to go to the police. I had no fucking choice!" His voice was a screech. "This whole thing was about him anyway. Christ! When I found out he was a homo, I just couldn't believe it. I just thought if he . . . I was trying to help him, after all—"

I stood up and lunged at him with a force that surprised me. Our relationship had never been particularly physical. But the physicalness of this was actually exhilarating—as well it might be. Years of frustration and hysteria were all being released. We must have been like that on the ground for ten minutes, rolling over and over.

I won't say I didn't have murder in mind.

I won't say he didn't defend himself, but after a while it was almost like he gave up and let me push him. We were standing up now, right at the edge, head and shoulders butted up against each other, feet planted far apart, maintaining that triangular balance, each of us fighting for our lives.

Alan lost his footing and went down.

I heard his scream echoing through the mountains before I even started forward. Then I stepped to the edge and saw my brother plunge downward, legs and arms flailing about like an injured bird's.

I watched as my brother was smashed on the rocks at High Exposure, nearly two hundred feet below me.

37

SUMMER 1969

THE WOODSTOCK MUSIC AND ART FAIR

BETHEL, NEW YORK

It was a tiny purple pill, about the size of half an aspirin. Purple Haze. "It'll make you fly," the man said.

He said his name was God, and he was wearing an iridescent purple cape and bellbottom jeans with an American flag patch on one knee. No shirt. He'd set up a concession stand with piles of pills in small blue cardboard boxes, all laid out in rows on a television tray table made of tin. Each box had a small, neatly printed label. METH $5. LUDES $2. ORANGE SUNSHINE $3. PURPLE HAZE $5.

"Why so much?" Ethan asked.

God smiled. "Hey, man, Purple Haze is the best there is."

"We heard there was some bad stuff floating around here," someone in the crowd said.

God put his hand across the smooth bare skin on his chest, laughed. "That's the brown acid. The Haze is the best you can buy. This stuff was made by a lab out on the Coast, set up by Owsley himself. No bad trips here. I guarantee it."

A short bushy-haired man standing in the crowd produced a ten. "Hey, man, that's good enough for me. I'll take two."

God handed the man and his girlfriend two of the purple pills, then looked around. "Anyone else?"

Ethan looked at Lana. "What do you think?"

"Ah, what the hell," Lana said.

God smiled when he took Ethan's money. "You won't be sorry, my man. Or your girlfriend either. Purple Haze is like nothing you can ever imagine. Before you're through, you'll know the true meaning of life."

* * *

The trip peaked just as the sky opened up, drenching the massive crowd in a ferocious electrical downpour. Lana and Ethan found shelter under a tent made of a huge American flag, and stood soaked and cramped, listening to the crackle of thunder all around them. It was there, under the tent, that Lana began to feel frightened. There were so many people jostling her, so many bodies, so close. They would all be electrocuted . . .

Finally the rain stopped and the music began again. Lana and Ethan emerged from the tent and began looking for a place to settle once more.

"How about this, Lana?"

They set their backpacks down on a knoll overlooking the vast crowd, looked out over the sea of heads.

"All these people, just like one big happy family," Ethan said. "All coming together to groove on the music. We're like a new nation, Lana. No past. No future. As if we were born right here at Woodstock."

Lana nodded. She was afraid to speak, afraid to tell him how terrified she was. Why was she still terrified when the lightning had stopped?

"Doesn't it seem like we're in a new reality? Like Comity never existed."

Ethan was always saying things like that. She nodded again. Her mouth was so very dry and her tongue felt swollen. She could feel the rush building inside her.

"I have to go to the bathroom," she said. Her voice sounded strange, loud, as if it were amplified.

Ethan laughed, looked around over the crowd, then up at the sky. A helicopter buzzed overhead, coming in for a landing.

"Where will you go?"

"There's a line of port-o-potties—"

"It'll take you hours to find them again." Joe Cocker was starting to play now.

"I have to, Ethan."

"You want me to go with you?"

"No, I'll be fine. I'll be right back."

He laughed. "Okay. You mind if I stay here?"

"I can take a piss without you, Ethan."

He laughed. "Well, it's a good thing, because just now I am completely stuck to this spot. Like I sprouted roots. See you later, love."

Lana began to pick her way through the mud-soaked crowd. It was funny how she'd never noticed the mechanics of walking before, one foot pushing off, then the other . . . There was a clump of trees near the pond. She could go there, squat down on the ground. Primitive. Just like they were supposed to be.

The ground was starting to swell. Whoa, boy. Maybe she should have stuck with Ethan. It was getting dark now.

Everyone was grooving on the music, closing their eyes, dancing, jumping around, swaying. But it didn't sound so great to her. It sounded like something leaking in from another world. Far out, man. Really far out.

Now what was it she had left him for?

Oh, yeah. A piss. She could feel her bladder pressing. Or was that something else, something awful growing inside her body? Like a tumor or something.

No. She had to stop thinking that way. The thing was to find a place to pee. No, she wouldn't go in those disgusting port-o-potties. They stank and they probably had shit overflowing, with all these people. The thing was to find the woods.

Oh, hell, she could go right here. Who the hell cared? Everyone was together here, all grooving on the music. But she wasn't. Why didn't the music sound groovy to her? Maybe because she wasn't human, like the rest of these people.

Maybe that was why she always felt different. Maybe she was, like, a dog, like Ellie? She was Ellie's child, so maybe she was a dog.

No. She was getting crazy. The Haze was making her crazy.

She stopped. The sky was threatening again. Why did she feel so hot?

Had she pissed? She couldn't feel the pressure on her bladder anymore, so she must have. Unless she'd entered a new reality. Unless she'd gone over to the other side.

Purple Haze.

Was she lost? Why did her skin feel like it was melting?

"Lana?"

The voice belonged to someone she knew. She opened her eyes. What the hell was Alan Wells doing here? How long had she been lying here? She couldn't deal with this now.

"Isn't this something, Lana?" He looked around at the people, then knelt down over her. "I'm with Randy. I lost him somewhere."

She had a vague impression that she was naked. Had she taken off her clothes? She grabbed hold of his sleeve.

He was looking down at her. "What are you doing here, Lana?"

She started to tell him she and Ethan had hitched up yesterday, but instead she started to cry.

"What's the matter, babe?"

She would tell him that she'd gone over to the other side, only she couldn't speak.

"You on something, Lana?"

"Acid."

"Wow, man, you look like you've seen a ghost."

"Bad trip."

"Why?"

"I feel so away from people. Like I'm not human."

"What are you?"

"I'm flying. I'm, like, a bird." Was she laughing?

He looked at her for a very long time—five minutes, six hours, eternity?

"What time is it?" she asked.

"What's the difference?" he said, staring at her. "Don't be hung up on meaningless things like time, babe." He laughed. "What if we could, like, stop time? Imagine it, Lana. Everyone would freeze and you could walk around and look at everything. You know what I'd look at? Bodies. All kinds of bodies . . ."

What was he doing?

Afterward, she lay there in the mud. Alan was gone. She was crying.

She felt very dirty, as if she had rolled around in filth. Maybe it was the acid. There was a lake. She sat up and looked around. Her dress was over by the tree. Oh, well. No one here cared. If she could just wash herself off . . .

There were some people bathing. She could wash him off of her. Then she might feel human again.

It took her until nearly dawn to find Ethan again. He was looking for her too. She begged him to take her to the hospital the Hog Farm had set up, but he told her it was over, everyone was leaving. He held her, helped her, saved her.

She had to tell him.

It was the next afternoon by the time their ride left them off on Route 6. God. Would this trip ever end?

"Let's go up to the meadow, Ethan," she said.

"Why?"

"I have to tell you something. Something I did."

"What is this big confession? I don't care, Lana. Whatever you do is all right with me."

They stood near the edge, where so many years ago she had let those boys—

"I'm sorry, Ethan. I'm sorry. When I went to find a place to pee, I saw Alan Wells."

"What the hell was he doing there?"

"I don't know. I think he raped me."

"Raped you?"

"I think we had sex."

"You think?"

"We did."

He grabbed her shoulders. "What's the matter with you, Lana? How could you do that?"

"I—I was confused. It was the acid, I couldn't stop him—I was a bird. No hands . . . feathers . . ." She heard her voice trail off. "I didn't think I would make it, Ethan."

"Why didn't you come to find me?"

"I *couldn't* find you. I was lost."

His face grew dark. "You're right, Lana. You *are* lost."

She began to cry, beg for his forgiveness.

"Forgive you?" Suddenly he was crying, too. "I could forgive anything, Lana. Anything but that." He turned and ran toward the path, leaving her standing there at the edge.

She had only been there a few minutes before Alan came with Randy.

38

The moment was forever frozen in my mind's eye; I see it even now: the look on my brother's face, the way he flailed about as he fell, the endless scream of terror, the long merciless echo.

And then, silence.

I stood at the edge of Devil's Meadow, trying to look anywhere but down, out at the sky, at the clouds, over the rich panorama of seven counties. I remember thinking that it was as if God as artist had painted the landscape in a patchwork of earth tones: greens, deeper greens, browns, fading to grays in the distance, all under a vast cool blue sky brushed with dark, threatening rain clouds.

I forced myself to lean forward, to look down. My brother had landed smack in the middle of the ledge. I couldn't see any blood. He almost looked as if he were sleeping, yet I knew he never slept peacefully like that. When he slept, there were always grunts, and movements, and fitful dreams. I know, because I learned to sleep through it all.

I remembered the way Mike Morino had described Lana's position on that same ledge so many years ago. I could envision her there, positioned with her legs tucked underneath her—apparently broken, Morino had said—and her arms outstretched, as if for flight.

Flight.

For a moment I had a vague fantasy that Alan, like Lana, might somehow have survived the fall. I thought of running through the woods and finding him there on the ledge, dazed but alive. Changed. He would have compassion, he would be filled with remorse, he would beg my forgiveness. And I would tell him that it was not my place to forgive, that it was Lana and Ethan who would need to forgive him. And I would tell him that even their forgiveness wouldn't be enough, but he would already know.

Or perhaps we could be boys again, and start over.

I stood there at the edge, tears now streaming down my face. I was unable to move to go to him, yet unable to turn away.

Was this to be the only peace my brother would ever have, the peace of death?

I knelt down at the edge, next to the briefcase full of money, and, for the first time in my life, I closed my eyes and prayed. I couldn't think of anything formal so I just kept saying, "God forgive me, forgive me." I listened to the sound of my voice saying the words, over and over.

After a time, I opened my eyes.

It was then that I noticed the transformation in the vista spread out before me. It *was* like a painting, but even from a distance a living landscape is never completely still. Clouds shift, cars move along a highway, leaves catch the light of the sun and shimmer, high grasses sway in a breeze. This landscape seemed completely—unnaturally—still.

I turned my head, shifted my focus from the distant tableau to the area closer to me. At the edge of the meadow, even silhouetted against the sky, the leaves on the trees were completely inert. No bird moved across the clouds. Not a blade of grass stirred.

And there wasn't a sound. No birdsong or chatter, no buzz of insects, no breeze. I couldn't even hear the sound of rushing water from the stream in the woods nearby.

I could hear the sound of my own breathing, my heart beating. And that was all.

Yet all of my other senses were alive, for what seemed the first time in my life. In that strange hushed stillness, I could see the majesty of the sky, the deep orange sun, the cool grass beneath my feet. But it was not primarily a visual experience; I could taste, touch, smell, feel.

It seemed to me as if time had suddenly ceased, as if it had all become a photograph that would remain the same forever, and in which I would be able to move about freely, taking time to examine, to understand.

I took a deep breath, filled my lungs with the fragrance of pine and wildflowers and mountain air. The air had a clean fresh smell, as if there had already been a rainstorm.

I remember thinking that I was hallucinating, having some strange delayed flashback to one of my LSD trips back in college. I'd never had one in twenty years, but I'd heard they were possible. I began to try to prepare myself, remembering the night-

marish trip I'd had the last time I took a tab of acid, when I was
a junior. I'd become convinced that my white blood cells were
exploding inside my body and that I was going to die an excru-
ciating, agonizing death. I had already met Donna, who was to
become my wife, and I think if I hadn't had her with me, I probably would have ended up in a hospital forever myself.

An altered state of consciousness, to be sure, but there was no
downside to *this* experience. This experience was good, natural,
loving, joyful, forgiving. For the first time in my life—despite my
grief for my brother and my guilt, despite what I had done—I
felt at peace.

My cheeks were wet with tears that I could not wipe away.

How many times had I been to this place and not seen it, not
felt this peace that could somehow contain my sorrow and my
pain, even lessen my burden? Was that what Sarah had felt here
so very long ago—her moment of flight?

My heart was so full, I had so many questions. Did God make
choices—who would live, and who would die? Had God intervened for Lana—provided a miracle, given her wings to carry her
safely to the bottom, given her Ethan to sustain her? And why
Lana? Because of the depth of the love she and Ethan felt for
each other? And why had it taken twenty years for her to come
back to life? Was that time a penance for her? Or was twenty
years only a blink of His eye?

I didn't know. I only knew that God was with me. And that it
didn't matter if I couldn't explain this miracle, or even understand. It was enough to feel.

Very soon, a cool breeze rustled the trees at the far end of the
meadow, passed over my face and my arms, filled me, renewing
me. The clouds were shifting now, too, moving overhead, revealing a flawless, very blue sky beneath. There would be no rainstorm.

It was over.

"Jack?"

I looked up slowly, still kneeling. It took me a moment to focus,
another moment to comprehend.

"Ethan?"

He wasn't an adult version of the boy I had known, but a man
with pale, pasty skin and a forehead that protruded dangerously
over his bony face. He was balding on top, but the rest of his hair
hung down past his ears, tied back.

Ethan Skitt glanced down at the open case full of money, then
took a step toward the edge and peered down.

"Police, judge, and jury, all by yourself—that right, Jack?"

I opened my mouth to speak, but no words came.

He stared at me for a moment, then said, "You feel it here, too?"

I stood up and wiped my eyes. My legs were shaking. All I could do was nod dumbly.

"My mother thinks this is a holy place," he said.

I nodded.

Ethan Skitt stood staring at me in silence for a long moment. Finally, I found my voice.

"I thought you were dead, Ethan."

"Priestman," he said. "Call me Priestman."

"That's what Scoggins called you."

"It was my way of surviving, man."

I couldn't help it; fresh tears were filling up my eyes again. I wiped them away.

"Surviving? I don't understand."

A fleeting smile passed his lips. "See, Jack, you all thought I was some bad kid because I was always getting into fights. The truth is, I wasn't a bad kid—just an angry one. But what was I in prison? Some skinny punk, scared of his own shadow, son of a religious woman. I became crazy Priestman. No one bugged him because he was crazy. Any Skitt knows how to act crazy—better than any of you ever did." He smiled again, this time more broadly. "But still sane enough to play this little game with you. And to win it, too."

"Game?"

"A dog, Jack," Ethan Skitt said. "It was a stray dog's blood you found."

"You set me up, then." It was a statement, not an accusation. I had no accusations left.

He shrugged. "I set up the scene in that apartment for your brother—he was supposed to be the one to find it. I figured if he thought I was dead he'd think he had nothing to fear from me. And he'd leave me alone. And if Lana said she didn't remember, he'd leave her alone too. At least for a while."

"But I turned up instead."

He shrugged. "You stuck your nose in where it didn't belong. I was protecting my own, Jack."

I took a deep breath and turned away, turned toward the open sky again. I knew Ethan Skitt was watching me as I looked down at my brother's body.

There was a noise then, the sound of footsteps. I turned around. Lana was coming out of the wooded area at the edge of the meadow, walking—then running—in our direction. As she came closer I could see she was looking at Ethan, as if there was no one else standing there but him. She had her arms outstretched, and tears were streaming down her face. And his.

I was to be a witness to their reunion.

Ethan didn't move. He just stood there watching her come to him.

When she was within touching distance, she stopped, stood still for a moment, then slowly reached out her hand and stroked his face.

"Lana," he whispered.

"What have they done to you?" Her finger traced his lips, brows, cheekbones.

"It doesn't matter, Ethan." She moved closer. "It doesn't matter. When Sarah told me you were alive this morning on the way over here, I . . . Why didn't you tell me you were alive? You could have come to me, told me."

"I couldn't, Lana. You had to believe I was dead or it all wouldn't have worked."

"I know. She told me about everything. The suicide note . . . how you used it to get Jack up here. And then she had me call Alan, tell him to meet me here with the money." She let her arms drop and peered over his shoulder at the precipice. "What happened?"

"Alan Wells is gone, Lana. We have nothing to fear from him anymore." He put his arms around her, said her name over and over again. They covered each other's faces with kisses, tear-stained skin soothed by kisses. And asked each other questions and made confessions.

"They told me you had hurt me," she said, "but I knew you would never have done that, Ethan. Even though I probably deserved it, after—"

"It doesn't matter now, Lana. It was the drug, I know that. I've long forgiven you for that."

"But why didn't you *tell* someone you hadn't tried to kill me?"

"I did. No one believed me, not even my lawyer. I told him Alan and Randy were lying. He was from the public defender's office—he thought I was guilty. There were two witnesses. Everyone says they're innocent."

"But you took the rap for Alan twice," she said. "Sarah says you made a tape, she says you recorded Alan killing Randy Slessenger. You could have turned the tape in to the police."

"If I had, you'd have rotted in that place," he said. "It was such a horrible place . . . when I went to see you, I knew I had to—"

"I knew you were there, Ethan, somehow I knew, but I just couldn't speak . . ."

"I had to use the tape to force Alan to get you the care you needed. Once I played the tape for Sarah, she agreed to help. It was a sacrifice, but everything worthwhile is worth a sacrifice." He pulled away from her for a moment. "Besides, what did I have to live for anyway, without you?"

They sank to their knees, embracing again, now locked in a deep passionate kiss. Perhaps I should have been embarrassed, but somehow I felt privileged to be a witness to such a perfect, uninhibited embrace. Had it turned into lovemaking, I think I would have stood there still.

Finally they became aware of me and broke apart, laughing. They looked up at me, stood up. Ethan still was touching her. He had his arm around her waist.

"Now do you see why I *couldn't* go to the police with you, Jack?" she said. "I *couldn't* say the truth, even if I did remember."

I nodded, then turned to face Ethan. "But why didn't you tell someone why Randy went along with Alan's story?"

"You still don't get it, Jack, do you? I didn't *know* why until thirteen years later. And I still couldn't prove it. Alan gave Randy back the pictures when they were no longer useful, and Randy burned them." He laughed. "Hey, man, don't get me wrong. I'm not sorry for living in prison for thirteen years, and then another . . . well, what is it total? Twenty years. I learned a lot there. For one thing, I learned what to believe in. I learned faith, I learned what I care about. And I learned about my karma. I lived out my karma—outlived it, you might say."

"And now you have your revenge."

"No, Jack. Not revenge. Justice. All I've done here is force you to do the right thing. See, I always thought of you as someone who never took a particular stand in life. That was your karma. You weren't evil, like your brother; you were just, well, the kind of guy who thought he could avoid taking a moral stand by denying there was a moral stand to be taken. It's pretty funny you chose to be a reporter. You just tell the facts, right? You don't have to take a stand. You were willing to exploit Lana just one more time in the name of your trade, isn't that right?"

I started to shake my head but Ethan Skitt put up his hand.

"And yet I always knew your instincts must have told you raping Lana was wrong."

"I didn't *know*, Ethan," I said. "I thought, well, I thought she . . . well, she wanted to do it. Alan never told me, he never told any of us." I looked at Lana. "Why didn't you?"

The man who called himself Priestman laughed. "Still looking for someone else to blame? Put yourself in her position, Jack.

She was fifteen years old. She was pregnant. He told her he would help her. She had nowhere else to turn."

"I know. And you're right. I think part of me always knew it."

"What do you think, Jack? Do you think your father would have aborted that baby?" He hesitated. "I don't suppose your brother would have even asked him, after all."

I looked away. There was a silence.

Finally, I said, "But why couldn't we just all go to the police now? With the tape. Before I—before all this happened. Alan would have served time in jail, surely."

"You have a rich man's mentality," Ethan Skitt said. "You think things are *fair* in this country, but the only thing that counts is who you know, what you look like, how connected you are. With a good lawyer, the best money can buy, Alan probably would have gotten off, or been out in a few years. No way. I wasn't going to rely on that."

I nodded and turned to go. For years, I had run away from the truth, from myself, from life. I had used whatever means were at hand: drugs, women, denial. Finally, now, there was nowhere to run. My path seemed clear. I would turn myself in, explain that I'd had a confrontation with my brother that had turned violent. Maybe they would—

"Jack, wait a minute."

I turned back to face him. He glanced at the briefcase full of money, took his hand from around Lana's shoulder, and said, "I'll make you a deal, Jack."

"A what?"

"Don't go to the police."

I felt a shiver pass through my body. "Why not?"

"Wait a few days. Someone will find the body—"

"But if I don't go to the police, they'll think *you* did it."

He shrugged. "Let 'em . . . They're already after me."

I stood there staring at him, the reality of what he was offering sinking in.

"Why would you do that for me?" I said finally. "You'll be running for the rest of your lives."

"We're already running."

"But *why?*"

"I'd do it because justice has been done. That's all I ever wanted, Jack."

"But what if they find you?"

He smiled. "If they do, I'll have your testimony, right?"

I nodded.

"And I still have the tape. Sarah kept it for me all these years."

I stood there. Could I really pretend none of it had happened, allow him to take the rap again?

"Take my offer, Jack," he said. "If you say you did it, the state will go for murder one, with intent, or at the very least, murder two. Your lawyer will say you were irrational at the time. Everyone will argue about the legal definition of insanity. In the end the jury won't buy intent, but they won't buy temporary insanity either. You'll be convicted of second-degree murder, or maybe, if you're lucky, your lawyer will be able to plea bargain down to manslaughter. Either way, you'll serve time in jail, Jack. No matter how or why it happened. I know how this works."

"You should hate me, Ethan," I said.

"Maybe I should. I used to."

"But you don't now?"

He let out a long low whistle between his teeth. "Man, I was an angry kid. I hated you all so much for choosing me as the butt of your demented little games, and at the same time I wanted to be a part of you. We're sick fucks, we human beings. I even cursed my mother for keeping me out of your world. I thought if only she hadn't been who she was, I could have been accepted by boys like you and Randy and Denny. And your brother. Can you imagine wanting to be included in a pack of jackals like you? Cursing my own mother, who's a warm, generous, faithful soul. Thing is, I don't have all that anger anymore. You see I've had the benefit of actually having seen God at work. It was God who saved Lana, after all. And it was Lana who saved me . . . No. I don't hate you. And I don't want to ruin *your* life too."

The three of us stared at each other; then he nodded at Lana and she smiled. He had made me a generous offer. I knelt down and closed the top of the briefcase, snapped the latches, then stood up and handed it to him.

"Take it. It's yours."

He took the case. They turned to go.

"Wait a minute," I said.

"What?"

"I want to ask you something, Ethan. Just one more thing. I told my brother on August twenty-fourth that Lana had come out of it, but I realized last night that Strother Brill already knew before that. He'd already gone to Drummond several days before, in fact—I remember looking at the register. August twentieth was the date of Brill's first visit as Enworth. How did Brill know? Did they call him?"

Ethan Skitt smiled. "You know, Jack, they let you make an occasional phone call from prison. Collect, of course. I called

Sarah the day Lana woke up." He looked at Lana, then back at me. "And Sarah made an anonymous phone call to Brill. You might say my mother has been the administrator of the Miracle Foundation."

I nodded. "But that still doesn't tell me how *you* knew Lana had recovered."

"I felt it, Jack," he said, then he smiled and touched his hand to his chest. "I felt it in here."

He put his arm around Lana, then they turned and walked into the woods, carrying the briefcase full of money with them. And I stood there for a very long time, watching the place in the woods where Lana and Ethan Skitt had disappeared from view.